Kate Grenville was born in Sydney in 1950 and holds degrees from the University of Sydney and the University of Colorado. She has worked as a film editor, a journalist, a typist and a teacher. Her collection of short stories, *Bearded Ladies*, was published to critical acclaim in 1984. Her novel *Lilian's Story* won the Vogel/*Australian* Award in 1985, and the Talking Book of the Year Award in 1986. This and her other novels, *Dreamhouse* and *Joan Makes History*, have all been published in the UK and the USA and translated into several European languages. Other publications include *The Writing Book: A Manual for Fiction Writers*, and (with Sue Woolfe) *Making Stories: How Ten Australian Novels Were Written*.

Kate Grenville lives in Sydney with her husband, son and daughter.

Other works by the same author

FICTION

Bearded Ladies
Lilian's Story
Dreamhouse
Joan Makes History

NON-FICTION

The Writing Book: A Manual for Fiction Writers
Making Stories: How Ten Australian Novels Were Written
(with Sue Woolfe)

dark places

Kate Grenville

PICADOR
Pan Macmillan Australia

Parts of this book appeared, in slightly different form, in the *Sydney Morning Herald*, the *Bulletin*, *Scripsi* and *Picador New Writing 1*.

First published 1994 in Macmillan by Pan Macmillan Australia Pty Limited
This Picador edition first published 1995 by Pan Macmillan Australia Pty Limited
St Martins Tower, 31 Market Street, Sydney

National Library of Australia
cataloguing-in-publication data:
Grenville, Kate, 1950–
Dark places.
ISBN 0 330 35641 0.
I. Title.
A823.3

Designed by Mary Callahan
Typeset in Plantin by Bookset Pty Ltd
Printed in Australia by McPherson's Printing Group

for Isobel

My thanks go to the Literature Board of the Australia Council for the Fellowship which assisted the writing of this book.

Prologue

THIS IS ALBION GIDLEY SINGER at the pen, a man with a weakness for a good fact. The first fact is always the hardest: you have to begin somewhere, and such is the nature of this intractable universe that the only thing you can start with is yourself. If I am nothing else, I am at least a link in the endless chain of proof which stretches back to a time when Albion Gidley Singer cannot even be imagined.

Mirrors show me a tall man with a splendid head, and a mouth that would never weaken. That person in the mirror has been so many solid things. He has always been a gentleman, and in addition he has been a son, a husband, and a father. He has been a customer in shops where long yellow gloves were laid out before him on glass, he has been a drinker on sawdust, and in the hushed leathery air of the best clubs. He has been a man in plus-fours, a man in a wing collar, a man in a nightshirt, a man in a striped bathing-suit. He has even been a praying man, staring at the dust between his knees and looking forward to lunch. He has been all these things with exceptional completeness, and has convinced the world, and himself.

I move from room to empty room in my house, inspecting the objects that I own. In the muffled air of the closed drawing-room I grasp a poker and hear it rattle against the grate; in the entrance hall, where no one enters now, I feel the marble of the hall-stand cold against my palm; in the gleaming dining-room I grasp the Dresden shepherd on the sideboard, and find the flute in his silly pink hand snapping off between my fingers: but these things remain strangers to me.

That dining-room is all chairs now, drawn up tightly against the table with the spindles grinning at me. Now that there is no one to sit in them, those chairs are multiplying, and the blank sheen of the table fills the entire room.

This is Albion Gidley Singer at the pen, locked in behind his mahogany, filling the silence around himself with the busy squeak of the nib across the paper. I will begin where I always like to begin, with a fact. Once upon a time, there was a man and his daughter, and all was well. There was a man and his daughter, that was a definite fact, and nothing a man need be ashamed of. I have never been ashamed of any fact, and I am not a mumbler: I like the way my face vibrates with the resonance of my voice as I declare a fact, and my chest swells. My voice fills the room completely, corner to corner and up to the ceiling like a smell.

I am in danger of becoming irrational. At any moment I will begin tittering. Grip yourself, Albion. Tell the story.

Part One

A Son

Chapter One

I WAS ONCE long ago a fat boy, and in the privacy of the bath I investigated my rolls and folds with interest. 'It is all muscle,' Father said. 'Do not slouch, Albion, muscle is nothing to be ashamed of,' and I said nothing, for if Father wished to have a son of muscle, I would do my best to please him.

I knew I was a disappointment to Father. He was a man of unbending lip, his fob-watch never far from his hand: stern reminders of how I must one day fill his shoes were never far from his lips, although he made no secret of his inability to imagine me doing so.

'Albion,' my father said, 'you must never forget that God is watching you. You are never unobserved.' Every tree, every fence and ditch, every soft sky above darkened houses, watched. God and layabouts watched from every corner. I was Albion Gidley Singer, son of George Augustus Singer, and had a position to maintain under so many eyes.

But who was Albion Gidley Singer?

He was a boy who learned early on how to tie his own

bootlaces and not to cry when he spilled his milk. He was a boy who was always big for his age, a boy who had learned to call his father *Sir*, and his mother *Mama*, he was a boy who stood when any of his elders entered the room, who doffed his cap when speaking to a lady, who learned how to conceal the various sounds and discharges of his body, and to lie down with a camphor cloth when the asthma came on; he was a boy who learned to say thank you to servants in just the right way, and to put the sixpence in the plate at Communion, and say his prayers for the poor people. He was a boy who knew all this: his various skills and knowledges armoured him so that life could never flummox him.

But Albion Gidley Singer was also a large and cumbersome suit of armour wheeled around the world, made to speak and smile and shake hands, by some other, very much punier person within: some ant-like being who did not know anything at all, an embattled and lonely atom whose existence seemed suspected by no one.

The only comfort in the existence of that microscopic Albion Gidley Singer was the certainty of facts. In bleakness of spirit, and in the confusion and panic of those times when the breath could not be forced in and out of my chest, a fact was a rock to cling to. As other boys collected stamps, my joy was in the accumulation of facts: I cherished and polished my collection, poring over *The Golden Treasury of Knowledge*, *Incredible But True*, and *Every Boy's Encyclopedia* until I ran at the mouth with greed for facts.

What a wealth of facts were in the world! When I was dispirited, or confused by my sister Kristabel's long green eyes and way of making me feel clumsy, facts were my best friends: in the uncertainties of childhood, facts alone could be depended on never to change, never to betray, and never to lose their charms.

How it comforted me to know that the average human skin measures seventeen square feet, that there are four hundred thousand words in the English language, that a single pair of rabbits can produce three hundred and twenty-four more rabbits in the space of a year, and that a man can live for a hundred and thirty-three days without food but only forty-one without water!

Before I knew better, and reluctantly abandoned the scheme, it had been my hope to know every fact in the world by the time I died. This did not seem to me impossible: even the *Encyclopaedia Britannica* held a finite number of facts. I envied those who had lived before me – ancient Greeks, for example, who seemed to know almost nothing, and who could therefore easily digest the entire store of facts in existence.

But I began to see that there was one fact I would never know: the fact of myself. I watched myself in mirrors, and saw how broad of shoulder, deep of chest, imposing of height I was, how utterly solid within all my fat, or muscle: I was a well-built young fellow, and anyone looking at me would have been sure I was as solid as I looked. They could not know that for all my massiveness, I was as insubstantial as a dandelion: and for all my appearance of strength, I could be reduced at any moment to a failed pair of bellows wheezing and squeaking.

I did a lot of watching of myself, and told my reflection its name: 'You are Albion Gidley Singer, you were born on the twelfth of January eighteen seventy-five, you have brown eyes and a mole under your fourth rib, you live at Rosecroft, 7 Palmer Street, Bayview, Sydney, New South Wales, Australia, the Southern Hemisphere, the World, the Galaxy, the Universe.'

This did not help: the reflection in the glass was unmoved, but the speck within was thrown into turmoil by the thought of all those stars, and the spaces between them that made the human brain reel to measure. There seemed no way to attach any kind of fact to that speck: the fact of its existence – the fact of myself – could be deduced only from my reflection in others.

◆　◆　◆

From Mother, for example. She brought comfort to my hollowness, filling it slyly every night. 'Here, Albion,' that lavender-fragrant mother would say, and bring a bag of fairy-cakes from behind her back. 'I know these are my boy's favourites.' I sat up in bed, watching her over my nose as it moved, set in motion by my chewing jaws. She watched every mouthful, and sighed when I had used a wet finger to pick up the last grains of sugar in the bottom of the bag. 'Sweet dreams, darling,' she murmured, 'the night-light will keep the ghosts away,' and she tucked me in as I lay down, queasy from such an engorgement of cake taken too quickly late at night.

Mother was something I never seemed to get quite enough of, delicious but unsubstantial like those cakes she offered, for it was borne in on me early that a manly sort of boy does not wish to spend time with his soft mother. I read and re-read the thick pages of the *Boys' Own Annual*, over *Chums* and *Ripping Yarns*, soaking this knowledge into my pores like a stain. I could not have pointed to the page where I learned this, but it was very clear: females did not feature in the world of boys except, now and again, as objects to be rescued.

I knew that the correct sort of behaviour for a manly young chap was winning blue-striped marbles from other lads, poking cats with sticks, and swashbuckling around with a wooden sword. Boys shouted each other down, boys jeered if you gave them a chance, boys could not wait to tell you what a *dill* you were, what a *thick-head*, how *yellow*, and how you *couldn't run for nuts*.

Mothers, on the other hand, did not wish to engage in any kind of bold action: they were people always sitting down, with a bit of tatting in their hand or a silver teapot, and soothing phrases always on their lips: *Never mind, not to worry, it is not as bad as it seems.* Mothers were people who spent their time in the company of other women, and if sons wished to be near their mothers it seemed it could happen only in those private moments when the world had its back turned. But oh, there were times when I longed to be spared all that marble-winning, all the cat-poking, and all that swashbuckling, all that puffing-up of yourself like a frog, to impress the others with how big you were, how fierce, how fearless.

No one needed to tell me that Mother's cakes were one of the things that were not to be spoken of to the other boys. No one needed to tell me – somehow it seemed I was born with the knowledge – that they would mock. Had Mother ever said, 'Do not tell your father, Albion,' as she handed me cakes, or had I always known this was a secret between us? Those cakes were the currency of the love between us: sweet but flimsy, a private transaction of which the evidence soon vanished.

When Father was present, Mother suppressed her sighs as well as her smiles, and only watched when Father prodded me in the chest and exclaimed, 'No mollycoddling for you, Albion. I will not have you malingering, it is just a matter of will-power.' So I straightened up and tried to please by being board-like in erectness and blankness of feature, and kept my eyes on the middle distance, concentrating on keeping the breaths steady in and out of my chest, and on not letting Father see that his poking of me made me want to cough.

I certainly had no wish to be a cissy, in spite of that longing to feel Mother's arms around me now and then. Father said, 'No cosseting, Angelica, the boy will become a *milquetoaste*!' and Mother would agree, 'I would not dream of it, George,' but later there would be a bag of cream puffs, or bull's-eyes, and her soft eyes watching while I ate.

◆　◆　◆

Then there was my sister. Had we been a pair of brothers, Kristabel and I might have got on, for we were alike, but as it was she could not forgive me. I was the boy, so I was sent away to one of the top schools, and was given the benefit of Greek and Algebra, and I would be groomed for the business, later on.

Because she was a girl, Greek and Algebra were kept from Kristabel, and she did not have to master anything more baffling than a little polite French chit-chat, a few Kings and Queens, and a tuneful tinkling on the piano. Perverse as she was, she did not see her good fortune. 'Why does he get to do all the interesting things?' she would demand loudly of Mother. 'I am better at sums than he is, any day of the week,' and she sulked for all that Greek and Algebra, and did not believe when I told her she would not want to have anything to do with it. She envied me, and was sure she could have done better than I. 'Say something in Greek, Albion, go on,' she would say, and sneer when I tried.

Mother did not seem able to warm to her eldest, that skinny girl with her scrawny freckled arms and bumpy elbows, who had nearly killed her in coming into the world so reluctant and awkward. 'Just look at the state of you,' she exclaimed, and tweaked and tugged at Kristabel's skirts. 'And what in Heaven's name have you done with your hair?' Mother and Kristabel spent long hours with Morgan the dressmaker (Kristabel surly, standing sullen while they circled her with pins), and she made her lie in darkened rooms with slices of lemon all over her face and arms, and walk around with books balanced on her head.

But Kristabel remained all sharp angles, rough elbows, lumpy-knuckled hands: her skirt always hung awry on her angular hips: she remained unalterably plain, and so much lemon seemed to make her freckles darker than ever. All Mother's labour and worry – hurrying home from a tea-party with a new kind of poultice that Mrs Adams swore by, to try on freckles, or a flesh-increasing diet recommended by Mrs Phipps, and all the calling to the kitchen for bowls of cucumber and oatmeal, or the yolks of four eggs in stout – poor Mother: after all this, her daughter was as bony and freckled as ever. Into the bargain she was now sulky, sullen, grizzling: 'Let me be, Mother, it is just the way I am made, it cannot be helped.' There was never a soft look for her poor mother, or a smile.

Although so plain, skinny, and short, she never had a day's illness, and could run and climb and jump with nothing worse to show for it than a red face and wild hair. *Just breathe, Albion*, she would say. *Look, like this*, and would demonstrate with her own fleshless chest how to breathe.

But Kristabel, for all her inadequacies, was a female, and shared with Mother the underworld of women, from which I was forever excluded. What were those secrets they shared, Mother and Kristabel, murmuring away on the corner of the verandah, that made them fall silent when they saw me? 'Some things are just between us girls,' Mother might murmur, and wink at Kristabel. 'We girls must be allowed our little secrets. Mustn't we, Kristabel dear?'

They seemed to think they had some sort of superiority to me with their women's vapours. For no visible reason, without being feverish, or wheezing, there were days when Kristabel would not play tennis, would not even walk, would do nothing but lie on the chaise-longue saying, *I am a little indisposed, Albion, just at the minute*. She would whisper to Mother, and disappear mysteriously below-stairs with some little bundle in her hand. They made me feel frumpish and

stupid, with their secret knowing glances at each other –
We know, but he does not. I was made tiny by their freemasonry
of femaleness.

To spoil Kristabel's poise, then, was a necessary relief. She
might be as smug as a coiled cat, but I could cause her com-
placency to crumble, oh yes indeed! The calm and pallor of
my skinny sister could always be transformed by her brother
Albion, and Albion could deduce the certainty of his existence from his sister's frenzies under his fingers.

'Albion,' she shrieked throughout our childhood, 'Albion,
let me go!' She was a wanton one, with a red mouth full of
teeth gasping for me, and her eyes lost in flesh when she cried
out. 'No! No, Albion, or I will tell!' She loved nothing more
than my hands tickling her, under the pinafore, into her ribs,
under her arms, her belly. 'Albion, stop, I cannot bear it!' she
shrieked, and I heard the passion in her voice that made a lie
of her words, and I would not have thought of stopping until
the tears ran down her red blotched face, and her voice became
reedy. Sated, crazed with pleasure, she sat doubled up over
her crumpled pinafore, breathing hard, hunched over on her
own pleasure.

'You love it, Kits,' I whispered into her hot red ear. 'You
love it more than anything.' Kristabel would shake her head
– 'No, no, no' – and I would laugh at her game of pretending
to hate it, and tickle more if I had energy to spare. She, the
wanton, gasping and crying out, arching and writhing under
my hands: it was her pleasantry to tell me it was no pleasure.

Chapter *Two*

THERE WAS A particular smell of school that made my heart
sink and my brain go slow as soon as I smelled it, of many
boys packed together, of chalk, of forgotten food in the backs
of desks: a smell of extinguishment. It was one of the top
schools, as we were forever being reminded, and our fathers
paid some of the top fees, but I could not seem to *make the
most of my advantages*, as I was always being urged to do.

How I envied the less blessed boys, at the despised govern-
ment school: they said *haitch* when they meant *aitch*, and
grasped their dinner-forks like spears. But they were not sent
away three times a year to live among cold-eyed strangers. No
amount of grammar, no number of gentlemanly ways with
knife and fork, could be worth the dormitory, the chilly sharp
edges on everything, the bells cutting the day up into bits,
and the way there was no escape, for day after dreary day.

Poor Mother did her best: in the holidays I gorged, and
her cakes followed me to school: thick fruitcakes with paper
around them, that I hoarded in my locker, and gobbled under

the gaze of other boys whose mothers did not think to send them cake, and who did not warm to me more because I received cakes from home, even on those occasions when I handed slices out all round: they took the cake, but I was still Albion whom no one liked much.

Father, although such a slapper of shoulders, and such a mocking poker of fat, believed that a boy should not be kept short, so there were plenty of humbugs and cream buns from the sweetshop across from the headmaster's house. It was a comfort, among such a smell of chalk and of too many years of boiled potatoes in the air, to cram my mouth full of something sweet and crunch it, so that I could not hear the shouts and cries of boys developing team spirit out in the playground, and could imagine myself somewhere else altogether, somewhere warmer and lavender-scented. They were like a promise that home was still there, and that I would be returning to it before too long.

The masters were mostly dust-coloured ageless men billowing along briskly in tattered gowns of which they were proud, with a vague way with boys such as myself who were neither bad nor good, neither quick nor slow, but simply the pudding-face in the third row, who could never remember how to find a square root no matter how many times he was told.

There was another type of master, but I feared them even more than the ablative-construing and square-root querying ones: these were robust young ones, who had been seniors themselves only a few years before, who bullied us around outside, devising from week to week another way of making us stumble across paddocks, sweating our way over fences and down the sides of gullies, and generally suffering in various manly ways.

These dreadful cross-country torments were considered suitable for the boys with *chests*, and so was a little slow cricket, but we were let off the worst of it, and did not have to mill around in mud trying to kick a slimy ball. But we still had to stand watching the ones who did, and pretend enthusiasm, and were despised as well, for being *girly*, not up to any rough-and-tumble.

Nights were the worst; the days were not much fun, but at least no one gave you time to think, or to feel. I lay in my bed, hearing Chester Junior snuffling in his sleep beside me, and some other boy having a dream about his dog: 'Fetch! Go fetch, Blackie!'

I lay under the coarse cold sheet, with no possibility of arms around me, and felt a fear like no other, a fear that squeezed cold tears out from under my tight-shut eyelids. 'I cannot bear it, I cannot,' I tried to tell that fear, but it would not leave me, but froze my heart with its emptiness, left me sucked dry and shivering, a dead leaf in the wind. I lay very still and tried to resist that nagging fear, like a flow of cold water, that was never far from me, the fear that this was what life was, for ever and ever until you died: being locked up within yourself, all alone, having to pretend all the time, every minute, that you were absolutely perfectly all right.

In fact, I was far from being all right. I was ashamed of my large-knuckled red hands, ashamed of the way my voice was by turns squeaky and rumbling, ashamed of the blemishes on my face which no amount of scrubbing seemed to remove: I loathed my coarse boy's body and my coarse boy's clumsiness.

More than anything that could be seen, though, I was ashamed of certain alarming mysteries of which I dared speak to no one. What were those dreams from which I awoke stifling and gasping, with my nightshirt strangely soiled? And what went on within my trousers at times, so that they were caused to bulge out as if there were a grapefruit in there?

I knew that I knew nothing, but there were other boys, bold boys with cold eyes, who knew. There was Morrison, for example. He was a boy none of us would have invited home for the holidays, for he tended to say *anythink* when excited, and it was rumoured that his father had made his pile in tallow. It was obvious that Morrison had not had as sheltered an upbringing as the rest of us: Morrison was one of the knowing type of boy.

We gathered around Morrison in the glum corner behind the bike-shed, where a sharp smell of burning rubbish always filled the air from the incinerator smouldering there, and Morrison told us what he knew about females.

Their *titties* hung down to their waists, he said, so they had to strap them up, and he brought an engraving of some primitive wrinkled female in Africa to prove it. Some, he assured us, had dugs so long they could toss them over their shoulders or knot them together. *Down there*, Morrison told us, whispering hoarsely so we all had to strain forward to hear, women had a gaping slit like a mouth. There was nothing there, he said, only a lack, a gap, a hole where any proper normal person had a thing you could hold in your hand. What was more, the lips of this unimaginable mouth drooped:

'I have seen the lips hang down just about to their knees,' Morrison claimed. 'The old ones, you know, the old ones like your Mums.'

There was silence behind the bike-shed at this, as each boy thought of his mother and this frightful hidden thing about her. Morrison sniffed – he was an adenoidal boy who sniffed day and night, winter and summer, and even one of the best schools had not succeeded in getting him to use his handkerchief – Morrison did not care, for his mother had died when he was little, but we other boys would never look at our mothers with the same eyes again.

'What's the difference between the Jenolan Caves and an old woman?' he asked, but spared us trying to answer: 'The Town Hall wouldn't fit in Jenolan Caves!' He told us of the way women could take hold of a man's organ with this hole and refuse to let go, strangling a man's manhood while he struggled in her grip. And were there teeth? Listening to Morrison, we were not quite sure. I thought of my sister, Kristabel of the mocking eyes, and was struck with the likelihood of what Morrison was telling us. If Kristabel knew she had something between her legs that could tear a man apart, no wonder she thought herself so superior! Morrison told us of the insatiable appetite of women for men: 'They don't, you know, have a squirt and be done with it, they can never get enough of it,' Morrison whispered, and not a boy crouched on the scuffed dirt would have been the one to ask, 'What is this "it", Morrison?'

◆   ◆   ◆

When we arrived back from holidays one term, there was a new master. Cargill was tall and thin, and walked with a faint shamble, as if he was wearing feet a couple of sizes too big. He was a loosely put-together individual with a permanent rash on his jaw where his starched collar rubbed the skin; his slow smile showed a crooked tooth and his large face was mild and attentive. He was a man whose academic gown was stiff and new, whose laurels still sat unfaded on his brow. He had been a prodigy, we heard, and would go far, and was full of schemes to get his boys developing team spirit. Under Cargill's direction, we boys with *chests* were no longer to moon on the edge of the football games hugging ourselves in the wind. 'You are all part of the team too,' Cargill shouted over the grunts of the players. 'You will barrack, and I will teach you to barrack as you have never barracked before!'

He took it seriously, as he wanted us to. Once a week he sat us in the assembly hall, among the rows of dusty chairs, and directed us from where he sat right at the back of the hall. 'Project,' he would declaim, 'project, boy, I want them to hear you in Broken Hill!' and we would try again:

> 'Rovers Rovers red and blue,
> Rovers we are counting on you,
> North and South and East and West,
> Rovers Rovers you're the best!'

If we could not get the hang of projecting our thin voices as far as where he sat, he would stride down through the chairs with his long legs, bound up onto the platform, and grasp a boy around the waist to demonstrate the existence of the diaphragm.

I was that boy once, and could hardly breathe, let alone project, as he stood behind me, one hand in the small of my back and the other on my stomach. 'Push, Singer!' he exclaimed. 'I want to see my hand move out as you take in air, go on, push, boy!' I pushed, and we all watched as Cargill's large hand was moved outwards by the volume of air I had taken in. 'Now, project, Singer, on that chestful of air,' he urged, and I found myself filled with a resonant and steady voice which filled every corner of the chalky hall. 'Well done, Singer, well done indeed, that is quite a voice.' Cargill said, and let go of my back and my stomach, but gave me a smile into my eyes that made the world warm for the rest of that day.

It was Cargill whom I began to adore, and longed to resemble. 'What are you slouching for, Albion?' my stern unfriendly father demanded when I went home for holidays, and jabbed me in the button of my jacket. 'Stand straight, boy, be a man.' I would not tell him, or even myself, that I was being Cargill, that I was trying out the skin of another being who I longed to be one with. I felt my toes turn in and I took the long gangling strides that Cargill took, and was at peace and in a tumult of excitement both at once, because I was feeling what it was to be Cargill, and to leave lonely Albion somewhere else.

Cargill's smile was a leaf caressing the sky. It was a bird through blue, it shaved the stone away from the world and left soul shining through. In the angular and bloodless cold world in which I lived, Cargill was the moment of warmth in it, the only moment when it felt acceptable to be Albion Gidley Singer. Stony boy that I was, with a reputation for being one for tittle-tattle and going to the authorities, disliked as I was for my stiffness and prissiness, and too much insincere politeness: this stony boy could melt when he thought of Cargill's smile turned towards him.

I turned out to have an aptitude for bellowing the Rovers' warcry across the churned mud. I even embellished the simple roar with several yodel-like variations of my own, and schemed for those moments when I could produce a new sort of noise that would cause Cargill to look at me, with his smile that turned me to water inside my vest, even though I felt myself to be an empty bell, my throat producing volumes of sound out of a centre of blank air.

In the classroom, where we laboured over gerundives, Cargill bent over me to examine what kind of botch I had made of my parsing. With his hand over mine, he guided my foolish pen so that it drew the correct lines and loops and arrows, splitting the sentence neatly into its parts, and as he did so – I, breathless, feeling every molecule of my hand where it was touched by Cargill's – I saw between us one of his hairs slip down on a current of air and settle on the edge of my book. When he had moved on to some other desk, some other boy for whom I had to choke down envy for being so close to Cargill, I laid my palm over that hair: gently, so it would not take fright, I captured it. Cargill turned and met my eyes as he spoke in a humorous way of the split infinitive, and all the while I had to leave my hand awkward over the hair, and I saw his eyes linger on me, watching and wondering why I sat so stiff and wooden, with my hand ablaze, covering my treasure.

One Sunday in our free time after dinner, I was alone on a cliff mooning at the unfriendly polished surface of the sea. I stared glumly at where grey sea met grey sky and wished for the holidays to arrive: failing that, a tidal wave would have done. All at once there was Cargill, coming towards me with his awkward long-striding walk over the bumpy grass, the wind lifting the hair from his forehead. My heart thudded in my chest and I could not breathe; but he was definitely coming towards me across the wet grass with a smile on his face, his eyes looking into mine.

I had allowed myself to dream of Cargill's arms around me. On countless nights I had rescued Cargill from burning houses, swum through whirlpools to save him from drowning, sucked the venom from the twin puncture-holes in his ankle. Together we had stared up at Victoria Falls (six hundred thousand cubic feet per second), gazed down from the Eiffel Tower (nine hundred and eighty-six feet, with a lateral movement of five inches in a high wind), and shaken each other's mittened hands at the North Pole (lowest recorded temperature, minus seventy-two degrees Fahrenheit).

Now Cargill was beside me, not in dreams but in flesh, beside me in the wind, sharing the same cold air, and while it was what I longed for, I feared it as well. Up close, all my difficulties began.

Far below us on the sand, two men were straining at a boat that was stuck like a rock in the sand. At the bow the man in black tugged so hard we saw his hat fall off his head, and I heard myself laugh my unpopular laugh; and at the stern, a man in yellow was a tiny hopeless machine, nearly horizontal in his pushing. I laughed and stood beside Cargill, glad of a pretext to laugh aloud, because my breathless joy was forcing its way up and out of me, and just for a moment the void was spinning off harmlessly beyond us.

'I am pleased to see you here, Singer,' Cargill said out of a long silence into which my laugh had been absorbed. 'Very pleased indeed,' and I glanced up to see whether there was some detail of gerunds or the subjunctive that he wished to share with me. His mouth was a trifle strange, as if he were trying to smile and not smile, at once. His eyes met mine and slid away: I could not guess what was in his mind, but it did not appear to be gerunds or the subjunctive. I was awkward then, standing thick and sullen, with only the most unhewn and clumsy words coming to me in a moment that I knew was one requiring delicacy, and if words at all, then words of a flute-like fineness.

Cargill and I stood so close I could sense his body swell with each breath he took, although we were not touching, except perhaps that the fluff of his tweed might have been brushing the fluff of mine.

A gull wheeled by below us and shot suddenly up into the air so I saw the sun illuminating it from behind, a lambent gull soaring, full of light. We watched birds squeaking across the sky in pairs, home to their plump branches. Those birds beating their way slowly across the ash-grey sky had my envy, for I knew they were together for always, or at least until death.

If a genie had appeared to me at that moment, my wish would have been to be able to melt into another, without any kind of fuss or embarrassment, the way one ice-cube could liquefy and become one with another. But I was no simple ice-cube: I was a complex lump of boy whose large body was a burden he could not escape. I knew that I was about to be put to the test, and knew already that I would fail.

'Well,' Cargill said, and I heard the sigh, and a shudder in it. I felt my lips creak apart with the effort of thinking of something adequate to say. All at once Cargill turned and pressed me to him, so that my face was drowned in the heat of his chest and air rushed out of my body in a moan. He turned my face up to his, with his hand under my chin, and I felt how he trembled as he touched me.

What possessed me, that I flailed out then against Cargill, choking on fear, feeling my hand strike his face so he flinched? What terror filled my mouth with vile words like stones hurled into his face? In an ecstasy of anguish, I ripped myself out of his arms and stumbled across the grass. Gulls followed me, screeching and flapping like creatures of doom, and the earth tilted and rocked beneath my clumsy running feet, and behind me I knew Cargill stood watching, and knew he would have held out his arms to me in welcome if I had heeded those gulls and the tilting earth, and turned back to him. But I could not. I struggled on in despair, throwing my feet out under me, further and further from where Cargill stood watching with the wind blowing around him.

What was my fear? Was my fear the worst of all, of finding paradise and then being expelled from it? I had watched

Cargill bending over other boys, their brown heads close to his, so close they seemed to be touching, and I had seen Cargill even take the skinny hand of other boys as he took mine, to guide it over the shape of a tricky sentence: I had seen, and been filled with pain.

I knew that there must be boys of the past on whom Cargill's musing eyes had smiled, and knew that there might be other boys in the future. To be locked into myself, hungering for the paradise of his arms, was a lonely and comfortless place; but I could bear that, could go on living with a few warm dreams at night in my thin bed.

But if I unfolded the petals of my embattled self to Cargill, if I allowed his arms around me, his whisper in my hair, and the fondness in his eyes: if I let myself be undone by all this, and stand naked in the blast of love, I would risk the worst death of all. I would not survive such a death as that, as Cargill having opened my soul and then with his mild manner moved on, leaving me flayed. It was pride and deepest fear, and it left me dry-eyed and stony-hearted later, leaning on a fence, thinking with despair how much life I had still to live.

Chapter *Three*

WHEN THE HOLIDAYS CAME, Mother and Kristabel continued with their normal lives, as if nothing out of the ordinary was happening. The fact that I was home did not seem to be important enough to interrupt their endless little projects: pinning bits of cloth together in the drawing-room to make dainty things, disappearing together for periods of time into Mother's room, and calling endlessly on other ladies. Kristabel was surly through it all, impatient with the pins, preferring to be out in the garden rather than murmuring with Mother or the tea-time ladies, but there was no choice for her as there was none for me, and I heard her laughing with Mother sometimes too, and taking seriously the matching of one blue to another. 'Oh, Albion,' Mother would say, 'Kristabel and I are just busy for a few moments, can you entertain yourself for a while, dear?' and I would leave the cosy dimness of the drawing-room and its fascinating scraps of cloth, and drift aimlessly back outside into the sharp sunlight. Finally I would tire of waiting for the women to have time for me, and would wander the streets with a stomach full of cake and my pockets full of humbugs to suck on.

I watched women with ostrich-feathers in their hats getting onto trams, I watched men taking up a lot of the footpath, standing legs a-straddle discussing one thing and another, with their hats on the back of their head and their hands in the pockets stretching their pants tight over their buttocks. I watched bearded rough men guffaw outside public houses, and women in calico aprons looking cross and hurrying along with bundles wrapped in cloth. I watched runny-nosed children with scabs on their faces playing knucklebones in the dirt; and once I saw the streets of the Chinese, but I went away quickly because I had been told plump white boys like myself were considered delicacies for a Chinese dinner.

And it had been with a sticky pocket of my Norfolk jacket full of fluff-covered humbugs that I had been frightened in Roden Street by an odorous skinny woman. 'Boy!' she called hoarsely from across the street, and made to cross, so that I popped another humbug in my mouth for reassurance and walked faster. There she was, though, blocking the pavement in front of me now, inescapable, with a bony pointing finger and a glittering eye. 'Boy!' she cried in a hoarse voice like a bird. 'Stop, boy!' I thought of feigning deafness, but I had already flinched from her cry, and those glittery eyes had seen me hear her. I thought of feigning being foreign, and bamboozling her with some Greek, but with my mouth full of humbug I could not have done that. I thought of turning and fleeing from her crooked bony finger, but I was stuck to the pavement, and could not make myself move.

She was a wild-eyed woman with thin strands of hair falling down the sides of her face, and her skin was grey, her eyes set in dark rings, her lips the colour of a bruise; she was so skinny under her rag of a dress, and a rag of a shawl, she was like a bundle of rubbishy bits of stick; and against her she held a bundle that was a baby, of a nasty putty-colour, with lumps of hair stuck to its otherwise-bald head. 'Boy! Look!' she cried, and came closer, thrusting back the rags around the baby so I could see its face, wizened and pasty, and smell a smell of sour milk and femaleness: a rank, sharp smell of women and hunger.

She released me from her eyes and yelled something across the street, and I thought for a moment that she had already despaired of me and had found a new victim, but then I saw two tattered children run, all ungainly, across from a doorway and stand beside her with their feet bare and their ankles covered with scabs – had the sandflies got them on a picnic, the way they had got Kristabel once?

'Boy, we are hungry, look, these are starving away to nothin, see,' the woman cried in her hoarse voice, not like a woman's, 'and my milk for the bub here is all gone,' and her hands grasped at the opening of her bodice so I thought she was going to expose her titties to me, but she did not. 'We are hard-working and God-fearing Christians, boy, but we cannot manage in these hard times now when there is not work to be had.'

The humbug filled my mouth and I felt my spittle gathering in my cheeks, for I could not swallow, I was almost gagging, looking at these unpleasing and crusted beings. I felt how my cheeks puffed and popped with my humbug, I felt how the folds of fat around my neck glistened, I felt how the red blood surged under my skin, and I was ashamed.

How I loathed them in my shame, and wished for the pavement to open under them, and make them vanish! I thought to give them what I had, all my humbugs and the half-crown and two threepences in my pants pocket, to make them disappear and leave me alone with my full stomach, but I thought then that if I gave them all I had they would not disappear, but follow me. I pictured them trailing after me all the way home, with the woman's rough voice slicing my flesh with her words, and the silent children trudging, staring at my large buttocks moving up and down under the Norfolk jacket. They might stay then, sitting on the front steps or across the road, the woman's voice coming in at the windows as we sat down to our saddle of lamb, Mother and Father looking at me as a fool for bringing them home with me.

But the woman's hand, shaking, was stretched out, almost touching one of my buttons, and she would not let me go now. I could not seem to turn away from her tight stretched grey face, and could not have pushed past, for I could not touch that papery skin, those dingy bits of fabric, and I feared to touch the human body and soul within.

Their eyes all watched like small animals as I felt in my pockets and came up with my fists full: humbugs in one hand and coins in the other. Their eyes were not on my face now, but on those fists, and I flung them open over their heads so there was a clattering and tinkling on the pavement, and they all dived on them, sprawling over themselves to grab and scrabble. While they clawed on the ground, I ran, straining against my clothes, bursting at the underarms of my jacket, feeling my chest tighten and my breath grow reedy, until I was safely home.

'Why have you been running, Albion?' Mother wanted to know, coming out from the drawing-room all cool and smooth. 'Have you been fighting again, Albion?' In Mother's cool fragrant presence, ravenous-eyed women seemed a blasphemy. I felt shame at even having such images in my mind; they were like a shameful bodily function. All words stuck in my throat, and I could not tell my serene mother that I had been ashamed, and afraid, and nearly sick with some feeling or other, and that the world had toppled from its tidy axis for a few minutes.

◆　　◆　　◆

But the image of that woman nagged at my mind, and ranged itself with the shuffling men lining up outside the church, and sitting along the gutter with their boots in the mud, chewing slabs of bread.

I thought long and frowning over the idea of hunger, and decided to forgo my elevenses one morning so that by dinner-time I would know what it meant to be hungry. Under my jacket my stomach made petulant sounds, and there was a shaky sensation around my fat middle, and my mouth tasted of pennies, and I could not concentrate, and broke one of the masts of my best brig. I was glad, then, when I heard Manning hit the gong, and I could go down to the dining-room. That was hunger, then!

But, as I ate through my plate of cold tongue with pickle, and my slice of cold pie, and my pile of bread-and-butter, and my glass of milk, I wondered. There was always food. I knew that some kinds of food cost more than others, of course, but there was always bread, there were always eggs and milk, and after all potatoes grew right there in the dirt: there was always food.

I thought, then, to try to enquire of Father, in a man-to-man way, whether it was true that a person, or a woman, could be hungry, actually have nothing to eat, when, as I had established, there was any amount of food bursting out of the ground and being extruded from fowls and cows. As far as Father was concerned I was interested in an abstract question of political economy, and he was pleased to see me taking an interest at last.

'That is true, Albion,' Father agreed when I asked him at the end of breakfast the next day. Kristabel and Mother had left the table – I did not want them listening and exchanging glances across me – and Father seemed in a jocular frame of mind, having impaled his kidney on his fork and made some remark in Latin at which I smirked uneasily, trying to convey simultaneously that I understood but had no further comment to make. Now he chewed the kidney, nodding approvingly. 'That is all absolutely true, my boy, and it does you credit that you are considering such problems.' I swelled with pride: Father did not often find much to praise me for.

'It does you credit, Albion,' Father said, 'but consider this: what is it that causes a farmer to grow more potatoes than he needs himself? It is that others will pay him money for his excess, and with that money he will purchase, say, a pair of boots he cannot make for himself.' I nodded, I followed, and was even beginning to guess the next stage in the argument, when he continued. 'So you see, Albion, it would not work simply to give away the food, no one would bother to grow it.'

He looked searchingly at me, so I nodded, 'Yes, Father, I understand,' and tried not to blush at the memory of the humbugs and threepences tossed into the air, for that was the wrong thing to have done, it seemed: I should not simply have given them away.

But there was another part of the problem which I was trying to get clear in my mind. 'So,' I said, cautiously, unwilling to have Father think me a fool after such a promising start to this discussion, 'so, Father, there are people without the money to buy the food?' I was tentative, afraid his interested look would fade and he would dismiss me from his mind as a dolt: I knew Father's opinion of my brains was not high, so I had to go carefully, but he was listening blandly. 'Yes, Albion,' he said patiently. 'That is so,' and waited for my next question.

'Why do they have no money, Father?' I said, blurted rather, for I was ashamed of the nakedness of my question. 'They have no money because they cannot find work, Albion,' Father said, still patient, but I saw his finger begin to probe towards his fob-pocket for his watch, and I tried to be quick, before he lost interest altogether. 'Why cannot they find work, Father?' Father was pulling the watch out now and laying it on his palm as he spoke. 'They cannot find work because they ask too much for their labour,' he said, opening the watch and looking at the time. '*Tempus fugit*, Albion,' he said, and slipped his watch away, and I thought I would not get to the bottom of my problem after all.

But as he stood and buttoned his jacket, Father said, in quite a kindly way, so that I felt less doltish, 'You see, Albion, when they ask for wages that are too high, business cannot afford to employ them, so they cannot find work. When they ask for lower wages, business will find it profitable again to employ them, they will find work, they will have money, they will buy food, and all will be again as it ought be. Do you see, Albion?' and, as he was leaving the room, I rushed to follow him. 'Oh yes, Father, I understand perfectly, thank you, I see it all now,' I gushed, but Father had rung for Manning to fetch his hat and gloves, and was no longer listening, so I went away to my room to consider the beautiful logic of what he had told me.

I hoped never again to have an encounter such as I had suffered with my mouth full of humbug, but I also wished to rush out and find that woman with her accusing eyes, and explain the inexorable and impersonal logic of it all to her, and show her the way in which the answer to her problem was in her own hands.

Chapter *Four*

AS A YOUNG MAN of good prospects approaching manhood, one who was now starting to grow into his fat, and one who finally seemed to have outgrown the shameful asthma, certain social events began to be expected of me when I was home from school for the holidays: afternoon teas, mainly, with charades, and a game on the lawn later. Here I was expected to deal with the sisters, cousins, sisters' friends, and sisters' friends' cousins, of the boys who were at school with me. Reluctantly, and only because there was no choice, I went with Kristabel and sat in various drawing-rooms.

At home, Kristabel was always a square peg failing to fit a round hole: Mother longed for a dainty flouncy type of daughter, and although she and Kristabel made the best of it among the quilting and the tatting, Kristabel was never going to be that sort of daughter. But in other people's drawing-rooms, Kristabel blossomed, and her sharp remarks made people laugh, so she did not mind these afternoons. 'Oh,

at least it is a chance to get out of that everlasting house!'
she told me.

But I dreaded the visiting. I was awkward, all fumbles and
spills taking my tea, tipping the biscuits off their silly little
tray – the sort of biscuits, I discovered too late, that shattered
into many crumbs around one's boots. I did not quite know
what to do with my hands, or my cup of tea on these occasions. I watched myself leaning on things stiffly, trying to
look relaxed as the others did: I tried getting my hands out
of the way in my pockets, and found them bunching into fists
in the darkness there, so I took them out again; I tried crossing my arms, or sitting down and crossing my legs, but whatever I did my body seemed all thumbs.

I watched Davis, who seemed to have been doing this all
his life. Davis was a dab hand with a cricket bat and had a
hank of pale hair that hung over one eye. This hank of hair,
or something about the way he stood and smiled, drove the
cousins and sisters into a frenzy: they positively shouted each
other down, all speaking at once to attract his attention with
some saucy remark or other. They had not seen him, as I had,
picking his nose in Religious Instruction, and flicking the
snot across the room at the Map of the World.

◆   ◆   ◆

My trouble was, females seemed a race apart: human, I imagined, but not human in the way I myself was human. It was
the plumage of a different species, the way their hair looped,
folded, curled and fell; I could not understand how there
could be any room for their organs of digestion within their

tiny stiff waists; and although I had secretively studied various marble breasts, half-covered with marble drapery, on display in the Gardens, they had not been deeply informative. I could not imagine what bulges and ledges of flesh might be underneath the bodices of these sisters and friends of sisters.

Quite apart from the physical differences, there were others, even less comprehensible. How were the minds of these girls constructed, so they could keep up their trilling and exclaiming, and did not need to have anything of significance to say before they spoke? I could never have sparkled and tinkled to try to draw a smile from a young man scowling with shyness. I could not possibly have pretended all the phobias of which I learned: of spiders, of sunlight, of large birds, of tea gone cold, of draughts, and of yellow and green worn together. These girls did not laugh aloud when I committed some gaffe or other, only soothed and wiped up my slopped tea with a cloth, but I was abashed and found it easy to be surly. It was all too easy to imagine them tittering together about *poor old Albion* when I left the room; and was not all that soothing and mopping almost too solicitous: was it even possible that there was an element of parody?

Faces grew solemn when I joined a group of muslins and boaters, chat grew thin and lifeless, boys stopped doing droll things with their ties, and the laughter of the muslins faded. Silence grew like fungus around my facts when I brought them out and displayed them to these others. They nodded, they made sounds of appreciation behind their lips, but I saw their eyes growing distant and beginning to slide sideways over my shoulder as if someone might be approaching who urgently needed to be spoken to.

It was never long before I found myself no longer part of a large group, but part of a small group, one of three, or even two, edging away mentioning cups of tea. In a group I found myself watching faces carefully, like a deaf person, trying to work out what the joke was about Jocelyn's show pony. I suspected that it was not a horse they were speaking of, though I did not know what else a show pony might be. But everyone was laughing, so I laughed too, and hoped no one would ask me what was funny.

Like cleaved to like here, as elsewhere in nature, and dull Singer found himself settled within the dull group. There was MacDonald, no gadfly he, but a solemn young man in the year above me, who felt strongly about grammar, even at pimply seventeen getting himself in a state like some old blunderbuss with a red face and whiskers over the decline of the subjunctive. There was Gillespie: Gillespie was the other fat boy at school, and we had often been paired off in those atrocious pantings over paddocks. We hardly loved each other for being together in affliction, but it meant that we gravitated towards each other now. There was Parsons, who collected coins, and who liked you to turn out your change-pocket so he could check your half-pennies for the one that was worth two hundred pounds; and there was Singer, who could tell you the names of the countries in the world in alphabetical order.

◆   ◆   ◆

There was a young lady who seemed less flighty than the other giggling voiles and muslins: she seemed a serious type of person, and like me did not join in any of the banter. Like me, this cousin of a sister, or sister of a cousin, sat on the outskirts. On her face I recognised the same expression as on my own: haughtiness alternating with too eager a desire to please. This Winifred was a girl who came out with things abruptly, in a jerky way that sounded as if she were picking a fight, and she did not smile much: but I could see that like me she was simply stern with fear.

It was this young lady with whom I was teamed – others had seen how we were two peas from the same awkward pod – to play at some idiot game of shuttlecock and battledore. She did not warm to me for the fact that I was thought a suitable partner: we exchanged a remark or two, but her eyes were elsewhere as she spoke; her eyes were on Davis on the other side of the net, tossing back his forelock and turning from face to smiling face. He was surrounded by all the laughing ones, the ones who somehow had been born knowing how to *fit in*, and here on the other side of the net, awkward Winifred and I exchanged remarks on how long it was since we had played this game, how out of practice we were, and how all the best players seemed to be on the other side.

In the spirit of being a good sport I leapt and lunged as enthusiastically as I could, and played one or two good shots. When I missed an easy one, flapping at the air in a way that must have looked ridiculous, I turned to Winifred with a rueful laugh – Albion proving himself a good loser – and hoped for a friendly gesture. But Winifred did not respond with any kind of warmth. Instead she turned to me and in her most piercing and irritable voice said, 'What do you think this is, Bush Week, and you're the sap!' Before I could quite believe what I had heard, the rotten little feathered object came back over the net and struck me on the head – and Winifred laughed! Laughed at me, so that the spotty girls and the cross-eyed dolt, and all the sparkling beauties on the other side of the net, and Davis grinning away winningly – they all laughed with her, and I froze within, and burned without, with mortification. Desperation made me force out a hoarse laugh myself – a strained *ho ho* through stiff lips – so that I would not look even more ridiculous for taking myself seriously; but how I loathed them all at that moment! Afterwards, over tea and more of those hateful little explosive biscuits, our hostess, the girl most often and most charmingly at Davis' side, came up and put her hand on my arm. 'You must not mind that we laughed, Albion, I know you are a good sport, and it is all in fun, you know.' I was stung all over again that she could think I cared. 'Oh that!' I exclaimed. 'Oh, I had forgotten that, it was nothing,' and I heard my voice over-loud among the teacups.

It was not long before Winifred and I found ourselves teamed again with a dozen others patting a flabby ball about on the lawn, with a dispiriting collection of warped tennis-racquets and split hockey sticks. The ball came my way and I whacked it with my hockey stick (whose ruptured handle had already driven splinters into my palm) and watched it wobble crookedly over towards Winifred. She was well-placed to send the thing between the two tomato stakes that were our goal, and I saw her tongue come out between her lips and her cross frown deepen as she took careful aim with her ravelled tennis-racquet; squeezing that tongue between her teeth as if to bite it off, she took a great swipe at the ball, missed and staggered. A groan went up from our team, a groan and laugh mixed, and Winifred looked around rather wildly at everyone, and it was in that moment, in which her face was naked, that I said, loud enough for her to hear, but not loud enough for everyone, 'Is this Bush Week, Winifred, and you the sap?' Well, it was just a joke: one was supposed to take it in good part, and be a good sport, and see the funny side of it, and so on, but Winifred did not. Winifred shot me a look of desperation and loathing, a look like a physical blow. As I watched her fling away her silly ruined racquet, and walk stiffly off the lawn up to the house, I had to recognise that I had still not got the hang of these social exchanges.

I could see I had badly misjudged: Winifred did not ever look at me or speak to me again, and even the other young ladies seemed to look askance, and the young men seemed to watch me rather carefully, as if I might bite; I despaired, for it was clear now that just when I thought I had got the hang of this game, I had got it most deeply wrong.

Chapter *Five*

THE SIGN up above the door of the business, *Singer & Son, Stationers*, was like a reproach to me: for the eye that knew, such as my own, was conscious of the space after the word *son*, and before the comma, which Father had instructed to be left, in the hope of one day adding another 's'.

Entering by the ponderous front door, that swung closed behind us, cutting off the light and noise of the street, Father and I were entombed immediately in the aspidistra dimness of a tiled hallway with various appropriate dark-brown paintings on the wall, swallowed up in a stuffiness of rugs and furniture-polish. I had to grin and shake hands with various employees, and did not like the smiles they gave me, at once patronising and meeching, and the way I had to stand there then beside Father, tongue-tied as they spoke in figures and abbreviations I did not understand, ungracious when at last they turned to me with some well-meaning – too transparently well-meaning – question about school, or worst of all, some jovial remark about following in my father's footsteps.

The large face of Rundle had been known to me since I had first come here in short pants with Father. He had always seemed an old man in my eyes: he was someone it was impossible to imagine young. On my first piping-voiced visits to the business, Rundle was already a stooping coarse-pored personage who remarked wearyingly on how I had shot up, and how someone should put a brick on my head. 'Thank the Lord for Rundle,' Father would say when he was in a rare man-to-man mood. 'He has kept the business from going under more than once, Albion, though naturally I would never worry your mother with such things.'

Rundle was a man with a large sagging face like a dog's, who wore lumpy tweedy clothes with a suggestion of matted fur about them. His chin was cushioned around with a crescent of fat, but it was not happy fat: his was the awkward bulk of an anxious man, a worrier whose ambition would never rise above being someone else's right-hand man. He was an old-fashioned faithful sort of Fido, proud of being invited to dinner once a year by his employer, and ignorant of the laughter at the expense of his manner of grasping a knife, and of his yellow-charmeuse-swaddled wife, when they left. When called on to inspect a ledger and to point out some detail or other to Father, he would fumble at his handkerchief-pocket and draw out a pince-nez that perched on the end of his thick nose – no one could take seriously a man who wore such things! – and when he put the ledger down on a desk, in order to run a finger down a list of figures and stop at some significant one, the dog's toenail of his forefinger nail was hideously apparent: a brown curved piece of striated horn instead of a pale fingernail with a pink half-moon. Had he caught it in a mangle in infancy, or had he been born that way, and did his thick clothes conceal other hideous abnormalities?

The silence in Father's office, when I was installed in a corner with a humbug and a book, while Father and Rundle went over the figures together, had always oppressed me: my ears hummed, my heart beat too fast, and my palms grew cold at the thought of stepping into Father's shoes eventually, and spending a lifetime here.

Sitting on the hard chair in the corner, while Father and Rundle mumbled away together, I tried to remember who I was. Privately I knew myself to be nothing more than a wisp of unhappiness floating through space. But I reminded myself that in the eyes of the world I was Albion Gidley Singer, son of George Augustus Singer, the prominent and respected man of business. Albion Gidley Singer, I reminded myself, had a definite existence as a conscientious though mediocre student, an adequate medium bowler, and a custodian of a fact or two about almost any subject you could care to name. I ran through a few, like a consoling prayer: the four longest rivers in the world are the Nile, the Amazon, the Yangtze and the Niger; Reykjavik is the capital of Iceland; there are twenty-six bones in the human foot.

◆　◆　◆

I was a large lad now, who made the banister shake when I leaned on it, and these days over the leg of mutton the future of Albion Gidley Singer was often discussed. He would be going up to the University before long, and then, naturally, would go into the business under Father.

It was a comfort more consoling than Mother's fairy-cakes to have Father pass the newspaper across the table to me in the mornings. 'Here, Albion,' he would say, 'this will interest you,' and I would stare at the smudged coarse lettering and pretend to be so engrossed that Father would not query me on what I was reading, or make comments that would require an intelligent answer. At least I knew that, no matter what penetrating and intelligent questions Kristabel might ask, the newspaper would not be passed to her.

At such times I turned to my old friends, my facts, and occasionally I was able to produce a rare one that would cause Father to look at me with something like approval, though tempered with considerable surprise, and say, 'My word, Albion, you are a dark horse!' It was my greatest fear that Father would discover that the accumulation of facts was all I had: my great bank of facts was my capital, on which I drew larger and larger drafts, withdrawing and recklessly spending those hard-won facts.

However bogus I felt my new manliness to be, it seemed that it fooled Father. It was possible, too, that he wished to be fooled; or perhaps he hoped that clothes would succeed in manufacturing a man where one of the top schools, and every advantage, had not. In any case, it was a fact that I had crossed some frontier or other now: I had entered the section of life where fathers discussed the news with their sons, and took them to their tailor's to be fitted for their first adult suit of clothes.

'Chapman is a bit of an old woman,' Father warned me, on the ferry on the way to my first fitting, and I had no idea what he meant, but naturally was not so foolish as to ask. 'If the truth were known he should have retired years ago, but he would not know what to do with himself, I imagine.' Father guffawed, and I imitated him in a subdued way, feeling my palms clammy at having Father speak to me in such a natural way, quite as if I were another man, seeming to forget for the moment that I was his disappointing only son.

'Now, Albion,' Father said, and glanced around as if to check that no one was close enough to hear. The deckhand, a sharp-faced lad of my own age, stared back from along the deck, and I imagined how this wiry and competent person would despise the soft-handed youth standing there with his prosperous father, a person who could at last parse any sentence from Gibbon, construe any lines of Virgil, but could not have coiled a rope and dropped it neatly round a bollard to save his life.

Father lowered his voice, and moved a little closer. Generally, he was a father who kept his distance, so I felt almost embraced by his nearness now. 'There are one or two things you should know, now that you are coming on to manhood,' he said. Father had never spoken to me about anything of a bodily nature, but I was sure that he was about to speak to me now about the peculiarities my body was troubling me with in the most private of ways. Perhaps he would even clarify the mysterious little chats we had had at school from the housemaster on the subject of Purity. I felt a moment's panic, for I was not ready for any such initiation: the impressive husk of Albion Gidley Singer might have appeared ready, but I myself was not. And why had he chosen here and now, on the ferry, virtually in public, and with this knowing-looking lad, with his coil of filthy rope, staring at us?

But Father had no more wish than I to wax intimate on the subject of the body. As the foam sizzled away from the side of the ferry, he instructed me on the number of buttons a gentleman has on his jacket, the quantity of cuff that a gentleman must show, and the vulgarity of cuff-buttons, which no gentleman would ever wear. 'You may have my own silver cuff-links, Albion, until we can provide you with your own, they are the ones my own father gave me when I came of age.' He demonstrated on his own suit of clothes the fact that a gentleman never does up the bottom button of his waistcoat, and never fails to do up all the rest. 'Now, when Chapman is fitting you, Albion, it is a courtesy to stand quite still, and to make a little chat. A tailor is not the same as a shop-assistant, and will be treated by a gentleman with a certain respect.'

We were nearing the Quay now: the note of the engines changed to a deeper throb. Father drew out his gold double-hunter and checked the time, but absently, and as he put it away I felt myself grow even more self-conscious, for I could see he had something more taxing to say, which would require both of us to be at our most wooden and gentlemanly. 'Chapman will ask you, Albion, how you dress.' Father paused here, and coughed, and I felt every pore of my body congest and grow hot with the idea of stripping off (which was what this must mean) before Father, and before Chapman, and had not Father said that Chapman was a woman? I would have to stand shivering before them all, a shameful exhibit of naked-ness covered by nothing but goose-pimples, and everyone would see all I had.

'Yes, Albion, left or right, you must have happened to notice, do you dress to left or right?' I felt myself consumed with redness now, totally befuddled: had I somehow been getting dressed wrongly all these years? My mind was blocked, Father was staring, waiting for an answer, and I was failing the first test of my manhood.

But Father laughed, a great harsh laugh that made the deckhand stare. 'By Jove, Albion, I did not know either at your age, and my own father, your grandfather, let me go to the tailor's not knowing, and I was all of a flummox.' Was his look at my scarlet face ironic? 'It makes me laugh to remem-ber, but it was far from funny then, by Jove!' He laughed again: Father was seldom seen to laugh, and I watched the way his eyes became positively oriental as he did so, and how large and yellow, like a horse's, his teeth were.

To my relief, Chapman turned out not to be literally an old woman. He was a hunched and wizened dark man, horribly like a monkey, and there were large knobs on the knuckles of his hands such as I had not seen before, and coarse white hairs curling out of his ear-holes. He was clumsy with the pins and tape-measures, so that Dingle, the assistant who hovered close at hand, had to rescue various piles and tins of things several times. Chapman limped a little as he walked, making a great show of wincing at each step, his spectacles continually slid down his nose and had to be poked back up with a forefinger, and readjusted with regard to the bendy ear-pieces – generally he seemed even to the eye of one who had never before seen a tailor at work to be unnaturally slow and awkward, and forgetful as he shuffled through tissue paper and samples of dark cloth – 'Now this was the one, was it not, Master Singer? Or was it the stripe now?'

Father knew the right courtesies with which to fill the occasion, and Chapman replied at considerable length: 'Oh thanking you Mr Singer sir, the arthuritis is a great trial to me now, but I cannot complain, thanking you sir,' then going on to enumerate a great number of complaints of a more or less embarrassingly physical nature, so that I blushed as he sighed into my shoulder, chalking me up.

♦   ♦   ♦

A gentleman's club, like a gentleman's tailor, was something that was passed down from a gentleman's father, and once we had been released from Chapman's establishment, Father turned to me with over-loud heartiness and said, 'Lunch at the Club, eh, Albion? High time you knew your way around there.'

Everything in the dining-room seemed misted with the steam of a thousand roasts of beef and Gurney puddings, and there was an almost visible thickness in the air, that made every sound significant: the clink of two spoons on the other side of the room, as the elderly waiter helped someone to brussels sprouts, was an enormous sound, and when someone behind us lit a match for his cigar, the ripping sound almost made me choke on my custard.

In such a hushed and amplifying atmosphere, surrounded by solitary men chewing their way through three courses, it was even more difficult than usual to speak to Father, and all my resolutions – how I would get off on a fresh footing with him, being forthright and man-to-man – wilted, and I was reduced to churlish monosyllables and platitudes, trying to pitch my voice in this dense silence so that it did not ring around the room.

Yes, I agreed with Father, who was trying to do the right thing by his tongue-tied son, I was looking forward to finishing with school, and yes, a few years at the University would stand a man in good stead in any walk of life. How could I, in this greasy hush, punctuated with explosions of silverware, have shared with Father any of my uncertainties?

After lunch we withdrew, like the other gentlemen whose capacious stomachs were labouring to digest it all, to the Reading Room, full of serious men of commerce reading the business news as conscientiously as if taking medicine. Father and I sat down together and Father immediately turned to the stocks and shares page. I tried, but found myself surreptitiously turning back to the less serious pages, the ones in which tight-rope walkers plunged to their deaths, midgets took to Great Danes with carving knives, and babies' faces were discovered to have been gnawed by rats while they slept.

We sat firm in our leather chairs, which discouraged squirming or too much gesturing because of the rude way they tended to squeak and creak, and Father delivered himself of one or two pieces of advice.

'The race is to the swift, Albion,' Father said, and I was surprised to hear him wax poetic. I could see he was in a philosophical mood, and I would have liked to rise to the occasion, but could think of nothing more stimulating to say than, 'Yes, Father,' adding to make me seem more involved, 'I have often thought the same thing.'

Father gave me a look that was not one of admiration, and went on. 'The fact is,' he said, and I admired his authoritative way with a fact, 'that it is a fool's dream to seek equality in the affairs of men where there is none in nature,' and I nodded and murmured into my whisky-and-water, my mind quite blank of responses. Away from Father, I could at times come out with a rotund phrase or two myself, and hold my own in a conversation, and I was determined to come out with something or other now: I could not forever be the gormless son!

'It is a law of nature that the weak go under,' I said, and was pretty sure this was the right kind of thing, but I made the mistake of accompanying my words with a gesture appropriate to the going-under of the weak, that made the leather of the chair give out an unfortunate noise. Father glanced at me sharply, and an old gentleman with a monocle rattled his paper and cleared his throat, and Father said in a quelling sort of way, 'Indeed, Albion. Shall we go?'

Father was silent on the ferry on the way back, as if so much fatherly heartiness had wearied him, but as we neared the wharf close to home, and stood up to get off, he tweaked the front of my Norfolk jacket, holding me at arm's length as if weighing my worth. 'Yes, Albion,' he said. 'Yes, I am sure we will not know you when Chapman has finished with you.'

I was cast down all over again at the note of hope in Father's voice as he spoke of not knowing me. But I knew that no matter how beautifully Chapman cut and pinned, and no matter how scrupulous I was in the matter of waistcoat-buttons and cuff-links, I would never truly become that unrecognisable Albion he hoped for, the Albion who would have been made into a man.

◆   ◆   ◆

Mother's fairy-cakes began to make me gag now: the thick cream was sickening to me, the sugary mouthfuls unmanly and unmanning. 'No thank you, Mother,' I began to say to her offerings, peevishly, petulantly. 'No, really, Mother, I do not want them.' Mother's soft brow creased. 'Are you ill, Albion dearest?' she asked, and bent over me, all lavender and concern. 'No, Mother, I am not ill!' I almost shouted. I could not have said what it was that caused my monstrous impatience with lavender and fairy-cakes, but I wanted to strike this soft jelly of a person, my mother with her weak feminine shape, bending over me solicitously as if I was still an infant.

'Show me your tongue, Albion,' Mother said now, in a firmer tone, and sitting back as if she had seen in my eyes the thought that I wished to hit her. 'Come, Albion, do not be obstinate.' I stuck out my tongue rudely at her and she looked at it briefly without comment. 'Very well, Albion,' she said, and sighed, folding the fairy-cakes into their bag again. 'Good night, dear boy.'

There were no more fairy-cakes, and after a while, repelled by my chilliness and the way I drew myself away in the bed, there was no longer even a goodnight kiss: there was just her wistful smile, and a gesture of her pale hand over my head, and a smoothing of the counterpane over my feet.

Poor Mother! I was a man now, one who could speak man-to-man with my impatient father, I was no longer a child to be coddled and indulged with babyish sweet things. My mouth watered for the cakes, but I despised them too: they were woman's fare, children's fare, and must be put behind me now that I was a man. And that poor mother of mine: she was nothing but a spineless wisp who had to realise that her son no longer belonged to her.

Chapter *Six*

AT THE UNIVERSITY I was a young man in tweed doing his best to be like the others. I was determined to make a fresh start here: the young blades at the University had never seen me blunder on the lawns of Pymble, or sit tongue-tied with Father. With them I could act the man I wished to be, and perhaps if I acted the part for long enough, the act would become self.

I was realistic enough to know that social ease was never going to come naturally to me, but I was sure that being a man was something that could simply be learned, like canasta or waltzing: it was just a matter of acquiring a series of manners and a series of jokes.

I looked around me at the other men in my social circle: Davis was out of reach as a model for me, having too many natural advantages – that hank of hair, that face like a Greek god's, that winning smile – which I could not hope to emulate. But there was an Ogilvie whom I thought might be useful to me. When you peeled away his verve, he did not have any remarkable qualities. His ears stuck out of the side of his head, he was only just on the right side of being short, and his face was not the face of any Greek god. Yet Ogilvie was always the centre of things, always had a witticism ready, and just the right anecdote up his sleeve, was the man everyone wanted to join them.

More conscientiously than I studied Descartes and Milton, I studied just how Ogilvie did it. It did not take me long to notice that Ogilvie never gave anyone the benefit of a few interesting facts, and dignity did not seem to be something he worried over-much about. He had a way of hitching up his pants which I admired, and practised in front of my cheval-glass, and a laugh which did not involve the whole face, which I tried out on my own features. I parted my hair on the side the way Ogilvie did, and took up cigarettes so that I could stand as he did, lounging against something through a screen of smoke, and was even able to go one better when I discovered cigars.

On the subject of the witticism, I decided that forward planning was the thing. I made a note of a few good jokes that I thought I could manage, and spent many hours in front of my mirror, telling myself the one about the Irishman and the glass of water in a way that might strike others as amusing, or at least normal. I watched Ogilvie at the Empire, seeing the way he did not become sleepy and obtuse after a glass or two the way I did; so in my room at College I downed wine like medicine, training myself to become someone who could take his liquor.

I accepted that the thing would never come naturally to

me, but as I got better at it the encouraging notion occurred to me that all these breezy young blades were no more breezy and easy within themselves than I was: it was more than possible that we were all just scraping our shells against each other.

When I felt myself ready, I made sure that Ogilvie's group discovered that Singer, although not possessed of any great sparkle with an anecdote, could hold his own; and even better, that he was not stingy about calling for another bottle from his own pocket, or hosting a luncheon at Fort's. At length Singer succeeded in becoming a part – admittedly a somewhat shadowy and peripheral part – of this circle, which devoted itself to pranks of various kinds, and to entertainments.

And what entertainments! There were banquets upstairs in the private rooms of Juliana's, where the cigar-smoke hung in a cloud below the gilt ceiling and the bottles kept arriving while various entertainments were performed before us. There were more intimate parties of cards and whisky, in the college rooms of the bolder men, where we had to tiptoe out in the early hours onto crisp lawns without waking porters; oh yes, I was there, the education of Albion Gidley Singer was progressing apace.

♦   ♦   ♦

There was a particular evening, upstairs at Juliana's. It was an evening unclear in its precise shape, when many bottles of wine were opened and the cigar-smoke hung blue under the ceiling, and Ogilvie had done his imitation of a lady with a poodle better than I had ever seen it. I raised my glass in dozens of toasts, drained it again and again, confident after all my practice in my own room that I would not disgrace myself.

No: Singer, for all his residual awkwardness when stone-cold sober, was a stayer when it came to liquor, and I could see that they thought me much improved by a drop or two. When I rattled off an alphabetical list of the capital cities of the world, then in clockwise order the mountains of Europe, Ogilvie raised his glass to me solemnly, and Burgess actually laughed, not in an unkind way, but with drunken wonder. Under such approval, Singer blossomed. I was even bold enough to try the one about the blind man and the fish-shop: 'So he tips his hat and says, Good morning, ladies!' and there was general laughter. I caught glances between my companions that meant, 'Singer is not such a dull dog after all,' and I felt that at last I was making progress with this business of being sociable.

As the hour grew later, and the pile of empty bottles grew higher, the talk turned to females. I was the only one who did not join in their various boasts, though I tried to look as if it might be modesty that was keeping me silent, and I joined in admiration at exploits even when I was not one hundred percent sure just what one was supposed to admire.

Burgess boasted of three in a night, but Ogilvie laughed him to scorn and maintained that he had done six in three hours – *virgins at that*, he kept crying, *bona fide virgins, every one!* Before long they seemed to run out of figures, and Ogilvie began to talk of the real thing, of smuggling one or two females in, and was opening and closing a door which revealed and concealed, revealed and concealed, a bed, placed there for the convenience of parties of young bucks like ourselves. Ogilvie winked and grinned with fearful animation, and we all stared past him at the bed appearing and disappearing in a vertiginous way.

I felt myself growing sober with dread: beyond every hurdle there seemed always to be another. Ogilvie extracted pound notes from each of us and left in search of females, and I boldly called for a few more bottles. The mood had changed now. The room was quieter as each man appeared to be deep in thought, having to rouse himself to join in a bit of dispirited chat about what a young ruffian Ogilvie was. Delany began to swig down wine as if it were water, and Quince, who was not much of a drinker, took a huge tot of whisky at one gulp.

I was toying with the idea of a sudden bilious attack, or a shocking chest pain out of the blue, but others were ahead of me. By the time Ogilvie returned with three gaudy females, it was obvious that green Delany was about to disgrace himself, and Quince had lost control of his consonants. Ogilvie gave them a look that said he guessed, and despised, and glanced at the rest of us challengingly.

These smuggled females were another type altogether. I had not before seen such saucy eyes, such red cheeks and lips, curls of such contrivance, or such compressed melon-globes bursting out of bodices. There was more bare female flesh on show than I had ever seen before, and yet, whereas a mere glimpse of ankle or the soft inner flesh of an arm of those sisters and cousins seemed horribly intimate, the bold flesh of these females seemed no more personal than someone else's shoe.

Ogilvie was the first to disappear into the small room with one of the females; he was not there long, and emerged with a swagger and a wink. I watched the woman with curiosity: she followed him out of the room with a hand down the front of her dress, making an adjustment of some sort, then sat down and drank off her glass of port calmly, only complaining of a broken fingernail and asking for *a top-up, dearie*.

When Ogilvie had first returned with the females, I had been deeply fearful, and had kept up an animated conversation with Quince in order to be able to appear not to notice that a female with a great deal of chest on display was sitting next to me on the couch. But now Quince had let me down by sliding forward slowly onto the floor, and was now lying there smiling, too far gone to know that Simmonds was using his hip as a footrest; so, with Ogilvie's knowing eyes on me, I was forced to turn to the woman next to me.

This one had a tolerance for drink equal to my own: she had asked me to fill her glass several times while I was deep in conversation with Quince, and apart from an added brilliance of eye, she seemed unchanged. Her cheeks had been no less red earlier, and she had lounged against a cushion with her legs apart under her dress in just the same way.

Unlike all those genteel sisters and cousins, this female did not stand on ceremony. 'Anyways, I'm Valmai,' she said as if we had been enjoying a long and trusting conversation. 'I'm Valmai, love, and what do they call you?' What did they call me? They called me Singer, if they wore pants, or Albion if they wore skirts, but I found myself telling those rouged lips,

'George, call me George.' Valmai gestured with her glass, and when I had refilled it, she drank deeply and then put her face rather close to mine and said, 'Well, George, tell me something fascinating, eh?'

I did not know what she would find fascinating, so I tried her with one of my more grotesque facts. 'The human body contains twelve pints of blood, and the liver of a well-grown man weighs three and a half pounds,' I told her, and she squealed with horror and delight. 'Ah, garn! What's me big toe weigh then, tell me that, George?' We both gazed down at her feet, and it was I who boldly said, 'First the shoe must be removed, Valmai, then I will be able to estimate.' Valmai gave me a gusty laugh smelling of wine. 'Oh, I'm with you, George, better get me shoe off then, hadn't you?'

So it was that I found myself, purely in a spirit of scientific endeavour, kneeling at Valmai's feet and removing the shoe from the foot. I had trouble with the unaccustomed buckle at first: what was wrong with laces, such as an honest manly boot used? With the shoe off, there was still a barrier in the form of a stocking. From my position below Valmai, I looked up, uncertain what was to be done about the stocking, and found her grinning and nodding with approval. 'That's right, love,' she cried. 'Have to get that off too, won't you, love?'

I pulled at the toe end of the thing, then at where it stretched over the ankle, then at where it swelled over Valmai's substantial calf and hesitated at the barrier of skirt. 'You're a sly one, love, and no mistake!' Valmai shrieked and then to the room at large, in which everyone was now watching us. 'He's weighing me big toe, ever heard that trick?' Then she thrust her leg out and cried, 'Go on then, love, better get the stocking off, eh!' Gingerly I folded back the edge of her skirt, bit by bit, miming finicky scientific care. The stocking seemed to go on forever: was the thing one huge garment covering her entire body? Finally the stocking became thicker, and at the next fold of the skirt, flesh was exposed: jelloid pink flesh, dimpled like the surface of a river in flood.

I nearly abandoned the whole thing, but now the room was urging me on with cries of encouragement, so I wrestled with the rubber attachment until it snapped apart. I pulled, but the stocking was still attached and I deduced there was another rubber fastening at the back. Maintaining the expression of solemnity which was so useful, I gestured for Valmai to roll over to expose this second rubber item, and miming the obedient patient she did so, hiking her skirt up so roughly that I was presented not just with thigh, but with a large putty-coloured buttock, pink-striped from the pressure of folds of fabric, and seeming to my fevered face to be radiating heat like a water-bottle.

I turned away from the expanse of flesh before my face, and saw that my companions had formed a circle around Valmai and me, and were winking and making small signs with their hands, and Ogilvie was jerking his sideways towards the door behind which was the bed: there was no going back now. Singer was obliged to put a good face on it, and lead Valmai into the other room, winking and making small signs with his hands at his companions as he went.

But what did you do, exactly, to get the ball rolling? Did you make a little conversation, as you might in a drawing-room, or would they think that was eccentric? Did you undo their clothes – heaven knows where you started with all those hooks-and-eyes and plackets – or would they think that was rude, and slap your hand away? Did you have to kiss them?

I folded my jacket carefully and reminded myself of the pound notes I had given Ogilvie for the services of this woman, and their image restored me. I turned and eyed her boldly: a thing that you bought did not laugh at you.

In the end, I did not let Singer down. When Valmai removed some of her clothes – they seemed to fall away as easily as bark from a tree – and I was able to see the precise shape of what was under all those bodices and draperies, I rose to the occasion. Morrison had been wrong about almost everything: Valmai's *titties* did not hang down to her waist, and the lips *down there* did not hang down to her knees: in fact I could see nothing at all in that direction but a neat triangle of black hair. Once I had a look I could see that her body was simply a lumpy version of my own; I could not quite look her big bold nipples in the eye, but there was nothing that made me want to bring up my dinner.

And when I began – tentatively at first – actually to touch that flesh with my own, I surprised myself by finding it something I wished to do more of. Her flesh was so yielding that I could feel my fingers positively sink in: it felt as if my nails were actually penetrating that thin skin. I could hear the stubble on my cheek grate like sandpaper across her cheek, and when I lay down on top of her, as she suggested in a whisper in my ear, I heard the breath expelled from her chest with my weight.

She began to sigh and breathe heavily into my neck, like someone who had just run up three flights of stairs: it seemed that I must have found the place, for she panted louder, and I penetrated her.

At first I thought Valmai might break under my weight, or burst from my thrusts, but I became bolder as she neither broke nor burst, but whipped me on with sighs loud in my ear, and gusts of sounds which I recognised as words, 'Yes yes oh yes!' Her appreciation caused me to rise to new heights still, and to be less concerned lest she break or burst: I twisted her arm in its socket, I locked her leg under my own, I grasped her chin and forced her head back into the pillow, and I buried myself in her as far as I could go: still she sighed and breathed 'Yes yes oh yes' in my ear.

'Fleshpots!' I exclaimed, like stout Cortez on Darien, as I felt her warm slime around me. 'Fleshpots!' Even the English language, that I had taken for granted like air all my life, was made vivid in this moment: now I knew what a fleshpot was, and how it felt to be within the warm walls of one, the word made sense as never before. I was joined at this moment to generations of men before me who had made the same discovery, and from now on I, too, could use the word knowing just what it signified, unlike the innocents, who used it carelessly, as if it were nothing more inflammatory than *chair* or *table*.

Under my body, Valmai became puny, a person who took up hardly any space, a person whose voice was as insignificant as the rustling of leaves in a tree, a person who only existed as an extension of my own urges. She twisted under me, and gasped more loudly as my chest forced her down further into the bed, and the feeling of her bird-like framework of bones between my powerful hands made me a giant.

When I took hold of both her wrists and pinioned her to the bed, she could do nothing but turn her head from side to side on the pillow and breathe heavily: her physical strength was in no way a match for mine, and I was aware that it was not beyond the bounds of the possible that I could squeeze her hard enough to make her breathing stop entirely.

Now I knew what it was that fuelled the confidence of all the other men I had ever seen, striding and straddling and gesturing, booming out small remarks in loud voices, delivering themselves of opinions on this and that without a qualm of doubt: it was this, feeling a female body writhe like a skewered beetle under one's own!

I felt myself grow huge within Valmai, and I cried out at last to feel myself open like a flower slowly within her. In that long moment of amazement my blood swelled throughout every cell. My being expanded within the shell of Singer and filled all the space so that he and I were truly joined, and there was no hollowness left.

When I was returned to myself and the consciousness of lying on the bed, sprawled beside Valmai, who was scratching her scalp with a loud rasping noise, the world and myself seemed for the moment insufferable. 'Weary, stale, flat and unprofitable,' I found myself repeating in my mind. 'Weary, stale, flat and unprofitable.' I watched Valmai get up and put some of her clothes back on: now that I was feeling so weary, stale, flat and unprofitable, the flaccid skin of her belly, and the quivering dimpled flesh of her thighs, seemed like so much dead meat.

'Come on dearie, George,' Valmai said. 'Come along, dear,

there's work to be done.' She laughed a short laugh, and handed me my trousers, and although I would rather she had not, she watched while I dressed with clumsy fingers: buttons would not go into their holes, sleeves resisted hands being pushed down them. She watched, and helped, but in a way that did not encourage further intimacies. My body was now simply a problem of physics to her: how to get a hand down a tube of sleeve as quickly as possible.

As I entered the other room I was conscious of being the focus of all the eyes: what sort of fist of it had Singer made, I felt them asking themselves. How glad I was to be able to look them all in the eye, and give Ogilvie a triumphant wink! I would have liked Valmai to demonstrate some sort of admiration, but she plumped herself down next to the other female. 'Look at me blooming stocking, love,' she said, 'fresh on tonight and laddered to buggery, don't know why I bother.'

Ogilvie went over and ran his hand up and down her leg, making a show of inspecting the damage, and it was not long before Valmai was primping and smiling and calling Ogilvie dearie just as she had me; and not long after the door closed behind them for the second time I could hear her: 'Yes yes oh yes! Yes yes oh yes!' and a groan from Ogilvie. In this regard at least, Ogilvie's boasts were not hollow.

I sat with my arm expansively along the back of the sofa, considering afresh the question of women. Morrison had evidently been wrong about many things, but he had been right about one: women could never get enough of it. How could they, lacking the wherewithal for that blossoming epiphany? A man could only pity.

◆　　◆　　◆

Now that I had seen the true, strumpet-face of womanhood, I felt I could begin to understand those other, flutey-voiced unadorned ones who simpered above doilies in Daddy's drawing-room. I saw now with a wonderful clarity that there was no real difference in the ultimate transaction. Only the currency of exchange was different. In the drawing-rooms, the currency was of sighing, and hankering, and it was expected that the parties would do a certain amount of speechifying about love. In the drawing-room trade, the ultimate invoice was the engraved card: Major Such-and-Such (F.R.G. ret'd) and Mrs Such-and-Such request the pleasure of the company of so-and-so on the occasion of the wedding of their daughter. Upstairs at Juliana's there was no such sleight-of-hand: the currency was pound notes pure and simple.

Chapter *Seven*

FATHER DIED in the winter, and by summer he was nothing but a pinch of dust. Nature, the great rationalist, had ensured that the race was in a position to carry on now that Father had produced a son and heir, and Father himself was excess to requirements. All my life I had languished in his shadow, but it was my turn now: Albion Gidley Singer, that seed cold in the ground for so long, had taken a hold of life at last.

I took over Father's chair at the Club, and agreed with old Chapman as he measured me for my mourning that it was a terrible shame, a man in his prime, and what a burden to fall upon my young shoulders. I agreed, and made my face the right lugubrious length for a son in mourning; but my mind was not on dead fathers, but on the fall of a trouser-leg and the roll of a lapel.

Father had considered Chapman's way with the roll of a collar quite the last word in the elegant, but I knew better: things had moved on. 'Longer in the leg, Mr Chapman, they

are wearing them longer now, and the lapel somewhat nar-
rower, please, than the last one you did for me.' But Chapman
would not be told: he chuckled in a patronising way and said,
'Oh dearie me no, Master Singer, Mister Singer I should say.
Your father would turn in his grave if he knew I had given
you a lapel like a bit of string.'

I grew hot with impatience at that little chuckle, and the
way he was so pleased with himself: there he was, creeping
and creaking around his shop, taking forever to thread a
needle, and positively proud of being an old duffer. 'I am not
as young as once I was, sir,' this foolish bent man said, 'and
the arthuritis is shocking some days.'

I was a gentleman, so I could not be entirely blunt, but I
hinted, 'Young Dingle here seems to know his business, for
when you hand over to him.' Chapman creaked and threatened to snap, straightening so he could look me in the face.
'Oh dearie me no sir, I have my old age to think of, and my
own lads to see settled before I hand over to anyone.' I saw
then that Chapman was choosing to ignore what the laws of
life were telling him, and was clinging on like a shrivelled
leaf to a branch. Watching myself in his mirror, a fine figure
of a man splendid in mourning, I knew I could have no truck
with the shrivelled leaves of this world.

◆　　◆　　◆

On my first day of being Mr Singer Senior, I chose not to use
the respectable front door of the Business, as I always had
with Father, and the stuffy hall with the tiled floor. I came in
as an owner should, invisibly, through the back gate, seeing

for myself the life that lay behind the aspidistras and polished brass. Coming in through the big shabby wooden gates of the delivery yard, I felt myself entering the world I had until now been only preparing for.

The figures of those gadflies at the University, and the finicking lecturers in their billowing black, became as wispy as a bit of smoke in the crisp sunlight of this yard, where great lumps of men in blue singlets and braces exchanged shouts as they heaved boxes off drays, and the horses shifted their hooves around their piles of steaming dung. Every sound, every muscle, every hair had a mass about it that I relished: things here took up space, they sat indubitable under this shadowless light.

In Father's presence I had been bewildered by the activity of this organism called the Business – all those minions behind etched-glass windows, men in striped shirts and sleeve-protectors scratching away into ledgers, women carrying bundles of things, vague echoing shouts and thuds from lower regions – and I had been too wary of Father thinking I was a dolt, unfitted to fill his shoes, to ask the questions that might have made it clearer.

Today, Good Old Rundle gushed with too much eagerness, ushered me with too much obsequiousness, so that it verged on the parody, behind Father's desk, into Father's chair, and seemed prepared to exclaim all day on the remarkable fact of *Poor dear Mr Singer having been taken away from us, and now you, Mr Singer, sitting in his place!*

But eventually we got down to brass tacks, and he showed me various large books full of figures and lists. Mr Rundle appeared to know everything there was to know about the figures and the lists, and as he flipped through the pages, greasy with use, he remarked several times that poor dear Mr Singer, rest his soul, had left most of this day-to-day operation to him, Rundle, for it was purely of a mechanical nature and not necessary for a gentleman to waste his time on.

Listening to Mr Rundle I began to make out that Father had somewhat misrepresented his function in the business. It was borne in on me that Father had footled along, making money from a business he did not think it quite gentlemanly to understand. He had, I supposed, planned my gradual absorption into *Singer & Son*. Master Singer would have learned the names of his employees, as Father had been proud of doing; Master Singer would have had another mahogany desk like his father's, and learned to purse his lips and nod with an appearance of knowingness while Rundle explained: so that at last there could be a seamless and unremarkable transition from the rule of Mr Singer Senior to the rule of Mr Singer Junior.

But I was no blotter: to absorb was not my way. Listening to Mr Rundle I grew larger within my spirit, for I knew that I could easily follow the intricacies of the business, which was nothing but facts when you boiled it down. And unlike Father, I did not think there was anything vulgar in coming to grips with pounds, shillings and pence.

I did not distrust Rundle: Rundle would have no more robbed his employer than a rug would sit up and bite its owner's leg. But a man had a certain duty to make the most of his opportunities – even the Bible agreed on that – and I was pretty sure that *Singer & Son* could do better.

When Rundle had taken his ledgers away, some person in a black dress, with eyes red from weeping and an unpleasantly adenoidal way of talking through her tears, brought me a cup of tea – 'Your dear father's cup and saucer, Master Singer, Mister Singer I should say, and do you have your tea as your father did, with two lumps?' The tongs were already poised, but I said, 'No,' rather clearly, so that she looked up in a fright and dropped the sugar lump. 'No sugar at all, thank you, and that cup is too small for my taste, I will provide you with another.' In fact, I had always had two lumps until this moment, and had never before so much as noticed the cup it came in, but she might as well know from the start that the new Mr Singer was not in any respect to be confused with the old.

I resolved there and then on a posthumous portrait of Father: in a pink jacket and puftaloon pants, perhaps, dressed for the hunt, being handed up a glass of champagne as he sat on a horse with a big bottom. There would be a conspicuous contrast with his up-to-the-minute son at the desk beneath him, with his smart narrow lapels, making large sums at the stroke of a pen!

When I suggested to Rundle that he might like to show me around the place, he seemed surprised, but led the way down into the back regions. Here I was introduced to the dark underbelly of the prim shop I had always known. No one had told me that quite so many clerks would be packed into quite such a low-ceilinged room, scraping away into ledgers; no one had prepared me for the rows of peaky-faced women making up parcels in an airless room that smelt of the privy; no one had told me of the splintered floorboards, the unpainted walls, the pervasive smell of ink and paste, the cockroaches running over the piles of stock. It was a relief to stand again out in the yard, where there was a breath of air, and where the men cranking open boxes with crowbars had some blood in their faces.

But I flinched from none of it: I was determined to impress on all of them – Rundle and the sallow women in Packing, the pin-headed men in Despatch, the pimply clerks in Accounts – my rock-like indifference to mere discomfort, and the fact that, although the new Mr Singer was a gentleman like his father, he was a different kettle of fish altogether.

I had a continuous stream of shrewd questions for Rundle, and did not forget any of the answers. Females in the Packing Department were paid one pound four shillings and three-pence a week, they were allowed twelve minutes for a morning-tea break, thirty minutes for lunch, and eight minutes break in the afternoon; the hours were from eight in the morning until seven at night Monday to Saturday, and any breakages were to be paid for from wages. The youngest employee was thirteen, the oldest claimed to be seventy. Smoking was not permitted by staff, nor was spitting, coarse language, or sitting down. In an average year, *Singer & Son* sold forty-three thousand envelopes, one thousand and ten reams of best bond, seven hundred fountain pens, and, in the month of December, one hundred and twenty tooled-leather desk-sets.

I could see various shortcomings in the system, and a good number of my questions related to the prevention of pilfering and other abuses, and I made sure the workers heard me ask Rundle about these things. I wished the word to get around among the workers that the new Mr Singer would not be unfailingly blind and smiling as the old one had been.

In the shop itself, our last port of call, the air was sweet and calm, the various females very pleasing of aspect in their black, and one or two had a glance that I thought a bit on the saucy side as they stood behind their counters waiting to attend on customers, and sizing up the new Mr Singer out of the corners of their eyes. 'This is where your father spent a great deal of his time, Mr Singer,' Rundle said. 'He often said he loved to watch all the activity here, the dance of the shop-girls, he called it.'

Apart from the females, the shop interested me much less than those odorous regions behind: with Father I had spent many weary times here as he gazed complacently about at the long wooden counters, the high ceiling supported by nymphs and curlicued pilasters, and the upholstered chairs where customers rested between purchases. This was the sedate world he had enjoyed, the world of the end-product, but to me it was mere decoration, the showy icing: the real cake was behind, where objects were negotiated over and bought from sharp-eyed suppliers, where numbers were added and subtracted, and where unpleasing human types sweated and laboured, and a man such as myself had something to get his teeth into.

For the sake of completeness, though, I strolled between the various counters, and allowed myself to come to rest, in the most natural way, at the counter of the prettiest girl in black. Father had shown good taste in choosing these shop-girls, and I made a mental note to insert a few wood-nymphs into the hunting portrait.

I asked this girl a question or two about the sale of pens, and listened with a tremendous show of interest while she blushed becomingly, and gestured with her dainty hands, and tried to explain to Mr Singer just why a ten-guinea pen was a very much better buy than a one-guinea one. Her answer, in spite of her embarrassment at her public show, was quite satisfactory, at least to my ear, and on the strength of the girl's persuasion I would have bought two of them. 'Excellent, well done,' I said. 'And what is your name, dear?' 'Miss Gibbs, sir, Dora Gibbs,' she said, a bobbed a curtsy behind her counter, and I repeated the name to myself so I would not forget it, and noticed the way she coloured up so charmingly.

◆ ◆ ◆

I threw myself with pleasure into the business that Father had allowed simply to run itself. There was dead wood, for a start, that had to be removed. I was generous enough to the dead wood, giving out appropriate sums as pensions, and the kinds of trinket people valued – a watch or a silver-plated tray, those kinds of items – but I had my first lesson in the ingratitude of employees when they protested at being let go, and in a few cases actually wheedled me to let them stay on: 'For old times' sake, sir, for your father's sake, sir.'

Truckling was too ingrained in Rundle for him to be blunt, but I saw all the folds of his face become more pendulous with each of my reforms. 'I know he is a little slow, Mr Singer, but he has been with the business since he was just a nipper, sir,' he might venture, or, 'His wife is a sick woman, and there are a lot of kiddies, Mr Singer, it will go hard with him.' I cried out at those lugubrious dewlaps of his, creasing around hard-luck stories, 'Come along, Rundle, am I a charitable institution?' and then, since Rundle was puckering and creasing all over again and obviously had never heard of the rhetorical question, I went on quickly, 'You would not wish to see Singer's submerge under such a weight of hangers-on, would you, Rundle?'

Poor old Rundle: he was good at a hearty few words when one of the old chaps got his gold watch and his pension, he was supreme at just the right sort of laboured witticism when one of the girls got herself married; but he waded along through a miasma of woolly-hearted liberal impulses, and he had nothing to say now, only looked at me in an obstinate pleading way, like a faithful old fleabag being teased about a bone.

Once the dead wood was gone I had the satisfaction of seeing the business look altogether sharper. It was astonishing to see the way men in overalls moved so much faster, and how women in black bustled along so much more industriously after a few watches and trays had been given out.

As I set off each morning for business, I knew I was proving more than worthy of my inheritance. It was too late for Father to see, and to regret never having thought I would amount to anything. But I myself knew that I had, after my unpromising start, finally come into my own. Albion Gidley Singer walked tall now: I saw the light glancing off my boots, catching a button of my jacket as the breeze flapped it back, felt my soles ring on the flagstones. I was here, Albion Gidley Singer was fully present, a solid body at last. I stood waiting for the ferry, a man who had taken over the reins, and on fine mornings I felt like a newly hatched king. Water dimpled at my feet, green and so clear it was like something you could cut a slice out of; birds bobbed on the swell and eyed me, and I flung a handful of pebbles and almost laughed aloud, in spite of my serious suit, to see them flap up from the water. The phrase came to me, *The world is my oyster*, and on these winking and glancing mornings with everything shifting and swelling around me, the foolish platitude was plump and full of juice.

Part Two
A Husband

Chapter *Eight*

NOW THAT I was no longer a mere son, but a man, it seemed only right that I should take a wife. Around me, my school-mates were forging ahead in their professions, and making appropriate matches, setting up domestic establishments with sheets and maids and wicker hall-stands. I went to several weddings, and because of my reputation as something of a public speaker I was called on to say a few words at these gatherings, but afterwards I continued to see these newly married men at the Club as if, after all, nothing very dramatic had happened.

Since my education at the hands of Valmai and her many successors, the scales had fallen from my eyes. I knew now that the business of men and women was beautifully logical, and nothing a man need be afraid of: it was simply the smooth and cog-like operations of blind Nature, who knew of nothing but copulation, and had no purpose other than that of con-tinuing the species. A man of the scientific age, I could look at the whole business rationally, and after considering all the facts, I came to my conclusions.

It all boiled down to brains, and women did not, biologically speaking, need any. Women needed to entice, for otherwise the race would not continue, so they were supplied with various mechanisms of enticement: pink lips, fleshy bulges, and a thousand bolstering ways with a man. They needed to sit still while eggs swelled within them, so they were equipped with a disinclination for exertion, a weakness of ankle, and a fear of soiling themselves. How wondrous were the ways of nature! It was almost enough to make a man believe in a higher power.

As a male, it was my role to compete with other males. That way, the superior male won the superior female, and produced superior offspring to continue the species. In making a few enquiries among my books on how other species managed things, I discovered a most wonderful Aladdin's cave of facts. I took out subscriptions to various journals of a scientific nature, and read in considerable detail about deer, and seagulls, and ferrets, and even slugs and fruit-flies. The story was always the same. Male deer clashed antlers together, male bower-birds brought gifts, pea-cocks flaunted their tails, male slugs spun enticing tendrils of slime: in every single case I studied, all this flamboyant behaviour was nothing more than the mechanism by which the fit prospered, and the weak went under.

The human species was not equipped with antlers, or colourful tails, or even enticing slime. Our particular branch of the species did not even have spears to fling at each other.

But like any other species, our own had its ruthless rituals of selection: it was just a matter of recognising them for what they were.

If we had had antlers, I would have made sure mine were the biggest; if we had had spears, I would have made sure I learned how to throw mine the furthest. Things being as they were, I looked around me, took stock of the realities as a rational man does, and armed myself with a supply of romantic novels. The behaviour set out in these books was, clearly, the enticing slime of *homo sapiens* in the nicer suburbs of Sydney, Australia, in the last years of the nineteenth century.

Absorbing these books like so much nourishment, and cataloguing them on my shelves along with the scientific journals, I made many encouraging discoveries. First among them was the fact that a human male did not need to be witty, or wise, or good at telling amusing anecdotes or making snappy banter. On the contrary, reading between the lines of these books, it was quite clear that nothing more was expected of him than an interesting silence. Ideally, this silence was coupled with an unspecified sense of a mysterious and troubling past, but the great thing about a silence was that it could be eloquent of such things without actually telling any lies. I myself, for example, was not blessed with an interesting past, but I could certainly cultivate the kind of silence that suggested one.

The only other things a male seemed to need was a set of eyes that could *burn* when necessary, and a voice that could *tremble with passion* at the right moment, but could be relied on not to do so otherwise. I thought I could probably manage a bit of eye-burning, and I could probably go as far as getting a shake going in my voice at the right moment. The thing was basically all about something called *depth*, and the naturally stern folds of my face gave me a certain aptitude for *depth*.

Once I got the hang of all this, I turned out to be quite a success with the ladies. The trick was not to allow the manner to slip, even for a moment: the price of success was to banish self-doubt. It got boring behind all that dull silent *depth*, but it was worth a little boredom. 'Oh Mr Singer,' they cooed and clucked now, and their small weak hands fluttered around me as if to alight on some part of my clothing. Clusters of them no longer faded away when I approached, and my facts came into their own at last. Now that I was stern with them, and not trying to curry favour, they listened to my facts with their eyes rapturous, exclaiming, *Fancy! Who would have thought! Goodness me! And what about snakes, Albion, how do they go about it?* They drank in my facts, and encouraged me with their nods and smiles, and watched me sideways out of their shallow eyes.

I enjoyed the way they waited for me to turn and look at them: I learned the pleasure of letting them wait, and learned that the longer they waited the more fascinated they became. I was no longer Albion the outsider, Albion the awkward one, Albion the pitiable. I was like a grub freshly out of my chrysalis, gloriously arrayed in my new-hatched *depth*.

As a man who prided himself on a scientific approach, I read considerably about the whole matter of marriage. I read with some alarm that men who marry too young become *partially bald, dim of sight, and lose all elasticity of limb within a few years*. But as a man well into his twenties, I did not think that my strength would be drained by the duties of marriage. I also read that the rich are qualified for marriage before the poor, *on account of the superiority of their diet*, and approved of this logic. This seemed, in fact, to imply a certain responsibility to reproduce on those of us who were blessed with Nature's bounty. Otherwise there was a danger of the race being swamped by the inferior stock of the others, who leapt recklessly into marriage and produced more of themselves with the thoughtless zeal of hamsters.

I was struck, too, by the book in which I read that a husband and wife should differ from each other: 'The man of studious habits should marry a woman of spirit rather than erudition, or the union will increase the monotony of his existence, which it would be well for his health and spirits to correct by a little conjugal excitement.' Again, this seemed to me entirely logical: any offspring of mine would be equipped with plenty of brains, so that what they gained from their mother should be other qualities which I knew myself to lack.

Moreover, I was looking for a woman physically complementary to myself. The books agreed that, to make what is called a 'handsome couple', the female should be some three inches shorter than the male, and this was no problem, since I was taller than all the women I knew. Her thighs should be voluminous, and according to one rather technical book, *the cellular tissue, and the plumpness connected with it, should obliterate all distinct projection of muscles*. I thought of poor old Kristabel, who appeared to have no cellular tissue or plumpness at all, and who had always appeared to be all distinct projection of muscle, not to mention angularity of bone. However, Kristabel was not my problem. My problem was to choose, from all the sisters of friends, all the cousins of sisters, all the friends of sisters' cousins, which female would make the most appropriate complement to myself.

◆   ◆   ◆

It was the age of emancipation, and women, those ridiculous preaching dogs, felt it necessary to impress me. 'I do not wish to be impressed,' I could have told them, 'I wish to be charmed,' but they would not have listened, even if I had spoken. 'Ruskin, Mr Singer,' a skinny librarian said, pursuing me at one of the tennis parties. 'Do you not agree that Ruskin goes a little too far?' The skinny librarian, whose eyes were too bright for my taste, her mouth too eager to smile at me, leaned her chin on her hand and gazed into my eyes over the lemonade. With clever sparkling kinds of women like this one, I knew I would always be anxious.

Others knew better than to try to impress. There was a yellow voile called Betty, and there was a mauve voile called Norah, and one afternoon I found myself deep in someone's Daddy's Turramurra shrubbery with them both. All the other voiles and all the other boaters had been absorbed by this greenery: here where we found ourselves there was nothing to see but leaves and each other's eyes, nothing to hear but breath coming rather quickly, from laughing and hurrying. 'Close your eyes, Albion, quick, and we will hide,' one of them exclaimed, and obediently I closed my eyes. 'Up to fifty now, Albion, no cheating!' I counted aloud, rather conscious of my fine voice ringing out across the shrubbery, and almost forgot to stop at fifty.

But when I did stop, there was a great secretive silence which made my boomed numbers seem silly. It was quiet enough now for me to hear a beetle crepitate across some dried leaves near my foot, and my own blood beating in my ears. I made myself stop breathing for a moment but when I drew air in again I found that I was panting.

There was a fair spread of shrubbery: I had a feeling of it stretching away around me and found myself turning around and around in this clear patch and seeing only similar bushes before me. Had there been a tree, and a person up it, how they would have laughed to see me revolving in my little clearing! When I called out into the silence – 'Coming ready or not!' – my voice came back at me in a thin mocking way, a voice all on its own, speaking to nothing but leaves and twigs.

How easily I was still reduced to nothing, even after all that work on my depth! My depth was only a veneer: beneath lay all the old poisonous despairs. For now, hearing nothing but my own breath in my nostrils, I was stricken by doubt. It was all too easy to imagine the voiles already back in the house, covering with their hands the pink interiors of their mouths as they told how Albion – how well I could imagine the way they would drawl my name in a witty sort of way – had stood like an obedient pup and was still out there in the shrubbery, and might go on seeking till nightfall unless someone stopped him. For a moment I felt myself tumescent with rage, strangling within my collar. For a moment I felt again that gripe across my chest, squeezing out the air, and the breath grew stringy in my throat.

In the nick of time there was a flash of colour behind a shrub, a titter muffled by leaves, and sounds of feet between bushes. In an instant I was restored, a man once again, a man alone in a shrubbery with two women, and everyone knew what that meant. In an instant my depth fitted itself back over my void, and the gripe loosened its hold on my chest. 'Albion! Albion!' I heard one of them call teasingly. All at once, the afternoon was full of eyes watching me, and only pretending to hide.

It was the yellow that I caught first, crouching in a half-hearted way behind an oleander. She cried out, and covered her eyes with her hands as if to become invisible. 'Oh Albion, you have found me!' she cried on a sort of sigh. 'You must claim me, you know,' she said as I stood with my hands dangling, and came close so there was no mistaking that I was supposed to kiss her. But I took too long about it: should I approach on the left or the right, should the left arm go around the right shoulder, should the right leg take the weight, ought one to be aiming for lip or cheek? She was off before I had time to make my approach.

She vanished behind the bushes again, and when I set off in pursuit, I came across the mauve, caught in a cul-de-sac of bushes. This time I knew to claim her quickly. The right arm went round the left shoulder, the left leg took the weight, and you went straight for the lips, because of course it was part of the game that she turned her head at the last minute and all you got was a bit of left cheek.

Then, of course, the yellow sulked and pouted in a pretty way, so we played the game again, and again – left arm around right side, left arm around right hip, both arms together on shoulders, both arms together round waist, both hands together round hips, lip to left cheek, lip to right cheek, lip to nose, and – finally – lip to lip. Altogether, it turned out to be a very successful afternoon in the shrubbery.

◆   ◆   ◆

As the weeks went by, the mauve one, Norah, began to seem an appropriate sort of person. She was pretty, of course: Albion Gidley Singer was not going to attach himself to any Plain Jane. But unlike some of the others, her prettiness was not a matter of skinny little wrists, and thin little waists; it was not a matter of little nothings of feet, and a neck a man could snap off in his hand.

It could be seen that Norah strived for this flimsy effect, with artfully placed bits of lace, a cunning arrangement of tucks and gores, and a little quivering pair of ear-rings that distracted the eye from a neck as sturdy as a fence-post. Norah had learnt how to create a flutter about her person, a cloudiness of heaped hair, and a soft fragrance made up of lavender-water and laughing; she could hand a teacup like a jewel, and fill any awkward silence with a bit of rhubarb about *the days drawing in* or *the days drawing out*.

But like me, Norah was a sham. A man on the lookout for a bit of substance could see that there was more to Norah then met the eye. She was not a big person, but she seemed to be substance all the way through. From behind, in particular, she was a person to be reckoned with. Her waist was as fragile as was proper in a young lady offering herself as available, but her bottom, as far as could be judged under the layers of taffeta, was a pretty substantial piece of work. If a man took notice of that bottom, I was pretty sure he would not be disappointed. She might be a sham, but her sham complemented my own: she aped the fragile as I aped the solid.

It was Norah's silliness that charmed me most, and her lack of guile: she was as transparent as a window-pane. 'Oh Albion, what is it you see in me?' she asked earnestly, and it was no coquette's ruse: she really wanted to know. 'You are so clever and distinguished, Albion, and I could never understand Gibbon, and never got past the second book on the piano.' All this was true: she never attempted repartee, never tried to best me on a fact, and her jokes were as laborious as an army marching across a plain. But what she did not realise, and I was certainly not going to be the one to tell her, was that a man does not look for the same qualities in his wife as he looks for in himself.

So Norah was the woman I chose in the end. Choosing was no anguish to me, and if had not been Norah, it could just as well have been Betty or May or Violet. It amused me to think that women saw themselves as different from each other, when I knew them to be nearly as interchangeable as the bricks in a wall. I walked through the city and watched them frowning into the windows where dresses and shoes were displayed, I strolled through the shops where whole afternoons were consumed in matching ribbon to silk, or choosing the right shade of eau-de-Nil in gloves. The women in black behind the counters took it all gravely, holding things up to the light; sometimes one would even come out from behind the counter like a priest descending from an altar, to take a piece of ribbon or a scrap of *toile de soie* out into the daylight of the street. She might come back shaking her head like a doctor with a mournful diagnosis, and everyone at the counter would be serious and silent for a time, until someone wondered if the blue would, after all, be preferable.

Women, you fools, I wanted to cry. *You are all the same, you are all just flesh, easier or harder to win, fatter or thinner, passionate or cool: but you are all just the same, just flesh, no ribbons and silks make any difference.*

But they would not have believed. 'Oh, yellow is not my colour at all!' Norah exclaimed once when I pointed to something fanciful in a window. 'There are women who can wear yellow, Albion, but I am not one of them.' She was proud of that, thought herself very special in being unable to wear yellow. 'I am terribly sensitive to colours, Albion. Yellow really pains me. I hope you do not think me eccentric.' I could tell by her simper that she was proud of herself for being so sensitive, and so unusual.

To please her, because I had found that a pleased woman is a greater pleasure to be with than an unpleased one, I put away my yellow cravat with the black clock-pattern, which I had always liked, and let her know that I would no longer trouble her by wearing it.

'Oh, Albion,' Norah exclaimed and clasped her hands, 'how kind of you to humour my whim, I am a silly weak woman, I know, and you are truly kind to indulge me.' Her eyes met mine as she said this, met them rather insistently, and there was a particular sort of flavour to the smile she gave me, and a certain quality of leaning near to me as she spoke. I recognised that, in the language of our sub-group of the species, she was telling me, *If you want me, I am yours*.

Chapter Nine

I GAVE SOME THOUGHT to the where and when of my proposal, for I could easily imagine how such an event could be made ridiculous. That intimate moment could be interrupted by others coming in, who would guess what was happening, and put their fingers to their lips, and tiptoe out ostentatiously, and they would cock their eyebrows at me enquiringly later. And what if I had misread the signals, and she turned me down? Out-of-doors was the only possibility.

The weather co-operated, so we were able to stroll in the Gardens, where the colours of the autumn leaves made as good a pretext as any. We walked sedately along a path, making a little conversation about the various wonders of Nature before us. Norah seemed to know all the right things to say of a tree full of dying leaves, and kept up a steady stream of remarks about *the blaze of colour* and so on.

A certain tension was between us – like any normal man, I was a little anxious, and Norah was no fool in these respects, and knew what was coming. It seemed to me that other couples nudged each other when they saw us, and smirked knowingly, as if a sign hung around my neck: I AM ABOUT TO PROPOSE.

As the shadows lengthened, and the other couples hastened away to warm rooms and games of rummy, I became aware that Norah was allowing hospitable pauses to occur between her effusions. But like a swimmer dithering on the edge of a cold pond, I could not quite make myself plunge into any of her pauses. Somehow, now was never quite the right moment, there would be a better opening shortly. At the end of this path, I promised myself, I will speak. When we get to that palm tree. When those people down there have gone.

'Are you cold, Norah?' I asked solicitously, and hoped she might allow herself to shiver – she was flimsily dressed, and the breeze was cold now – and say, 'Oh, yes, Albion, let us go and have a cup of tea somewhere!' But she did not: in spite of the gooseflesh I could see on her arms, she said airily, 'Oh no, Albion, I am not someone who feels the cold, and it is so pleasant here.' She turned away on the last words – had she said, 'Pleasant here with you'? If she had, what better invitation could a man possibly have? Then again, perhaps she had not, and a man did not want to get it wrong.

So we continued to pace along, and Norah's ingenuity in thinking of yet another word for *blaze* and yet another word for *splendid* was remarkable. I agreed about how wonderful it all was, but I was made fearful by a sudden consciousness of the mystery of this other person called Norah. My palms prickled, my boots were made of lead, my collar strangled me: I could not give birth to the words I had prepared. While

I continued to go *Hmmm* and *Indeed* at regular intervals I was safe, but when the words stopped it would no longer be Albion Gidley Singer, man about town, taking a stroll with one of the young ladies of his circle, a young lady in mauve by the name of Norah. It would be merely me, myself, penetrating the amnion of another's otherness, and staring in the face the possibility of rebuff.

Suddenly a large yellow dog, smooth-haired and all muscle, bounded out of a bush and straight over to me. It leapt up, and before I could act it had wrapped its forelegs around my thigh, panting and slavering and pumping itself against me. I flapped and shouted at it, but the more I flapped and shouted the more excited it became, glancing up with a roguish look and humping away all the harder. 'Whatever is it doing, Albion, whatever is the matter with that dog?' Norah kept asking. 'It is terribly friendly, it seems to know you, Albion, does it belong to a friend of yours?' Finally, as well as wishing to throttle the dog, I also wished to throttle her and her comments. It crossed my mind that this woman was either more stupid than could be believed, or more knowing than any man could credit. Could it be possible that she was laughing at me?

Even after the loathsome dog had been whistled off by its master, who could not resist a suggestive remark about what a shine the dog had taken to me, Norah could not leave the subject alone. Was I generally good with animals? And had I had a dog when I was a boy, and was I good with horses too? And what about budgies? So that weeks had to pass before I felt equal to another stroll with Norah, when I could at last utter the by now rather over-rehearsed and stale words which led to her becoming flesh of my flesh.

'The fact is, there are women and there are men,' I said, sure of my ground there. 'And I wish you to be my wife.' Norah did not titter for once, but touched my skin, the palm of my hand, with her own, and tilted her face up to me. When she watched my mouth, as it shaped the authoritative words it knew, she did not doubt: she filled me with her belief in me. My hands moved, my lips opened and closed, sounds came out of my mouth, muscles in my face were put into operation one by one so that my face was made to smile. Her small hand in mine steadied my giddy hollowness. My mouth forgot its facts in the blaze of fire between our palms. 'Oh Albion,' she whispered, and it was done.

♦   ♦   ♦

At the other weddings I had been to, I had noticed that getting married was more than getting the words right and not tripping on the marble step. In even the best-planned wedding, there was the possibility that a moment would occur in which the rules dropped away from a man, a moment in which he might be called on for spontaneous action. I had watched Prentiss, for example: his hands had trembled so much as he lifted the veil that his bride had had to help him, and their kiss had been like a promise of a lifetime of coming to the rescue.

Or there was Mallory, poor boob: he had actually dropped the ring tinkling on the floor. Everything had to wait while he scrabbled around for it; but then he rose to the moment,

and held up the ring between thumb and forefinger for everyone to see, grinning all over his blushing face with silly
triumph, like a boy with a marble, and a ripple of good-
fellowship had gone around the church. Mallory had been
able, in that moment of mortification, to draw on some reserve
of self and make the moment his own. When he was dead
and buried, people would still be smiling at the way Mallory
had held up the ring.

On the morning of the wedding I woke with my heart
shaking the walls of its chest. If I were to drop the ring, or
fumble the veil, or fart audibly as Simpson had done, I knew
I would be lost: I was no extemporiser. If anything of that
sort happened to me, I knew I would simply be exposed.
Everyone would know that I was just a husk that had learned
a few tricks.

Mother certainly seemed to be on the verge of seeing through
me. 'Why, Albion,' she smiled at breakfast when I dropped
the jam pot, and knocked over the milk jug with my elbow,
'I think you must have a little touch of bridegroom's nerves,
my dear,' and she smiled warmly into my face, and laid a
hand over mine, and waited for me to lay bare my fears.

But I was a grown man in charge of a household and a
business, not a little boy about to break down and pour out
his troubles to his Mamma. 'Thanks, Mother,' I said, and
decided against any more breakfast. 'But I think I am all
right. If you have finished, I will ring for Manning and go
up, I think.'

Mother shed a few tears at the wedding, and Kristabel supplied her with a lacy hanky. My sister looked surprised when

she caught the bouquet, and clutched it ungraciously, as if catching it had simply been a reflex action, as well it might have been, for she had always been more interested in ball games than in marriage. Norah tittered and blushed prettily: women seemed to know instinctively what sort of thing was expected of them. But after the champagne she grasped my elbow in a bold way and cried, 'Oh Albion, I am silly with happiness!' I did not titter: it does not become a man, much less a bridegroom, to titter. But I was glad of my moustache to hide behind.

◆　　◆　　◆

We were married in the rain and my bride's hair smelled of orange water and rain when I deflowered her. Her pleasure in me was so great she writhed and arched beneath me like a hooked fish. 'Albion! Ah!' she cried, and I heard amazement in her voice, and the lust of every woman, for she had been hollow and now she was filled with my bursting passion.

Tears are the ultimate smile: Norah shed them on her wedding-night, ah, such tears, and as fast as I licked them off her face she produced more. I would have liked to say, 'Norah, how well your tears become you!' but, modest maid as she was, she covered her face with her hands, or turned away from me, so I had to grasp her wrists and force her arms down to her sides, and then I could approach my face to hers, and feel her tears cool on my own cheek, feel them salt on my tongue.

How I loved the feel of her arching away under me! How I loved to hear her hiss when I seized her delicate throat in my hands, and bent her backwards over herself, so her breasts became flat and her ribs tensed with strain! I grasped her like a stick across my knees and longed to snap her in two, such was my pleasure in her fragility, and the wire-sharp tension that filled her body in passion.

My own body rang with joy then, hearing her cry out with the pleasure of that pain, trying to whisper because she was a lady on her wedding-night: 'Albion! Please, Albion!' My love for her at that moment was a sickness that could have no relief: my passion was a fever that could not break, although if I had been able to forget myself enough to tear those arms out of their sockets, I might have felt some relief from what pressed against my being like a flood against a wall.

I shot my pulsing seed into her receptacle and lay panting and weeping beside her, feeling my own tears run into my moustache and be lost there. I was at my hollowest then, drained into the Norah-person beside me, and I wept at my emptiness. Life was not in my hands, there was nothing in my hands, it was this woman who had it all, now that she had been filled with my being. 'I am nothing, Norah,' I said, in a voice thick with tears, and felt her listening. 'I am a dry husk, an empty shell.' Around me and in my head the voids were beginning to spin and hum and I was full of nothing but fear: my being was whirling in great blasts of the wind of nothingness. 'I am nothing, Norah,' I said. 'My soul is all alone,' and I was seized with the panic of my emptiness and aloneness.

There was no way I could stop being alone except by a warm touch on my spirit, and I turned to the woman who was full of me, the woman I had filled from my own store of need and fear, and tried to warm myself at her flesh. 'Oh Norah,' I whispered through tears. 'Norah!' I could not find the words for my anguish of soul, and could only hold her against me and say, 'I am here, I am here,' to stop my soul sinking into blackness.

She lay, a minx ashamed. She did not speak, but wept. 'It is the pleasure,' I told her. 'You are a minx, and wanton, for all your titters and laces.' I laughed when she said, 'No, no!' and pushed at me with the palms of her hands. The tears ran down those cheeks of hers and into her mouth.

But Norah was a woman, and women's tears did not seem to well up from any dark and hissing void. Norah was a woman and an animal, and lived only at the level of her greedy flesh. 'Oh no, Albion,' she said, 'enough!' and she pushed at me with her palms, and thrust me away from her as I tried to comfort myself against her, thinking that I wanted to fill her again, not seeing that in my agony of emptiness I needed her to fill me. 'No, Albion, no!' she said, and I licked the salt tears off my moustache and swallowed them.

It was myself I loathed then, for my weakness, that she had seen and rejected. 'It will not happen again, Norah,' I said with dignity, tasting the salt on my lips, and I let her think that I meant I would not fill her again for the moment. 'Thank you, Albion,' she whispered, and I heard her sigh with pleasure, and curl into the bed, filled, replete, powerful, while I felt myself beginning to spin away into the panting fear again.

I felt my being shredding apart, and I seized my wife, because she was going to join me in fear if I had to suffer, and I shook her shoulders until she was gasping and trying to say 'Albion,' through teeth that rattled together, and her fear at last met mine, and I forced my way into her fear, and at last we were joined: she was weeping and fearful as I was, and my fear was divided by being shared with her. 'You are afraid,' I whispered into her ear as I thrust into her. 'You are afraid, afraid, afraid,' I felt her fear greasy under my palms on her skin and I could reject her then, roll away, thrust her away from me, and hear her sob and gasp beside me, and I felt no fear now myself, and could sleep at last. 'Flesh of my flesh,' I said just before I slept. 'You are my wife, flesh of my flesh.' Her tears soothed me like a lullaby into warm sleep.

Chapter Ten

THE BOOKS had warned me that *a houseful of women is like a cageful of monkeys,* but in the end, a houseful of women did not eventuate. Shortly after Norah and I were wed, Kristabel finally found a man who seemed to be willing to have her; perhaps catching the bouquet had done some good after all. They would make a strange pair, I thought; Forbes was a big windy guffawing man with a red face and powerful whiskers hiding a feeble chin, a man whose name I somehow found easy to forget.

I did not oppose, although I could not enthuse either. 'Well, Kristabel,' I said in my heaviest jovial way, 'I suppose you will be asking me to say a few words, will you, before too long?' But instead of being startled, and blushing, as any proper woman would have done, and exclaiming, 'Why Albion, I had not thought, you will have to ask Mother, or Forbes, I do not know' – instead of this type of response, my perverse sister simply continued stitching away at some bit of white stuff, and said calmly, 'Thank you, Albion, but we have decided to have the quietest possible wedding, and speeches are not permitted at the Registry.' I had begun to frame an apt phrase or two in my mind, and it took me a moment to realise that she had decided that she had no use for my apt phrases at all: the freckled vixen, laughing at me up her sleeve and stitching away like the soul of sweetness!

It was only right that Norah and I should now take over the master bedroom from Mother, but I had expected a fight about it, and had assumed that getting her out from among all her flounced bedroom furniture would be like winkling a beetle out from under a stone. But Mother astonished me even more than Kristabel had. She could not seem to turn her back on the master bedroom, or in fact the house itself, fast enough. 'I have it all planned, Albion,' she told me calmly. 'I am going up to Katoomba, to Daphne's, she has plenty of room and could do with the company.' Going to Aunt Daphne's! Without so much as discussing it with me, or doing me the courtesy of seeking my opinion! It was too late now, of course, and no arguments against the coldness of the place or the wrinkled unpleasantness of the sister prevailed against her obstinacy. It was *the reaction*, everyone agreed, from Father's death, although that event seemed positively ancient history to me. It took people in funny ways, everyone agreed, and she had her own means, of course, from Grandfather, so there was nothing anyone could do. 'Thank you for your concern, Albion, but my mind is made up,' she said, but mildly, so I could not accuse her of anything.

At the station, farewelling her, I experienced a pang. It was the same echoing sooty cavern where I had been the one boarding the train so many times to go to that loathed school. I had hung out the window for a last glimpse of Mother's hanky waving among the others, and in front of all the other boys had not been able to shriek, *Mother! Mother! Do not make me go!*

Was it an echo of all that grief, swallowed, stifled, flattened at the time, that caused me now to be glad of the folds of my face to hide behind? I watched Mother's lavender bottom labour up the steps into the carriage and the person within cried out in his heart, *Mother, Mother, do not leave me!* But now, as then, such thoughts were inadmissible: the boy crushing the tears rising in his throat had been practising to be this man, nonchalantly handing his mother up into the train that would take her away.

◆　◆　◆

Norah's first act was to get the dining-room *re-done*. 'It seems perfectly pleasant to me the way it is, Norah,' I said, but my reading had warned me to be patient about new wives and their whims, and I said no more. This *re-doing* occupied her for an astonishing length of time. There were endless holdings-up of strips of wallpaper, endless unpackings of Chinese vases and endless discussions about the merits of watered silk.

But when the room was finished according to Norah's taste, I regretted not having been firmer. In place of the embossed cream paper, and the gravy-coloured *Views of Loch Lomond*, Norah had gone radical. 'It is absolutely the latest thing, Albion, so much more dynamic than that boring old cream.'

The scarlet silk wallpaper was certainly striking, the new lustre chandelier certainly brilliant, the engravings of exotic faces on the walls certainly original: Kristabel and Forbes, invited over for the unveiling, agreed that it was a huge improvement. 'Oh yes,' Kristabel said. 'It was utterly awful before,' and I was reminded of how irritating her dogmatism was, as if no one could possibly think differently. Personally, I had always found the *Views of Loch Lomond* rather soothing.

Well, it might be original, and I was no expert in these things, but it was also possible that it was simply outlandish. I took my place at the head of the table with a certain misgiving. No one wanted to be boring, or to have a dull wife. But there was a limit to everything, and I decided that Norah's originality must not be allowed to encroach beyond the dining-room. As with horses and dogs, so with women: a firm hand has to be taken right from the start.

When it had been made clear to Norah that the rest of the house did not require *re-doing*, and Norah took up painting, I was pleased. A man did not have to eat his dinner in a picture. 'Very suitable, Norah,' I agreed, 'by all means, what a perfectly splendid idea.' There were various anaemic watercolours of *The Boats* and *Sunset over the Bay*, and I thought no more about it.

Before long, though, *a bit of painting* became *Art*, and things became less satisfactory. There were classes in the city, from which she returned with sticky oil-paintings of vases of flowers and arrangements of pumpkins. Art had begun by seeming a harmless enough occupation for a lady, but I grew to dislike the way her face lost its sunny little smile, and almost scowled with concentration, as she laboured over her palette, and the way she kept on fiddling with her picture and only paying me half her attention, as if her pumpkins mattered more than her husband.

'But Norah, have you ever seen a purple pumpkin, and what is this object here, is that supposed to be a leaf?' She held the picture up, squinting at it through half-closed eyes – she would get wrinkles that way, I made a note to tell her – and sounded quite smug and superior as she said, 'Oh, it is called Impressionism, Albion, the latest thing, you are not supposed to paint every leaf.' She made it sound as if painting every leaf, or even expecting a painter to paint every leaf, was a terribly boring thing to do, and continued to inspect the picture, holding it up to the light and humming as if I were not in the room.

As far as I was concerned, it was a lot of twaddle: either you knew how to draw a thing the way it looked, or you did not, and if you did not, you would do better not to try. And it was a fact, a simple fact of history, that there had never been any significant women painters. What was more, I was growing suspicious of these classes she went to. Naturally at the start I had made sure there was no nonsense about life studies, but the teacher had struck me from the beginning as a charlatan in need of a good haircut. Now it was transpiring that he could not even teach a person how to draw a leaf or get the colour right on a pumpkin.

I began to feel seriously encroached on by Art. As time went on, I was more than likely to come home at the end of a hard day at the business to find my drawing-room full of soulful-looking young women, and pale young men with hair in need of a good cut and big liquid eyes: it was like a roomful of spaniels. My wife would be radiant behind the teapot, her little red mouth shaping itself around smiles and exclamations, her little wet tongue flickering in and out, her head tossing and flirting so that her little ear-rings twitched and twinkled at them, and the men hung on her every word, nodding and curving their long fingers further around their teacups.

When the dynamic figure of Albion Gidley Singer burst in on a gust of nor'easter from the Harbour, their moonlike faces all swivelled around. A man could be made to feel an intruder in his own drawing-room.

'Why Albion,' Norah would call from her position at the head of the tea-table, 'you are just in time for a cup of tea, and Mr Reynolds here is just telling us of the fascinating paintings he saw in Paris, please go on, Mr Reynolds,' and courtesy would force me to sit and accept a cup of stewed tea and listen to some lisping little pansy come out with a lot of poppycock about pictures.

They all thought themselves artists, of course, although in point of actual hard fact they were simply students of painting, no doubt producing the same misshapen pumpkins as my wife. One of the young men wished to paint a portrait of Norah, while another sketched her profile as she sat over the teapot, and presented it to her when he left. The soulful girls nodded and looked soulful, but none of them seemed interested in doing a portrait of my wife.

It was a pang like the prick of something sharp to see

Norah's face light up in eagerness when she spoke to them. Her skin softened and warmed: she was like a wax figure coming to life. It made me realise how little she glowed and warmed with me these days, how cool and bland she was: she was politeness itself, but she never showed her eye-teeth to me the way she did to her artist friends.

When they spoke to me, it was in an over-polite and over-clear way, as you might to a foreigner who was more to be pitied than blamed for being so stupid. They showed me paintings, and engravings of other more famous paintings, and I saw only bunches of flowers in vases, or women pouring milk out of jugs, or ships sinking: I saw nothing in these but a representation, more or less accurate, of what I could see better with my own eyes.

It could make a man a little anxious, if he thought about it too much. Was it possible that I was lacking some faculty, in the way a deaf man cannot imagine sound, cannot even believe that sound exists? Was there, in fact, something in these pictures that others could see, and I could not? It was my student days all over again, with a circle of shoulders gently closing me out, the knot of people evaporating at my approach.

They were puffballs, but they were astute enough to flatter the provider of the elegant drawing-room and the plentiful ham sandwiches. 'How I would love to do your head in bronze!' Reynolds cried out at me on one occasion. 'Mrs Singer, you must agree, your husband has a head that would suit bronze.' I flinched from his cry, like the call of a mad bird in my own drawing-room, and stared everyone down as they turned to observe my head. Indeed, it was a splendid head, and probably well-suited to bronze. But I did not like the way Mr

Reynolds cocked his head on one side, considering me as an object in bronze, and the way he made little moulding gestures in the air beside my cheeks; even less did I like the way Norah stared and smiled, as if I were already nothing more than a bulb-eyed bust to have my nose tweaked and the size of my ears remarked upon. There was a little ripple of something very like laughter as they all stared at my head, which under so much scrutiny felt as hollow as a gong.

◆ ◆ ◆

Enough was enough. After dinner that night, I came to Norah in her room where she was brushing out her hair and staring dreamily at herself in the mirror with her hair electric around her. Whoever her dreams were for, they did not appear to be for her husband: when I appeared behind her in the mirror, she drew her wrapper up around her neck as if I were a cold draught.

'It is not the money I mind, Norah, or even the smell of turpentine, though that is peculiarly pervasive in the house. But my dear,' my voice was at its most reasonable, 'do you really feel you have the talent to make it all worthwhile? Can you really say you are in the same class as Mr da Vinci or Mr Rembrandt?'

◆ ◆ ◆

Embroidery turned out to be much more satisfactory. I liked to come home to an embroidering wife, and I liked to pause behind the plumbago before I entered my house, in order to watch my wife as she stitched at her petit-point, and sighed, and crossed and re-crossed her little feet and glanced at the clock, a wife with every hair in place, and every fold of skirt arranged for the delectation of a husband on his return from the shark-infested sea of business. The scowl faded from Norah's face: embroidery did not make her screw up her eyes, or become deaf to her husband's remarks. When she had filled the sofas of our own house with petit-point cushions, she started on Kristabel's. That sister of mine, even now she was a married woman, had not acquired any womanly graces.

Norah's became a small life of no real event. She made expeditions to Town, and could make a day's work out of choosing a new hat or some gloves, or of having luncheon at Bartholomew's with Mrs Longbottom or Mrs Cameron, and choosing another embroidery transfer at Mark Foy's. She no longer showed off her French accent over dinner, holding forth about *pointillism* and *palettes*, but listened while I told her little anecdotes about the business, and what Rundle had said to me yesterday, and how if the price of rubber kept going up we would be ruined, and by a process of association the fact that a rubber tree produces thirty-two pints of rubber sap per year, and that it takes three trees to make the bladders of a dozen fountain pens, and seven trees to make a gross of elastic bands. I would quiz her about the accounts, and she would try to tell me that two-and-six was cheap for mutton, and bring me the account book to prove it.

To my surprise she had turned out to be a pretty fair manager of the house. I had heard other husbands speaking in a tone of tolerant amusement of the inability of their wives to add up the grocer's bill, and I had been ready to step in every month in a jocular way to sort out a cash-book that did not add up. In fact it had been one of married life's little duties that I had almost looked forward to. But Norah did not ever come to me apologetically with a muddle of figures, and when I slipped the account-book out of her escritoire now and then, it seemed satisfactory enough.

Finally she turned out to be a most appropriate wife. She had a pretty turn of phrase with a thank-you letter, she poured tea with much display of now-plump wrist, and she could keep up a tinkle of graceful chatter about the price of tussore and the sullenness of housemaids.

◆　◆　◆

But there is a price to pay for everything in this life, and the price a man paid for a suitable tinkling and tittering kind of wife was a certain ennui.

She bored me to tears at times, with long dissertations over the relative merits of rice pudding or tapioca, or exclaiming indignantly to me about the housemaid over some failure to do with dust or grime. 'That girl will have to go, Albion,' she would tell me. 'I found her today literally, but literally, sweeping the dust under the rug, and oh she was so cheeky when I told her it would not do.' There was a flush in her cheeks: she was as excited at giving a housemaid her walking papers as if she were a general going into battle. Of such banalities was her life made up: and she had to think it mattered, for no one else ever would.

It seemed to take Norah some time to realise I was not interested in the shortcomings of housemaids, or the ingredients of tapioca pudding. I watched out of the corner of my eye as she sparkled and frothed away at me; I grunted now and then, I said 'Ah?' in a way that expressed little enthusiasm, and I allowed my eye to be caught by the corner of a newspaper, or if there were no words at hand, I became engrossed in a speck of mud on my trouser-cuff, or the way my thumbnail needed trimming. Do not think that I meant to hurt. But what was there she could tell me that could engage my interest? Details of her dresses or her coughs, the romances and squabbles of her twittering lady-friends, the price of spotted batiste: how could such things interest a man? I did my best, I sat as long as I could bear, I filled my 'Ah?'s with as much verve as I could muster: I tried, I could not be blamed. But my mind could not be expected to engage itself with the things that filled Norah's mind.

Norah prattled on, no longer waiting for my chilling 'Ah?' but rushing on into some new tale; her voice grew thinner, the tales lost conviction; and at last she fell silent, fell to working on an embroidered parrot or fiddling with her combs, and after a silence she would get up and ring the bell for tea, or for the fire to be lit, or a fly killed.

She might do that, or I might forestall her: the speck on my cuff or my ragged thumbnail might engross me so far that, in the middle of some desperate bit of sparkle of hers, even as her hands were sketching the shape of the climax of her tale on the air, I might rise and leave the room, murmuring words I did not bother to shape properly, leaving her there as if dropped in mid-air. Later when I came back, all smiles and innocence, I would find her gone quiet, subdued, monosyllabic, engrossed herself now in her silly petit-point, or the way the cushions were arranged on the sofa. Then I could be gentle with her: then I could charm and flatter, and cajole and beam, until she thawed, and would embark on some enthusiasm about Mrs Turnbull's dahlias or the proportions of Mrs Fleming's drawing-room.

It was not what she had expected, or what she liked, but she did not run deep enough for any feeling to last long. How I despised her for that thawing, that forgiving! To a person so shallow, nothing could do serious injury.

A wife was not supposed to be a Valmai, but for all the titillation my wife knew how to provide, a man might as well have been in bed with a teapot. She pitied me my passion as if it was a disease that must be humoured, and handled carefully, and smiled about afterwards like an illness that was over now, but would return.

But she was a tease: she loved to provoke me, lying on her chaise-longue, acting the modest maid. 'No, Albion,' she would say. 'No, no, Albion, I am feeling poorly, Albion dearest.' I laughed, because this was a good joke, the joke that she did not want it. 'You are a rutting creature in heat,' I said, and I took her there on the brocade. I loved the game, and so did she. 'You are a modest maid,' I would tell her as I embraced her, 'waiting for the touch of a man, and here I am.' She would keep up the fiction of her headache, or her backache, or her indisposition, as long as she could, lying as unresponsive under me as a lumpy pillow.

But I could not put up with that, for her limpness stole my manhood away from me. Until she was alive and full of protest I was nothing more than a blunt tool questing and finding nothing.

I would have to shake her and prod her, and cram my

fingers into her hungriness, until she writhed and gasped, pulling away from my hold on her, like a chorus insisting, 'No, Albion, Albion no!' but all the while twisting under me in an ecstasy of pleasure. Her 'No, Albion, no!' was the same, I realised, as Valmai's 'Yes, dearie, yes yes yes': the words of women were not to be taken too seriously, but what their bodies told a man was the real story. When Norah began to call out, and arch herself under me, I was restored to myself, and became again a man with his wife.

◆   ◆   ◆

I came to her one night by surprise. She was sitting up in her bed with her embroidered parrot on her lap, staring at nothing. When I came in she made a great show of being busy with the parrot, bringing great clumps and skeins of cotton out of the embroidery-basket, laying them side by side, squinting at them up against the light. 'Oh, Albion,' she exclaimed when I was right up beside her, 'you startled me, I did not hear you.' She frowned as if she had made a mistake, and said again, 'I am busy *here* so I did not *hear* you,' and she might have gone on wondering, had I not put her out of her misery. 'Norah, lend an ear, since you are in the mood for a jest,' I said, 'lend your ears, for I am thinking of heirs,' and I laughed to show her I had made a pleasantry, and she showed her teeth in a smile.

At close quarters, which were the quarters at which I preferred her, she was like a peach, in need of a shave. The down softened the contours of her features and gave her a vagueness that I liked, and I enjoyed the feel of that fur under my fingers. 'My peach,' I said, and she never guessed why she was my peach rather than my angel or my rose.

She watched me closely as if for more, so I found myself speaking in my most coaxing and winning way, and sitting beside her knees on the bed, feeling the warmth of her flesh through the bedclothes. 'Tell me, Norah, how is a woman to be made happy? How is she to be made whole, or rather how is she to be made no longer hole?'

I had to laugh at my joke, and being so witty made me feel gentle towards those warm knees, which I knew to be dimpled and white, and connected to other dimpled and white lengths of soft flesh culminating in the whole of my wife's hole. I laughed, and continued to smile, and shifted a little closer to those knees: I was warmed from within by the thought of what was about to happen, so that I knew I did not look stern and manly, but was demonstrating the manner in which a truly manly man can allow the softer sentiments to take their place when appropriate, and how much more appropriate than when leaning against my wife's white and dimpled knees, connected to her white dimpled thighs, and etcetera?

So, although as much of a man as ever – more so in fact as I felt the effect of my wife's white dimpled etceteras upon the manhood within my trousers – manly as I was, I was sweet for the nonce, and Norah trusted. She laid down her silly silks and tangles and said, 'Oh, Albion, could you not be gentle with me? A woman likes a gentle touch, and a little romance.'

Romance is a cheap trick for shop-girls, Norah, I would have liked to say. *Romance is a fiction invented for the convenience of men.*

I said none of this, however. 'Norah,' I said, 'you are the only one, you are my angel, my cherub, you are the stars that rule my life.' I stared into her eyes, pressed her cool hand, drew closer, in a horizontal sort of way, to where she lay in her white dimples. 'My Norah,' I murmured, 'let us discuss the nature of my void, and yours,' and I took her in a loud sound of sighs, and the other sound that only I could hear, of my own amusement.

Chapter *Eleven*

NOW AND THEN Norah quizzed me about my friends, and I had to give the impression that they were unsuitable, or had moved to Melbourne, or died suddenly but painlessly far away, for I was aware that a man was supposed to have friends.

Ogilvie was the nearest I could claim, although I knew myself to be a very peripheral figure in Ogilvie's life; but under Norah's persistent questioning, our friendship blossomed somewhat in retrospect. When we bumped into Ogilvie outside Bartholomew's, and he invited us home to meet his wife, Norah was most enthusiastic.

I remembered Ogilvie as a bit of a gay dog, and expected a lively evening within which I could imagine Norah and I coming across as rather dull, unable to keep up with smart worldly gossip. But Ogilvie's house turned out to be one in a dull street of similar houses, each with a frangipani or an oleander in the corner of the small front garden. It was not a street where anything much would ever happen. It was a street of perambulators, and men in singlets sweating over the lawn-mower of a Saturday, and talk over back fences, under lemon trees, of joints of meat and ways with beaux.

Norah, that tiresomely appropriate wife, was already making conventional twittering sounds of praise and pleasure as we pushed open the gate, which swung loose from one hinge, so that I could not help frowning: this was slovenly. 'Oh,' she murmured and exclaimed. 'Oh, lovely, frangipani, what a nice quiet street, and look what a dear little brass bell.' This was the kind of thing I had married Norah for, but tonight her girlishness irked me, for I imagined Mrs Ogilvie to be silky and sophisticated, with high-arched pencilled-on eyebrows, and an interesting nose: beside her, Norah's artless charms might seem simply infantile. 'Quiet, Norah,' I said in the moment before I rang the dear little brass bell. 'Quiet, Norah, their frangipani is no better than any other, do not prattle, Norah, I beg you.' She fell silent then, and my finger pressed the dear little brass bell, and we stood side by side in silence, listening to it ring.

Ogilvie opened the door to us, beaming in an avuncular way that I did not recognise. In fact, this was an Ogilvie who was altogether strange to me: this was a tooth-showing Ogilvie of many smarmy phrases as he took Norah's coat, and my hat, and hung them in the cupboard. 'Now come and meet Marjorie,' he cried in a social way I cringed from. Norah twittered away and finally sat, still murmuring amazement and pleasure to be shown to one end of a chintz sofa and be given a sherry. I saw Ogilvie bending over her, offering things on little plates, twinkling away at the rather splendid display of upper chest that was one of Norah's greatest assets. She smiled, showing the dimple in her cheek, and I was pleased to have a wife whose charms were so apparent.

Then, on a cloud of steam and in an aura of roasting meat, Mrs Ogilvie came in from the kitchen, flushed, a lock of hair coming adrift: she was no sophisticate in black satin, with a cigarette-holder and hooded eyes, but simply a skinny woman with a plain face that shone from her exertions in the kitchen, dressed in a brown frock that frankly did nothing for her complexion whatsoever. She came up to me and shook my hand like a man, staring me boldly in the eye and telling me, 'How much Jim has spoken of you, Mr Singer,' quite taking charge, as if Ogilvie were only an onlooker.

Mrs Ogilvie – 'Oh, do call me Marjorie, everyone does' – Mrs Ogilvie was a woman altogether too bold. What a thing of bones and sharp edges she was! Not a single womanly grace: next to her, Norah seemed watery and more than a little silly, but at least was a woman with a curve or two. Nothing about Mrs Ogilvie pleased me, and I could not make myself call her Marjorie: it would have been a kind of intimacy to call her Marjorie, and the thought of intimacy with this sharp-edged glinty-eyed female was about as attractive as the idea of intimacy with a pair of scissors.

I could only pity Ogilvie, for finding himself trapped with this unlovely woman. Poor old Ogilvie! There must have been a sudden child, I assumed, or a nice lump sum from Mrs Ogilvie's Daddy, or some such tale; I reminded myself to try to get the story out of him if we found ourselves alone, and was beginning to look forward to Ogilvie making some private admiring remarks to me about my own choice of wife, and perhaps even revealing a degree of envy.

'As you can see, Singer, we are in a fairly small way here,' Ogilvie said, and glanced around at the gaudy chintz, the scuffed piano and the monkey of a wife. She gave him a glance as if to reproach him for apologising for their life, and then he drew closer to her, took her arm in fact, and tucked it up under his own so that she smiled up into his face. 'But we get along very well with our few books and our music,' he announced heartily, and seeing that I was not going to nod and smile, he turned to Norah. 'And Mrs Singer, do you play, yourself?' Norah, with many a dimple, many a flash of white teeth, and much becoming modesty, made a little story of it. 'Oh, it was attempted,' she laughed, so that her throat in its pearl choker was offered charmingly to the room. 'It was agreed on all sides that since I could not sing, I must therefore of necessity be a fine pianist – but after eight years I had only got up to Book 2,' she twinkled at Ogilvie and Mrs Ogilvie in a confiding humorous way, 'and to this day Book 2 has proved to be a mountain I could not climb!' This was not terribly funny, even less so to me, as I had heard it all more than once before, but Ogilvie and Mrs Ogilvie laughed as if it were the best thing they had ever heard.

'Marjorie is very musical,' Ogilvie said. 'Really very talented you know, Singer.' I did not wish to hear of any of the virtues of that skinny charmless woman with her bold man-like stare, and did not reply. But Norah rushed in to fill the silence I was leaving. 'Oh, how wonderful that must be!' she cried. 'I do so envy you, Mrs Ogilvie!' Mrs Ogilvie appeared to be making an effort to charm Norah. 'And tell me, Mrs Singer,' she said, taking Norah seriously in a way she was not used to, 'are you taken up with charity work at all?'

Charity work indeed! I would permit no such fiddle-faddle from any wife of mine. Norah shot me a look and began to twist her gloves together as if to strangle them. 'Not at the minute,' she said. 'I have been thinking about it, I have been looking around, but what with one thing and another . . .' I sat clenching my glass, willing her into silence, and she did finally subside, and began to smooth out each finger of the gloves on her knee.

To get myself out of the embrace of chintz, I went over to the piano in desperation and jabbed at some notes, and Mrs Ogilvie was beside me all at once, smoothing a bit of the crazed varnish with the tea-towel she had in her hand – 'You must take us as you find us,' Ogilvie had said, but I had not thought he meant tea-towels and palaver!

Oh, I wished to go home! I could not bear the thought of sitting here, observed by Marjorie Ogilvie, and by Norah too, suffering an evening's chit-chat and hearing this woman call him Jim, a quartet of suburban husbands and wives grinning and chattering away at each other.

The food was brought. Ogilvie stood in his place at the head of the table, carving, and Mrs Ogilvie, shinier than ever, doled out greasy potatoes.

'Marjorie is very active in all kinds of ways,' Ogilvie said with a pride I found nauseating, and Mrs Ogilvie nodded, her lean face gone serious, not to say dour, and I realised with a burst of understanding like a door being flung open, that Mrs Ogilvie must be an Emancipist, and was probably working to make sure women became engine-drivers and Prime Ministers. Now I understood her: I understood her sexless brazenness as she stared me in the face, thinking herself as good as

I; I understood her leanness, her sexless wiry energy of form.

Ogilvie! I thought, you are not the man I thought you! I began to notice everything with rage and contempt – the thick china we were eating off, the inferior silver, the overdone beef – and my heart began to harden against Ogilvie. I had a moment's vision of him in bed with his wife: there was no question in my mind as to who wore the pants in that relationship, and as Ogilvie stared at me I could envisage all too clearly that greyhound Marjorie astride him, whipping his lumpen flesh on until it responded.

◆ ◆ ◆

I was an unpleasant guest. I was at my most churlish, I refused everything offered to me, picked around at the food on my plate in an insulting way, and hardly spoke. Time had reversed our positions, and Ogilvie, who when we were mere students had seemed to inhabit the pinnacle of success, was exposed in the light of maturity to be nothing more than a shabby little man with frayed cuffs.

I watched coldly as Ogilvie tried to woo me with wit. 'Singer!' he exclaimed, with the bottle of only-passable wine in his hand. 'Singer, let me fill you up!' I shook my head and put a finger over my glass: I was keen for this meal to be done, and the less we ate and drank the quicker that moment would arrive. But Ogilvie would not take no for an answer. 'Come, Singer!' he coaxed. 'Alcohol, Singer – one of the greatest of human inventions!' He held the bottle up to the light and stared at it as if it was a great vintage. *You would do better not to draw attention to it, Ogilvie*, I thought unpleasantly. He swooped down with it to my glass and filled it before I could stop him, crying out, 'A greater invention than Hell, Singer, greater than the bullet, greater even than the sock-suspender!' His voice, full of far too much cheer, was loud and forced in this small quiet room.

I downed the wine quickly, as if it were medicine, although I did not go so far as to grimace. At last plates were removed. Mrs Ogilvie did not actually scrape them at the table, but she stacked them with a great slattern's clatter. Trifle was brought and I ate mine so quickly, mad with impatience now, that Mrs Ogilvie was sure I must have enjoyed it, and would want more: there was a tedious exchange with a trembling spoonful of the stuff hovering over my plate.

When Norah accepted a second helping I had to clench my feet inside my shoes in rage. 'Fool woman!' I shouted in my heart. 'We will never be done!'

That lot of plates was cleared; a dish was heard to slide off the top of a stack in some further room, and smash in a satisfying way, and Norah began a titter, and looked around for support, but I was giving her none.

Mrs Ogilvie returned smoothing her hair and smiling as brightly as if she was as pleased to see her ugly dinner-set broken as I was. She did not sit down again at the table, but on the piano-stool, spun it around, and played a chord. 'Mr Singer, I am a tyrant, you know,' this bony woman exclaimed, and I stared, for she seemed capable of anything. 'Mr Singer, with a name like yours I feel sure we can expect some entertainment from you.'

Other feeble males might be prevailed on by twittering

females to stand at the side of the piano and stick a thumb into the waist-band of their trousers, strike an attitude, and sing. For myself, I did not know how a man could stand showing his tonsils to a roomful of people. 'By no means, Mrs Ogilvie, will I be prevailed on to sing,' I said. 'And Norah, as she has said, does not play.' Mrs Ogilvie did not shrink back from my stone-like tone: she continued to gaze into my face, but she looked coldly now.

In the event, no one sang. I could see that Ogilvie had finally allowed my chill to penetrate his heartiness, and that Mrs Ogilvie was now animated, pink of cheek and gleaming of eye, by dislike for me. I glanced, not very surreptitiously, at my watch, but saw that even such an ungracious guest as myself could not leave just yet.

Mrs Ogilvie decided on a different stratagem now, seeing that a jolly night of music was out of the question. 'Would you care to look at my glasshouse, Mrs Singer?' she asked. 'It is my pride and joy.' Norah was not a woman that any Emancipist could warm to, but I could see Mrs Ogilvie reminding herself that Norah was a sister.

Ogilvie lost no time. 'Well, Singer, perhaps I could show you my study, there are one or two items of interest there.' I had no wish to see Ogilvie's study: I was prepared for fancy paper-weights in the shape of the Eiffel Tower, and vulgar elaborate pen-sets, birthday gifts from Mrs Ogilvie. I was prepared for a room attempting the grandiose, as so much else this evening had, with thousands of books, all worthless, lining the walls and some kind of self-important tooled-leather desk, saved and scrimped for: I could imagine it all, of a piece with the chintz and the dinner-set, and looked forward to finishing off the last of my illusions about Ogilvie. 'Nothing could give me greater pleasure,' I told Ogilvie, and got to my feet as slowly as possible, so he had to wait to usher me through the door.

To call the room a study was to overstate the case: it was simply the glassed-in back verandah, where the light rained down onto the desk and a few leaning bookcases. I turned to the books as a refuge, and Ogilvie did too. 'I observe the same law regarding my bookshelves as I do in the rest of life,' he said grandly, running his hand along the spines of his thin little collection, 'namely, that competition is the mechanism whereby excellence flourishes. If I do not consult one of these books in the course of a year, it has not earned its shelf-space: it has become a parasite, and I weed it out.' He fiddled on the desk for a moment before saying in a different and less confident way, 'Of course, Marjorie cannot bear to see a book thrown away, she salvages all my rejects and keeps them on her own shelves; we differ in such things, Marjorie and I, we do not see eye to eye on everything. But,' he stopped fiddling over the pens on his desk and looked me in the face, 'in spite of that I am devoted to her, Singer, we are joined by the strongest of intellectual bonds.'

I could forgive Ogilvie now: he wished me to know that he had not become a fool. As clearly as I could myself, he could see the difference between Norah and Marjorie, a gulf almost as between different species, but he was man enough to declare his loyalty to her. Now he glanced at me, as if fearing skepticism in my face, and said, 'My life is not a wealthy one,

Singer, as you can see, but I count it rich for having a wife of intelligence such as Marjorie.' The night fell very still as if to receive this declaration. I considered the matching declaration I myself could make, that my life was becoming wealthier every day, but I counted it poor for having a wife of silliness such as Norah.

Unlike Ogilvie, however, I was not prepared to unburden my soul to a man who was, after all, really a stranger to me. I began, 'Well, Ogilvie,' preparing a few banalities about *married bliss* and *better halves*, but he came halfway to meet me in my difficulties. 'Oh, I did not mean to burden you with my entire life-history, Singer! I am a terrible gasbag, you know.' And there was the old Ogilvie shining through now, charming me with his smile and his way of leaning in towards you as if you alone were the special one. 'My word, Singer, I am glad we met again,' he said, and all my churlishness dropped away. As a pair of gentlemen, there were few outlets available to us in this moment, but we used to the hilt those we had. I slapped Ogilvie on the back, he shook my hand at length, and we spoke together the phrases we were permitted: *Good man, jolly good show, damn fine, by Jove eh.*

◆　　◆　　◆

When we returned to the wives and the chintz I looked at them in a new way. I looked at watery Norah, each of whose shallow depths was quite transparent to me; and at Marjorie Ogilvie alongside her with her clever eyes, and her mouth that seemed always on the point of a wry or ironical smile, and that seemed to conceal who knew what surprising thoughts. Just for a moment I was seized with a pang. Had I done the right thing, after all, in snaring the daintiest and most adoring of those muslin gowns? Had I done right to go for chatter about grosgrain, and a graceful way with a saucer? Or was it conceivable that I had short-changed myself? Should I have found, as Ogilvie seemed to have, a witty ironical comrade full of surprises, someone to bring a bit of fun into life? Could I have found someone to share the dark solitude of self?

The thought was like a door opening out of a dark wall, letting out laughter and music, the sounds of others finding joy, while I myself was left out in the cold, all alone. It was a freezing pain such as I had never felt, all the worse because, until this moment, I had not even guessed at the possibility of such a thing. There was a bleak void at my heart, and a sense of outrage. Why had no one told me a man could hope for more? Why had no one told me a wife might bring joy?

But, no! I closed the door: I looked at Norah as she sat neatly against a corner of the chesterfield, her cheeks prettily flushed, her skin gold in the lamplight, her eyes soft and admiring as Ogilvie and I came in and stood before her. We would shortly go home, Norah and I, and I would come to her as she lay in her peach satin nightdress, and she would be soft under me, her eyes closed, her limbs mine to do with as I wished. Whereas – I looked hard at Marjorie Ogilvie, and tried to imagine her in her nightgown, hair spread out on the pillow – she would still have her ironical smile and her clever eyes hiding surprising thoughts, and I was not a man who wished to find himself in bed with an ironical smile and clever eyes.

Chapter *Twelve*

SOMETHING WAS BEGINNING to be required to be proved.
People were starting to comment, in a sly way: hints began
to be dropped, glances began to invite confidences. Kristabel
was the only one who minded her own business, and that
was because she and Forbes were also failing to do the
expected. Mother, casually, and not as if it concerned anyone
she knew, began to speak of various old wives' tricks she had
heard of, and I was growing anxious enough to try them.

Against Norah's protests I tried tipping her up on end like
a bottle, I tried large quantities of oysters and stout taken
beforehand, I tried tincture of belladonna introduced into the
cavity; I even employed a ridiculous person, a hypnotist, who
spent an hour with Norah in a darkened room, charged me
five guineas, and went away laughing! Norah actually tittered
in my face when I tried Mother's waxed-paper trick, but it
seemed that this was the one that finally bore fruit.

Norah began measuring her neck in the mornings. I felt
cold fear the first time I saw her with the tape-measure around

her neck; was she measuring herself for the noose? I said nothing, but the next day once again she had the tape-measure ostentatiously in her hand as I passed, and leaned forward to the mirror so she could read the figures. It went against the grain to have to ask Norah anything, especially since she so clearly wished me to ask, but there was nothing for it.

'It is one of the best early signs, Albion,' she said, with a peculiar simper, and I was forced to ask, becoming more irritated, 'Signs of what, Norah?' But even then she would not give me a straight answer. 'Oh Albion, can you not guess?' she smirked and mewed, and I could imagine my hands grasping her around that neck and squeezing: her eyes would bulge, her cheeks would purple, but she would finally come out with it.

As if she saw this look written on my face she said quickly, 'A baby, Albion, a thickening of the neck is one of the first signs that a woman is with child.' *With child!* Something in me flinched from the dignity of the phrase: it was true that I wished for a son, but I did not feel that Norah had any right to become a person of substance, as she did in describing herself as *with child*.

'That is good news, Norah,' I said evenly, 'and, if I may say so, high time.' Norah, whose face had brightened when she had announced herself as being *with child*, deflated, and her forehead creased. Creased and deflated was the way I preferred Norah, and I put my arms around her as a mark of approval that our demeaning bedroom practices had finally paid off: as a reward, I was willing, for a few minutes, to be that romantic gentleman she wished for.

• • •

It turned out to be a wild kind of night when Norah was brought to bed. The tempests of wind and rain beat so furiously against the roof and the windows that I could not hear Norah as she said something from the end of the dining-room table during dinner. 'I beg your pardon, Norah, you will have to speak up,' I mouthed down the table at her, but her eyes slid over me without seeing; she got up quickly from her chair and without a word to me moved in an awkward sort of way, bandy-legged under her skirt, towards the door.

As she went through the doorway I saw that the back of her grey gown was darkened, and darkening further even as I looked, by some flood. Was it possible that my wife had wet herself at her own dinner-table?

I waited, but Norah did not reappear, only finally flustered Alma, the new maid, poked her head around the doorway, as if I were a tradesman owed some money, who did not require proper courtesies, and shouted out hastily, 'It is coming, Mr Singer, the baby is coming, sir!' and was gone again, leaving me sitting in foolish pomp at the head of an empty table, with an uncleared clutter of plates around me.

I had known for years, especially at my own marriage, that a husband is the least important accessory at a wedding. The gown, the bridesmaids' gowns, the going-away outfit, the flowers, the choice of hymns – all were more important than the bridegroom. Now I discovered that the unimportance of a man at his own wedding is as nothing compared to the unimportance of a man at the birth of his own child. I sat in the parlour, where the fire was dying away for lack of coal in the coal-scuttle, and submerged myself in the sober facts of the *Sydney Morning Herald*, lit a cigar and let it go out, poured myself a port and drank it too quickly, and sat hiccuping, crouching lower and lower over the creaking coals.

But no matter how many solemn pieces of news I read, no matter how I puffed, swallowed, hiccuped and crouched, I could not fail to hear the sounds from the room above. All my study of the statues in the Botanical Gardens, the books on *The Sacred Bond*, Valmai and all the rest of them, even the various textures of my wife, had in no way prepared me for those sounds. At first I thought the screams must be some aberration of the wind in the shutters, and went around the room checking each one. Then I wondered if what I heard was not a large sound travelling some distance, but a tiny sound close up, and I poked and prodded at the embers, in case some bit of something damp was setting up a tiny squealing. I could not believe for a very long time that the sounds were definitely coming from upstairs, and it took me even longer to comprehend that they must be coming from the dainty throat of my wife.

Nothing I had ever experienced made it possible for me to believe that any human being could make such noises, and certainly not a lady. And it was simply not credible that it should be my soft-spoken wife, immaculate and modulated at all times of day or night, whose voice was never raised, whose control over the various operations of her body was total, and who would be embarrassed beyond words to hear sounds like these.

These sounds were made by a person who did not care what anyone thought: they were made, could only be made in their dreadful coarse frankness of pain, by someone who had forgotten that they were part of the human race: they were sounds made by someone entirely alone with the unbearable.

Around the time of the arrival of the midwife, the timbre of the sounds changed to something more like hoarse cries for help. By the time the specialist had arrived, solemn in his whiskers, brushing past the ineffectual hovering husband on his way up the stairs, the sounds Norah was producing were a kind of agonised mooing.

I had long since stopped even pretending to read the *Sydney Morning Herald*; I had lit several cigars, poured more port, lit every lamp in the room, paced up and down like a man in a cartoon: generally I had not known what to do with myself. Finally, frozen in the bleak room, I went out myself to fetch coal and ran into Alma, heaving a great kettle of hot water up the stairs, panting, wild-eyed: the look she gave me could only have been one of accusation. 'Oh, Mr Singer, it is bad, it is real bad,' she said, then set her mouth tight and went on slopping the kettle up the stairs.

I went down to the scullery, feeling that nature was being turned on its head on this wild night. That grubby and illiterate maid-of-all-work was full of power tonight, and Albion Gidley Singer, man of expensive and extensive education, of spotless linen, beautiful manners, and a considerable way with the ladies, mattered about as much as a puppy underfoot. Alma was mistress over the master tonight: she was invited into the room upstairs, while I was not. Alma could look at me with barely disguised scorn because she knew the facts of what was going on up there, and I did not. I knew the orifice the child was likely to emerge from, that far simple logic could get me, but beyond that I had not the slightest image of what the thing involved.

As the hours passed and a second coal-scuttle was emptied, the sounds from upstairs found a new tone. There was no longer fear or despair in them, no longer a pleading cadence. Now they were the sounds of a being in outrage. There was an element of astonishment, and an element of muscular rage. They were now the cries of someone doing battle, someone becoming more furious and more determined with every new blow: someone in whom mere pain had been transformed into adamantine will.

The chill that I was beginning to feel around my heart now was not entirely due to the lateness of the hour and the coldness of the room. There was another private and shameful chill, of knowing that I would not be able to survive what Norah was now surviving. Man and all that I was, I would have despaired, would have laid down my burden and died rather than go on, and on, and on, with this thing that seemed to get nowhere. That flimsy, silly, timorous woman Norah, who had to summon me from the next room to kill a spider, who ran screeching at the sight of a mouse along the skirting-board, who collapsed in a heap if her pink moire got a drop of rain on it: this little nothing of a person had found within herself some warrior who could go on doing battle all night.

Chapter *Thirteen*

MY CHILD, a large pink daughter of many wrinkles and folds, was the most indubitable fact I had ever seen. She shocked me, lying naked and lewd on a sheet: her cleft was swollen, pink, pursey. The women watched me, to see what I would make of this creature with its privates as shameless and swollen as a libertine's, but I betrayed nothing. Norah stared with her biscuit-coloured eyes, Alma gawped and breathed, and the midwife in her bloodspattered white would not leave me alone with her eyes. 'Look, what a beauty, Mr Singer,' they crowed. 'Look, look, look!' and they thrust her tiny cleft towards me, and wanted to see me hold it.

Like any man worth his salt, and especially one in charge of a family business, I had wished for a son and heir. I had had various names in readiness, and had been enjoying small scenes in my mind, of introducing my manly young chap to acquaintances, and hearing them exclaim at what a fine fellow he was and how much he took after his father, and other no less comforting scenes of handing over the business at the end of a long and successful life to a son full of respect for his venerable father.

I had never thought of a girl as a possible event. The birth of my daughter was a harsh reminder to me that dreams are not facts, and dreams are not worth a pinch of dust.

How could it benefit me, I cried to the dead gods who had left us spinning here alone, to have a female child? 'Lord,' I would have cried, had I been able to believe in any Lord. 'Lord, how could'st thou?'

Such an unlooked-for event shook me somewhat. The steady world around me, in which a mile always contained 5,280 feet, and a table was a solid thing that hurt your knuckles if you struck it, took on for a while the unsteady quality of betrayal.

❖   ❖   ❖

Babies were women's business, so that apart from gazing at the face surrounded by lace in the crib, I did not have much to do with Lilian the baby. Once or twice Norah handed me the white bundle, but there seemed nowhere to get a grip on the thing, and the way the head lolled backwards and forwards alarmed me: what if my daughter's head snapped off its shoulders while I was in charge?

On the occasion of her first birthday a celebration was thought to be in order, so the family assembled. Mother came down from Katoomba, where she had flung herself into good works and temperance. 'No, Albion,' she replied blandly to my enquiries. 'I do not find the cold a problem, I just make sure I have my combinations on, and thank you, but Daphne and I seem to see eye to eye on most things.' Certainly the air, or something, had put a flush in her previously pasty cheeks and given her a liveliness of eye I did not remember her having. Norah saw the change too, and exclaimed with a tactless astonishment, 'My goodness, Mrs Singer, how wonderfully well you are looking!'

Certainly she exuded rude sinewy health now, but was rude sinewy health really what one wished for in a lady? Her stride as she crossed the room to see her granddaughter was robust enough to set the knick-knacks on the occasional table a-quiver. Her hair was no longer arranged in an intricate construction of combs and pins, her clothes were plain to the point of ugliness, and she seemed to have forgotten that a lady does not monopolise the conversation about her own interests, and not in such a loud and dogmatic voice.

Ambitions to better the world were laudable, but they appeared to do nothing for a lady's charms. I made a note: Mother would have to be warned that she was in danger of *letting herself go*.

She swooped on Lilian with great crows and cries of delight, rattling rattles at her with inexhaustible energy, and exclaiming over and over again the very things I felt might be better passed over in tactful silence: 'Look at these great big fat legs! Look at the size of her chest! And goodness, how strong she is!'

To tell the truth, I was wondering whether Norah had not been stuffing the child like a goose, she was so very large and muscular-looking, and flung herself around in people's arms in such a determined and vigorous way. It would have been more natural for a girl to have something delicate about her, something winsome, something altogether more yielding.

Kristabel was there, playing the fond aunt, though she made no secret of the fact that she was not the motherly type. She admired Lilian from a distance, making remarks about how advanced her niece seemed to be, but was uneasy when given her to hold. It occurred to me to wonder whether my sister was simply barren by nature, or whether, being such an unnatural woman, she was *taking precautions*. I had heard the phrase, and naturally I knew what it meant, but *taking precautions* was another of those slimy female mysteries that a man was supposed to nod wisely about, and not enquire into too closely. I thought it was not a bad idea. It was hard to imagine the weird and wonderful progeny that might have come from the union of a woman like a man and man like a woman.

For Forbes was full of what one could only call maternal feelings. He clucked and sang at Lilian, and played *this little piggy* with her toes, and did *this is the way the ladies ride* with her on his knees: altogether making a monkey of himself.

I tried to think of the way I had seen other fathers deal with their children: surely a man was not expected to do this type of thing? I watched Forbes with embarrassment, but also with an uneasy knowledge that I could not have delightedly lost myself in a child the way Forbes could, even if it had been expected of me. He was not simply acting the part of the fond uncle, he was actually taking joy in every moment, relishing every smile she gave him, full of gladness when she laughed. Something in him was able to blossom with a child, and when I searched my own heart I knew I was lacking such a thing.

When Lilian, in the middle of all the excitement, suddenly

went still, became very red in the face and began to grunt
like an old woman, it was Forbes who laughed fit to rattle the
ornaments, and exclaimed, 'By Jove, she is busy down below,
that's the girl, Lilian!' I kept myself very cool about it all, but
I could not help feeling it was something like having an
animal in the room. From the area around Lilian there came
a pungent smell. I was prepared to pretend it did not exist,
but Forbes did not seem to have learnt the same sort of manners I had. 'By Jove, that is a rich aroma, Singer,' he blared
out shamelessly. 'That is a healthy system at work!' Kristabel
and Mother and I pretended a matter-of-factness about it all,
but I could not help feeling that there was an obscene relish
in his enjoyment of the bodily functions of my daughter.

When the nursemaid brought Lilian back it seemed that it
was my turn. The proud father was handed his daughter, and
while everyone looked on, staring as if wanting to see me
make a fool of myself, I tried to dandle her on my knee. But
she was an awkward child to dandle. She heaved around,
arched backwards in my hands, flung toys across the room
when I offered them to her, and was generally as wilful and
uncomfortable as a lapful of monkeys.

They watched and watched, Mother and Kristabel and
Norah and Forbes and the nursemaid, all their eyes on me.
I grew more and more awkward, because as well as being
restless, it seemed to me that my daughter was being a tease:
yes, at one year old somehow she was already a flirt! Her tiny
feet trampled into my lap, and however often I took her feet
in my hand and shifted them onto my legs, they went straight
back to the area of my groin: she stamped and fidgeted there,

and laughed into my face to see me wince. She laughed, showing gums and a few lonely teeth, and collapsed against me so that I felt her wet hot mouth pressed directly against my own, cold saliva running down my chin, and it took a considerable part of my strength to prise her away from the embrace. Titillation of a male seemed to come as the earliest instinct, before speech, before locomotion, almost before thought!

I felt myself becoming flushed with the consciousness of all those eyes watching while my daughter toyed with me, and it made me remember what I had not thought of for years, that occasion of similar awkwardness during my courtship of Norah, when that yellow dog had humped itself against me as if I were a bitch on heat, and Norah had pumped away with her questions, artful or artless I would never know.

It was the same confusion I felt now, not knowing what any of these women were thinking, or how much they might know about the male physiognomy. The women all stared and laughed and murmured comments to each other that I could not hear over Lilian crowing in my ear; the nursemaid stood grinning, Alma stared and nodded like a dolt, and Forbes was smirking and exclaiming as if to egg Lilian on, and winking at me.

I was growing hot and bothered within my worsted, and felt myself all awry: Lilian had grabbed at my tie, plucked at my hair, dribbled on my shoulder, and altogether in her hands I felt that I was becoming a dishevelled figure of fun. 'Thank you, Miss Adams, I think Lilian has become a little over-excited, perhaps you would take her back to the nursery,' I said, and as Lilian was removed, why was it that my word *excited*, perhaps a poor choice, seemed to be repeated by everyone in the room as they glanced at me, the word repeated over and over as if in mockery, until I strode to the bell and rang for tea. Whether they were mocking me or not, they would have a stop put to it.

◆　◆　◆

When Norah became *with child* again, I knew better than to subject myself to the sounds of her being brought to bed. This time her pains started in the morning, and it was not difficult to ensure various pieces of business that would unavoidably keep me out of the house until late. The midwife was there, the specialist was on his way, Alma was running up and down as before with hot water and sheets: I had no wish to be the supernumerary husband once more, and left them to it.

This time Norah earned her keep in managing to produce a son. 'A boy!' the nurse cried, panting with excitement. 'A son for you, Mr Singer, you must be pleased,' this foolish woman babbled at me, staring and crowing, wanting to see me undone by the fact that she had brought me, wanting to see me full of womanly hysteria, and grateful to her for being the one to bring the glad news. 'Mr Singer,' she cried, louder now, thinking I was deaf perhaps, because I was refusing her the satisfaction of seeing my triumph, 'A boy, Mr Singer!' She was yellow now in her desperation, and was becoming ugly. 'Quiet, woman,' I snapped, and she clutched the white starch over her flat chest. 'Why should it amaze you that I have a son, woman? Half the world is sons.'

But from the beginning, John was a puling plaintive creature. Could this really be a son, I wondered, this spindly mauve baby lying in the cot, bulbous of head, blotched of face? Was this hairless head bobbing on its puny stalk of neck the head of a son? As if guessing my doubt, they unwrapped it, and held it out so I could not miss that purple bundle between its legs, so unlike Lilian's fat cleft at birth, but also so unlike my own appendage.

Norah lay pallidly with her eyelids drooping and her hands palms-up, supplicating, on the bedcover, but I felt the others watching me, all those nurses and midwives with their nipples under starch, as I wondered if my son and his handful of bruised flesh was normal. I was conscious of how they must by a logical association of ideas be thinking at this moment of what lay between my own legs: all those pairs of nipples pressed tight against starch must be wondering what my own organ of generation was like, to have produced what was on display before us. I thought of it, too, hanging proudly in front of me, and I could see none of that in what was between my son's legs.

'He is such a finely made little chap,' one of the starched females cried. 'Oh you must be so proud of him, Mr Singer!' and I was reassured then that they were staring in admiration rather than pity, and that eventually this sad little bunch of grapes would develop into my son's manhood.

In private I had to walk out on grass and feast on my joy. I knew what a son of mine would grow up to be, no matter how inauspicious his start. I could see his face already, my own face although of course smaller, and lacking the moustache for the moment. My son would soon grow out of the shell of that mauve monkey lying squalling upstairs, and would grow into a manly little chap who would square his shoulders, meet my eye with his own, and listen, nodding and saying, 'Yes, Father, I understand.'

How I looked forward to storing the mind of a male-child with facts! I felt myself at this moment in my life to be ready to seize a son and fill his spirit with all that was admirable from my own. I began to plan how I might best oversee the growth of a well-equipped mind, free from any cant and delusion, and of a body trained to the harmonious domination of dogs, horses and women.

Chapter *Fourteen*

I HAD NEVER HAD any natural talent at camaraderie of the bar-breasting tall-tale-telling variety, but with Ogilvie it seemed possible, at least away from his home and wife, and our acquaintance slowly blossomed into further friendship.

To the superficial eye it was an unlikely union. On the one hand was Ogilvie, a man of ready wit, a man with a charming easy smile, a man who could do justice to an anecdote and was full of bold plans about this and that; and on the other hand was Singer, no one's idea of the life of the party.

My grave face and slowness with a smile had always been enough to persuade most men that I was what I appeared to be, a serious man for whom a joke was something you brought out only on the rare appropriate occasion, like the best china. That was true, but in the company of Ogilvie, I was aware of other alternatives. In my heart I had to admit that it was not so much that I disapproved of jokes, but that I was afraid of them. If I were more confident of telling a joke, or even of understanding one, I would not have had to hide behind such a solemn manner.

Ogilvie treated that manner as if it were an unfortunate handicap I had, like a limp or a stammer: something that a good friend would overlook or overcome with encouragement. Like a woman he joked and jollied me along, until in spite of myself I found myself unbending. His charm was a kind of seduction, and it was not too often that anyone had set themselves to charm Albion Gidley Singer.

Ogilvie became a regular guest of mine at the Club. I did not embarrass him by suggesting that he become a member, for I knew he could not afford it, and in any case it gave me great pleasure to sign him in as my guest, and usher him along in a proprietorial way, my hand under his elbow. I did not bustle, did not fuss, made no womanly palaver: we sat firm in our chairs, a pair of gentlemen whose minds were in harmony.

Outside, it was a splendid spring day. Even here in this dim room in a shaded street in the middle of the city it was impossible not to be aware that outside the sun was shining away, breezes were playing with the leaves of trees and the skirts of women, and there was a sweet sad smell of jasmine in the air. The long windows at the end of the Newspaper Room were open so that the impertinent breeze even penetrated this leather-smelling fastness, ruffling our newspapers and making the portraits of past members rattle on the walls.

I submerged myself in my paper, and became absorbed in the details of Dalgety's stock prices, but Ogilvie was restless. He twitched at his newspaper, crossed and uncrossed his legs, sighed, and generally fidgeted until suddenly he exclaimed, in that voice of his that never spoke except in an exclamation, 'By Jove, Singer, but it is fusty in here this afternoon, let us get out, eh, how long is it since you have been to the races?' He winked a larrikin wink at me, and I was filled with some kind of rather breathless warmth that I had never known before.

Behind us, pillars of the community rearranged their newspapers ostentatiously and cleared their throats, but Ogilvie had more life in him than the whole of the Club put together. He had more life, and he had more wisdom, too, because he had guessed, as no one before him ever had, that within the dour personage of Albion Gidley Singer lived a wild fellow who was dying for someone to come along and lead him astray.

◆   ◆   ◆

Only a man who failed to understand the laws of chance would be a gambler. We sat in our seats and watched the unshaven men down at the rails flinging their arms up and down and jumping on the spot: from our dignified distance they were not quite human.

Around us were thin men – for gambling did not make you fat – men in their shirtsleeves and greasy cloth caps; they were men sharp of elbow and chin, men with large hungry ears sticking out of the side of their crudely cropped heads as if to suck in luck, they were men whose hands were never still, reaching into their pockets for another handful of silver, or fidgeting with their betting-slips, and going wild when the race was on, shrieking like women, dancing up and down, pounding on the rail, or into their own cupped palm: like ants, or crabs, or praying-mantises in a frenzy.

I stared off after a man in a shirt with the collar half torn off, clutching his ticket as if it were gold, staring with haggard face ahead, not seeing the backs and fronts of people, but seeing his own salvation or ruin: seeing wads of greasy notes thumbed off from the bookie's roll, or his ticket torn into shreds and trampled, and an ache in the belly, of remorse as well as hunger. These men were blind with their fantasies, knocking into you as they hastened to fling good money after bad.

Ogilvie threw himself into it as he threw himself into anything, with tremendous verve, making me join him at the fence of the Paddock to point and talk about fetlocks and withers. I suspected that Ogilvie knew no more of fetlocks and withers than I did myself, but I could see that he was exhilarated to be here with me; I rather wondered, too, whether Ogilvie might even be trying to impress me with his knowledge of a fetlock, and the thought pleased me.

'Ogilvie,' I said, and permitted myself to touch his arm, 'Ogilvie, do you come here often, then?' Ogilvie laughed and without answering cried, 'Oh Singer, we will have some jolly japes together today, I am sure of it.'

At last he decided on some set of fetlocks or other, and propelled me by the elbow over to where the bookies stood above the crowd with their yawning bags slung before them; beside them their numbers-boys flickered and twitched their hands in signals as quick as thought; beneath, punters eagerly handed up their money and walked away with a bit of scrawled-on paper as if it was a good exchange.

'I would not have taken you for a gambling man, Ogilvie,' I remarked as he stood watching this one-way trade. 'I would have said it was too illogical for your taste, which goes to show one never plumbs the depths of another human being.'

'Ah, but Singer,' he exclaimed, 'your equation is missing a factor: you have forgotten the pleasure element. I have been thinking about you, Singer, and I have decided that what your life needs is a little more of the thrill factor, and I regard it as the greatest privilege to be the one to perform your initiation.'

He gave me one of his smiles, eager and charming, and I felt the blood rush into my heart to swell it at the thought that he had wondered about me, reflected on me, guessed at what I would or would not do. I smiled back and winked, a reckless sort of activity I hardly ever indulged in, but my full heart had to have expression somewhere.

Ogilvie, in his eager enthusiastic way, was flushed with the thrill of the wager, and we hurried back to our seats in order to watch his set of fetlocks finish the race next-to-last. He did not appear humiliated, as I would have been, by this defeat, but cheerfully handed me his binoculars and pointed at the Members' Stand. 'Take a look up there, Singer,' he said, 'and tell me what you see.'

I had never used binoculars before, and saw nothing at first, but Ogilvie leaned over me and fiddled with the things while they were still against my face, so that I felt the warmth of his large hand over my cheek. All at once I could see with astonishing clarity the gigantic face of Sir Arthur Mackenzie, the steel man, popping a sandwich into his mouth like a lizard snapping down a fly, 'Mackenzie,' I cried, and heard Ogilvie beside me say calmly, 'Yes, Singer, and who else?' The binoculars jerked along a little further, past several women showing a lot of fine chest, who did not look like wives, and came to rest on a face I recognised from the papers, Sir Walter Bleasdale, the newspaper man, and next to him Sir Angus Worrall, the cattle king. They were all gesturing with their sandwiches and their glasses, cheering on some bit of horse-flesh or other. I watched them from time to time over the next hour, and never saw them downcast, although it was obvious that they could not all be backing winners every time: they opened more champagne, talked and laughed around mouthfuls of chicken sandwiches, and cheered in an indiscriminate way at the end of each race.

As a general rule I was not a man to display ignorance. Long ago, with Father, I had perfected the non-committal nod, the grunt that might mean *yes* or *no*, and the way to wait for answers to present themselves. Asking questions had never been my way. I dreaded exposing my ignorance to Ogilvie, perhaps to see the smile fade from his mouth, the glow leave his face, as he turned to look at me with eyes from which the scales had fallen: 'Singer, are you serious? Surely everyone knows *that!*' But as I considered further, I saw that Ogilvie had brought me here to astonish me, and to fill me with wonder at all the things he knew: it was a kind of gift he was making to me, and the appropriate gift in return was my unfeigned curiosity. In the end it was easier than I would have thought, simply to ask: 'Ogilvie, are all those peers of the realm up there larrikins like your good self? What is the attraction to them of subsidising the educations of bookies' brats?'

Ogilvie threw back his head and laughed, and I was pleased I had taken my time about arranging my question. He leaned his head so close to mine our cheeks almost caressed, twisted his mouth like a fish's and hissed, 'A precise answer might involve me in a suit for slander, Singer, but let me ask you to consider two facts. One, winnings at the races are not taxed. Two, no one can query sudden accumulations of cash in a man who is seen frequently at the races. Gambling is for fools, Singer, as you and I agree, and those men up there are certainly not fools.'

A little later we made our way to the buffet, and I saw that Mackenzie and his party were heading that way too, and that we would arrive simultaneously at the door. I hung back somewhat, for although Mackenzie and I had chatted at the Club a few times and agreed that the Club's steak-and-kidney was the best in New South Wales, I was not confident that he would remember me now. And if I spoke, and he did not remember me, I would be utterly humiliated in front of Ogilvie.

Mackenzie stood gesturing us through the door first, but did not actually look at us: his face had the bland benign expression of a man used to being recognised in public. But to my horror, I saw that Ogilvie was pressing forward, was catching Mackenzie's eye, was about to address him! I willed him not to: Mackenzie must spend his days being unctuously greeted by men he could not remember, and I did not wish to be labelled as a gusher along with Ogilvie. I could imagine only too clearly the way Mackenzie's large face would go more bland than ever, the corners of his enormous mouth stretched fractionally by muscles within: he would look at both of us, only too obviously trying in vain to remember who we were, and he would finish by giving us the most remote of smiles, as one might to a servant, and would sweep in ahead of us without a backward glance.

'Sir Arthur,' Ogilvie was beside me, crying out. 'Great day for a punt, Sir Arthur, is it not?' Schemes flashed through my mind to disassociate myself from Ogilvie – ideas of bending to tie my bootlace, or having a sneezing-fit into my handkerchief, or simply turning away as if I had heard my name called. But there was no time for any of these measures. Mackenzie's eyes slid over both of us, and I was stiff with mortification.

But to my astonishment his massive face creased and spread into a smile, and there was no mistaking the fact that he gave Ogilvie a wink! 'I find most days are good days for a punt, Mr Ogilvie,' he said mildly, and Ogilvie let out a graceless cackle which Mackenzie seemed to appreciate. He directed his smile at me for a moment, but blindly: I was simply The Man With Ogilvie. It was clear that I had no existence for him as a man whose opinions of the contents of a steak-and-kidney pie he had appeared to take seriously.

In the bar the crush of gentlemen baying at each other over the din was enormous. I could see that Ogilvie was excited by it, as if it was a bit of a lark that we were here among important men. He acted as though we were here by some sort of accident or trickery, like children sneaking in the back of the circus tent, and I was torn between being a man of dignity with every right to be here, and joining him in being what was much more stimulating, another man-about-town off the leash for the day.

I allowed Ogilvie to breast the bar on our behalf, and established myself in a corner. I busied myself staring at the surroundings, while I could hear Ogilvie crying out, 'Hoy! Hoy!" to attract the attention of the barmaid, not caring who stared, and I admired him for not caring.

We had a high time of it all afternoon. I was finally persuaded to try the thrill of the wager, and saw just what he meant when, in spite of my resolution to stay completely calm, I found myself shouting, 'Go, Blue Streak, go!' and experienced a wonderful rush of blood to the head to see my horse actually come third! Ogilvie clapped me on the back and cried, 'My word, Singer, I knew you would have an aptitude for this gambling business! Well done, my dear fellow, well done!' His praise made me warm, and I found my tongue large and inert in my mouth. Sheer gladness had swelled it into stillness.

Chapter *Fifteen*

NORAH RUSHED to and fro with napkins and bonnets and grew more and more hectoring with the nursemaid. She began to sigh theatrically when the children could be heard crying from the nursery, and she would fling down her napkin and leave another meal to congeal: what heavy weather she made of being a woman! Bearing children was after all no great achievement, but something which millions of illiterate primitives did every day of the week, and thought no more about it.

What a perversity there was to life! Norah, weak and winsome Norah, who had once admitted to me that she could never remember how many feet were in a mile, much less how many inches there were in a rod, perch, or pole – that silly Norah had become possessed of the ultimate fact: other beings out of her own flesh.

The injustice of it all! My wife had looked within herself and seen a living being; I looked within myself and saw nothing. Oh, there were plenty of facts which I could tell over to myself when the world began to spin: I knew how many feet there were in a mile, and how many inches there were in a rod, pole or perch, and I even knew the number of fluid ounces in a gill or firkin. From my now extensive researches, I could inform Norah that a Russian peasant woman had been independently assessed as having produced sixty-nine children, over twenty-seven confinements; that the common tenrec of Madagascar could produce thirty-six offspring at a single birth, whereas the most a female of the human species had ever produced was eight, and all died within fourteen hours. I could even tell her of the Asiatic elephant, with a gestation period of over two years, as compared with the human's mere nine months. All this should have put things in perspective for Norah, but she did not seem to realise what small beer her two children were in the big scheme of things. She remained unimpressed, and although I bought more and more books of a scientific nature, and began a complex filing system for my facts, I knew I could never be filled, as Norah had been filled. I might know every fact in the universe, and was even seriously considering assembling a book from those facts, but I could never create such a colossal fact as my soft-headed wife could do effortlessly in simply fulfilling the laws of her animal biology.

I had to remind myself that it was my own vital spark that had allowed all this to happen within Norah. Out of my own loins, my own homunculus had travelled into the darkness of Norah's interior. I imagined millions of tadpoles, each with my own face, squirting into Norah and doing battle with each other so that it was only the strongest, the swiftest, and the cleverest that managed to burrow into the blank egg within her.

But at those times when all my achievements were nothing more than a puff of air, this was not enough to reassure me. I peered into myself to see more, but saw nothing: there was just this emptiness surrounded by a series of correct facial manipulations and appropriate phrases, going on for a little span of time. Down there along the tunnel of the future, the will operating the facial manipulations and the phrases would wink out like a light, and after that there would be nothing more, ever. The thought drove me up to my study, where I drew paper towards me, filled my pen with my darkest ink, and made a start. *Chapter One*, I wrote in my fine hand at the top of a page, and began at the beginning: *Man (homo sapiens) is a species in the sub-family Hominidae of the super-family Hominoidea of the sub-order Simiae (or Anthropoidea) of the order Primates of the infra-class Eutheria of the sub-class Theria of the class Mammalia of the sub-phylum Vertebrata (Craniata) of the phylum Chordata of the sub-kingdom Metazoa of the animal kingdom.*

Further than this I could not seem to go for the moment. I laid down my pen and decided that more research was needed: the facts had to be all at my fingertips, and then the writing-out would be a simple enough affair.

Such thoughts did something to still the agitation in my heart, but were not enough. I was still conscious of the fact that Norah, tending to the children, would always be a part of them, and of their children, and their children's children, and so on into eternity: *Mother*, an image graven on every heart. When Norah's being winked out, she would live on in the beings she had created. In bringing forth flesh from her own flesh, Norah had succeeded in locking me more tightly than ever into solitude. I felt something like panic: Norah, my own wife, had rendered me more hollow than ever.

◆   ◆   ◆

Before we were wed, I had had some idea that a wife might, over time, look into the being of a husband, and would come to love what she saw there. But Norah had never attempted to look into my being: she had always been happy to take me at face value, and see only the Albion she wished to see. *You are such a strong silent type, Albion*, she would cry teasingly, or, *Oh Albion, how kind you are, how handsome, how this, how that!*

I had been happy enough in the beginning for her to adore the manufactured Albion Gidley Singer, although there had been times when I had felt stifled by so much adoration. But now that the children filled her life, adoration had got a bit thin on the ground, and my hidden self ached with invisibility like something toxic.

'Norah,' I wanted to say, wanted to beg, to plead even, 'look,' I wanted somehow to say, 'this is the person I am, Norah, look into my heart and take me in.' But I did not know of any words a man might be able to use, to ask for what he needed, and I stayed silent.

Norah was replete, now, and she began to turn away from the husband who was becoming a shadowy figure to her. When I began to finger her upper arm in a way which she and I both knew to signal an approach towards other more intimate parts of her body, she drew herself away in the chair and turned her face away. More and more often she took refuge behind headaches and indispositions, and quoted the doctor at me – did I imagine her smugness? – who had, she said, told her most particularly to avoid any type of *amative excitement*. 'Albion dearest,' she said in a flat way, 'I feel I must conserve my strength, for the sake of my milk,' or, 'the children have quite worn me out,' or, 'I must just make sure Cook has got Lilian's arrowroot mould right this time.'

I would hold myself with even more than my usual up-rightness as I left the room after such a rebuff, and yet I found the word *slinking* coming into my mind, and the humiliating image of a cur kicked away from a bitch on heat. 'But Norah,' I cried out in my heart, 'it is not just a body I want: I want, I need, I beg you for something more than that,' but if she did not know, there was no point in telling her.

Norah was managing to make malingering into an art-form. She lay for days on end on her chaise-longue with the blinds lowered, sucking on cachous, with her various tonics ranged beside her on the table. I was exasperated by her endless little ladylike indispositions, and the fact that I was forced to pander to them because of what everyone referred to delicately as her *troubles*.

And finally I tired of the game: a man could not be forever wrestling open the door that should have been standing hospitably open at all times. She had cried *No, no Albion!* once too often. I knew she meant *yes*, but that lewd and teasing wife of mine, who had never given me the satisfaction of admitting she enjoyed it (but why else did her nipples grow hard like my own organ, why else did she writhe and cry out?), could be taken at her word and go without. She would be the loser, not I.

In fact, I could hardly remember now why I had wished to try to rouse Norah to passion: how had I ever found her tantalising as she lay fending me off, so that I had steamed and fumed over her until she had cried out? She was as attractive to me now as a clod of dirt. I looked at her, down-turned of mouth, sallow of complexion, altogether without charm.

Her voice alone was enough to irritate me now, a voice at once plaintive and triumphant: the voice of a person who has won, but in an underhand way. It sometimes crossed my mind, as I was forced to fetch a cushion, or ring for tea, or bring her her embroidery from the next room, that Norah was wearing the pants now in our household, exerting the tyrannical power of the weak. Sometimes I looked at her face, which had grown strangely swarthy since she had given birth to John, and wondered if she was even growing a moustache to go with the pants.

It was a victory for Norah, but I was determined it should not be a defeat for myself. In my more clear-headed moments I recognised that this was Nature's law. Norah's enticement had done its job now: there was no need of further entice-ment on her part, or further fever on mine, because we had reproduced ourselves: the race, as represented by Albion and Norah Singer, was now in a position to continue.

Was this why Norah's adoration had faded and gone mouldy? Did she think I was expendable now? In her eyes, was I no more than the sum of my sperm?

What she did not realise – what no woman can realise,

perhaps – is that Nature operates with a considerable margin for error. She equips the male of the species with a compulsion that exceeds the strict requirements of the case. The world was full of normal women who longed for just such a man as myself: it was nothing more than the safety-net with which Nature provides herself.

Chapter *Sixteen*

AT THE END of a certain narrow laneway in a certain part of town, there was a house where I was always made welcome. In this house a certain Mrs Smith sat near the door to open it to anyone who happened to knock, and behind Mrs Smith, Agnes and Una sat in the front room, cosy and frightful with wallpaper and pampas grass.

'I will just be out for a little, Norah,' I would say, and leave a space in which she could look at the clock, look at the darkness of the night beyond the curtains, and ask, 'Why Albion, wherever are you going at this hour?' I had my answers ready. 'Oh, I am just going to pay a visit to some friends, Norah,' I would say, slightly emphasising the *pay*, and would stare at her until the penny dropped and she would look away. But she never asked, never once. She yawned, she stretched herself, she glanced at the clock, but all she said was, 'Well, I will turn in, Albion, I will see you in the morning.'

'Oh, Mr Smith!' exclaimed Mrs Smith (it was a house full

of Smiths, this one). 'Is it to be Agnes tonight, or will it be Una?' Mrs Smith was positively oily in her welcome. 'Have a look, Mr Smith, and let me know.' Over the time I had been visiting this house, Agnes and Una had undergone several changes as to colour of eyes and shape of mouth, but Agnes and Una were always spry little fillies, marble as to shoulder, and melon as to breasts, and Mr Smith had never failed to be satisfied by them.

Agnes and Una exclaimed over me, and patted my arm, and laughed at nothing very much as they ushered me along the hall past the artisic prints. 'Dear Mr Smith,' they cooed. 'Such a pleasure to see you again, Mr Smith,' they clucked.

Agnes and Una were women of much movement, given to gesturing with cigarette-holders and making much play with fans. They were not such fools as to pretend, as Norah did. They did not lie on brocade, fatigued by nothing, with camphor-cloths on their foreheads, nor did they languidly finger the keys of an insipid piano. Agnes and Una, the dears, were full of raucous laughter like birds, and their flesh was not trammelled with corsets, but flowed and shook beneath kimonos covered with tiny mirrors stitched all over them, that fell apart at the breasts and parted at the thighs.

Oh, how Norah would turn her nose up at it all! How her upper lip would wrinkle, and the word *common* would hang in the air around her. However, there was no possibility that Norah would ever see these rooms. I guessed that she did not even dream of their existence. Did a lady know of such places? Or was she so ignorant of the needs of the male that the idea did not occur to her?

Agnes and Una fluttered and caressed, brought me little drinks on little trays, rubbed my feet, made me laugh with little silly womens' stories of this and that, uttered charming ripples of laughter at my own little stories of the business world; I always felt my spirit expand in their company, and realised how little I was appreciated elsewhere.

In the house of the Smiths, I was a giant among men, and afterwards I stared into the tiny mirrors stitched onto the silk of Agnes' wrapper, each one smaller than my own eyeball, and saw a dark glooming shape I knew must be the reflection of my own eye. Eye to eye with myself, I lay in bliss with Agnes – or was it Una who wore the mirrored wrapper?

Chapter *Seventeen*

THE BUSINESS ran like clockwork now as long as I paid a few surprise visits to the lower regions once in a while, and made an example of any employees I found to be wasting their time and mine. *Singer Enterprises*, as it was called now, held no secrets from me. I knew how many pounds of tea and sugar my employees consumed in their morning and afternoon tea breaks, and how many times a day the female employees used the privy; I knew the exact state of health of the father of Rawlinson the clerk, who had once been impertinent to me, but was a changed man now he had an ailing father; I knew that a dozen envelopes wrapped in blue paper with a white band around it and the *Singer* emblem embossed on it was worth threepence more a dozen than the same envelopes sold loose out of the box; I even knew how many bales of hay the horses consumed per week, and what the lad who mucked them out was paid, and when he had last asked for a new shovel.

I was no gentleman dabbling in business with his face turned aloofly away, who thought it vulgar to speak of pounds and pence: I was a worker like the rest, doing his job to the very best allowed by his talent, and was entitled to my reward.

Young Mr Singer had seen fit to abandon most of the traditions his father had started within the walls of *Singer Enterprises*. In the face of steady resistance from Rundle, we stocked lined notepaper now as well as the linen-faced variety, and the very same cheap japanned document-cases that I could remember Father pointing out to me with horror in the window of Anderson's, and there was a new line of scented notepaper with violets printed on it which would have made Father's blood curdle.

But there was one tradition which I continued, and that was the tradition that Mr Singer should sometimes seat himself in the padded oak chair at the end of the shop, and watch as his business was performed around him.

There were my clerks, those grave adenoidal cautious fellows; one was wrapping up three dozen of the finest monogrammed envelopes for a gentleman with a cane, not exactly dallying, but being sure to take his time about it, so that the gentleman with the cane also found that his eye was caught by the leather writing-cases. At the next counter, pen nibs and pen-nib wipers were being gravely handed around and commented on by various unhurried gentlemen under the supervision of a pimply but respectful youth.

And, more interestingly, there were my shop-girls, charming their way into the purses of dowagers, laying out a fan of deckle-edged on the counter as gently as a diamond necklace, inclining their trim heads murmuringly towards their customers, making up neat bundles with flicks of string and expansive gestures with sheets of brown paper.

All those pretty little slips of girls in the shop, hand-picked by Father, were precisely the kind of thing I would have chosen myself. Little Dora Gibbs – I had not forgotten Miss Gibbs of Pens – was not the only pretty one. There were several pairs of moist cushiony lips, and more than one globular bosom that made black fabric gleam and swell in fascinating ways.

It was the most natural thing in the world that Miss Gibbs should accompany Mr Singer one day into the stockroom at the rear of the building, to discuss pens. I had already had Miss Patterson and Miss Dimpleworth (wonderfully well-named, to those in the know), in the stockroom, to inspect envelopes and sleeve-protectors respectively. Now it was Miss Gibbs' turn.

Mr Singer was no sneak: he made no secret of his visits to the stockroom with his girls. *Miss Patterson and I will just run our eye over the new consignment,* I would tell Miss Gumble, or Rundle if he was there. Or, *I will just take Miss Dimpleworth in the stockroom,* and the faces of Miss Gumble and Rundle would go respectfully blank, and they would nod, *Very good, Mr Singer sir.*

◆　　◆　　◆

Back there in the stockroom, the air was always cool: beams of sun slanted in from the big dirty window overlooking the street, breaking the dimness up with bright shafts full of dust-motes. Above us we could hear the continual tramp and creak as the clerks up in Accounts walked backwards and forwards,

backwards and forwards, on the bare boards. It was a disturbing noise, sudden and close, the sort of noise that makes you
glance over your shoulder for no good reason; but in other
respects the stockroom was ideal, for the stairs up to it crackled like gunfire when walked on, so that in spite of the con-
stant distraction of the footsteps above, there was no way in
which one could be taken by surprise there.

In this brown light, with the late sunlight making the
shadows soft, little Dora was like a beauty in a Dutch painting: her skin was like a ripe fruit, her fine bosom buoyant
under its coverings. Was it my imagination, or did Miss Gibbs
point that fine bosom towards me rather more than necessary? Was there even a certain amount of thrusting going on
in the bosom region?

Miss Patterson and Miss Dimpleworth had been found to
be straightforward enough propositions, worldly girls who
could take anything in their stride, girls who knew which
side their bread was buttered. But I could not quite get the
measure of Miss Dora Gibbs, and I went carefully. She was
very young, and there was a guilelessness about her which
was appealing. But there was a strong possibility that she
might be a knowing little piece of work, just the same. There
was a way she had, of tilting her face up to me, that might
have been a child's artless way of looking up to a fatherly
employer; on the other hand it could just as easily have been
something she practised in front of the mirror. Damned
women, that you never knew where you were with! What if
she ran shrieking down into the street crying accusations?
On the other hand, what if she laughed at me for failing to

get on with the job: *Come along, Mr Singer, no need to be shy!* So I proceeded with the greatest caution.

Miss Gibbs was nearly young enough to be my daughter, and I was the picture of the bluff and fatherly employer. I was a gentleman whose mind was on pens and ink, and who was quite unaware of the fragrant proximity of Miss Gibbs; I was a gentleman who had quite lost track of the time in his enthusiasm for the new filling mechanisms. He was far too engrossed in the new shipment to be aware of anything as trivial as the time: he needed to try all the new nickle-plated nibs, and see if the new type of bladder in the Stylus range filled properly, and consider the merits of the various colours.

Miss Gibbs would have seemed a very poor sort of employee if she had drawn Mr Singer's attention to the time. Once or twice she glanced uneasily towards the door, so I came around beside her and insisted that she try a few out, sitting at an old desk there, in order to see how they worked *in situ*, as I said. I could tell that she wondered what I was talking about, and her uncertainty suited me.

The robust sounds of *Singer Enterprises* at work gradually died away: doors slammed in distant corridors, voices called out farewells, footsteps hurried along the linoleum towards home, and the startling noises from the ceiling fell silent. Dusk settled pleasantly around us; on all sides the orderly rooms were silent.

An indefinitely extended discussion on the relative merits of platinum or gold nibs did not seem likely to advance the cause for which Dora and I had come together, so when all was quiet outside I took the plunge. 'You have very dainty hands, Miss Gibbs,' I said, and took one of them, and before she could snatch it away, if she had intended to, I exclaimed, 'By Jove, Miss Gibbs, just stand quite still, there is a little spider,' and brushed my hand against her hair. She did not recoil, but stood under my ministrations like a patient child having her plaits done, so I went a little further, placing my hands on her shoulders to direct her backwards a step or two, so that she was gently impelled to sit down on the old settee (what was an old settee doing up here, I wondered, and thought again about Father).

'My word, Miss Gibbs, that beam of sunlight lights up your hair so that you look quite like an angel, upon my soul!' I cried in a hearty avuncular way, and stood in front of her admiring the picture she made, conscious of how my trousers were on the level of her eyes. While I ran on, remarking on how pleasant it was back here in the stockroom, and what a good spot it was, how pleasant to have a few minutes alone here, alone that is, in such very pleasant and charming company, I saw her eyes flicker down to the region of my flies, and I knew then where I was with her.

Her eyes darted away and up to my face, but against her will they were drawn back and back to my flies: she was like a bird beating against a window. I watched her, and under my gaze she could not stop herself twisting her hands around each other, rubbing her palms together, tucking her fingers into her armpits, crossing her arms over her breasts: and with each movement betraying knowingness.

'Stand up, Miss Gibbs, if you please,' I said, and I planned a little confusion of feet and knees, and an awkwardness with elbows, so that I would have to lay hands on her and steady her so that she did not fall. But she was ahead of me: she positively leapt out of the chair, and before I could put into action my scheme of ankles and feet she had sunk back with a hand to her forehead. 'Oh, Mr Singer, I am a bit faint all of a sudden, it is that close in here.'

Ah! I was sure now, or almost sure. There was still the possibility that she was simply faint, such a skinny little thing, and probably not eating a proper breakfast, although there were still other possibilities: I could imagine her regaling her friends, *Oh, I thought he would never work himself up to it!* and all their little mouths laughing at a man of doubts.

I crossed to the window, wrestling with a lock gone rusty but finally able to fling back the dirty window so that pigeons fluttered up in fright. Then I could help Miss Gibbs over to the window, my hands under her armpits so that I could feel the stuff of her dress tight over her hard little breasts. 'Stand here, Miss Gibbs, and get some of this fresh air,' I said, and like a child she was obedient to a fault, taking the air as if it were medicine, in great gasping breaths. 'Oh,' she laughed suddenly, pink in her cheeks and peach-like. 'Oh, Mr Singer, I am come over all dizzy now, it is all that air,' and she stood with her hands balancing on the air in front of her breasts.

I looked out into the dreary street, given a moment's glamour by the golden late-afternoon sun that made even the peeling paint of the warehouse opposite seem picturesque. Down on the street someone must have spilled a bag of wheat, for directly below us a sea of pigeons seethed, a shoal of silver backs churning and cooing. 'Look,' I exclaimed, and took advantage of the moment to lay my hand along her arm, as if she could not see those roistering birds. 'Look, Miss Gibbs, doves!' I leaned out, and tightened my grip on her arm; I could feel her tremulous through my tweed. I felt myself becoming a man in my trousers, feeling her quivering against me, and said, 'It is their courting ritual, Miss Gibbs, they are preparing to copulate.'

Ah, what an unscrupulous rascal I was! I felt Dora flinch, but she did not fling away in disgust, did not even remove her arm from the grasp of my hand. I took her hands and pressed her against me, saying, 'Miss Gibbs, I am overcome, Dora, oh! Dora!' and other exclamations under the cover of which I wrapped my arms around her. 'You are loveliness itself, Dora my dear.' I spoke into her hair and against my fine woollen chest I could feel the thrust of her breasts, heaving up and down against me in an inflammatory way.

Nothing stopped her from removing herself from my embrace: nothing stopped her from saying *Kindly keep your hands to yourself, Mr Singer*. No, she stayed where she was, and proved herself to be just another trollop.

I knew I could have her now, on the table strewn with pens, or on the settee, or even on the splintery floor. I went ahead, naturally, and did not let myself down; but something within me had lost interest. It was all too easy: a man needs a difficulty or two, to make his satisfaction more piquant.

◆　　◆　　◆

And did Norah never wonder at her husband's irregular hours, or the way he radiated a certain kind of glow on his home-coming on certain evenings? Did she never wonder where her husband disposed of his excess of virility, now that he so rarely coupled with his wife?

No! She did not wonder, because she did not care. Her husband was nothing more to her now than the provider of Wedgwood and spotted batiste, the figure in the other armchair with whom a wife was expected to exchange a few banalities in front of the servant.

'By Jove, Norah,' I might say, 'the business is certainly thrusting ahead now,' and she would say in that languid condescending way she had, 'That is good, Albion, I am so pleased,' and suck the end of her cotton to thread the needle for a bit more rose petal. 'Pens are coming along very nicely,' I went on. 'I was working on Pens just tonight, and my word they are well worth looking at,' but Norah only squinted at her needle, poking the thread at it, and when she spoke, it was only to tell me that Lilian had cut her forehead, falling out of the jacaranda, and she had the gall to pretend surprise when I shouted, 'What the devil were you doing, Norah, letting her up in the jacaranda in the first place?'

Her lack of interest in my doings verged on the pathological. It made me wonder. I looked across at her, pushing the needle through the linen, sighing a little, feet neatly crossed at the ankle as she had been taught as a girl. Norah's promise of solidity had been fulfilled: although not a large woman, her weight in the chair was measurable, her presence in the room indubitable. Here was a wife, a mother of two: Norah was a fact. As I watched her bland insistence on her rose petal, her obstinate silence about my own doings, it crossed my mind to wonder whether, behind the fact of Norah, behind the fact of those children she had produced, there might not lie other facts.

Those homunculi of mine, for example, that had made their way into the heart of my wife's emptiness and taken root there: were they all that met the eye? There was no question about Lilian, for she was already the image of myself, but what of John, in whom I looked in vain for the slightest resemblance?

With a determination not to flinch from any possible fact, I toyed with another possibility. On those mornings when I had left the house for the ferry and the city, Norah might have waited to see her husband's back, my back, walk down the hill to the ferry and then have sat, waiting, winsome and lustful, for some other man. Out of the hydrangeas he might have come, smirking. He might have taken my wife's soft palm in his and have crushed his vile pink mouth against hers. He might have heard the cries that should have been mine, and the embroidered rose might have fallen to the floor. 'Oh yes,' Norah might have sighed, or, 'Oh no,' inflaming him as she did me. He might have been engorged past bearing, and beyond bursting there might have been the tears running into my wife's lewd mouth, the sobs of her abandon. Later, full of another man, she might have sat and embroidered on, pricking her finger as she waited for Albion her husband, so the rose became speckled with blood.

It was possible. Either it was so, or it was not so: it reduced me to hollow rage that I could never know for certain. The doings of women could never be reduced to fact, could never be anything better than speculation. I scrutinised Mother's face when she came down *to do the shops* every few months; I stared at Kristabel, who stared back rudely as if she thought I had no right to look at my own sister's face. We were at their mercy, because no matter what we did, we would never know for sure.

◆ ◆ ◆

The charms of Miss Dora Gibbs turned out fairly quickly to be finite, and before too long I was ready to move on.

Dora was sharp in some ways, but in matters of the heart she believed everything that twopenny novels and the shop-girls' magazine told her. Other women I had known had tortured themselves from time to time with the thought that I would leave them, or tire of them. 'But do you still love me a little, do I still please you?' they would tiresomely pester as I loved them less and less. But Dora did not seem to consider that I might tire of her. Dora had not heard of the word *philanderer*, and in the world of her novels, love was ended only by death, never by ennui. To a person such as this you could not simply say, *Dora, I have finished with you now.*

I had always prided myself on an artistic way of ending an entanglement: I loathed all the awkward scenes, with women becoming red and blotched with tears and having to be given a handkerchief. They did not seem to realise that it would be better all round to avoid these ugly noises and uglier noses. In addition, the handkerchief was never returned, I knew that from several experiences: the handkerchief was gone for ever.

I sat at my desk with my feet up on a drawer, considering how I might put it to her. *Dora, you have ceased to amuse me*, I considered, or, *Dora, my wife has discovered us*, or even, *Dora, the doctors have given me a week to live, this is to say goodbye.*

In the end it was simpler to do nothing at all: I sat in the oak chair as always, but I no longer suggested that Miss Gibbs look over the new stock with me, although it was imperative that Miss Pearson (Betty to her friends) should run her eye over the new lines of blotting-paper.

It was disgraceful how a young lady could let herself go. In no time at all, Dora degenerated into someone a man would not glance at twice: she became pale, with a red nose – had she taken to the grog? – her face became puffy, her complexion rough, her eyes seemed to have shrunk, and there was no hint that that cheek could ever produce a dimple. Usually so immaculate of dress, she took to wearing a coarse skirt with the hem coming undone at the back, and she walked around slouch-shouldered, dusting things in a mournful way, and ignoring the customers. No man would give her a second glance: how could I ever have picked her out for my special attention? *You are a guy*, I thought to myself in amazement. *You are a guy, Dora, and I was fool enough to think you beautiful.*

She needed to pull herself together, but she did not, and it was nothing to do with Mr Singer when Miss Gumble, in charge of the girls, came to me in confidence and wondered if perhaps Miss Gibbs would have to be let go, her appearance and the quality of her work in general had fallen off so greatly of late. 'Oh?' I was all concern and surprise. 'But she was one of our best workers, was she not, Miss Gumble?' Reluctantly, Mr Singer was persuaded that Miss Gibbs was now something of a liability in Pens. When pressed, Miss Gumble confessed to having given the matter thought, and felt that she could wholeheartedly recommend Miss Smythe from Despatch, who seemed an ideal type of lass for the job.

I did not bother with any silver-plated tray for Dora, but instructed Miss Gumble to give her a week's wages in lieu and wish her well. Miss Gumble could be relied on not to mince words.

Chapter Eighteen

SINGER ENTERPRISES was fifty years old, and Rundle had suggested that some sort of celebration would be in order. To tell the truth, I would not have thought of it: as far as I was concerned, *Singer Enterprises* had begun with me. Father, for all his pendulous cheeks and substantial waistcoats, had turned out to be easy to forget

'A buffet type of a thing, Mr Singer, perhaps,' Rundle suggested. 'The staff would be as pleased as Punch.' I did not care much about pleasing the staff – surely it was their job to please me rather than the other way around – but it seemed easier to agree.

But when I mentioned it to Ogilvie, his eyes lit up. 'I would urge an elephant or two on you, Singer,' he said. 'And a brace of monkeys, the winsome kind.' I could only stare and wonder what sort of joke this was, and he went on, 'A net of coloured balloons, or even better, pigeons, I know a man who will be able to help you there. You will need the police, of course, but there is a set fee for such things.' I could smile now, I had the hang of it, this was one of Ogilvie's bewilderingly original ideas, and although I could not quite leap after it agilely, I was sure a smile would be appropriate. 'Inside, maids with canapes of course, but something a little different: medieval wenches, perhaps, or a mermaid theme? And nothing much on display, Singer, tantalise them: just one ream of best bond on a snakeskin, a bottle of ink in a fishbowl.'

'By Jove, Ogilvie,' I cried, 'I must say I had in mind something a little humbler!' I found a terrible windy laugh coming out of my mouth, as if to make him admit that the elephants were going too far, but his face did not waver in its seriousness. 'Look, Singer,' he said, 'an elephant is guaranteed to make the newspapers, and making the newspapers guarantees trade, and guaranteeing trade is what being in business is all about. A few clerks dropping oysters on the floor in a shop full of blank paper is not going to make the newspapers.'

In the event, elephants proved unobtainable. We settled for two camels, the wisdom of which I privately doubted, and three unpleasantly hairless monkeys; but we managed a live python with a gentleman's desk-set in its coils, which proved a great success with the ladies. Norah, for one, could hardly be dragged away from the python's cage, watching with lips ajar as the python engaged with the ink-well in a grotesque way.

◆　　◆　　◆

It was a good enough gathering: the high society of Vaucluse was well represented, and so were the professional men of Macquarie Street and their wives. There must have been an acre or two of gleaming silk, and several furlongs of best

worsted, moving to and fro under the new chandelier. Everywhere I looked I saw the powerful shoulders and the bull-
necks of Sydney's successful men, heard their braying laughs.
So much massed achievement was not unlike a roomful of
cattle. Even the women, showing their plump creamy shoulders and their substantial arms, made you think of slabs
of beef.

The chandelier was a stroke of genius, and gave the shop a
particularly brilliant effect. I would not have thought of a
chandelier, but Ogilvie had not come down in the last shower.
'I am told it is the most flattering light for the ladies, Singer,'
he assured me. 'A female who feels herself exquisite will lay
about herself lavishly, but if she catches sight of herself looking plain in a shop-mirror she will close her purse and go
home.'

Ogilvie was in his element with a glass of punch in his
hand, standing in front of the massed banks of hydrangeas.
There was some intimate thing about the way Ogilvie leaned
in to speak to people, which I saw that others besides myself
responded to. It was a quality I was somewhat conspicuous in
lacking, and it made Ogilvie the perfect foil to myself.

Vaucluse and Macquarie Street warmed to his bonhomie,
and even the reptilian gentlemen of the press watched and
listened with some interest: the python and the camel would
certainly make the newspapers, and *Singer Enterprises* would
be remembered as a go-ahead and surprising sort of place.

I watched and admired him: what a man of parts he was!
With dull worthy Rundle he could be dull and worthy, wor-
rying away at a bit of conversation; with Norah the perfect
lady he was the perfect gentleman; and with those cold-eyed

hacks he was – well, I could tell by the quirk of his eyebrow and the shapes his mouth was making that he was entertaining them with something a little racier than the new improved bladder of the Bismarck fountain-pen.

Norah did not do too badly as the wife of the owner. She circulated and gushed conscientiously, quite the society hostess. I could see her exclaiming with pleasure and astonishment, and grasping the other gloved hands of other ladies, and puckering her lips in the air near their faces, as if sucking up their smell. This was the kind of thing Norah was good at, and I was reminded of why I had married her when I saw her shrinking away in a charmingly affrighted way from the camels as they rolled their eyes at the crowd.

I noticed Sir Jeremy Jones, that ancient fraud, who stood up in Parliament and like a Red advocated the unions, while sitting safe on his grandfather's fortune. I saw him take Norah's arm and his lips mouth 'Mrs Singer!' in his trumpeting demagogue's way; and Mrs Jeremy Jones, with whom Norah often exchanged women's chit-chat over their Royal Doulton, reached out a gloved hand as if to touch the closer camel, and had to be reassured when it turned to her with its black lip curling. I overheard Norah cry above the din, 'Do tell me about your work, Sir Jeremy, it must be so very interesting.' Norah had no more idea of what *work* might be than a fish would have, but she had various phrases of a conversation-starting kind at her disposal: in private she verged on the imbecilic, but I was pleased to see how convincingly she scrubbed up in company.

But her sparklings and bubblings were pathetic, for they

were so sadly misguided. Poor fool, she thought it mattered that the old fraud Jones had come. How could she know – as even the least observant member of the Club knew – that he was to be seen anywhere the booze was laid on? She sparkled away at him, no doubt under the impression that Jones – leering down at her chest in a rapacious way – was admiring the cut of her gown, when any male in the room could have told her that he was not thinking noble thoughts about her gown, but dirty ones about what the gown just failed to reveal.

She glanced over and caught my eye for a moment, and I nodded at her, and let her see my teeth, so that she went back to listening to Jones with an extra flush of pleasure on her face, and she would never guess that it was contempt that was softening her husband's face.

By contrast, Ogilvie and I worked the room like a couple of professionals. Here he was, bringing up one of his journalists to ask the proprietor a few words; there was I, introducing Ogilvie to one of our account customers, and watching him lean forward and do that gently electric intimate thing he knew how to do. Several times Ogilvie rescued me, with a judicious *thing needing your attention, Mr Singer*, from some bore who could be of no use to *Singer Enterprises*. Several times more he came and stood shoulder-to-shoulder with me, helping me endure some other bore who had to be sent home happy.

When the crowd separated us, some part of my skin seemed always to know where Ogilvie was. When things grew desperate, and my smile became a rictus, I knew where to look in order to exchange a restoring glance with him. We worked like clockwork all evening and, now, as I let the din of laughing and talking wash over me, taking a breather between bores, I winked across the room to Ogilvie, and had his own larrikin wink in return, and I could never remember being happier.

Vaucluse and Macquarie Street did not stay long, moving off in shoals to their smart dinner engagements. But they had come, and what with the python, Norah's dress, and the camels (one of which had finally spat at a gentleman with a cane, and got him fair and square in his starched shirt-front), *Singer Enterprises* had made its mark.

❖   ❖   ❖

It was fitting enough for women to step into cabs and be driven home after such excitement, but it did not do for me, or for Ogilvie. My blood was hurtling through my veins, my tongue was loosened, and I was at last finding it easy to laugh, and even to make others laugh in a surprised sort of way.

The last thing I wished to do, as I saw the last of them off the premises, was to go tamely home with my wife. Ogilvie and I were at one in this, as in so much, and we retired up to my office with a bottle of brandy and a box of best Havanas. In the glow of the good evening's work behind us, Ogilvie and I sat over our brandies until the stars were small and sharp in the sky outside. It was a warm feeling, two men together enjoying the best in the way of company and cigars: I was at last like a cup or bucket, a receptacle filled to every edge and corner, with not a pocket of hollowness anywhere.

We both leaned forward in our chairs at the same moment to reach for our brandies. Our hands did not touch as we picked up our glasses, but they nearly touched, might have touched, and our eyes met. 'Well, Singer,' Ogilvie sighed on a smile, holding my gaze. 'What now, Singer, how can we round off such an evening as this has been?' he tilted his head back to drink and I was sure – almost sure – yes, quite sure – perhaps – I saw an eyelid drop over an eye for an instant. I was almost sure that Ogilvie had something on his mind.

But I was shy of rushing in too foolhardy: I watched him put the glass back on the table, and thought before I spoke. 'I have some friends I am sure you would like,' I said, and almost regretted it, for the open look of surprise on Ogilvie's face as he wiped his moustache where brandy lingered.

I wished I had not spoken: I felt a blush rising to my face, and Ogilvie watching in what I was sure was amazement. I could wish, but I could not make the words unspoken, so all I could do was go forwards, but I could feel mad blood pouring up from my chest, racing up my neck and into my cheeks as I went on, 'They would be glad to welcome us, I know.' Ogilvie continued to stare with what seemed unbelievable obtuseness, and I floundered on against his silence, feeling myself blurting out the words like some pipsqueak schoolboy with a dirty mind, 'Little friends, you understand, Ogilvie, charming little friends.'

Was Ogilvie stupid, after all? Was he a secret Methodist? Or did he adore his shrewish wife? Why was he continuing to stare in that unnerving way?

'Singer!' he exclaimed at last, and I felt heat prickle on my palms; but he was smiling, although still not quite sure. 'Why

Singer, are you suggesting a visit to your friends, your *little* friends, at this hour?' He was positively grinning now, almost certain, and when I fought down the blood flaming in my face and said calmly, 'This is their finest hour, Ogilvie, I assure you,' he let out a great rude guffaw, the like of which *Singer Enterprises* had never heard, and stood up. 'Let us go, then, Singer, let us rise to their finest hour!'

We sat in silence as the cab jolted us towards joy. I could feel Ogilvie's thigh, Ogilvie's hip, jouncing against my own, and wondered if this was what people meant when they said they were *beside themselves with happiness*. Several times I began the movement of turning to Ogilvie, to say, 'The curls of their hair are like a tame creature in your hand,' or, 'The tiny mirrors on their wrapper make my head spin,' but I was afraid he might think me soft-hearted, and did not.

Mrs Smith never let me down: there were dear Agnes and Una, rather younger than I had remembered them, and even more marble as to shoulder, and melon as to breast. They exclaimed over us, and patted our arms, and laughed at nothing very much as they ushered us along the hall past the artistic prints. 'Any friend of our dear friend Mr Smith,' they cooed. 'Such a pleasure to meet another gentleman, Mr Brown,' they clucked.

As I had hoped, Una – or was it Agnes? – had on her wrapper with the tiny mirrors, and they made us sit down on the squashy couch, *to catch our breaths. Catching my breath* before we got down to business, with cheeky little bosoms slipping and sliding out of the folds of a mirrored wrapper, was one of the things I most looked forward to at Mrs Smith's.

One of them signalled the end of preliminaries by standing up and stretching in a way that reminded us of the shape of her chest. 'We are going to have ever such a nice time, dearies, I feel it in my bones,' she said with a wink from one of her artfully darkened eyes. 'In your bone, dearie?' the other one cried. 'Well, dearie, if that is what you would like to call it,' and she placed one finger, with its long nail of brilliant red, beside her nose and gave Ogilvie one of her bold looks, and I could see that Ogilvie was prepared to enjoy the bold looks of Agnes and Una as much as I did.

Oh Ogilvie, how my heart swelled to see you, and know you my friend! 'Indeed, Una,' he said with his engaging smile – and he seemed to have sorted out which was Agnes, which Una, within minutes, whereas I still had not got it straight in my mind. 'Indeed, I do believe I am beginning to feel it in my bone too!' and Agnes and Una positively shrilled at this, and nodded and smiled at me, congratulating me on my choice of intimate.

I could not be outdone, though: Ogilvie was the companion of my soul, but I could not have him outdoing me in my own house of pleasure! 'Well,' I said in the sort of tone that signalled another witticism, 'I am pleased to have extended your *circle* by the addition of another *member*.' I was conscious that my wit was not quite in the same breezy spontaneous class as Ogilvie's, but they all turned to me and appreciated my effort: Ogilvie touched my shoulder in a suggestion of a manly slap on the back, Una sagged and needed to be supported, and generally the whole thing was off to a fine start.

There were two back rooms at Mrs Smith's: one was tricked

out in a sort of Bedouin tent effect, with stuff draped across the ceiling, and cheap Turkey rugs on the walls, and gimcrack brass tables and lamps. The other was what the girls called the Marie Antoinette boudoir, with frills and furbelows, bits and pieces of petit-point and little gilt mirrors.

As the guest, Ogilvie was given the choice of Bedouin Tent or Boudoir. 'Oh, I have a Moving Finger that is itching to Write something tonight, so it had better be the Bedouin Tent,' he said. It was a joke I had used myself under the canopy, and I was struck again at how much we were in tune with each other.

As Agnes and I – or was it Una and I? – got down to business, I could hear noises from the next room. I listened, and held a hand over Agnes' or Una's mouth. She was making moaning noises, of the *yes yes oh yes* variety, but just this once I did not find them inflammatory: I wanted to hear the sounds from the other side of the wall. Ogilvie and I were separated only by the flimsiest of lathe-and-plaster partitions; I clearly heard a buckle strike a piece of furniture, a spring cried out as weight came down on it, and there was the rumble of a male voice.

I answered. I made sure that my own shoe struck the wooden floor, made sure that my voice also rumbled, and although in the normal way I was a discreet driver of a bed, tonight I bounced and thrust so that the bedhead tapped against the wall and the underparts tinkled and creaked symphonically.

It was a delightful duet. I tapped, he tapped in response; I clinked and tinkled, he clinked and tinkled too; and was that him I could hear panting so hard? We tapped and clinked and tinkled, and in due course things became dim about me, and I felt myself about to lose myself, and at last there was a cry, but I could not have said whether it was from myself or from the other man on the other side of the wall.

◆　　◆　　◆

Mrs Smith was not one of those who hustled visitors tactlessly on their way. When I emerged with Agnes or Una, Ogilvie was sitting *catching his breath* again on the spineless sofa, and I sat down beside him. Post-coital, Ogilvie was a man softened: there was an appealing languor in his movements, and his laugh was lazy now, like a hungry man after a good feed. His eyes met mine and kept hold. 'My word, Singer,' he said, and made a fluid circular sort of gesture. 'My very word, Singer!' I felt I had never looked as deep or as long into anyone's eyes as I now submerged myself in Ogilvie's.

Chapter Nineteen

WITH MY WIFE sitting smugly on her own flesh, I was empty sounding brass. I could set Albion Gidley Singer in motion, make his lips utter the right kinds of banalities, make his cheeks crease into smiles or frowns as the moment demanded. But upstairs in my study, wedged behind my heavy desk, padded around with the soft piles of alphabetical facts, about lemurs, seagulls and Emperor moths, that multiplied each day, enwombed in my facts, I was no mere gesturing husk.

Emperor Moth, I would write in my best copperplate at the top of one of my index cards (yellow for Lepidoptera). *The most acute sense of smell exhibited in Nature is that of the Emperor Moth, which can detect the sex attractant of the female at the range of 6 and four-fifths miles upwind.* I would then take the card over to Filing Drawer 37 of Filing Cupboard 6, and insert *Emperor Moth* between *Elephant Beetle* and *Firefly*.

My research was coming along very nicely: from time to time I got out *Chapter One* and looked at my opening sentence, but saw no way in which it could be bettered. One day

I would write all the rest, but the important thing was to have all the facts at hand before I started.

The curves and graces of the silver lady who strained to hold up my desk-lamp were a consolation to me when times were lean. I could sit at my desk with my pen in my hand and my colour-coded filing boxes around me, and enjoy the comfort of her little thrusting breasts, and little clenched buttocks, in the privacy of my trousers. Of all the good things about her, though, the best was that she was nothing more than a bit of furniture, and only a mad person would suspect a man of lascivious thoughts about his table-lamp.

Up here in the privacy of my study I waited for the arrival of the day's mail, and whiled the time away in watching the way the light caught her folds, and fingered her pointy little breasts until I was no longer a man sitting on a chair inside his trousers. I became some other being, watching from a great distance as Albion Gidley Singer became a creature consumed entirely by white lust. The smile of my silver lady seemed to congratulate me warmly on the vigour of my blood.

When there was a knock at the door, I was thrown into a minute's confusion. I was pleased it had not occurred just a few minutes before, but now I was simply a gentleman having a small adjusting fiddle with the desk-lamp in his lap, and calling out, 'Come!' to someone on the other side of the door.

'It is the letters, sir,' foolish Alma said, peering around the edge of the door as if I might bite. 'They are come a bit on the early side today, sir.' She stood in the doorway breathing hard over the silver tray of letters: what a slattern she was, with the hair coming out of her cap, and a frightened sort of grin on her red-blotched face. She was a coarse sort of woman, like a piece of bag. How was it that other wives managed to find housemaids pert, alert, upthrusting of bosom, square of shoulder, saucy of eye, while Norah had found only this slope-shouldered drab?

'Well, bring them over here, Alma, I cannot read them across the room,' I said, and laughed at my joke to see her bare her teeth in a kind of laugh too. Poor dolt, I had confused her now, for yesterday I had told her never to enter my room, but to leave the letters by the door. She came across the room with an awkward self-conscious walk, and laid the letters on the desk with a nervy jabbing motion as if I might be too hot to come close to.

I saw her tongue as she put them down, and it was pink and lewd, and she seemed to lean rather closer to me than necessary as she put them down. Perhaps it was the exertion of coming fast up the stairs, or the sense of being scrutinised by her employer, but something had brought a flush to her cheeks, and I looked at her with a moment's curiosity: her blushes and confusion made me realise that under her uniform she was generously endowed. In fact, now that I looked I could see that this generous endowment thrust against the starch so hard that it strained the buttons. As a man of the world, a man of wide experience with women, I recognised that Alma was highly conscious of the proximity of a man such as myself, and could very well turn out to be another strumpet.

I had assumed that Norah's inability to choose a stylish maid was just one more example of why women could not be relied on to do a thing properly. But watching Alma now, another more interesting possibility occurred to me. Was it possible that Norah had chosen Alma not from stupidity, but from guile? Knowing her husband to be the man he was, had she chosen her housemaid expressly for her redness of knuckle, brownness of teeth, and cheesy insipidity of feature?

If so, she had failed: being a woman, and believing in romance, she did not understand that a female does not have to be pretty, or young, or gracious, to rouse a man's blood if his blood is prepared to be roused.

The thought of poor Norah and her failed schemes made me jovial. 'Thank you, Alma,' I said, and tried to fix her eyes with my own, to test my new idea. But she could not meet my eye: her mouth was wet and shiny, her eyes darted everywhere except towards myself. Yes indeed, I was not mistaken. Alma was overtaken with a particular kind of fluster, and could only have a certain kind of thing on her mind.

◆　◆　◆

What a woman of wantonness Alma turned out to be, in her smell of yellow soap! She was a secret artist of passion. And oh, so clean! I knew her the first time at her cleanest, her most provoking, and the breath gasped in and out of her mouth as she surrendered to me.

I had made myself as light as a wish to go silently down into the scullery, and there she stood before the tub, waiting for me with her hands in the pile of lather on top of her head. Her breasts thrust and strained against the camisole that was all that covered them, her shoulders were as smooth as a well-turned bit of statuary: she needed only a bit of drapery to be one of those solid marble women who had been my first teachers about the female form. I saw the darkness of her underarms, where the hair was thick and secretive, and felt her lust transmit itself to me from the lewdness of that hair.

Alma did not writhe or gasp as pale Norah did, inflaming me with protest. Alma did not lie under me arching in passion like a fish. 'Sir,' she said again and again. 'Oh sir, oh Mr Singer sir!' Her gratitude was touching. Her breasts were cool in my mouth, the nipples engorged with her longing for me, and I felt her under my hands, shivering with the pleasure of it, and I thought of how demure and modest this minx seemed, serving a potato from a trembling spoon, or setting down a plate as if it was an egg, and how she was not demure at all, or modest, and must have been waiting since she had first come to us for this moment when my hands would force her down to her large knees on the scullery floor and she could cry out, 'Oh sir, oh Mr Singer sir!' until her mouth was too full for words.

There was ecstasy, but later it was only disgust I could feel at some housemaid with her hair falling in wet soapy strings around her blotched face, wiping her mouth with the back of her hand and pulling up the grubby straps of her camisole. Her flesh was cold to me now, and a nasty raw colour, and she leaned like a sack against the tub, staring at the floor.

Dinner in our echoing dining-room was not usually an affair to engage the interest of a man of the world such as myself. But on this night I was so eager that I came down early;

Norah made a show of putting away her embroidery in surprise and checking the clock.

Alma came in then, tiptoeing hugely around the table, handing dishes, breathing unsteadily with a whistling sound through her nose as she managed the peas and potatoes in their bowls: I heard her holding her breath, ashamed of the noise, as she crouched around the table, sliding food onto our plates like secrets. When she bent over Norah, serving her, so close that her arm almost embraced Norah's shoulder, what a private thrill I experienced in my trousers! Norah, my wife, addressed Alma, speaking in her vague way of salt and parsley, and Alma, my mistress of the scullery, nodded *Yes Mrs Singer, no Mrs Singer*. Poor silly Alma fell all over her words, answering, because of me watching and listening, knowing what Alma was like when undone by lust, with the soap shiny on her breasts.

I sat back waiting placidly for my dinner while my maid-of-all-work exchanged a few words with my wife. Alma looked at Norah, whose forehead was still puckering with the difficulty of making herself quite clear about the quality of the peas, and Norah looked at Alma, red in the face, holding the dish of potatoes at a dangerous angle, unable to decide whether the right answer to Norah's question was *Yes Mrs Singer* or *No Mrs Singer*.

At last she made a convulsive gesture that caused the serving-spoon to smear Norah's silk shoulder, and with an unusual spurt of temper Norah cried, *Alma! Whatever is the matter with you tonight, for Heaven's sake?*

How could that demure wife of mine guess that not twelve

inches from her face was the pair of breasts that her husband had so recently clawed to himself? I was moved, I was humbled by the mystery of all things: I felt the universe spinning about me in the wonder of seeing Norah speak to Alma and not know that Alma had held my joy until it burst like a grape.

When Alma left the room, I began to speak of her: I praised Norah's perspicacity in hiring her, praised Alma's thoroughness with the dust, and indicated that I thought she was a very fine figure of a woman, and did not Norah think so too? 'Why, Norah,' I exclaimed, 'I sometimes look at Alma, and do you know it crosses my mind that if you put her in a decent frock – your amber taffeta, for example, our Alma would cut quite a graceful figure.'

But Norah's face, always blank, grew blanker with every word I spoke. 'Really, Albion,' she murmured, but was obviously not hearing, or at least not listening. 'How interesting, taffeta, yes, but excuse me, Albion – Lilian, do not hold your knife as if you wish to strangle it, please,' and the moment passed: Norah was not prepared even to do me the courtesy of listening while I taunted her.

I was not going to be bested, though, by the inattention of a woman. I knew how to get her to listen, and tried a different tack: and in all these years, Norah had never learned to resist thawing in the face of attention. 'And did you go to your concert today with Kristabel?' I asked – how many husbands would be able to keep track of their wife's doings to the point of remembering a concert?

As I had predicted, Norah brightened at this like a fanned fire and said, 'It was a very fine band, Albion, but we did not fancy the music, it was rather bullying.'

She looked up at me and the light fell flat on her face in a way that showed every pore, but she smiled as though she thought she had been rather clever to call the music *bullying*, and thought that I would think she was clever too.

On another day, with a different sort of wind blowing through my heart, I might have. But today was not that day. In my mildest way, in my sweetest tones, I took out the knife and inserted just the very tip into her, so quietly that she did not know it was happening. 'Norah, do you not think it is rather wrong to condemn the music like that? It might not have been to your taste, but that is no reason to accuse it of bullying.'

Norah had not felt the knife slide in, for she was expecting no knife. 'Oh no, Albion,' she exclaimed in her arch hostessy manner, which the other ladies thought so amusing. 'It was positively like being hit over the head with a blunt instrument! Kristabel agreed, and I promise you, Albion, you would have hated it too.'

I became cold then, and slid the knife a little further into her unsuspecting flesh. 'Norah, I have my own opinions about things, and I would thank you not to tell me what I think.'

Ah! Now she felt it at last, the first stab! Her face clouded, she looked down in confusion, and her hands went to her hair in an anxious way. But when she looked up again I saw she had decided it was one of her husband's jokes, and she cried with a smile that had only triumph in it, 'Oh, Albion, I have heard you say much worse!' It had been a long time since Norah had roused me to passion, but now I felt a throb of excitement as I prepared to do something decisive with that knife which she had dismissed.

I turned away from her, I drew myself up, and I dusted an imaginary fleck off the table between us. It was sorrow, not anger, that I wished to convey, so I softened now, in order to open her for the deeper penetration of the blade, and said, 'I am sorry, Norah, but as a husband, it is my duty to warn you that this mocking of others, and this imposing of your own view, is something which, frankly, I have never liked in you.' I saw her face bleach to a putty-colour and her lips part, and pressed home the point. 'And, Norah, I have to tell you that others do not like it either, and have gone so far as to mention it to me.'

Poor Norah's brief moment of sparkle was now altogether extinguished: she glanced at the children, who were staring with food unpleasantly visible in their open mouths, and pressed her hands together, and began to mumble, 'I am sorry, Albion, I did not mean, I only meant, I would not dream,' until I left her there, relishing the authoritative sound of my footfall on the floor, and brushing aside Alma as she blundered up from the scullery and almost ran into me. 'I am going out for a short time,' I called back over my shoulder. 'Please do not wait up for me, I have a couple of *little things* to attend to.'

◆   ◆   ◆

It was a fact that Agnes and Una, lovely ladies in kimonos, with white buttery thighs and breasts that smelled of vanilla, loved me, Albion Gidley Singer and all that was within him. 'Do you love me, Agnes?' I asked. 'Una, do you truly love me?' and they knelt at my feet, those lovely fleshy women with their slits moist for me, knelt at my feet and whispered and murmured until I lay back and saw the darkness of Albion Gidley Singer's closed eyelids, murmured and soothed, and while they spoke they were interfering with me in the way they knew made my life a joy. 'Mr Smith, of course I love you,' said Agnes or Una, 'such a clever and distinguished gentleman, and so athletic too, why Mr Singer, how can you doubt that I love you ever so much.'

Of course there were the pound notes that I slipped under the vase at Mrs Smith's elbow, but it was me they relished, a man with whom they did not have to feign delight. 'Oh,' they cried, when they found the pound notes as if by accident, tidying up as I was putting on my hat and gloves to leave. 'Oh Mr Smith, you are too good, really you are, you are a naughty boy, very naughty, to be so extravagant!' How I loved their charming exclamations, and how I loved the way they stood at the door of the house waving and blowing kisses as I left, to go back to my wife. Norah was certainly a lady, but she never tapped the end of my nose with a spit-wet forefinger and exclaimed, 'Naughty boy! He will have to be punished!'

I did not doubt, but like any normal man I wanted to be sure. I could not come straight out and ask: 'Agnes, am I doing it right?' or, 'Una, how do I compare with other men?' At the Club I had discreetly checked, while at the urinal, that I was normal in respect of size, but I could not be sure of anything else. I had heard men talking about it, late into the whisky-and-sodas at the Club, and although I had nodded, and smiled, and exclaimed, 'My word yes,' I had wondered.

Dark Places

Were they all like me, pretending that the whole thing was somehow a larger experience than it was? Or was it possible that there was something to be done other than what I did, that made a man wax genuinely lyrical over it afterwards? That made men even court scandal and ruin rather than forgo such a pleasure? Nothing I had ever experienced with a woman had even begun to be worth scandal and ruin, and I had to wonder.

Of course I did not doubt, but it had crossed my mind to wonder what might happen if I should ever leave without slipping the pound notes under the vase. Several times, I felt so invincible in the house of the Smiths that I nearly put it to the test. Once, I was so sure of myself that I was actually on the doorstep before I thought I caught something in their eyes, and my hand went to find my wallet.

I went home trying to forget that moment's look in the eyes of my fan-fluttering mistresses. That look was the look of the world gone hollow and loveless, a world where Agnes and Una might stand at the door of their house with no vanilla breasts showing at the tightly bound necks of their kimonos, a world where smiles and warm words would turn into tight pinched mouths. I wanted to know, but I did not think I could bear living in a world in which it was, after all, only the pound notes that stood between bliss and being turned away, without love, into the night. In the end, the pounds were always under the vase, and I could never know.

Part Three
A Father

Chapter Twenty

I HEARD men in the Club: 'Now, I am a family man,' they would announce. As if being a family man established their credentials, they would clear their throats then and deliver themselves of some observation on the price of wool or the fecklessness of the working classes.

I had tried it out myself, in front of the three-faced pier-glass in the bathroom. 'Now, I am a family man,' I rehearsed. Should it be 'I *am* a family man', or 'I am a *family* man'? In the end I decided that the most significant part of the equation was the manhood part of it. 'I am a family *man*,' I told myself, watching my moustache move under my nose as I pinched my lips together for the word *man* – and in the end I came to believe.

Breakfast in the Singer household was something of a production, attended by Alma, who had still not learned how to live up to such a blaze of silverware, and presided over by Our Lady of The Platitude, my wife. Poor old Norah still clung to some fancy of herself as *artistic* and she had read in one of her tiresome arty journals that the *al fresco* breakfast was all the rage with the smart set in London. On balmy mornings the entire breakfast paraphernalia was trundled out to the verandah, and as we chewed our kidneys we were watched unblinkingly by various sharp-beaked beady-eyed specimens of birdlife.

Alma did not approve, panting in and out of the house with trays of things, and flapping away at wasps and flies, and trying at the same time to catch my eye, offering me things insistently. 'Jam, Mr Singer? More jam, sir?' I did not want jam, and I did not want Alma either. She was turning out to be exceptionally slow at cottoning on to the fact that Mr Singer had been interested once, but was not interested now.

Alma did not approve of breakfast out of doors, and I did not approve either, but over the years of our marriage it had been borne in on me that a husband does best not to dissipate his energies. A wise husband knows that it is the war that has to be won, not every single little battle, and that if a fight is to be undertaken, he must be completely sure of winning it. The matter of breakfast did not quite seem to me to fall into this category, so I had been careful never to let Norah see how little I liked it. There were advantages, I could see that: it was true, for example, that the various noises and smells made by the children were diluted by the open air, and a person could busy himself admiring the jacaranda when John brought up his porridge over the tablecloth, or Lilian knocked over her glass of milk again.

◆   ◆   ◆

As long as no one looked too closely, it all looked just as it should be for a *family man*. There was my wife, pale but well-groomed, crumbling bits of toast on her plate in a way that set off her slender fingers, and addressing her husband now and again, as one would expect of a wife, 'More tea, Albion?' or, 'Would you be good enough to pass the jam, Albion?' I did not know whether all wives, in the privacy of the family circle, were quite this polite with their husbands but it seemed satisfactory enough, and what went on behind Norah's eyes was her own affair.

Then there were the children, also satisfactory enough, at least at a distance. For the longest time, Rundle had insisted on calling them my *pigeon pair*, until I had pointed out that pigeons were paired in order for them to copulate. He had not used the phrase again.

At seven, my daughter was a clumsy fat girl, bursting at the seams with herself: her skin was taut with the amount of Lilian packed within it. Her legs were solid tubes of flesh, her fingers bulged, her very ears seemed fat. When she walked up the stairs the pictures trembled on the walls, and when she plumped herself down in her chair at the breakfast-table I could hear the snapping of wicker.

John sat over his plate like a toad, staring glassily with a strand of dribble still hanging from his chin. He was never going to amount to much. He sat in his little chair, goggling, his eyes set in pink flesh like a pet mouse's, stunned by the faces and talk around him. I could see none of myself in him. I had kept hope alive as long as I could, but now I had to face the fact that John was never going to grow out of being as puny as a bit of string. He was his mother's child, with his knobby knees, his plaintive little squeak of a voice, his large moist eyes that went into a panic at any little thing. Any dog, for example, even Kristabel's dreadful little lapdog, threw him into a state of hysteria, and it was always his mother he ran to, hiding in her skirts, and if I tried to prise him off her, and make him stretch out his hand for the dog to smell, and stand up straight like a man to look the dog in the eye, he set up a wailing as if I was poking him with needles.

I wondered at how different John was from the Albion Gidley Singer the world knew. He was like the other Albion made flesh: I might bury my weaknesses and fears beneath layers of manliness, but here it all was sprouting back up again in the form of my son, a buried weed sending up a sickly but obstinate shoot. I saw men look at me and look at John, and when they smiled at John it seemed to me there was something patronising there for me: *Poor old Singer, he seems right enough, but you only have to look at the boy to see the real story.* Had I been as bad as this when I was a boy? I could remember Father's impatience with me, heard myself using the same tone and the same words with John, and knew that, much as I hated the thought, John was the self out of which the splendid edifice of Albion Gidley Singer had created himself.

Lilian took a gigantic forkful of kidney; her cheeks puffed and bulged as she worked on the mass of food in her mouth, and as she did so she wriggled and gestured, her eyes winked and rolled: it could be seen that Lilian wished to speak. She forced the food into submission with her powerful jaws and

swallowed like a snake gulping down a hen, and on a spray
of kidney-fragments shouted, 'Father, what is a gentleman?'
She watched me minutely, waiting for an answer. 'A gentleman is a man such as myself,' I answered, but she did not
seem satisfied, and went on staring at the reflection of herself
across the table. 'Do not stare, Lilian, it is rude to stare,'
Norah told her, and tapped her thick wrist, and her small
eyes slid away from mine at last, and she fingered a smear on
the front of her pinafore.

But she was like a moth drawn back to a flame: her eyes
crept back to my face. 'Father,' she said in a wheedling way,
and I said, 'What is it, Lilian, speak up,' briskly, because I did
not want my daughter to become a wheedler. 'Can I be a
gentleman too, Father?' she asked. I heard Norah laugh in an
indulgent way, but there was a quality of startle in her laugh,
as if she had longed for the same thing in her most private
heart. 'No, Lilian, I am afraid that girls cannot be gentlemen,'
I said, and smirked across at her.

'Why not, Father?' she insisted. 'Why not?' Her curiosity
was becoming repellant with eager spittle, but she did not
realise, and looked at me brightly – *questioning is the mark of
intelligence*, I had once told her, and she had taken me literally
– and rushed on, her voice growing louder. 'Is it because of
titty-bags, Father?' and, in case I did not know what a *titty-
bag* was, she pointed with her grubby finger at Norah's chest.
'Those, Father, gentlemen never have those, do they?'

Norah made little gestures with her fingers at her from the
end of the table, and creased her face into shapes that were
supposed to make Lilian drop this line of enquiry. But I

believed in calling a spade a spade, or, as in this case, a *titty-bag*. I chuckled in the way I had heard fathers chuckle at the drolleries of their children, and announced, 'No, Lilian, but here is a fact that will interest you: the human titty-bag, or breast, is equipped with the same erectile tissue as the male organ of generation.' This gave rise to an associated fact in my mind, and I went on, over Norah's pipings of 'Albion! Please!' from the end of the table. 'Furthermore, the organ of generation of the stallion, Lilian' – how splendidly those two words rang together! – 'is over two feet long, and perfectly humanoid in form.'

Norah had few weapons, but those few she had, she used to the hilt. As so often before, she silenced her husband not by logic, or wit, or even by an appeal – it was some years now since Norah had tried the appeal – but by ringing the bell for Alma. We watched in silence as Alma chipped a cup, slopped the milk, and upset John's abandoned porridge-bowl, trying to get it all onto the tray with the master and mistress watching. I could hear her breathing loud in the silence; Alma was not a person who could be said to rise to an occasion.

Lilian seemed to have lost interest in titty-bags now, and got down from her chair. 'May I be excused, Father?' she remembered to say, but did not remember to wait for an answer, and began to march up and down the verandah. Her feet thwacked down at each step so that her fat cheeks shook and the railing trembled.

Norah turned in her chair to watch her. 'She has told me that she is being you,' she told me, 'when she stamps her feet like that,' and she watched me as if for a weakness. But my face was a good one for giving nothing away. 'Yes, Norah,' I said without lifting my eyes from the newspaper. 'She has told me too,' although in fact this was the first I had heard of it.

◆　◆　◆

Women had always been the mysterious other, but Lilian was no other. Embedded within that gross casing of flesh, blurred but unmistakable, were my own features. As Rundle, that master of the wearying repetition, exclaimed whenever he saw her, she was *a chip off the old block*, and he was right for once: she was myself in miniature. Already the flesh of her heavy cheeks was beginning to form into magisterial grooves beside her nose, and it was all too easy to imagine her with a moustache.

Norah thought she understood all about the way my daughter took after me. *Oh, she is a real little echo, such a funny thing to see*, I had heard her gushing to Kristabel, and Kristabel had nodded, and looked hard at Lilian. 'Yes,' she agreed. 'She is very like Albion was as a boy,' but she gave Lilian a particularly warm and personal smile as she spoke, as if to say she forgave her, and added, 'But you know, Lilian, your father was never as good at his Kings and Queens of England as you are, he always got muddled when he got to William and Mary,' and Lilian smiled back into her aunt's eyes.

Our resemblance was nothing so demeaning as *funny*: this was just Norah's way of belittling what she could not share. She tried to pretend that it was merely something rather quaint that Lilian should be a tiny feminised version of myself: something on the surface, a matter of mere noses and chins, and play-acting at ways of walking and talking. She could not begin to imagine the way we felt ourselves slide in and out of each other's beings, gazing into the distorting mirror of each other. That was something private between a father and his daughter, which no prying wife could have any part of.

But how could Norah be expected to guess at anything other than surfaces? She was content with the surface of her daughter – forever tweaking and pulling, the way Mother had done with Kristabel – as she was content with the surface of her husband.

It was me that Lilian adored. She could not respect her mother – what child of brains could respect a person with as much character as a glass of tap-water? I had listened to them speaking together at times when they did not know I was near, and was surprised to hear Lilian's gentleness with her mother, the soothing fibs, the reassuring but meaningless stream of small phrases: it was for all the world as though Lilian were the parent, and Norah the tetchy child.

With me, Lilian was not gentle. With me, she was invigorated by opposition: our minds wrestled in the best kind of intimacy. Give a fact to Norah, and it would disappear without trace, like a stone dropped into the sea. But offer a fact to my daughter and it would come back polished and warmed by challenge. What Norah had from Lilian was the gentleness of pity: what I had was the ferocity of love.

◆　　◆　　◆

'Family men are on the increase,' I stated in my clear fact-voice when we were all seated again, and Lilian was gouging the flesh out of a boiled egg. 'There are thirty percent more family men than there were five years ago, and the number is rising by one-half of a percentile point per annum.' This was a good fact, and I chewed on a large rubbery piece of kidney while my family absorbed it.

My daughter watched me with small calculating eyes over her champing mouth, and finally spoke. 'So, Father, there must be thirty percent more family women too.' She knew that an exchange of facts was what I loved best of all, and watched with a bright eager look as I prepared to parry and thrust another one at her. 'Ah, but Lilian,' I crowed, 'you are not in possession of all the facts. The fact is, women lack will, and do not live. Family women die out. Family men live to grand ages.'

Lilian looked at her plate, Norah shifted and coughed, John ground away obliviously at a crust. 'The average age of death of a family man is sixty-eight,' I strode on, and no one would have tried to disagree. 'Whereas women lack will, and have an average age of only sixty-four and a half.' My daughter watched me with admiring eyes, and I heaped facts upon her like caresses.

John had continued to champ blankly through all this, and champed still. When I exclaimed at him, 'Stop that din, John, and let me hear the months of the year!' he stared in a fright and swallowed with a terrible gulping. 'Yes, Father,' he said, because he knew better than to be silent when spoken to by his father, but was completely stumped by the months of the year. 'October, June, Friday,' he suggested at random. I could see Lilian itching to tell him: she squirmed against her chair, longing to rattle off the months of the year, and steal a little more approval from her father, while John sat staring at the tablecloth, his narrow white face blank with stupidity, and I seethed and frothed within.

'Oh look,' exclaimed Norah, in the special sweet little piping voice she used to talk about sweet little piping things. 'Look at the sweet little sparrows, look, they want to join us for breakfast. Look, Lilian!' Lilian glanced over at the sparrows without interest, but Norah was determined; her voice grew more shrill as she insisted on her little bit of whimsy, and tried to make Lilian join her in it. 'Look, Lilian, do you think that big one is the Daddy? And that one with the bright little eyes must be the Mummy, Lilian, look!' In her own velvety way, Norah could hector, every bit as well as I could myself.

But Lilian was too much her father's daughter to have any interest in this kind of twaddle. My heart swelled with pride as I heard her say in a flat, matter-of-fact way, 'Yes, Mother, and the Daddy has just done number two on the step.' Norah's head drew back into its neck and her coaxing smile congealed; but now Lilian was interested. 'Oh look, Mother,' she cried eagerly. 'Look, a dead one!' She sprang up from her chair, and ran down the steps, scattering birds before her. A moment later she ran back up, holding something that she laid next to Norah's plate. 'Look, Mother,' she cried. 'Look, it is dead.' The fledgeling she had carried up to the terrace was nothing more than a slack grey sac, with a small beak hopelessly ajar on air, tiny dead claws clenched, dead enough for ants to be investigating the jelly of its eye. 'Look, Mother,' she shouted enthusiastically. 'The skin is so thin you can see its guts, look!'

Poor old Norah, with her silly little rose-blossom prettiness about everything: she had nothing to tell Lilian about dead birds and their guts. 'Dear,' she said faintly, a hanky at the ready at her mouth, 'young ladies try not to think about such things.' She appealed to me. 'Albion, will you get rid of it, please?'

God is said to note the death of every sparrow, but I myself would note the death of this particular one. 'I disagree, Norah,' I said. 'Even young ladies should know the brute facts of nature. Putting your head in the sand is a coward's way.'

I turned to Lilian, who was now poking at the flabby corpse with a piece of twig. 'Regard, Lilian, how wonderful are the ways of Nature: in that nest a sparrow hatched more chicks than she could feed, and here we see Nature's iron law being acted out.' Lilian nodded and flipped the thing over with her twig so that it quivered as if alive. 'The fact of the matter, Lilian, is that the world only needs a finite number of sparrows, and this particular sparrow exceeded that number.'

She nodded. 'Yes, Father, I see.' Her eyes were fixed on mine as if physically sucking in the wisdom I had for her, and under her admiring gaze I warmed to the occasion. 'It is a well-known fact, Lilian, that a sparrow eats three times its body weight each day. Imagine, Lilian, if you ate three times your own body weight each day!'

Ah, my gigantic daughter blinked at that, and suddenly smiled at me. 'Oh, but Father, I probably do!' With a side-long look at Norah, she said, 'Father, you know the scalpel you gave me for the frogs, can I cut this up with it?' Norah was beginning, 'Absolutely not, Lilian,' but I rode her down with my orator's voice. 'Splendid idea, Lilian, but do it soon or it will start to smell.'

Lilian and I both glanced at Norah: she had shrunk into her clothes, bowed her head, and was now snapping a piece of toast into four perfectly equal pieces, and buttering each one fastidiously. Lilian and I watched her until she glanced up at both of us and pushed the plate away with a little shudder.

The bringing-out of a fact was always such a pleasure! I thought of another one I could share with my clever daughter. 'Did you know, Lilian, that the human brain weighs three pounds one and a half ounces? That is about the same weight as a man's foot. The female brain is naturally smaller, weighing only two pounds ten ounces.' I saw her face cloud, and was quick to reassure. 'But you yourself, Lilian, have a good-sized brain-pan, and probably have almost as good a mind as a male.'

Norah looked up from her toast. She was going to try to get into things again. Her own head was a particularly small one, under all that hair and those gigantic silly hats. The smallness of Norah's head had been one of her greatest charms, back in the days when I had found her charming. Today it was looking particularly small, with her hair not yet in the full flight of its loops and heaps. She was unwise to take issue with me, but she was always unwise to take issue with me, and yet never learned! 'Surely, Albion,' she said, 'brains are not a matter of mere volume, but of quality.'

I cleared my throat and paused impressively. I was going to enjoy this. 'I would not expect you to agree, Norah,' I said, speaking very slowly and clearly so she could not fail to follow me, 'for the following reason: your very refusal to see the logic of my case is, in itself, overwhelming evidence that I am right.' How fluidly my voice wrapped itself around each word, ringing out over the lawn! What a deft and elegantly executed *coup de grâce* I had just delivered!

I let the silence extend itself so long that even John realised something was happening, and gawped up at us. We all watched as Norah slowly flushed darkly around the jowls. She said nothing, but set her lips tight like someone suppressing wind, and avoided looking in my direction. Everything went still, watching and listening in silence; there was only the secretive whispering of the leaves of the jacaranda, and the moth-like rustle as Norah pushed back a strand of hair.

I glanced across at Lilian and moved my shoulders in a way that might have been nothing more than a man settling the muscles of his well-made shoulders inside his coat. Only someone looking for trouble would have mistaken it for a shrug. Lilian smiled back at me, and I surprised myself with a thickness around the interior of my nose. I loved to make my daughter smile, and what a magnificent acreage of face she had when she was pleased!

Chapter *Twenty-One*

NATURE HAD DEALT Lilian a nasty blow in making her a female, but I was not going to be cheated of her. She was *a chip off the old block* in every respect but one, and I was going to make sure that one flaw did not spoil the rest of her.

The first rule that I had made, which had caused Norah to sulk over her embroidery for days on end, was that Lilian was to have no dolls until she could read *Mackie's Primer*, and the rule had paid off: she had been a precociously early reader. I kept a close eye on the books that came into the house for her. She had to be allowed to open and look at the ones given on her birthdays by Kristabel and Mother, but I made sure that accidents happened to happen to all those winsome little pink and white books: why should my daughter's mind be wilted with pap? So they were accidentally left out in the rain, or taken on picnics and accidentally left behind, or accidentally fell down behind the chesterfield.

In their place I supplied the things that were worthy of her mind, the same things that had equipped my own: the sum of man's knowledge lay at her fingertips on the shelves of her room. There was the Encyclopedia, there was the Dictionary, there was even the Bible, for although I discouraged God, I felt that an educated person should know who Noah was. There were *Great Men of History, Man the Masterpiece, Men of Science*: there were the books on birds, insects, mammals, steam engines, levers, the circulation of the blood, the countries of the world, their principal exports, their mean annual rainfall; and, of course, the matched sets of classics: Milton, Dickens, and Byron.

The Byron had been a cause of open conflict between Norah and myself. Norah knew a few lines from Byron, had charmed me, in fact, by quoting somebody or other's declaration of love, from some poem or other, when we were courting, that day in the Gardens. It was only long after we were married that I had discovered that those few pretty lines were not a small sample of Norah's literary accomplishment, but the entire stock. 'Some nicely illustrated children's book, perhaps, Albion,' she had urged. 'Surely she is a little young for Byron.' I had looked at her fidgeting with her embroidery, unable to tell me what she really thought: not simply that Byron was full of long words, but other objections she knew I would have no patience with. *Byron is rude*, she was probably thinking. *Byron is full of things that are not a bit nice.*

There was a particular thing she did with her nose when she thought *unpleasantness* might be arising, and she did this thing with her nose now. 'When I was a girl I had a lovely leather-bound *Gems from the Poets*, Albion. Just highlights, you know, much more suitable for her age.'

I gave her a look which caused her to shrivel somewhat. 'Yes, Norah,' I said, with an exaggerated show of patience. 'I am sure it was just the ticket for you. But no daughter of mine is going to be offered mere emasculated fragments.' Norah did not answer this, but went on sipping her tea and smoothing the fine hairs on her forearm. She was not good at much, but she had entirely mastered the art of sulking.

◆　◆　◆

It was a great satisfaction to watch my daughter's mind develop along the correct lines. Like her father, she came to love a list. *Rivers of Australia, Clockwise*, she would announce, strike a pose, and launch herself. *Oceans of the World. Parts of the Body in Alphabetical Order*. Her father always applauded heartily, the more so for knowing that Norah did not care to hear about intestines over dinner.

Like her father, she relished the lovely definiteness of numbers. 'Lilian,' I would say, 'a human body, if baked until all moisture is evaporated, is reduced in weight as 1 to 10: a body that weighs 100 pounds living, will weigh how much when dry?' Her eyes would brighten with the chance to impress me, and she would stare at the wall above my head – she had never been allowed to count on her fingers – until, usually with an unfortunate blurt of over-eager spittle, she came up with the answer.

She had quickly grown out of her first little table and chair, and for her ninth birthday I bought her a proper desk and chair for her room, plus a desk-lamp the twin of my own. As I sat in my own study, with my silver lady beaming her light down on my page, it gave me great pleasure to know that, in her room, Lilian was sitting at her own desk with just the same glow on her page.

She had the best pen that *Singer Enterprises* could supply: Miss Cunningham had been quite flustered, blushing all over her pretty little neck, going through the nibs with Mr Singer's daughter, as she had gone through them the week before in the stockroom with Mr Singer, and had had a little *discussion* with him later on; but she had made sure that Lilian came away with the very best. In the drawers of her desk lay reams of best bond and bottles of best India, rubber-bands, paper-clips, manila folders: nothing would come between my daughter and the cultivation of her mind.

I did not permit flim-flam of a purely decorative nature, so on her dressing-table were none of the frilly little things that adorned her mother's: there were no china ballerinas here, or blown-glass pussy-cats, or lace-trimmed pincushions embroidered with pansies. Instead there was her plaster model of the brain, her bottled taipan, and her collection of lead soldiers.

I had come up against certain ingrained difficulties on the subject of the soldiers. Her set was the one I had had as a boy, supplemented by new Boer War issue, and it was a beauty. However, it had taken me quite a time to teach Lilian how to play with it properly. At first she had been inclined to treat the soldiers rather as if they were dolls: I would come in and find them leaning up together to drink tea out of a thimble, or on their backs under a handkerchief being put to bed. Teaching her was not easy, but I persisted. I supplied her with new forts and model landscapes; but it was when I found some corpses and puddles of bright-red lead blood that I got her interested. Finally she got the hang of it, and she even learned to do a rather snorty version of my own cannon-noise.

◆   ◆   ◆

Over the years I had got into the habit of coming up to her room after dinner to check on how she was getting along. On a particular night soon after her tenth birthday, I came in as usual, but instead of turning to me with a glad smile, and some amazing fact about aardvarks, she jumped when I came in behind her. 'Oh! Father!' she gasped. 'I did not hear you come in,' and was it my imagination, or was there reproach in her voice, as if she thought I should have knocked at the door?

Her fluster made me suspicious, but the things on her desk spoke only of innocent intellectual endeavour. Her geometry set was spread out, although I saw with disapproval that she was not trying out problems from the Euclid I had got her, but using the compasses to draw symmetrical flowers and colouring them in with her mapping inks. She made a move as if to cover her work with her arm, as well she might, wasting her time on mere decoration, but I jerked her arm away, off the desk. Something flew out from under the silly flower, and fell on the floor: a book that sprawled face-down, buckling like a thing in pain. Even as I bent to pick it up, I could tell from her stiffness that it was something forbidden.

Strictly speaking, it was not something forbidden. Norah's

romances were so entirely vapid, so utterly silly, so completely lacking in merit, that it had never occurred to me to forbid them to Lilian. Yet here it was: *Lo, the Dawn is Breaking*, open at chapter twenty-seven: 'How Strong Were His Arms'.

'Lilian, how dare you read this tripe?' I demanded. 'I thought I had taught you to know better. And sneakily! How dare you?' I suspended the flaccid little book by thumb and forefinger and stared down at her face, turned up to mine in the lamplight. She should have hung her head, should have been ashamed, should have mumbled something apologetically, regretfully, remorsefully. Instead she answered back very pertly, 'But why not, Father? Mother said it would be all right.'

Ah, it was that woman behind it, undermining me at every turn! Ignorant, illogical, bigoted and credulous, with a brain which had made sheer stupidity into an art-form! But ah, she was cunning, too, in a low animal way: cunning enough to know how to seduce Lilian away from me, and to make her as silly and sentimental as herself.

'How dare you answer me back like that!' I exclaimed – God Almighty, how quickly the rot had set in! – but she stared very saucily and said, 'I am not answering back, Father, just answering your question,' and for an instant on her fat red face I saw the same smug expression I saw on Norah's when she thought she had floored me.

It had always sickened me to punish Lilian, because I knew it was her triumph, not mine: I could spank till my arm ached, starve her till she was as pale as paper, confiscate her best books – I could do all this, yet I was impotent in the face of her impenetrable female will. She had long known the power of silence, and had many times endured being sent to bed at three in the afternoon through some enraging refusal to confess, or explain, or simply speak when spoken to.

Where had such strength come from? It was true that I myself was a man of iron will. But as a child, I had been fearful of punishment, and sly in devising ways to avoid it: a small chronic fear like an ache had hung over my childhood. I had taught myself strength as another man might have taught himself ballroom-dancing, had learned strength as a way of dealing with my weakness. But Lilian seemed to have been born with unbreakable will: it was not something she needed to learn. How had such a fearless spark of a child sprung from between the glass of water of her mother and the hollow drum of her father?

'Lilian,' I roared, and heard my voice around the room. 'Lilian, how dare you!'

In theory I did not believe it necessary to strike women, but I struck Lilian now. In a passion of outrage I slapped her so hard that she fell off her chair, knocking her plaster model of the human brain down with her to the floor. The plaster broke, but not my fat daughter, who lay under me, breathing loudly as I freed layer after layer: the pinafore, the skirt, the white bloomers, and there at last was her dimpled white buttock-flesh, quivering under my hands.

'There! There! There! There!' I could not prevent myself braying with each sound of my flesh against hers, and when at last I stopped, the room continued to pulse with the echo of my cries.

What indignation and pain she feigned then! She roared and shrieked, wailed and wept and provoked me into slapping her more. On the cool whiteness of my daughter's buttocks, the marks of my hand were as pink as a peach. When I stopped, she fell silent and stared at me from under her untidy hair with a pout that seemed to invite more of the same. I thrust her away. 'Get away from me, Lilian,' I cried. 'I am engorged with you!' – meaning, of course, that I was enraged with her. I listened as she ran heavily out of the room and along the hall, and could hear the ugly sobs she was producing as she ran.

Alone among the accumulated knowledge of the ages, I was filled with a kind of airy confusion, as if the self that lived within was evaporating from every pore. I took hold of the edge of her desk to remind myself that I was a thing, separate from this construction of wood, I too was a thing that took up space in the world, but I felt myself to be as insubstantial as a ragged leaf spinning down from a tree. Rage had blossomed, slapping had occurred, shouting had taken place; but could it have been myself that had done these things? The rug stared back at me blandly, outside frogs honked to each other. Life flowed back over the slapping and shouting I had done as a pond swallows a stone: I had left no mark behind me.

Whereas – Lilian had planted those wide feet of hers apart on the rug as solidly as if she had taken root there. There was the chair she had overturned, there were the pieces of brain that she had brought down with her; and along the corridor in Norah's room, she was not watching her hand, wondering if it was part of her, she was not kicking her foot at a table-leg to check that she existed – no! My daughter could be struck hard enough to fall over, she could be shouted at loudly enough to burst her eardrums, she could be shaken until her teeth cracked in her head, but my daughter would never be hollow. Her fullness mocked me, her eyes full of herself mocked me, her echo.

Chapter Twenty-Two

I HAD NEVER been a gregarious man, and it was not often that I invited anyone, even Ogilvie, to visit me at home. But these days my house seemed full of beings foreign to me. Norah and her friends had always made distracting noises from downstairs when I was trying to concentrate, up in my study, on the mating habits of the Great Crested Grebe. And now there were other noises as well: Lilian thundered up and down the stairs, called out querulously to Norah, shouted at John; John squealed and wailed, and Norah had to raise her voice to make peace between them: generally a man's home was hardly his own any more. A visit from Ogilvie, then, seemed the right kind of antidote to all this, a reminder that the house was, after all, mine.

On the day of his visit I was full of anticipation like an itch. I found myself watching at the window listening for the front-door bell, wiping my damp palms down the side of my trousers. But by the time he had been in the house for ten minutes, he had made me laugh three times, told me five things I had not previously known, and listed twenty-three reasons for not believing in God: and I was relishing his company like a fresh breeze on a stagnant day.

Outside, down below on the lawn, I could hear Norah feebly piping, 'Alma! Alma! Hot water, Alma, where is the hot water?' and how it filled me within my clothes to be up here discussing large ideas man-to-man with Ogilvie, while the pointless world of women unreeled its paltry thread below us!

Ogilvie peered and poked around my study, as he had on the other occasions he had been here – his frank curiosity about things was one of his continuing charms for me – ran his finger along the colour-coded files, listened with interest as I explained my system of classification, admired at some length my opening sentence, and agreed with me that a man had to have all his data in order before he started to write. In return, he advised me to get in on the ground floor with calculating-machines, and gave me a couple of tips on up-and-coming stocks; over the years, Ogilvie's tips had been a mixed bunch, but I wrote down the names and thanked him.

Down below, Norah's voice could be heard again, with a different refrain now, but probably just as ineffectual. She nagged on and on, 'Lilian, come and change your frock for dinner! Lilian! Lilian!' and I was reminded that the day was waning. 'Ogilvie, you will join us for dinner, of course,' I said, adding, 'I will not take no for an answer, Ogilvie!' in what I intended as a copy of the bluff forthright manner I had heard friends use to each other, but Ogilvie glanced at me in some surprise, so I wondered if it had sounded simply peremptory. 'I should be delighted,' he said, without further ado – and how I warmed to him all over again for not going into all the silly palaver about *imposing* and *intruding* that many another would have felt necessary!

It was Norah who mentioned Mrs Ogilvie, and suggested in her most tiresomely genteel voice that we should telephone to *enkwayer* whether Mrs Ogilvie might care to join us.

Frankly, I had forgotten Marjorie Ogilvie, but there was no need to worry. 'Thank you, Mrs Singer, but no: Marjorie does not generally expect me for dinner on a Tuesday, and is often out of the house herself then.' I could see that Norah was curious at this arrangement, which sounded a little slapdash to her, and to forestall some endlessly tedious conversation about these domestic details, I quickly ushered Ogilvie into the dining-room.

As we sat down to dinner, I found myself proud of being the family man, surrounded by children, wife and servants producing a meal that was orderly in surroundings that were well-regulated, in perfect taste, and conducive to rational thought. John was tucked quietly away behind the napkin at his neck, Norah ladled soup deftly, and Lilian sat up straight, looking across brightly at Ogilvie.

'Good evening, Lilian,' I exclaimed, and was pleased that she looked into my face and said, 'Good evening, Father,' in such a frank and forthright way. Lilian was now suffering what Norah quaintly called *puppy fat*, her new teeth were still much too large for her face, and she was as awkward as a seal flapping on a rock; but she was undeniably bright, and had a vocabulary well beyond her years. I surprised myself by feeling a glow of pride when Ogilvie spoke to her: he was that kind of man, to take the trouble even with a lard-faced child – and she spoke up smartly in response.

'And what projects are keeping you occupied at present, Lilian?' he asked, and Lilian faced him across the table, fixing his eyes with hers as she had been taught, and projecting her words across at him like tennis balls. 'Oh, I am learning the Encyclopedia by heart, Mr Ogilvie,' she said. 'Father gave me the whole set for my birthday.' Ogilvie did not smile patronisingly, as many another would have done. 'You could not do better,' he said approvingly. 'And what are you up to now?' Lilian put down her spoon, wiped her mouth on her napkin, and announced so the room rang: 'Of living birds,' she began, 'that producing the largest egg is the North African ostrich (*Struthio camelus camelus*). The average egg weighs just under four pounds, measures seven inches in length, and requires forty minutes for boiling. The shell is one-sixteenth of an inch thick and can support the weight of an eighteen-stone man.'

When she had finished, Ogilvie applauded, and glanced down the table at me with a warm smile. 'A chip off the old block, Singer,' he said, and coming from him the words were a delight.

'Do tell us, Mr Ogilvie, about your work,' said Norah. I had heard this formula from her so often I could not for the moment remember whether she had ever used it before on Ogilvie. I could only hope not, and he gave no sign of thinking anything strange in the question. He was a man who understood about singing for one's supper, and did not need further invitation to keep us entertained on the subject of the various pamphlets he was writing. 'I must hire my pen to whomever can pay, Mrs Singer, and am concocting a very weird and wonderful little piece for the flat-earthers at the moment, and another for the nudists, who make up for having no clothes by having endless layers of solemn ideas.'

I could see Lilian was interested in this, and asked in her penetrating precocious voice, 'And do they wear clothes when they come to see you, and do they make you take your clothes off, too, Mr Ogilvie?' From the end of the table, Norah was making hushing gestures at her, but I was not ashamed. I was a family man, but I was not some tame family man who swaddled his womenfolk around with pretty lies.

'No,' Ogilvie said, taking her seriously, 'we all retain our clothes. And Mrs Singer, I believe you are involved with charity work these days?' Ogilvie turned his full face and attention to Norah as he spoke, as if she was really worth listening to. What a man of tact he was! Norah shot me a glance, and said, 'Oh yes, Mr Ogilvie, I think my husband does not altogether approve of charity, but I do what I can to help others.'

She smiled in that winsome way she had always known how to turn on, to take the sting or the stupidity out of what she was saying, and I saw Ogilvie give her in return his charming face-creasing smile. I could not let her get away with this, and said in a way that was intended to be humorous, 'As you know, Norah, it is not that I disapprove of charity, but that I believe it is the lint that clogs the machine of progress.' I glanced at Ogilvie: yes, he appreciated this little *bon mot*, but Norah stared coldly, and came at me with her fuzzy-headed do-gooder's arguments. 'But Albion, why should we not help those who are scraping dripping on a crust of bread, when we can afford our rack of lamb on Wedgwood?'

Oh, that wife of mine was becoming a thorn in my side! I was conscious of Ogilvie watching with some interest as this little marital difference unfolded itself before him, and savoured many replies to Norah's question. Of replies there was no shortage: I could, for example, have the cheap satisfaction of inviting my well-cushioned wife, already halfway through her second serving of rack of lamb on Wedgwood, to go down to the kitchen and find some fat to scrape on a crust, and take her plate of food to some indigent on the street.

But such a cheap triumph was not the kind of triumph I wished to have over my thorn of a wife in front of Ogilvie: the cleverer course was to pincer her in logic. 'But Norah,' I said in my smoothest way, and laughed a little, the more to disarm her, 'you must think the thing through, my dear. It is a matter of simple common sense. If there were no eaters of rack of lamb, then there would be no one to provide employment. And without work, Norah, you will admit, there is not even bread and dripping to be bought. No, a moment's thought will show you that the eaters of bread and dripping need the eaters of roast lamb to continue doing so.'

I was enjoying my voice, so fluidly wrapping itself around each word, given resonance by this echoing dining-room. I glanced at Ogilvie: he was nodding vigorously as he chewed, and watching Norah to see how she would return the ball.

But Norah, like all women, would not take a man on in a fair fight. She stared at her Wedgwood, empty now, and would not say a word, but the set of her mouth as she tucked a strand of hair behind her ear said that although she knew better, she would not deign to reply.

I could not let her get away with that: there was Lilian, watching me with a smear of gravy beside her nose, and there was Ogilvie, who was a good fellow, but it was easy to imagine him telling the others at the Club about *poor old Singer, his wife wears the pants, you know.*

Alma came in then, her feet and breathing loud in the silence, and I saw my chance. 'Where does our dripping go, Alma?' I asked, and after wearisome repetition, and explanation, she finally replied, 'Why, into the dripping-tin, Mr Singer.' I was determined that Norah should see that she did not have a monopoly on kindness towards inferiors, and displayed no impatience as I said, 'Yes, Alma, very good, but where does it go after that?' There were laborious exchanges then, about dripping for the breakfast eggs, and dripping for the Sunday joint, and Alma had to agree that the Sunday joint itself created more dripping, so the net effect was a gain of dripping, not a loss. Finally Alma's mind took a visible leap, and she cried, 'Oh well, Mr Singer, when the folk come to the kitchen door, you know, to do the kindling and that, and the other poor wretches on their beam ends, well, Cook will often give them a bit of bread with a scrape of dripping on it.'

She was not sure if her leap of imagination had led her into dangerous waters, and I made a mental note to have a short sharp word with Cook about charity at the back door, but for the moment her leap suited me nicely. 'Norah!' I cried, and it was intended to be jovial, but I saw her jump in fright. 'Norah, there you are, were it not for us eating our roast lamb, the poor wretches at the back door would leave empty-handed.'

I let a silence fall then for my statement to sink in, and watched the way Norah flushed in a mottled away around the jowls. She was too trained in social hypocrisy to go on arguing in front of a guest, but I could see that her breathing had become shallow, and she placed her knife and fork alongside each other with mathematical precision, staring at her hands as they did so as if she was afraid of what they might do. She was obstinacy itself, Norah, as hard as a lump of coal under all the soft soap.

I was full of good feeling now, warmed from within by the completeness with which my argument had filled every chink in Norah's case. I was pleased to be able to demonstrate to Ogilvie that, although I might appear to be ensconced in the most perfectly conventional suburban comfort, surrounded by all the gimcracks of bourgeois splendour – electro-plated silver cake-stands, mahogany chiffoniers, cutlets with paper frills – I was not afraid to take a firm hand. From the other end of the table, Ogilvie met my eye, and it seemed to me that his smile congratulated me in the warmest terms on my handling of this little family mutiny.

Chapter *Twenty-Three*

LIKE A business, a household benefits from vigilance. Lilian's surprises had been kept to a minimum since the day of *Lo, the Dawn is Breaking*: while she was off at school there was plenty of time to check her room for rubbish. I was afraid that at school she might read on the sly the romances of her little friends, and had had several discussions with Miss Foote in which I made my views perfectly clear.

John had never been capable of surprising. He was off at Miss Birtwhistle's now, and Miss Birtwhistle assured us that he was *a lovely dear boy, no trouble at all, never a peep out of the dear little fellow*. Reading between the lines it was obvious that John was as gormless at school as he was at home.

And Norah? Norah may conceivably have surprised me in the past: a man could never be one hundred percent sure, especially when one of his children seemed to be almost a different species from himself. A man had heard too many stories: that poor boob Sutherland at the Club, for one, had apparently arrived home a few minutes too early one day, and been most unpleasantly astonished. So vigilance, and the unexpected visit, remained a habit with me.

The afternoon still blazed as I made my way home. It had been a day to make a man feel truly a man; I strode up the slope from the ferry, at one with Albion Gidley Singer. His cane pirouetted before him vigorously and his boots planted themselves strongly on the earth; sunlight was something you could take a handful of, leaves applauded in the tops of trees, birds pealed and cried: it was an afternoon (after a morning on which the Rawlings contract had been sewn up, and young Philips put in his place) when a man felt that the world was eating out of his hand.

◆　　◆　　◆

Mine was a house of many openings where a man might enter unannounced. It was full of traps, too, but I was not caught out. I knew that the hinge of the back door squeaked if you pushed it slowly, so I gave it a single decisive thrust, and it was silent under my hand. I knew how to step from rug to rug on the polished wood of the hallway, and never forgot now just where the squeaky boards were. I glided into the heart of my house causing not the faintest ripple in its stillness: I was like a paradox from geometry, a man become a flat plane, turned sideways to the air, a man of length and breadth but no volume whatsoever.

I stood quietly at the foot of the stairs, a man invisible at the core of his house, and listened to its life. What did they all get up to when I was not here? No matter how many times I had compacted myself between the particles of air in my house, I had never satisfied myself. Something was always just out of reach, something had just that moment fallen silent, someone had just left by the front door as I had come in the back – why else were the dust-motes dancing in the light of the coloured panes? – or it had been yesterday, or would be tomorrow, that it would happen.

It did not seem to be today. I held my breath and listened, and all seemed innocent enough. From the kitchen, I could hear Cook clashing things together: she was getting hard of hearing, and it reassured her to get a clatter out of her saucepans. There was no mystery in Cook.

Closer at hand I could hear an irregular swishing and thumping, and craning silently round and looking up I could see Alma at the top of the stairs, crouching in a cloud of dust, flicking a rag between the banisters. I had had occasion to speak to her about the banisters not long ago, and saw now with approval that her tongue was poking out in concentration and she was flicking away mightily, and was too completely absorbed by her task to notice a man like a sheet of paper standing edge-on to her and watching.

From the drawing-room I heard the tinkle of best china upon best china, the rattle of a teaspoon in a saucer: there was Norah accounted for, entertaining ladies, elaborating the drinking of a cup of brown water into a whole afternoon's project.

As I stood listening to the various types of sounds made by the various types of females under my roof, it occurred to me that, with John away at Miss Birtwhistle's, mine was the only male organ on the premises. This ratio of men to women –

about one to six – seemed, purely in scientific terms, to be about right. To waste the possible seed of one man on a mere one woman, who at best could only produce offspring once a year, was a reckless waste of resources. In theory, a man could service dozens of females at once, and sire thousands of children in the course of his lifetime! Only the day before, I had noted and filed the fact that Fateh Ali Shah, Emperor of Persia from 1797 to 1834, had fathered a total of one hundred and fifty-four sons and five hundred and sixty daughters by his many wives. If the world destroyed itself in the next moment, and left only Rosecroft surviving, the human race could get going again from just the few specimens of it here.

Naturally, restraints had been imposed upon this potential, but they were constraints of a purely social and artificial order, and beneath them, the pulse of biological compulsion beat away steadily. There were times, in fact, when it was almost audible. And at this moment, in this house of women, I was vividly aware of the animal maleness of me tucked away beneath my clothes.

A sudden loud burst of female laughter came from behind and startled me. I took a step back, gave myself a fright with my reflection in the mirror, stumbled on the rug, knocked into the hallstand with my elbow, dropped my hat. And of course it was just a trick of the acoustics in this hall: there was no one behind me, watching and laughing to see me in disarray.

'Oh Mr Singer, you gave me such a fright, sir,' Alma squeaked at me, peering around the corner of the stairs. 'I never knew you was home, sir,' and she guffawed meaning-lessly, and seemed prepared to elaborate on the subject of surprises and frights, standing up now with the rag in one hand, the other on the banister, like a parody of a belle making a grand entrance with a fan in her hand. 'Indeed, Alma,' I said. 'As you see, I am home, and will be checking those banisters shortly,' and she crouched down again and bowed her head to her duster.

Another gust of mocking laughter came from the drawing-room. There was something about standing here in this gleaming draughty place, hearing laughter on the other side of a closed door, I did not like: I had to resist the impulse to check my fly-buttons.

◆ ◆ ◆

A man does not sidle into his own drawing-room. I flung the door wide and stood there until I had their full attention. The room was a long one, as befitted the drawing-room of a man in my position, and the women were gathered at the far end, in the curved bow-window. My eyes had accustomed themselves to the dimness of the hall, for picking out fine details of dust-motes and rugs: the blast of light pouring in these windows was an assault. The huge radiance engulfed the women, reducing them to insubstantial silhouettes, so feathery that they hardly interrupted the flood of light. There were three, or was it four? When they moved against one another it was hard to tell, all faceless, filmy, nothing more than smudges marring the great chord of light.

By contrast, I was conscious of the bulk of myself, the solidity of my footfall on the wooden floor, the massy darkness of my garments sucking up the light. As I came down the room towards them, the silhouettes became still: the laughing died completely away, and dimly I could see that all their faces were turned toward me, waiting for me to speak.

As I drew near, the figures resolved themselves into individuals, and there was Norah, there was Mother, there was Kristabel, and there was Lilian. Norah's hands flew about her person, smoothing her hair, smoothing her waist, smoothing the brooch at her neck, positively caressing herself as she gave me a wavery social smile. It would have been appropriate, I thought, for Norah to have told me what they had been discussing with such a lot of mirth, but she could only fiddle with the buttons of her blouse in a suggestive way and flounder, 'Oh, Albion!' Her astonishment and agitation at seeing me in my own drawing-room could not have been greater had it been Marco Polo standing on the rug before her. 'Albion, oh, we were just . . .' But she could not quite locate the idea of what it was they had all just been doing, and glanced around at the others.

'Oh yes,' Kristabel said quickly, in what I thought was far too loud a voice for a lady in a drawing-room, 'We were just . . .' but she caught Lilian's eye, and could not go on for thinking of how terribly funny the thing was, whatever it was, and the others all laughed again, so hard their faces twisted: if they could only see how ugly they looked! They knew – oh, they knew! – that I did not know what was so amusing, so that I had to stand there awkwardly, someone who had not got the joke.

'Oh Albion, take no notice of us silly girls!' Mother cried through her hysteria, and Norah tried to call out, 'A cup of tea, Albion?' but even in asking me, her voice was choked with laughter, and her eyes were not really paying me attention.

'I see,' I said in my most chilling way, and loudly so that it was clear that I intended to take the reins of this moment back into my own hands. 'No, Norah, no tea is required.' Norah shrank away, curving her hands around the teapot as if to warm them.

That tiresome Norah had recently developed yet another enthusiasm, which was no doubt the reason for the tea-party today. The smeary watercolours and the pumpkins in oils were long gone, and so was the lace-making, the petit-point, the china-painting and the flower-pressing. In their place the fallen girls of Sydney had been installed in Norah's empty hours. My drawing-room had now become a kind of factory for the production of tiny coarse garments in calico, and hand-knitted pilches and leggings, each one a slightly different size from any other, so that a man could not even sit down on his own Chesterfield without first moving great bundles of them. Other women's little interests seemed to stay within tidy bounds: why could my wife's not do likewise? There had been times when I had even felt that the all-pervading smell of turpentine of our early married life was preferable to the all-pervading skeins of silks, the endless bobbins of lace, the tangles of wools, and now the piles of small garments encroaching on every horizontal surface.

Norah was the centre of bustle and fluster about her responsibilities as to pilches and bootees, with lists of names and tasks spilling from her hands, her hair awry, her skirt hanging crooked – I did not like to see any wife of mine letting herself become so slatternly – consulting her lists and getting into a tangle about whether Blue Group was supposed to be stitching fifty calico smocks and knitting twenty pairs of pilches, or was it supposed to be twenty calico smocks and fifty pairs of pilches? She made heavy weather of it, but how could the efforts of a few well-meaning but leisurely ladies in their elegant drawing-rooms possibly make a difference to all the bastard children of New South Wales?

Mother was ancient now, a woman long since past any biological usefulness, and in this light her neck was as loose-skinned as an elephant's knee. But Mother was still a woman: under the folds of dress, under the petticoat, under the silk drawers, lay the same unsatisfying, ungraspable, hidden bit of flesh that all these women sat on all day: that swallower of men's organs, that spitter-out of greasy babies. It troubled me to know – I knew it in my brain, but could only reject it in my heart – that I had once been such a blood-streaked blind bit of tissue being expelled from between those very thighs. It had been many years since I had thought babies arrived in the beaks of storks, but it was a much prettier idea than the reality.

Kristabel had turned out – not altogether to my satisfaction – to be fond of Lilian. The girl appeared to enjoy her company, even visiting her at home, although I did not encourage this, as Kristabel was not the best influence for a young girl. But I could not go so far as to forbid, and here she was now, winking at Lilian like a gypsy.

Kristabel and Mother had been uneasy with each other years ago, but as their lives had gone on they seemed to draw somewhat closer, and now they had widowhood in common. Poor old Forbes had turned out to have a weak heart under all that red-faced hail-fellow-well-met carry-on, and apart from providing my sister with her independent means, poor silly Forbes had not left as much as a ripple on the surface of the world.

Marriage had never done anything to make a woman of Kristabel, and widowhood had done even less; but today she was wearing some sort of thing with a nipped-in waist that made the most of her slenderness. It was no accident – oh no, Kristabel had no womanly bust or behind, but was cunning enough to have got together with her dressmaker to tease with the little she had – no, it was no accident that my mind filled with images of grasping and seizing and snapping in two!

I looked at her, standing with her back to the window so I could not see her face: there she was, flesh of my flesh since I could remember, and a sad figure. Poor creature, she had never really got the hang of being a woman. Even Lilian, looming very large beside her, was more feminine than she was.

Lilian should not have been there. I made a mental note to find out why she was not at school: a man did not work his fingers to the bone to pay Miss Foote's fees to have his daughter stay at home sipping tea!

At thirteen, Lilian was a massive body of flesh: she had grown immense on a diet of facts. What great slabs of haunch lay beneath her muslin! What volumes of bone, gristle and lung were enclosed in that torso of hers! I thought of sieges and castaways, and the eye of my mind watched a knife slicing into her soft meatiness.

It was a ghastly thing for a female to be so enormous. In particular, her breasts, or *titty-bags*, were far too big. I could hardly bear to look. In the past I had occasionally taken Lilian to lunch at the Club, but I did not feel at ease doing so now. *Did you get an eyeful of Singer's daughter*, I imagined. *Did you get a look at the chest on her?* The sallow face of Morrison came back to me, and I smelled again the sharp stink of burning rubbish and forbidden cigarettes. *It is scientific fact*, Morrison had said. *Big tits mean they love it*.

I had brought it up with Norah one evening, although aware it was not a father's place to have to remind his wife of such things. But Norah had laughed, actually laughed in my face! 'Oh no, Albion!' she crowed. 'You will find it is quite normal,' she said smugly. 'You will find she will grow out of it, she will slim down in due course, take my word for it, Albion.'

◆   ◆   ◆

Now the women watched me in an expressionless way, and rather pointedly did not say anything further. The silence extended itself; there was a clicking of knitting-needles as Mother got on with something in pink, her lips pursed in the way they always had when she was concentrating. Norah had retreated behind her eyes, and Lilian stared at something in her lap. It looked to me rather as if they might be waiting for me to leave, so I sat down and made a space among the pilchers on the table for my elbow.

'Lilian!' I cried, and they all paid attention. 'To what use are you putting your day, Lilian?' I asked. Finding Lilian at home was not the surprise I had expected when I had decided to come home early, but I intended to make it clear that I did not approve of her being here wasting her time with these women and their gossip and giggling.

'I am a bit poorly today, Father,' she said, and suddenly blushed. We all watched as blood poured up her neck and into her cheeks, mottling her like a sausage. She struggled on, 'So Mother and Nanna are teaching me to knit, I have done half a pilch already.' She held up a bit of knitting that was full of holes, and hung warped off the needles. Her pride in it was obvious, and her pride filled me with rage. Knitting, crocheting, tatting and petit-point were all things I had expressly forbidden Lilian to learn, also cross-stitch, edging, and applique. 'But Albion, it will not hurt her to know how to knit!' Norah had wheedled, but I had had the scientific answer, as usual. 'Norah,' I said evenly, 'the human brain is finite. Some human brains, of course, are more finite than others,' I added, and let a significant silence fall. 'But even the best brain is finite. Fill it with piffle, and there will be no space left for thought. Even you, Norah, cannot deny the logic of that.'

Norah argued less these days. She had perfected a sort of grey neutrality and a mild way of turning away that I could not challenge. She was not convinced, never convinced, but she was too cowardly to have it out with me. 'Very well, Albion,' she had said. 'As you wish, Albion,' and when I had added, 'That goes for tatting too, Norah, and that thing you do with knots,' she had nodded, 'Yes, Albion, I understand.'

But I had known in my heart even then that she was only biding her time.

'Lilian,' I said now in my quietest voice, in which fury lay concealed like a spider under a stone, 'this is terribly interesting. Moreover, you are obviously a terribly talented knitter. But Lilian, let me ask you this: if you are well enough to sit here turning good wool into rubbish, why are you not well enough to go to school and learn something that matters?' My voice had risen, although my control over a sentence remained perfect, and I watched the blood drain now out of Lilian's face. She sat stricken, with the knitting clutched in her fist.

But now Norah was coming to her rescue: I was forever being undermined. 'Lilian has stayed home from school today for a reason, Albion,' she said with mysterious meaningfulness. 'A good reason. A very good reason.'

I saw her face radiant with smugness: she coddled a secret. Almost visibly she swelled with satisfaction in knowing something her husband did not. She looked at me, and I saw her face convulse into a huge unpractised wink; she sat nodding and winking as if she had been stricken with palsy, and jerking her head in the direction of our daughter.

'Do you not notice anything different about Lilian today, Albion?' she asked with a simper. I could see – Blind Freddy could have seen – that Norah was longing for me to make further enquiries, to be puzzled, to press her, to implore so that she could resist. *Lilian? Different? Whatever do you mean, Norah?*

How dare she try to fan up a bit of a mystery at my expense?

This was a person with hardly even a shadow to her name, and yet here she was, attempting to put me at a disadvantage in front of these women. Out of the corner of my eye I inspected Lilian; she was sitting beside me with half a pilch still dangling from her needles. She was as huge as ever, and she still seemed to have more knees and elbows than anyone else: nothing about her looked any different from any other day.

I was not going to walk into Norah's little trap, so I began to inspect the stitching on a pair of leggings. I set my inner being into a state so hard and stony that, if necessary, I could spend the rest of the day examining seams and stitches, and resist the slightest betrayal of interest in Norah's secret.

◆   ◆   ◆

Poor old Norah! She had never learned to drive a hard bargain: even a waiting game was beyond her. I had only to sit for a few moments picking at a flaw on a pilch, and she was beaten: she hastened to squander her tiny coin of power, did not know how to hold out for any profit at all. She announced to the room at large, as ringingly as if to a public meeting, 'I have something very important to tell you, Albion. This morning our little girl became a woman,' and sat back smugly.

I felt a pang like a cold blade. Only yesterday Lilian had been my own clean girl, who could make her father's blood warm with pride at what a brain she had, almost as good as a boy's. Only yesterday her mere flesh had not mattered: she had warmed me with her smile, had turned her face, the twin of my own, towards me, soaking in all that I had to share with her.

Now she was one of theirs, sliding away into the foreign country of femaleness. At this very moment, even as I watched her, she was doing that secretive dirty thing of bleeding into rags. I knew now that they really did that: Morrison had not been making it up. I knew it not from any woman, of course, but from men: I had heard enough jokes over the years in the bar at the Club, to piece together some kind of theory of it. But it was not something I could actually imagine, in its mechanics, and it was certainly not something I had any wish to be reminded of.

It was happening: she was actually doing it. Furthermore, she and Norah must have had a conversation about it. She would have known not to come to me about it. For the first time, she would have seen that it was her mother, not her father, who could answer her questions about this particular thing. To Norah she would have looked for explanation, instructions, perhaps even reassurance; and Norah would have explained, instructed, and congratulated: an intimacy would have happened between them, murmuring behind a closed door, from which I had been utterly excluded.

Moreover, this was only the beginning. From now on, my daughter would turn more and more to Norah for the things she knew, would be privy to more and more revolting secrets of female flesh. It was only a matter of time before she would be initiated into the ugliest mysteries of all. Sooner or later, she too would puff up with a gross distended belly, would make those noises that the female of the species makes while giving birth to its young, and would have something suck milk out of her *titty-bags*.

I thought of all the breasts I had tweaked, all the thighs I had pinched, all the mouths I had crushed under mine; I thought of all those orifices, slimy or dry, tight or flaccid, and I saw them in a sudden blazing new light. My own daughter, the child whose brain I had nurtured, whose tempers I had punished, whose quickness with a fact had brought a flush of pride to my heart, had, overnight, joined them. One day some man would tweak her breasts, pinch her thighs, crush her mouth, and force his way into her flesh. In his mind, and perhaps with a few friends at the Club later, he would compare her with others, laugh at her enthusiasm or her modesty, advise his friends to *give her a whirl* or not to bother: he would describe her as *a good handful of a woman, know what I mean*, or *a big fat cow like a tub of lard*, depending on which he thought would raise the best laugh. And it would be my flesh and blood he would be talking about!

It was all a shattering sort of thing to land on a father in the middle of a sunny afternoon; but my sorrow was for the privacy of my own heart alone. Norah, obviously, expected a satisfying display of astonishment, bewilderment, whatever she thought was appropriate. She was sitting up alertly now: the colour was back in her face, her spine was straight, her eye unflinching as she met mine. She was reminding me – and not for the first time – that no matter how many facts my daughter and I might share, and no matter how little my daughter respected her mother, they were united in their femaleness, which I could never penetrate. Lilian might bear my own face and my own brain, but Norah loved to rub my nose in the fact that a daughter was a foreign language to me, which my wife could speak, and I could not.

On the other hand, was she quite as innocent as she appeared? Was she trying to make me blush in front of everyone? Was she hoping for an Albion all flustered and embarrassed? After all, was this quite the sort of bodily fact that was spoken of in mixed company, even when the only male involved was the actual father? Did she hope to see me flinch?

Be that as it may, I made sure my voice was as silky as it had ever been. I was a study in scientific detachment as I told my wife, 'Norah, may I remind you that a gentleman's wife does not trumpet her daughter's intimate particulars from the rooftops. Lilian is biologically ready to mate now, like any dog or monkey coming on heat. That is simply all there is to it.'

A certain kind of silence settled around our little tableau at this point. Norah sat glassily, Kristabel stared into her empty cup, Mother put a hand up to her cheek as if to make sure it was still there. The room was so quiet we could hear a flurry of wind in the jacaranda outside, and a bird somewhere letting out a cry like a cat.

Then Kristabel raised her head, and I saw Mother's hand come down from her cheek. They were about to claim the moment for their own, so I rose quickly. I cleared my throat to cover a half-formed word from Mother, tapped the table where the pathetic pilches were lying half-made and neglected, and spoke over Kristabel as she started to say something, 'You have dropped a stitch here, Norah,' I said. 'It will all have to be unpicked.' Norah snatched up the knitting and began to throttle the life out of the ball of wool, winding it tight, and I turned on my heel and walked back down the room.

But as I reached the door I heard one of those light woman's voices say something, and there was a blurt of half-stifled laughter. Were they still laughing at some silly women's joke? Or was it possible – was it conceivable? – that they were at this moment winking at each other, and laughing not at some frilly little schoolgirl joke, but at me, the man, the one who did not know things that they knew? Were they all watching my back, exchanging glances, winking, waiting for me to close the door so they could laugh out loud? Pride forbade me to turn around and squint into the light, but the air in front of my face grew dark and the muscles of my face froze. I closed the door on them with loathing: a loathing born of despair.

Chapter *Twenty-Four*

THE SINGER Christmas Picnic was becoming something of a legend. Each year it had become more opulent: it was now so extravagant that it verged on the vulgar. As far as Singer himself was concerned, the Singer Picnic was a bargain. I would not have wished my employees to know this, but I got it all very cheap from Baldwin's, who owed me a favour over a certain little business to do with manila envelopes. Whatever the reason, there was no doubt that *Singer Enterprises* was the only establishment in Sydney to have smoked salmon at its picnic, and ham all round.

The thing had become something of a sacred cow, and Norah waxed lyrical, not to say hysterical, on the benefits of a day communing with nature. Personally, I had no interest in picnics. What thrill could there be to sit among ants, eating gritty bread-and-butter, and scalding your lip on milkless tea out of a chipped enamel mug? All right-thinking people agreed that vegetation was simply one of the impediments nature had put in the way of civilisation, and should be ignored where it could not be subdued.

◆　　◆　　◆

Be that as it may, one sultry morning the entire kit and kaboodle of *Singer Enterprises*, and all its employees and family, set off through the bush on carts, everyone cranky in the early sun and slapping at flies. These picnics brought out the absurd in Rundle. He was kitted out like some pioneer of old times – *It is only a picnic, we are not looking for the Inland Sea, you know, Rundle!* – in enormous boots and moleskins, and a cocky's hat that sat oddly above the mournful flaps of his face; he even had a Bowie-knife on his belt, and a compass on a string round his neck. He and I led the way in a cart with the marquee and a couple of muscular lads from Despatch, and in the spirit of goodwill towards all men I nodded and made noises of agreement as Rundle boomed on and on in my ear.

Rundle was a man with a systematic approach to conversation. He began by reminding me of all the spots he had chosen in previous years for the picnic, then went on to tell me about the spots he had considered choosing this year, ticking off on his fingers their various advantages and disadvantages; he wound up by speculating on the spots he might consider choosing for next year, and running through a few of their features. It was only nine o'clock in the morning, and already I was sick of the whole thing, straining to remain gracious with Rundle. A day of utter tedium lay ahead.

In spite of all Rundle's laborious decision-making, the place was simply the usual kind of place. There were large red trees of irregular shape and inadequate shade, there was a patch of tufty grass, no doubt home to snakes, there was a small brown creek, and there were clouds of flies: all was according to tradition. I sat myself on a fallen log and watched dourly as the marquee was unpacked. Rundle pointed and perspired, and the muscular youths from Despatch, ant-like under the enormous lumpy trees, pulled and pushed, and shouted *up a bit your end, mate*, until the thing was perched on its poles, and then they stood back scratching their heads under their caps and batting away at flies.

Next to arrive was the Singer entourage. Norah sat up at the front of the cart, staring around at leaves as if they were interesting, with a slight superior smile on her face, as of one who considers herself in harmony with nature. Crouched behind her, hanging on grimly as if he thought he might soon be sick, was John, on whose face anxiety looked like bad temper. Lilian was leaning over the back of the cart with her bottom in the air, watching the dirt pass between the wheels.

Looking at her now, as the young men from Despatch were doing, I could see that Lilian was turning into something embarrassing. Norah dressed her nicely in sprigged this and spotted that, trying to minimise the balloons on her chest and the vast rump on her. But all the carefully chosen lace collars and smocking, all the discreet blues and muted pinks, all the expensive pin-tucking and darts, had a look of the grotesque on the great hot undeniable fleshiness of my daughter. She was like a piglet in a lace nightdress. Norah's daintiness could make you forget the seamy femaleness beneath, but Lilian was a coarse parody of the feminine, a mocking reminder of what really lay under all the laces and lavender-water.

Now she was sitting in the cart with her legs wide apart, easing her flesh like some old slattern, without a thought for how she looked. She did not seem to realise that she should make an attempt to control, or at least conceal, her flesh. Had Norah taught her nothing about being a woman, that she was so entirely without shame?

Moreover, in spite of her lack of womanly charms, she was cultivating none of the shy attractive ways, none of the eagerness to please, none of the fluster and blushes that a plain woman does well to learn. She did not even seem to realise that incompetence is one of a woman's essential graces. 'Oh no, Father, I can get down myself!' she called out when I offered her my arm, and jumped down so heavily that the trees rocked in their very sockets. She stood beside me, exuding animal warmth, and gawped at the young men from Despatch, wrestling now with trestle-tables, tripping over guy-ropes, and swearing audibly. I felt her take a huge chestful of air and suddenly hoot a *Coo-ee!* – 'to see if there is an echo, Father,' she said – that made everyone turn to stare at Mr Singer's large and surprising daughter, and I caught a smirk exchanged between two of the lads.

And now my damned wife was summoning me from her chair. 'Oh Albion dearest, could you come here a moment?' She had already made her way across the creek to where

Rundle had set up the all-too-folding chairs in what little shade there was, and sat with her swollen ankles and everlasting fan, with the crease between her eyebrows that I hated, and that whine in her voice that made me want to trumpet in her face like a rogue elephant.

'If something could just be found to raise my feet a little, Albion, the grass is damp, you know, and my legs ache so.' Rundle and I scurried around, finding a hamper that was too high, and a box that was too hard, and finally a stool that was acceptable.

Lilian galloped over the tufts to us, and startled me by suddenly laughing a gusty laugh and pointing – 'Look, Father, that tree is just like a person, look, it has elbows and everything, look, it even has a . . .' But she stopped; she had spoken the truth, but the truth had swept her a little further than she dared to go. For the tree was indeed like a person: to be exact, it was like a fat female with her clothes off. There was dimpled pink flesh that was as plump and smooth as the inside of a thigh, with busy creasings and foldings around angles in the branches like elbows and knees. What had silenced Lilian was a dark puckered orifice in the trunk not far above Norah's head, the skin of the tree bunched around it like the neck of a bag, a thing humanoid to the point of obscenity.

My eyes returned from these puckers and plackets to my pasty-faced wife. 'Look at the dimpled flesh, Norah,' I said, 'on that tree,' and Norah looked, but blankly, seeing only leaves and branches, and wondering aloud about the possibility of bird-droppings.

◆   ◆   ◆

We sat tilting on our chairs in the sandy soil, and waited like galahs for Rundle to *boil the billy*. I had suggested a good supply of vacuum-flasks, but of course *boiling the billy* was the high point of a picnic for Rundle. We had to go through the whole drama of gathering up the sticks, being scientific about laying it – *a fire needs oxygen*, Rundle reminded us as we sat in a row watching him balance one twig on top of another – then there was the puffing and blowing at the smoulder until it lit. Smoke swirled around our heads, Rundle wiped at his streaming eyes, the billy tilted and nearly put the whole thing out, but Rundle stood back as triumphantly as if he had just invented the wheel. I sat consumed with irritation like an itch: what was the point of all our heroic pioneers having been so uncomfortable, if not to spare us this sort of thing?

At last the great table was set up, only slightly lopsided, under the marquee, and Rundle came over. 'Ready, Mr Singer?' he asked, positively purple with the responsibility of it all. What a freak of nature Rundle was, especially with the smudge of ash on his nose, and the Bowie-knife which had now swung around on his belt so that it dangled lewdly into his groin. *Look sharp, Rundle*, I wanted to say. *You are not doing anything for the dignity of Singer Enterprises, man!* but I replied calmly to set an example which I hoped he might follow, 'Yes, Rundle, I am quite ready.'

The next bit was the only part of the Singer Christmas Picnic that I enjoyed: I knew I had the right kind of carrying voice for my task, and a grasp of the suave platitudes appropriate for the moment. How it warmed my heart to see their faces crease with laughter at my little jokes! I swelled with the knowledge that I was the ultimate head of the ultimate family. They were gathered around me, laughing obligingly at jokes which in cold blood even I would have admitted were not terribly funny. Everyone nodded, smiled and greeted with applause the various achievements of *Singer Enterprises* over the year: the introduction of the window envelope, the installation of the Pneumatic Cash Railway, and the marriage, finally, of Miss Freeman. I felt myself expand under the trees, matching them in sheer bulk and solidity: I had never felt more substantial, knowing that the boots of every man here, the corsets of every woman, the bread in every child's mouth, were all thanks to me.

After the proprietor's speech of welcome, the next thing was the parade, and this was the reason for the purple panic on the face of Rundle. I looked away discreetly as he hissed various last-minute instructions, and pushed and prodded at workers until they formed ragged lines. Then he waved his arm in a wild way at the band of St Brendan's (of which Rundle was apparently a pillar), and with a colossal fart from the tuba, the parade began. Rundle led the way, but was unable to resist anxious glances back over his shoulder, so that the *Singer Enterprises* banner he held – embroidered and gold-fringed by the ladies of Notepaper – dipped and twisted dangerously. Courtesy of Mr Singer, each female had been provided with a corsage (cheaper in bulk) so that every bosom crawled like a nest of spiders, and each man had a buttonhole, even though the weaselly fellow who did the privies did not in fact seem to own a buttonhole in which to poke his button-hole, but had put it in a convenient rip in the front of his shirt.

A parade is a thing calculated to stir the blood: amass a crowd of people in ragged lines, get them behind some embroidered banners, make sure there are tubas on hand, and it would take the soul of a reptile not to be stirred. My daughter was no reptile: her feelings flowed so close to the surface they could be read on her very skin. She said – shouted, rather, for the tuba was assertive – 'Jolly good, Father, isn't it?' and watched with her hands clasped at bosom-height, over-acting her ecstasy, I thought, and drawing attention to her chest in an unfortunate way.

The workers marched and wheeled in a ragged sort of order before us, and when they had finished, we set up a patter of applause. Rundle bowed, wiping perspiration off his brow and actually laughing with relief, I cut a symbolic slice off a leg of ham, and the picnic was launched.

◆　◆　◆

We ate our way through ham and mustard, and beetroot, and potato salad; the keg of beer was broached with much spurting foam, and Lilian went around with plates offering bits of the famous smoked salmon. I grew weary of standing on the bumpy ground with Rundle telling me how many pounds of mustard he had bought, how many hams, how cheap beetroot was when you bought it by the bushel; how could he think Mr Singer would be interested in the price of beetroot?

I murmured my marvelment, I hoped not so enthusiastically as to encourage him to go into how he had arrived at the precise number of potatoes, but he was not to be stopped.

He told me how he had sat down, by way of a scientific experiment, with a plate of ham before him, to see how large a smear of mustard the average man needed for the average plate of ham. From this he had ascertained how many smears of this size were to be got out of a jar, and thereby – Rundle did not spare me any detail of his mathematics – by multiplying the number of smears by the number of employees, and dividing that figure by the number of jars – or was it dividing the smears by the employees, and multiplying by the jars? – thereby arriving at the number of jars of mustard the picnic would need.

◆   ◆   ◆

Esprit de corps was the name of the game at the Singer Picnic: what the parade had started, the afternoon games were to continue. Rundle produced a number of chaff-bags, and a number of soup-spoons and china eggs for the Ladies' Heats, and cricket paraphernalia for the men, and Miss Morgan of Fastenings was deputed to round up all the girls.

This was a delicate matter: when does a girl cease to be a girl? The matrons of *Singer Enterprises* were naturally not expected to hump themselves along in sacks or scurry with eggs, but it was thought appropriate that the young ones – the girls from the packing room, and the junior sales staff – would throw themselves into the spirit of the thing. The delicacy was in drawing the line, which is why Rundle handed over to Miss Morgan.

Miss Morgan herself, with her liver-spotted cheeks and her quivering dewlaps, was clearly not eligible, while little Miss

Connie Entwhistle of Fastenings – her cheeks as pink as a man could wish, and I could personally vouch for the rest of her being equally pink – clearly was. But what about Miss Spragg, who in the soft light of Envelopes was a peachy enough proposition, but who in the crude daylight here could be seen to have a pucker between her eyebrows that was nearly a wrinkle, and pouches of flesh starting under her eyes? And what of Miss Parkinson? She had won the egg-and-spoon race last year – Miss Parkinson was built on the same lines as a wading-bird, and had more or less waded her way to victory on her long shanks – but this year there was a certain indefinable change in her. I happened to know – Mr Singer liked to keep track of his staff, and Rundle could be relied on to keep me informed – that a young postal employee was showing interest. Would Miss Parkinson be wounded not to be asked, and wish she could join the fun, and perhaps win again? After all, the egg-and-spoon race at the *Singer Enterprises* Christmas Picnic might well be the only thing Miss Parkinson would ever win. Or would she feel she was above such childish amusements now that she was spoken for? Would she be offended to be invited, as if the postal clerk and all he represented did not exist? Only Miss Morgan could have any hope of charting a course among all these delicacies.

And Miss Morgan rose to the occasion, as always: Miss Morgan would have made a fine diplomat. I saw that Miss Parkinson, her long cheeks flushed with excitement, had been entrusted with the starting-pistol, and Miss Spragg was fussing around the finish line with a notepad, a pen and a stopwatch – clever Miss Morgan!

Miss Entwhistle, Miss Baxter, Miss Flaherty, all known to me from the stockroom, one or two others with whom I was not yet familiar, and Miss Singer, were definitely on the humping-and-scurrying side of the invisible line that divided the female species. The young ladies from the shop stood holding their eggs gingerly, their cheeks flushed with having everyone looking at them. One of them dropped her egg before the starting gun went off, and giggled as if it were the funniest thing in the world, picking it up with a dainty little bob, and Miss Flaherty showed all her fine little teeth, laughing along with her, and they both tucked the hair behind their ears with a graceful gesture.

By contrast, Lilian was all frown, concentrating. She had gathered her skirt up in one hand so that she could run efficiently, as if she did not know that a young lady does not expose her meaty calves to the gaze of the world, and that efficiency is not the point in a ladies' egg-and-spoon race. Did Norah teach the girl nothing? We all watched, and Miss Parkinson waited with the gun in her hand, as Lilian experimented with the best technique, whether it was better to hold the egg out at the end of your arm, or clutch it up against your chest. Finally she was ready, and waited for the starting gun crouched like a jockey, with her tongue poking out of the corner of her mouth as if it all mattered. 'Lilian must think she is in the Empire Games,' I remarked to Norah, but to my surprise Norah came back at me rather tartly, 'She wants to win, Albion, and why should she not?'

A good crowd was gathered to watch; on rugs on the lumpy ground all the shop-ladies were gathered. Some reclined, others sat bolt upright, depending on the ferocity of their underpinnings. Behind them, caps on the backs of their heads, legs a-straddle, arms akimbo, stood all my awkward lads, in their greasy cloth caps, and their pants too short in the legs.

The day had grown hot, and the cask of beer had grown empty, and under these influences the young men from Despatch had taken the liberty of removing their jackets. They were all well-built. I employed them scientifically, on the basis of their chest measurements; there were employers who believed in the fallacy of wiry strength, it was often debated at the Club, but personally I believed in muscle you could measure. Their bodies were their glories, but above their necks there was not much worth looking at. Their features were jammed together in the centre of their faces like an afterthought, and they all stared out woodenly at the world, as if it cost money to have an expression on your face.

One young chap, a gingery fellow with a neck like an ox, the pearl-white skin of his shoulders almost luminous, was particularly conspicuous, having stripped down to his under-shirt so that his particularly fine pectorals could be clearly seen. When he passed close to us I caught the sharp animal tang of his fresh sweat, and saw Norah pick it up too, and follow him with her eyes as he joined the other young men. I caught Rundle's bloodshot eye, and by a meaningful jerk of the head and lift of the eyebrow, instructed him to get the young man's shirt back on: it might be a picnic, but it was not a free-for-all!

Miss Parkinson took up a threatening stance with the pistol, and Lilian watched every move, positively scowling with concentration, so that Miss Parkinson's finger had barely squeezed the trigger before Lilian shot off, egg a-tremble. When the shot was fired, Miss Entwhistle gave a jump, squealed, and dropped her egg again; Miss Baxter began to waver forward in a sort of zig-zag, as if chasing her egg rather than propelling it, and laughing away fit to burst: they were in a state of quite delightful flush and titter.

Lilian had never looked less delightful. Her large pink tongue was now protruding so far from her mouth that she could have caught flies with it, and her thick red cheeks shook at each step she took. While all the others tripped along calmly and daintily, their skirts flouncing nicely around their ankles, Lilian was galumphing along like a rhinoceros, her flesh shaking around her at each step and her chest bobbling along under its muslin.

I became aware that I was not the only male watching her over-eager efforts with her egg. The gingery lad had put his shirt back on, but was now standing taking up a lot of space on the grass, his eyes devouring the breasts of my daughter. This thick-necked ginger lout had the face of a cockroach. There was something greedy in the way he stared, and when he muttered something out of the side of his mouth to the youth next to him, I knew precisely what sort of thing he was saying.

Miss Entwhistle came gracefully last, puffing in the prettiest way: the exertion had put a charming colour in her cheeks. Lilian was the colour of Rundle's beetroot, and was blowing like a whale. She won by a good margin, and the oafs unlocked their hands from over their chests, clapping rather more enthusiastically than I thought warranted by a ladies' egg-and-spoon race, and Lilian, sweaty and dishevelled, grinned around as if she had never heard of mockery, and waved at me as if she might have escaped my attention. I clapped, as faintly as I could, but the cockroach was actually cheering her.

I was a democratic man of business relaxing with his employees, and I intended to roll up my sleeves later for a game of cricket with these lads, but one could carry informality too far. I strode over, casually but quickly, and said in a voice not intended to carry, 'Lilian, you have made a spectacle of yourself.' The laughter dropped away from her, and how hideous she now looked, scowling, with her cheeks scarlet and her nose shiny! I was overwhelmed by the dreadful vigour of the blood in her face and her sheer coarse bulk.

With a hand under her elbow – I could feel the heat of her pulsing against me – I steered her away from where the eyes watched from under the cloth caps, and handed her a dipper of water from the bucket and a comb from my pocket. 'Set yourself to rights, Lilian,' I said. 'And remember next time that there is no need to try so hard.'

◆　　◆　　◆

Like Lilian, I did not believe in coming second in a race: a person might as well come last if they were not going to win. I had to admit that, had I been unlucky enough to have been born a girl, I might have been as Lilian was. In that sense, I could understand Lilian's refusal to tuck her animal fleshiness away, and join the simpering hypocritical games: I could see that without realising it she was trying to tear at the tissue of lies going on around her. I should have been pleased that she had the wit to see through it, and that she was not simply another in the vast herd of human blanks.

But the point was that I had not been born a woman, and what was proper in me was mortifying in my daughter. I saw now – too late! – that I had not done her any favours, in encouraging her intellect. My daughter had grown into a freak of nature, a misfit with the brain of a man in the body of a woman.

When John was chivvied along by Norah to join us for another cup of the everlasting tea, I was struck afresh by the perversity of life, for he would have made an excellent girl. He mooned around at the edge of things holding his cup and saucer crooked, so that tea splashed on the cuffs of his creams, his head sat at a cringing angle on his neck, and his shoulders were hunched over as if to make himself shorter. He had refused to go in any of the games at all, saving us all the embarrassment of seeing the way his feet appeared to flap on the ends of his ankles when he tried to run, and how his elbows stuck out like a chook in a fluster.

The problem was that in spite of John's frog-like look, his pale damp skin, his fears, his silences, his stupidity in the face of even the simplest building-block or golliwog – in spite of all this, John was a male. It was hard to imagine he would ever amount to much of a man, but he was male; whereas Lilian, no matter how brave and no matter how bright, would always belong to the secondary sex.

I thought ruefully of all the muslins and voiles from which I had chosen Norah: it was clear to me now that I must have ignored some signal from nature, and had picked an unsuitable set of genes. It was a bitter irony. I had approached the problem systematically, researching the latest scientific ideas and thinking the thing through logically, and yet had ended up with such a failure that my line was likely to end with me. Others – fools – had merely let their fancy dictate their choice to them: they had swallowed all the nonsense about love, and chosen their mates on great gusts of blind feeling – yet these fools had produced manly young chaps and sweet-voiced little girls who would all reproduce themselves copiously – there was a monstrous injustice somewhere!

◆　　◆　　◆

Cricket was another of those manly accomplishments I had long ago made sure I was competent at, and during last year's picnic, although Mr Singer's team had lost with a good grace to Mr Rundle's team, Mr Singer himself had put up a fine show. In fact, he had actually driven the ball so hard into the cleft of a paperbark that it had had to be left there for the tree to swallow. Efficient Rundle had produced a spare ball, and what a cheer had gone up for Mr Singer!

I had felt last year that Rundle was uncomfortable at trouncing Mr Singer's team quite so thoroughly. When the subject had come up during the months that followed, I noticed he hastened to remind everyone of the ball stuck in the tree, and several times he had got up to demonstrate in front of the desk, with a rolled-up newspaper, just the kind of action Mr Singer had used to get it there. 'Classic cricket,' he would repeat. 'Absolutely classic cricket.' This year, Rundle announced that he would not play: he appointed himself umpire instead. 'Oh, I am getting on, Mr Singer,' he twinkled at me, as if this was an amusingly original phrase, 'time to hand over to the younger ones now, sir,' and it was the gingery lout with the pectorals who was going to open the bowling against me.

Nature had been kind to Rundle, providing him with a dusty patch of flat ground among the trees. Sunlight poured itself down all around, insects droned away in the afternoon heat, and the leaves far above shook themselves together spasmodically in a flukey breeze. The clearing lay expectant under the sun: the wicket, hammered into the hard ground with the back of Rundle's axe, gave the patch of dirt a human meaning.

I strode to the wicket feeling my muscles moving pleasurably under my shirt – a gentleman knew when it was appropriate to remove one's jacket, and that time was now – and limbered up with a few swings. I was no muscle-bound bruiser, but I was a fine figure of a man, a man in his prime. Over on the rugs under the trees, the women watched me. Norah began to clap her hands together; she did not actually go so far as to produce any sound, but the other women soon took it up. I saw Lilian beating her palms together as vigorously as if knocking the dirt out of a rug, and Miss Baxter and Miss Entwhistle going at it conscientiously, keeping an eye on Mrs Singer so they would know when to stop. They worked away at it in their different ways as their males gathered in the clearing, ready to perform before them, but the bush swallowed the sound they made so that it was as insignificant as the rattle of a beetle through leaves.

Up at the other end, the ginger boy was snapping at his

braces where they bulged over his chest, and grinding the ball into his groin. He stared down the pitch at me, but I could see that his blank insect-eyes were not registering his employer standing at the other end, or the father of the girl he had ogled as she galloped over the grass with an egg. This boy's eyes saw only a problem of distance, speed, and angle: Albion Gidley Singer was nothing more to him than a thing in front of a wicket.

As he walked back to start his run, I took up my stand, thumping the end of the bat into the dirt, flexing my wrists: I was already relishing the percussion the ball would make as it connected with the bat. From far, far away across the sunlit grass, I saw him begin his run. He had started much too far back, like all beginners. He was positively small in the distance, crabbing towards me with the sweat-stains showing in his armpits, and his boots beating up the dust. A bird warbled abruptly and swooped low over the wicket; he was still miles away, and I was still readying myself, gripping and re-gripping the bat, when I heard a clatter behind me, and Rundle was braying 'Out! Out!' The fool, did he not see we had not even started yet?

It could only be a mistake, or perhaps a joke. Who had knocked the wicket over so that it sprawled stupidly on the grass? What was this silence, in which I heard the wind in leaves? What was this stillness, everyone moonfaced, watching me? 'Out,' Rundle said again, but quietly. 'Clean bowled, Mr Singer sir, I am afraid to say,' and there was young Parkinson from Accounts already coming towards me and reaching out for the bat.

'Jolly bad luck, Father,' Lilian trumpeted as I sat down, 'he was as fast as anything, wasn't he, Mother?' I wanted to crush that red face, to stop her loud artless voice from going on. My chest was aching with the outrage of it, my throat stringy with suppressed tears. *How dare they, how dare they*, my heart repeated, but just who it was that had dared, and just what they had done, I could not quite have said.

The thick-necked ginger lout had the face of a cockroach, but he was a dab hand with a ball. I recovered my equilibrium somewhat when Parkinson was dismissed for 2, O'Malley managed a mere 5, and Gorman was out for a duck as I had been. With each of my team-mate's disgraces, my own shame faded. 'Oh, he is awfully good,' Lilian cried after watching him deliver a sizzler to McAllister, who frankly ducked. 'He is amazing, Father!' and I was recovered enough to be gracious. 'Yes indeed, Lilian, I happen to know the poor lad has never learnt to read, so what a good thing it is that he can throw a ball.'

When the cricket was over, Mr Singer made sure he led the applause, and was to be seen nodding and smiling, and making a remark to the young lady beside him. Our sweaty genius of the ball stood luminous with sunlight in the middle of the clearing, grinning and rubbing the ball along his thigh as if he did not know how to stop. In fact, Mr Singer had to go out onto the pitch in the end, to shake him by the hand and more or less usher him off the pitch and over to the refreshment tent. I saw Miss Flaherty get up from the grass and start over towards him. But off the pitch, out of the sunlight that lit him up, and with the ball removed from his grip by Mr Singer, so that he stood with his large hands dangling, he was simply a sweaty gawky lad in pants too short in the leg, and I saw her falter, reconsider, and turn away.

◆　◆　◆

The day finished as it had begun, in a colossal tedium of folding things, and packing things, and installing things and people into carts, and jolting back through the dusk with a headache. For many a weary mile, Rundle exclaimed at the performance of my daughter. 'My word, Mr Singer,' he said, and said again, and then said once more, 'she will not be beaten, will she Mr Singer? My word, Mr Singer, your daughter certainly does not mind exerting herself,' and so on and on. Was Rundle simply a blind mule of a man, with not an idea in the wide world of the things a father might not welcome in a daughter? Or was Rundle a sneak, mocking me in his meeching way? I nodded and did my best to assemble an agreeable expression on my face, but I wanted nothing better than to forget the way my daughter had wobbled and joggled her way to victory, and to forget, too, the way her father had been vanquished without even lifting his bat to the ball.

Chapter *Twenty-Five*

I HAD never believed in the concept of the birthday. Everyone is born on one day or another, and what could it matter if it were this day rather than that? In my own childhood, they had forever been pestering me to agree that I felt different now that I was seven, or ten, or whatever it was, and I had always refused to play their game. 'No, I feel no different at all,' I had always said, and watched them recoil.

When Lilian turned sixteen, Norah felt strongly enough to urge some kind of celebration. 'Sixteen is an important moment in a girl's life,' was as much as my silly wife could attempt by way of reasoning. 'It is traditional, Albion, for a girl.' A man such as myself could see why, and I had no hesitation in telling her, 'Yes, Norah, and the reason is that at sixteen the female of our species is biologically at her peak. From then on it is all downhill. It hardly seems something to celebrate.'

Occasionally Norah could surprise me. Although I knew where she had got the phrase – I had also read the piece in the paper on the rituals of the blacks – it was still a pleasure to have my wife say something a man could respect. 'It is by way of being a rite of passage,' Norah said pompously, and since this was clearly all she could remember from the piece, she said it again. 'A rite of passage, you know, Albion, she has a right to a rite.' A frown creased her brow then, and she went away puzzling.

◆   ◆   ◆

But she had succeeded: seen purely in the light of reason as a rite of passage I was willing to agree to a birthday party with a few of Lilian's friends. A new frock was ordered from Kennedy, invitations were issued to all the Ursulas and the Enids, to all their mothers, and to sundry Dicks and Edwards, and trestles were set up under the jacarandas.

We hired a man to do the lifting, and there was a woman from down the road got up in a black dress and a frilly apron, to hand the cake around. The day was all it should have been, with sun in reasonable quantities and no wind; the gaudy tiers of azaleas gave the garden an appropriate magnificence, and apart from a last-minute bird-dropping on the damask, all went according to plan.

A great deal of effort had gone into Lilian. Hours had been spent with Kennedy the dressmaker, and I knew that this white muslin, so cunningly pleated and gathered so as to make her seem buxom rather than elephantine, would end up costing an arm and a leg. Her hair had been pinned up in honour of the coming-of-age, so that she seemed quite foreign to me, and to herself, a little girl play-acting at being a lady with her hair up, mincing in her mother's high-heeled shoes.

She stood around on the flagstone terrace as the last-minute arrangements were made, putting a hand up to the back of her neck now and then, feeling the way the hair was pulled up the wrong way into its arrangement on the top of her head, smoothing the secretive underneath hair that was suddenly exposed.

'Stop fiddling with your hair, Lilian,' I told her, trying to be friendly, but hearing my tone abrupt. 'People will think you have nits.' She glanced at me to see whether I was joking, and I forced my face into a show of smile: Albion Gidley Singer, every inch the paterfamilias, giving his daughter a little tip on correct behaviour.

Norah hurried around, pointing for the men to lift this, carry that, move the other; she ticked off points on her fingers to the woman in black, and the woman in black smoothed her frills and nodded obediently. She hastened from the tea-table under the jacaranda to the flower-arrangement, from the sweeping of the verandah one last time to the cutting back of a bit of intrusive bougainvillea.

Mother was there, with a little apron on over her bottle-green costume, and met my eye: I was not sure if she had heard me speak to Lilian, but Mother's ears had always been sharp. 'It is her big day, Albion,' she came over to me and said, and I could not tell if this was simply one of her unanswerable trite remarks, or a reproach. 'And your next big day, much bigger than this, my dear,' she smiled at Lilian, 'will be your wedding, and you, Albion, will be giving her away.'

Giving her away! I wanted to retort that a man of business never gives anything away, but the humour would not be appreciated by my present audience, and I reminded myself to work this little witticism into my next conversation with Ogilvie.

All the same, it brought me up short, and I looked again at Lilian, standing patiently now while Mother tweaked at her seams. I could go so far as to imagine her dressed in white lace, leaning on my arm for that last walk down the aisle, but beyond that my mind simply would not go. Some man, whispering sweet nothings in her ear as he penetrated her garments one by one, some man waking up next to her in the same bed? No, the thing was impossible. 'Plenty of time to worry about that, Mother,' I told her briskly. 'Let us get one thing done at a time, shall we?'

But the hint was lost on both of them: Lilian interrupted me, crying, 'Look, Aunt Kitty is here!' and rushed off across the lawn, heedless of the way her skirt caught on the plumbago as she passed it, and flung her arms around Kristabel with what I thought was an over-done demonstration of affection. Kristabel hugged her back, and got out something wrapped in coloured tissue, and suddenly there was a little clutch of women all exclaiming over some trinket, and I was left alone on the lawn with my words falling emptily on no ears but my own.

When they had finished exclaiming over Kristabel's gift, and when every cup had been dusted, every chair-cushion plumped up, Norah came over in her sky-blue silk from Kennedy – another arm and another leg – and stood beside me. She laid a hand on my arm; I could not remember her having made such a gesture of affection to me in public since the memorable day I had proposed, when we had appeared among the aunts and mothers to announce the event. It was so unexpected I had to try to turn my flinch into a cough. She said with unaccustomed warmth, 'Oh, Albion, it is going to be such success, I feel sure.' I could feel the warmth of her flesh through the fabric of my sleeve, and remembered what I had not bothered to think of for a long time: that the inner skin of Norah's thighs was hot, and so soft that a thumbnail along it could leave a mark. Later on, perhaps, I would personally supervise the peeling-off of the sky-blue silk, and the examination of that inner skin of the thigh.

I was conscious of the picture we made: the charming Mrs Albion Singer and her husband the distinguished Albion Gidley Singer, happy married couple, proud parents of a brace of children, affectionately arm-in-arm: what a delightful picture for anyone who did not look too closely! I placed my hand over Norah's to retain it for a little longer, and wished Lilian and the woman in black were not the only audience of this moment.

'Well, Albion, what a significant day,' she was beginning again, but in the nick of time I heard the gate open, and could become the perfect host, excusing himself intimacy with his wife in order to greet his first guests, a clutch of Lilian's little friends.

Oh, Lilian and her little girl-friends! I went down the path towards them with a sense of weariness, but summoning the avuncular manner I had developed for these occasions. Now, was it Ursula who had the rheumatic mother, I tried to remember, or was it Enid, and was this one Enid, or was it Myrtle?

But I was in for a surprise. Only yesterday these creatures had been simply little girls, skinny or tubular, freckled or dark, with yellow hair ribbons or blue ones. Overnight they had revealed themselves to be females. Here was little Ursula, for example: she had always been the pretty one, and now that I looked, I could see that she was coming along very nicely indeed under her spotted batiste.

Enid had always been a big wooden sort of girl with a muscular neck that strained the seams of her muslin, and now she careered through the gate like some big runaway bit of machinery, all elbows, crashing against me and blurting *Sorry! Sorry!* But she, too, was no longer a child: there was a humid fleshiness about her as she disentangled herself from me, mottling darkly around the neck and panting from our encounter, and the way she stood with her arms crossed tightly over her chest made you aware that there was a certain amount of meaty charm going on under there. Enid was not going to be one to set the pulse racing, but she was a tryer. Her hair bore the marks of the curling-iron, and had been painstakingly arranged so as to cover her great domed forehead: she was going to give it all she had. A man who knew a thing or two could see that Enid, by dint of sheer application to strategically placed curls and ruffles, would eventually succeed in finding some young man who did not mind a wife built like an ironbark.

Somehow, the layers of fabric of these other girls' frocks

caused a man to speculate on what lay beneath: those artful tucks and flounces hinted at things unseen, half-concealed possibilities, and drew the interested male eye to things that were all the more enticing for being hidden. The essence of the feminine lay in that concealment: a man knew there was flesh there, but it was flesh imagined, not seen. How different from Lilian's frank bulk!

Last time I had seen them, these girls had looked on me simply as Lilian's father, a person in a suit who might startle them now and then by asking them how their mother was, or quizzing them jovially on the number of gills in a firkin, and they would stare blankly at that person in the suit and do their best to answer his questions. Now what a pretty flutter they were in!

Silly little things, they had no conception of why speaking to Lilian's father should suddenly throw them into such confusion, and make them blush so hot. But their bodies knew what their minds did not: that, in conversing with me, the female in them was responding to the irresistible call of the male. I felt myself rise up to meet such a clarion-call from biology, and all at once the day promised well.

◆   ◆   ◆

Nothing had changed at this type of tea-and-cake pimping. The tallest boys still danced attendance on the prettiest girls, and out on the periphery the stunted boys, the beanpole girls, and the ones whose clothes had been handed down from someone else, tried to make do with each other.

On chairs in the shade, a flotilla of majestic-bosomed

mothers sat with eyes as hard as china, exchanging remarks from lips that barely moved. They assessed the blood-stock on display before them: the good figure of one girl was weighed in the balance against her plain face; the cheerfulness of this one weighed against her tallness; the pimples of this one weighed against the fact that she would come into the Carmody fortune. The young men could be handsome or plain, short or tall, pimpled or smooth: none of that mattered. What the mothers saw when they looked at them were the bricks and mortar, the grassy acres, the pounds in the bank of which these young men were the promissory notes. The flinty mothers sitting with their reticules beside them were not taken in: like me, they recognised a piece of business when they saw it.

We knew this was business, but we had to pretend. Ursula fluttered and tittered and pursed her little red mouth at her cup of tea, and showed her little pink tongue, popping in another piece of cake. Like all the best pretty girls, Ursula pretended to think she was plain. 'I hope to go to the Teachers' College, Mr Singer,' she mouthed earnestly at me. 'I think a teacher has so much to offer.'

Ursula knew, quite as well as I did, that she would be snapped up in no time to become the better half of some young man, and begin doing what Nature intended for her: reproducing the species. But modesty is at its most charming when it issues from a succulent little mouth like a ripe peach.

Poor Enid was a realist. 'I have my sights set on the Teacher Training, too, Mr Singer,' she told me. 'A girl has to have something to fall back on,' and I could hear an echo of some sighing parent. 'She had better have something, Fred,' I could imagine, 'just in case, Fred.'

Young men had deteriorated since my day. These were terribly feeble things, in striped blazers that made them look like some kind of beetle, holding tiny spoons with huge red hands, trying to find a way to stand that did not make them look as if their underwear was strangling them. They nodded and smiled too much, they blushed and shifted from foot to gigantic foot, while the girls frothed on, running the show: at least in my day we had known better than to let the girls rule the roost.

It was a father's job to get the measure of the young men who came to his daughter's house, so I chose the nearest one, and began by asking him in a friendly enough way about his plans for the future. Of all these spindly boys, he was the spindliest; there was something disorganised about his face, as if he had borrowed each part from someone else: the mouth was too big, the eyes too small, the ears from a giant, the nose possibly off a bird.

'Oh,' he said, and jerked so that the tea slopped into his saucer, and I was already beginning to regret my choice, and wish I had spoken to the boy with the bat-wing ears, at this moment listening respectfully to little Ursula. 'Oh yes,' said this one, as if reminding himself of the existence of a future that needed thinking about. 'Well, Dad has got a property, Mr Singer.' I could see this boy, Duncan was his name, squirming with his cup of tea and his pikelet – he did not dare take a bite, in case I came at him with another question and his mouth would be too jammed to answer – so he stood

clutching his pikelet and the teacup like a clown about to
start juggling.

'A property,' I prompted, all patience, perhaps rather visibly
all patience, and Duncan seemed to gulp, so his long knobbly
neck convulsed like a goanna's. 'Out West, Mr Singer, out
Collarenebri way, do you know Collarenebri at all, sir?' and
he stuffed the pikelet in his mouth, clearly hoping that I
would make some lengthy answer on the subject of Collarenebri. 'No,' I said, and watched in silence as his freckled
cheeks distorted around the pikelet.

When he had finally swallowed, I said, 'And is that where
you see yourself, in the years to come?' Thinking this rather
a dainty way of saying *when your father is dead*, but Duncan
was not a boy to appreciate a nuance. 'Oh, well, you know,'
he began – how I hated this modern habit of prefacing everything with a fanfare of meaningless phrases! – 'well yes, he
hopes I will take over the place when he dies, and I suppose
I will, but poetry is more in my line, really.' I let a short
silence fall before I repeated, 'Poetry?' But instead of flushing
and thinking better of this, Duncan opened his wide mouth
and laughed a big silly laugh. 'Oh yes, I have written reams
of the stuff!' He seemed to have no shame, so I went carefully; you never knew when some no-hoper might turn out
to be a prodigy. I could not ask bluntly, *Are you any good?* but
I knew the polite code, and asked, 'Oh? And where have you
been published?' Duncan took a gulp of tea, audibly rinsed it
around his mouth, and said cheerfully, 'Oh, none of it is
published, Mr Singer, and it is probably no good, but it is
what I enjoy.'

I was rendered speechless by this: it was like talking to someone from Mars. The worst of it was, Duncan appeared to be quite unaware of the embarrassing nature of what he had said: it was as if he thought it was the right thing to go on doing something as unproductive as poetry, although you were no good at it, just because you *enjoyed* it! I watched him as he glanced around; he was entirely untroubled, the clown beaming around in the moment before his pants fell down.

It was hopeless: I could only trust that not all of these insects in stripes were as bad as this one. I would come back to the others later, but I could not bear any more of them now.

I strolled over and stood close to a little knot of the girls, fiddling with a fresh cup of tea while I listened to them cooing and billing away together. Like the boys behind the bike-shed with Morrison in my own younger days, these females were concerned with only one thing: the opposite sex, and how to get hold of a sample of it. But there was a difference: the fascination for these shallow girls was the romance angle of it all. I could see, watching them smirk and titter, that they had swallowed hook, line and sinker every lie that had ever been invented to sugar the pill of biological necessity. *Lo, the Dawn Is Breaking* and its ilk had taught them all they knew, so they naturally thought they were experiencing love, or despair, or some such large noble thing, because *Lo, the Dawn Is Breaking* told them they must be. What a pack of gulls they were, all of them, when this strutting was about nothing more or less than copulation!

I was immensely glad to be no longer young. It was not a bashful youth, his body a burden to him, who stood now among the teacups, but a solid block of man-of-the-world in a dark suit, not ashamed to take up plenty of space among these wisps of virgins.

◆　◆　◆

Now the basilisk-mothers were forcing tennis-racquets into the hands of the young folk, and propelling them off to the tennis court. These pimping mothers seemed keen to encourage the girls and boys to be alone on the court and in the tennis-shed, unsupervised by any adult eye. But I saw no reason why risks should be taken on the Singer property. I appointed myself umpire and chaperone, and tried not to creak as I swung myself up to the top of the umpire's chair.

That Duncan was a fool in flannels: the racquet stuck out awkwardly from the end of his arm, and balls fell out of his hands before he could toss them up in the air for a serve. This was contemptible, but what seemed worse to me was that he did not mind. 'Oh, what a duffer I am!' he exclaimed and laughed, missing another easy ball from Lilian with a wild swing that made him stagger. 'Could we try using a football, and I might have half a chance!' he called out, and I thought it was a pretty feeble joke, but Lilian laughed fit to burst. He floundered, and ran after balls he had no hope of hitting, and I was embarrassed for him.

I sat up in the umpire's chair calling out, 'Fault, fault,' time and again; or, when the miracle happened and he got the ball over the net, 'Out!' He took it all with a silly smile, but Lilian took his part, and protested when a ball was close to the line, 'No, Father, I saw it, it was in, it was definitely in!' I did not wish to argue with her in front of guests, but sang out, 'The umpire's decision is final, those are the rules.' Lilian called up, 'But Father,' her face unpleasantly red from running to Duncan's wild balls and laughing, 'we must give the poor fellow a chance, and turn a blind eye now and then, or there will be no game!' From my height, the top of my daughter's head was odiously pointed, ugly under the sun where the hair lay flat on her skull. And what an idiotic idea! If winning was not the point of playing a game, what point could there possibly be?

Just the same, I could sympathise with Lilian. No woman should win a game so resoundingly against a man: it is not a good thing for a woman to show a man up, even a man as foolish as Duncan. I softened at this proof that my daughter had, after all, some sense of the proper. But although in defending Duncan she was upholding the dignity of one male, she was undermining the authority of another, and that could not be allowed.

'If you go on disagreeing with the umpire, Lilian, he will have to leave,' I warned, for I had no wish to look ridiculous, perched up there umpiring nonsense. Lilian looked up at me, squinting into the sun so I could not see her expression, and I thought she might argue, but she returned to play. At the next ball I called again, 'Out!' My voice was crisp: it was a pleasure to hear it cutting out so cleanly across the court. But Lilian was beneath me again, calling up, 'No, Father, I assure you it was definitely in, there is no possible doubt about it, I must disagree with you.'

She stood there squat and foreshortened, obviously prepared to make difficulties with me all day. 'Very well,' I said in a pointedly quiet way, and climbed down from the chair. 'Very well, Lilian, then you must do without an umpire.' I walked off the court without looking back, sure they would call out and ask me to return. But Lilian was too obstinate, and Duncan too ineffectual, and was in any case a guest, and no doubt reluctant to take the initiative. I did not give Lilian the pleasure of seeing me hesitate as I entered the house, but walked into the cool, blinded for a moment in the deep shadow of the hall.

A voice came from the darkness, the voice of my invisible wife. 'That was a very quick game, Albion, to be finished already,' and as we stood in the dimness and I saw my wife's shape in the doorway I said, 'Lilian must learn, Norah, that rules must be obeyed, and that a game without rules is simply nonsense.' But in the silence after I had spoken we heard the hollow mocking sound of a tennis ball hitting one racquet, then another, backwards and forwards, and then the thin silly sound of people laughing out-of-doors.

❖   ❖   ❖

Later, when everyone was reassembling for more tea and cake, I did not want to be close to Lilian and Duncan. Lilian was more fat and freckled than I could believe, and her stringy mouse-coloured hair was loosening itself in wild strands around her face. I saw with distaste that there were large circles of sweat beneath her arms: surely this perspiring person could be no daughter of mine! She stood swinging her racquet between two fingers so it bounced on her knee in its muslin; she smiled and wiped the hair and perspiration off her face, and stood much too close to Duncan, who probably had no more wish than I did to be too close to such an over-exerted female.

Although, when I looked, I saw that he too was showing the signs of vigorous movement in the hot sun: he panted and grinned not unlike a large well-intentioned dog. It would hardly have surprised me if he had begun licking things with a thick rough tongue.

Duncan brought her a cup of tea, and perched on the arm of her chair, and they sniggered together over an album of postcards. What a sweaty animal warmth emanated from them!

Deep in the armchair, Lilian pointed to something, laughing up at Duncan, inviting him to laugh with her. I did not care for it. Hers was the sort of smile that might – in another woman, in another set of circumstances – have been an invitation. I made a mental note to take her aside at some point and tell her a thing or two about smiles, their temperature and duration, or she would find herself being misunderstood.

A cup of tea was inserted into my hand and I accepted it, though I waved away the pikelets thrust into my face by some silly woman bursting out of royal-blue watered-silk. I knew a pikelet could be trusted not to explode into a thousand fragments around your boots, but I had long ago made it a policy never to eat on social occasions. She billed and cooed at me about what a splendid place I had here, and what a lovely sight the young folk made, and my word just look at the blue of that jacaranda out the window: all these mothers had an inexhaustible store of platitudes to keep the shallow river of chatter tinkling along.

When I looked again, the corner where my daughter had

been was empty. The album of postcards was lying open, abandoned on the table like something broken.

'And where is Lilian?' I asked, in what I had intended to be the most casual of enquiries, but I saw mothers turn, and realised that I might perhaps be bellowing. One of them, a withered-up affair in drooping navy that showed the chicken-flesh of her upper chest, spoke up loudly, as if on a stage, and said, 'She may just be powdering her nose at the minute, Mr Singer,' and she actually winked at me. How dare they, these dough-like women, these pimping mothers, how dare they mock me, making a female conspiracy out of every little thing?

I sauntered away to find Lilian. I had not outlaid good money for her to hide away powdering her nose when she ought to be getting down to business like the rest of them. But I came across John before I found Lilian: his head was down and he was coming out of the middle of a bush. When he saw me, it looked as though he would have liked to retreat back into the bush, but it had closed behind him like a valve.

'Where is your sister, John?' I asked. There was not much male shoulder-to-shoulder comradeliness in our household, but finally I got out of him that she was in the shrubbery. 'By herself?' I wanted to know, and John thought, and said, 'I am not sure, Father,' in his toneless way, unable to decide whether Lilian would get into greater trouble if she was there alone or with someone else.

I made myself very silent and slipped through the shrub-bery, until my eye was caught by a flutter of white under the trees beyond the tennis-court. Over there, hidden from every-one, Lilian was jumping up and down, trying to catch a feather. In the tumid green of this space, with bushes crowding in all around, and the trees as dense as thatch overhead, the little feather was uncannily white. Laughing Lilian sprang in an inefficient way, so that the feather eluded her, buoying itself up on the currents of air she was producing. She was laughing so much that even from where I stood, I could see her fine pointed teeth, and how she was rosy and sparkling from her efforts. She leaped and bounced, and her hem flounced around her thighs and her bosom jumped up and down as if with a life of its own.

I watched, and was about to call out when I saw that Lilian was not alone under the tree. The young man called Duncan stood there, the stripes of his blazer lurid in the syrupy shade, staring at her with his mouth hanging open.

She called out something to him and he went over to her; as they stood still together, looking up, the feather wafted down between them and with one decisive movement he had it caught in his hand. He handed it to her and she stroked her cheek with it, looking up at him. Her pink mouth grimaced and stretched, smiling and pushing words out at him, playing with the feather in her hands. I could not hear, but I could see the fluid shapes that her mouth was making.

'Lilian!' I called, rather louder than I had intended. They jumped when I spoke, and stepped back from each other, which made me realise just how closely together they had been standing; Duncan hung his head, but Lilian stared pertly at me, still caressing her cheek with the feather.

'Lilian, you are being remiss about your duties as hostess,' I called out, but I could hear how my voice sounded puny in this vaulted green space, how lisping all those sibilants sounded. 'Come along, Lilian, if you please,' I said in a lower and less shrill voice, and waited until they passed in front of me. 'And give me that rubbish,' I told Lilian, taking the feather from her hand. 'You are not a child any longer, Lilian, kindly take a grip on yourself.' As I walked along behind her huge white bottom working up and down against its muslin, I could not stop my mouth forming a smile so wide I could feel the air cool on my teeth, at the idea of Lilian taking a grip on herself.

Chapter *Twenty-Six*

THE HERDING OF FACTS into my brain had been my consolation for many years now. That void at the heart of things shrank away in the face of so many facts brought to heel, and a man could find a way to go on, while he told his facts over to himself and devised new kinds of colour-coding, new ways of cross-referencing, and new combinations of the alphabet.

My facts had long since overflowed my study, had taken over the spare bedroom entirely, and were still expanding. What was happening brought on a sense of vertigo: I was making the discovery that there was simply no way to get a grip on facts, no matter what a man did.

It was not that facts resisted me. On the contrary, they clustered eagerly around me, each fact splitting off more and more facts from itself, each split-off fact branching out into sub-facts of sub-facts, and sub-sub-facts of sub-facts. Every moment created its own fact needing to be recorded, but the recording of the moment itself was another fact needing to be recorded, and the recording of the recording was yet another fact, and so on dizzyingly, sickeningly, into the void of infinity. There was no way to keep up, no matter how fast you went, but if you stopped, the thing would overwhelm you: I was like a man holding back the tide with his bare hands.

It takes a man of powerful will to hold back the tide with his bare hands, and I had to apply myself to it pretty fully. For a time the figures of my children and my wife receded into pinpricks in the distance, the operations of my house were of no importance to me: even Rundle with his ledgers was just a shadow mouthing at me while I got on with trying to get a grip on the ocean.

I triumphed at last: that is all that matters, and all that needs to be said. It was a fact, though, that while I had these other concerns on my mind, my control over the operations of family life had been for a time less than absolute, and when I was again in a position to take up the reins of the Family Man, things had undergone a subtle shift.

My jaw was as authoritative as ever and my boots rang out as satisfyingly on the planks of my house. My wife still gave tea-parties for ladies, though the Fallen Girls had gone, and been replaced by something to do with a notebook and a stopwatch that involved hours sitting on the terrace. John was now a young man whose pimples alone indicated that some change was occurring in his chemistry as he inched towards manhood; and my daughter was now a huge girl who had exceeded all expectations in her exams, and had started at the University.

But things were crumbling from within in a way I could not seem to arrest. Norah looked all right to the naked eye, but she was coming apart at the seams. She was such a thin sort of person now that I found myself checking on the ground for her shadow.

I picked up her notebook one morning as she sat alone at the breakfast table on the terrace waiting for the rest of the family, to see what it was she was getting up to: but what she was getting up to was nothing more revealing than page after page of numbers, column after column of figures.

'Oh Albion, it is my researches,' she said, and fumbled with her pearls, watching the book in my hand as if I might be about to eat it. 'My researches, Albion, which I am conducting with my stopwatch.' And there it was, Norah's stopwatch warm in her hand, custodian of every passing second.

I experienced a pang of loss, of hatred and envy. Not only did my spineless wife have – or had once had – the power of life and death, but she had now also usurped the fact to end all facts, the fact of time itself. It crossed my mind that this assembling of facts was a kind of parody of my own beautifully catalogued battery of information, arrayed floor to ceiling in my study, and now entirely under my control once again. But it was hard to believe that Norah had the brains for parody.

I snorted and laughed a nasty laugh. 'And what researches are you conducting, exactly, Norah?' She shook in the blast of my voice, and I went on, so that my loss and hatred began to recede in so much authoritative sound. I reminded myself that Norah could conduct no researches of much significance from the wicker chair in the shade where she spent her days, while I was a man who daily breasted the world, and who –

it would be any day now – would sit down and assemble all his researches into something definitive.

But Norah recovered, raised her head and looked into my face. I knew, having seen it under all expressions in my mirror, how very daunting a face it could be, but nevertheless she said strongly, 'I am researching the times of the ferries, Albion. When the wind is from the nor'east they are one-and-a-half times faster.' She lost faith then, and could not look any more at my face, which I could feel stone-like and unwelcoming. 'And other things too,' she said vaguely. 'Other researches of various kinds.' She had one last spark of pride: 'Of a confidential nature,' she said, trying to be bold, but I laughed in her face and saw her shrink.

'Well, Norah,' I exclaimed in a woundingly jovial way, 'may you have every success with your researches. Every success, and do let me know when they are published.' I turned my back on her there folded into her chair with the silly silver stopwatch in her hand. I could feign heartiness, but I was dismayed: always watery, my wife was now in some way slipping through my fingers.

♦ ♦ ♦

Then there were the children. They sat up straight at the table, and had been taught how to *keep the ball rolling* in family conversation over dinner. But in a way I could not quite put my finger on, the sedate family dinner, with all faces turned to the head of the household sitting at the top of the table, was being eaten away silently and invisibly from within.

When we met around the dinner-table now, Lilian would

not look me in the eye, and there was something I did not like happening with the muscles around her mouth. She watched me sideways, her mouth wry.

And there was John, sniggering with Lilian instead of paying attention to questions his father might put to him. John had recently taken up the tuba. He sat for hours in his room now within the embrace of its brass coils, filling the house with a hoarse hooting that he must have known was maddening to anyone engaged in important researches. The tuba seemed to have gone dangerously to his head. He did not always listen to me as attentively as I would have liked: and now, down at the end of the table, he exchanged glances with Lilian in a sly sort of way, as if they were sharing a joke at my expense. When he shook out his napkin and it flew out of his hand onto the floor, both of them actually laughed aloud.

I was not to be made a fool of at my own board, under my own roof. Ah, Lilian, my daughter, you glanced at my head at the end of the table, so substantial with facts and its own magnificence, and you did not find me beloved, although you did not fear me either. Perhaps, worst of all, you found me only ridiculous.

◆　◆　◆

I dated the beginning of the rot to the day of the beggar in the street: some faith in the solidity of the world dropped away from me then, the day my daughter turned her back on me.

The sight of a beggar in a torn jacket, with the sole of his boot flapping, and three days' growth on his chin, with his eyes screwed up in a dirty face and a clumsily lettered sign, *Blind*, around his neck, was not calculated to stir any pity in me. A man such as myself could see at a glance that the fellow was a fraud. I had to work hard for my living: why should this man simply sit on a street corner and have it handed to him on a platter, or to be precise, in a dented tin cup?

I pointed him out to Lilian, who was travelling in with me on the ferry. 'Look at that fraud, Lilian, will you? Perhaps we should tell him that the genuine blind do not screw their eyes up like that: how can the light hurt their eyes? They cannot see the light!' and I was preparing to have a moment's enjoyment with my daughter on the subject of this beggar.

A tram crashed past at that moment, and when Lilian said nothing I thought perhaps she had not heard. 'What do you think, Lilian, will I tell him, or will you?' But when I glanced at her I saw that her lips were so tightly compressed she had a crone's wrinkles around her mouth, and I saw that her eyes were full with a woman's quick tears, and glittered dangerously in her face as she glanced again at the beggar, his shaking hand holding his tin cup.

I was not going to allow any daughter of mine to get away with tight-lipped silence: she would agree with me, or have the courage of her convictions and speak out! 'Well, Lilian, what do you think? Did you hear what I said?'

I thought I heard her say, 'Father, how can you?' and when I turned to see what she meant, she turned her eyes, bulbous with tears, on me, and cried in a theatrical way, 'Have you no pity at all, Father?'

Her face was red with feeling; her nose shone repulsively,

and the tears threatened to spill down her thick cheeks. She had never looked quite so much like a side of beef. But unlike Norah, who at least knew what was proper, Lilian did not have the decency to turn her face away or conceal it behind a handkerchief. I had never before seen Lilian do the trembling-lip feminine thing on me: she had never copied her mother, in going all to jelly when I challenged her. But now she was proving herself just another silly female, and not even one with a dainty lace hanky up her sleeve.

'That man is without a doubt richer than I am, Lilian,' I told her. 'Mark my words, a Rolls-Royce will pick him up at the end of the day and take him to Vaucluse. Take it from me, Lilian: your pity is wasted.'

She did not give me the courtesy of a reply. She did not even look at me, but reached into her handbag and gave the man five shillings – five shillings, mind you, not a threepence or a sixpence, but five whole shillings hard-earned by her father! – and walked on without waiting to see if I was beside her.

Oh charity, thy name is Self! Lilian, gone all damp and defiant, thought she was a fine soul. We walked a block in silence, and I saw that Lilian was determined not to be the first to speak. Further, it was obvious that by this means she was expressing disapproval, or even distaste, at my last remark: she was attempting to rebuke me. Meanwhile, the charlatan we had just witnessed was no doubt laughing up his sleeve at how he had duped the young lady in the mauve, the one with the fine-looking father.

'Lilian,' I said, without rancour, 'Lilian,' I said sweetly, 'Lilian, let me ask you a question, if you would be so kind.'

Lilian stopped. 'Yes, Father?' she said, oh, she was at her mildest, but I saw a glint in her eye, a glint that said, *I am finer of spirit than you*, and I was going to crush that glint. 'Lilian, I am curious, you must just tell me why you gave to that man back there: I ask purely as a matter of interest, you understand.'

Lilian grew more deeply flushed than ever. 'Heavens, Father,' she cried, 'have you no feelings?' But I would not be baited, I would not deviate. 'I am probably the best judge of my feelings, Lilian,' I said in my driest way, 'but be that as it may, I would like you to think, and to answer.' Lilian thought: it was visibly apparent, from the corrugations on her brow, that thinking was taking place. At last she came up with an answer, but in a somewhat bewildered way, as if she was already against her will seeing the trap I had laid. 'I gave because I have everything, and he, poor wretch, has nothing, and I could just as easily be in his position as mine.' This was no answer, to my mind, and I persisted, 'But you have not answered the question: what, precisely, made you give to him?' This time Lilian did not stop and think: she should have given the matter a moment's consideration! 'Well, Father,' she said loudly, 'if you must know, I gave so that he can eat a square meal, and pay for some kind of bed, and that means I can sleep easier in my own.'

Ah! For the sake of the nice symmetry of phrase, Lilian had completely delivered herself into my hands. I could become silky now, and soft, for I had her cornered. 'So, Lilian, you gave in order to make yourself feel better, you are saying?' I did not bother to pause and watch her flummox and bluster: I went straight on, wishing to screw her humiliation into her. 'Lilian, you have just proved that charity is simply another form of commerce. The commodity bought is no less pleasurable for being intangible: it is that inner satisfaction as you walk along with your purse a little lighter. Altruism is really just another type of self-interest, Lilian.'

She had condemned herself from her own mouth. And yet she would not yield. Her chin set tightly under her face, her mouth went thin, and her eyes stared coldly at me as she came at me with her do-gooder's nonsense. 'Father, your logic is faultless, but nevertheless you are in the wrong. It is surely better to be moved by another human in distress, and help him, than to argue your way out of lifting a finger.' She did not look at me, but adjusted her hat as if her righteousness had caused it to lift off her head, and walked off ahead of me towards her tram without looking back. I was left with the choice of hastening, positively running, after her, or watching her grow small in the distance.

Watching her grow small in the distance was very much the preferable of these courses of action, but I was taken aback by the whole experience. How dare she? How dare she try to make out that I was her moral inferior, and waltz off before I could catch my breath to prove how wrong she was?

◆　◆　◆

And now here they were, being disruptive down at the bottom of the table. 'John!' I called, and saw them both straighten up quickly, and the silly hysteria drain out of their faces. 'John, I am speaking to you, kindly do me the courtesy of listening!' I said, hearing my mouth smack around the words in a satisfying way, and I saw his Adam's apple rise up his throat. 'Yes, Father,' he mumbled. How I would have loved him to be a manly boy who could look me in the eye! How I would have welcomed a few facts from him, no matter how wrong! But this boy shrank into his clothes and hunched over his plate as if to get right into it: his resistance to me was palpable, like a magnetic field around his body.

I was determined, though, and was prepared to seize that jaw in my hands and force speech out of his mouth if necessary. 'John, how long is the Amazon?' I asked, because answers can be demanded of questions, and I was determined to make him speak to me. 'How long is the Amazon?' I cried at his deaf, closed face, and saw him flinch. 'Come, John,' I said, more mildly. 'Come, John, if you do not know, I will tell you.' John shot a look at me and I made my face bland and welcoming. 'I do not know, Father,' he whispered at last. 'I do not know.' He closed his face again then and thought he would have to say no more, but I was determined that my son would speak to me. 'Then guess, John,' I said, and tapped the table beside my plate. 'Guess, boy!'

Oh, what a desperately feeble boy he was. He stared at me blankly, and when he saw I would not give up, he said, 'One hundred miles, sir?' and I snorted, but I would not let him off so lightly. 'Guess again, John,' I cried, and kept him guessing, one number after another, and saying, 'No, guess again,' in triumph, until Alma came in with the vegetables, and made a distraction with her clattering and breathing, and asking people whether they was wanting the potato or the carrot. I was sick of the frog-like clammy boy stuck to his chair with hopeless numbers coming out of his mouth, and said in my authoritative way, 'The Amazon, John, is three thousand nine hundred and fifty-three miles long from source to mouth.' The lavishness of it made me smile. 'By Jove, John, you were far off the mark!'

When Alma had left us in peace at last, it was time to turn to my daughter and deal with her. I laughed a little, the more to disarm her, and remarked mildly, 'Lilian, did you know that by the age of sixty the average woman is a dead seed pod? The oldest woman ever recorded as having given birth was fifty-seven years and 129 days old.'

Lilian stared and John coughed his mealy-mouthed cough, but I would not be swerved. 'By contrast, Lilian, and John, you should pay attention to this, a man at seventy, even seventy-five, is still full of animal spirit.' *And sperm*, I would have liked to shout in triumph, but I heard Alma coming up the stairs from the kitchen again and was afraid such a robust word might make her drop the water-jug, and my rhetoric was parching me.

But Lilian watched me down the length of the table, and waited until Alma was in the room, creaking over to the sideboard with the jug. Then my daughter spoke. 'Also sperm, Father,' she said loudly, and Alma rattled something tremulously behind me. 'A man of seventy is still full of sperm, Father, that is a fact.' I saw that my daughter was attempting to make me foolish, having the last word on this sperm business, and being brazen about it in front of the servant.

My laugh shook my water-glass. 'Since you are interested in these things, Lilian, let me share an intriguing fact with you on the subject of the male organ.' Alma snatched up the empty gravy-boat and left the room, Lilian stared at me in a glassy sceptical way I wished to galvanise, Norah hem-hemmed at me from the other end of the table, and John stared at his napkin-ring and ground away with his molars at a piece of food: a boy more like a cow was hard to imagine. 'Something that may interest you, Lilian, is that the sexual entrance in the female pig is normally sealed shut. Pigs love mud, as you know, so Nature has ensured that the reproductive cavity does not fill with mud and putrefy.' Out of the corner of my eye I glimpsed Norah bring her hanky up to her mouth. 'Now this would present a difficulty for the male of the species when servicing the sow, and Nature has come up with an efficient solution. The organ of generation of the male pig is curved, and as sharp as a knife. What he does is to more or less slice his way into his sow.'

My daughter looked most like me when she frowned as she was doing now. A flush rose up her neck into her face, but she did not flinch. Her own flesh was safe at this moment pressed against, in the first instance, Mark Foy's best pure silk cami-knickers, and then against Hordern Bros' figured muslin, and then against the cut velvet of Ball Bros, Uphol-sterers. But behind her stony face she must be imagining how it might feel to have a man cut her open.

My obstinate daughter did not recoil. But with terrible choking sounds John was stumbling out from his chair and with a hand to his mouth was running in a jerky way from the room. Norah rose and flung her napkin on the table like someone throwing down a gauntlet. 'Really, Albion!' she exclaimed, but coward that she was, she would not challenge me more precisely than that. She knew that I would have my answer ready: 'Do not blame me, Norah, for the facts of life! Would you rather have your children live with their heads in the sand?'

So Norah said nothing, and Lilian and I were left alone in the room, glaring at each other. At last she looked away, and in a voice that started off hoarse, so that she had to cough to clear her throat, said, 'I shall ring for Alma to clear away, shall I, Father?'

Chapter *Twenty-Seven*

WHEN NORAH TRIED to tell me, it was easy to shrug it off as just another proof of her decay. It was one night, when Lilian had gone up to study, and John had faded away into the wallpaper somewhere. Norah and I sat together in a tableau that might have been called *Family Harmony*, except that it was a parody of that: we were a pair of souls opposite each other in our armchairs, close enough to hear each other's breathing, yet as foreign to each other as two stones. I got up to poke the fire, and Norah put out a hand in my direction, without actually touching me, and said, 'Albion, there is something I must tell you.' She looked up at me with those eyes of hers that were always a little elsewhere. 'Albion,' she murmured, and I spoke loudly, for I would have no truck with her dreaminess, 'Yes, I am Albion, your husband of twenty-two years and two months, still Albion after so long.'

This silenced Norah and she opened her notebook and pretended to read the columns of numbers in it. I watched the top of her head, saw grey hair, the pink of scalp, and felt

nothing but revulsion for this dry withering piece of womanhood, who had once been flesh of my flesh.

But she was not to be deflected: she said again, 'Albion,
there is something I must tell you.' It was so long since Norah
had had anything to tell me that I stood, feeling my thighs
taut with power, my spine upright, and placed my hands –
fine hands, hands capable of anything – across my groin,
like a sympathetic clergyman, to demonstrate how ready I
was to listen.

My wife grew nervous at this, and flustered into her notebook. But she seemed to find there what she was looking for,
for she said, in a clear elocution-class voice, as if reciting from
memory, 'Albion, I am worried about our daughter Lilian.
She is not herself. She has become unladylike, and is loud.'
Norah, my pathetic wife, looked up from her notebook and
said in her own wistful voice, 'And Albion, I have seen her
wearing blue and green together.'

She was alarmed then, and shot a glance at me standing
there so attentive, unnerving my nerveless wife with my
powerful hands across my powerful body, and she turned back
to her book, but I could see there was nothing more written
on the page after *loud*, which was underlined. 'Loud,' Norah
said loudly, and as if she had the hang of it now, began
reading again, this time as ringingly as if to reach across
the bay, 'Albion, I am worried about our daughter Lilian.'
I seized her bird-like wrist, I could not bear it, and I shouted,
'Norah! Stop!'

From being a little erratic, it was obvious that the woman

had become unhinged. I had heard of these things happening at Norah's time of life. There were mothers, for example, who came to hate their own daughters. There was an inexorable symmetry about the whole thing: Norah could see Lilian ripening into womanhood just as she herself was shrivelling, a dry pod from which the seed had fallen. It was all understandable, and she was fortunate in having a husband who was so rational on the subject. All the same, I made a mental note to have a word with that old quack O'Hara.

O'Hara was quick to diagnose that what my wife needed was a rest and a sea voyage with one of her lady-friends. It seemed to me that Norah had been *resting* for the last twenty-odd years, but I was sick to death of her in every corner of my house now, staring at me with her mooning eyes. The cost of a South Seas Cruise seemed a low price to pay to be rid of her for a time.

She cried when the time came for her to leave, clung to Lilian, could not remember what she had done with her hat-pin – 'Hat-pin, Norah? What will you want with a hat-pin in the South Seas?' I demanded, but as usual got no answer from her – but finally she was bundled into the back of the cab and the three of us, Lilian, John and myself, stood on the front steps waving her off, the picture of a happy little family. 'I will be back soon,' she could be heard still calling out from the back of the cab, as if to reassure us. 'I will see you again soon.'

I surprised a certain fullness around Lilians' eyes as she waved, and a certain reluctance to answer when I exclaimed robustly into the silence of her mother's absence, 'Well, Lilian, it is just us now, just us!' With Norah gone, fetters seemed fallen away from me.

◆　　◆　　◆

But when Rundle tried to tell me, I was forced to listen. I was sitting considering the latest column of figures in the latest ledger Rundle had left on my desk, when Rundle himself knocked on my door and came awkwardly in, filling the room like an embarrassed St Bernard who has just wet on the carpet. 'Mr Singer, sir, might I have a word with you?' he asked, and I was every inch the gracious host as I came around the desk to fuss him into a chair, and rang for the woman to bring us a cup of tea.

We crouched over the wretched books as usual, although it was not the books that Rundle had come about this time. But he seemed incapable of coming out with what was on his mind, and to hasten the process, I tried to put him at his ease by a little chat about the fine weather we were having, the activities of Rundle's Sundays, and so on.

'Oh yes, Mr Singer, the bitch is getting old now, but she is still a bit of an interest,' Rundle said. I stared at him: had I misjudged Rundle all these years? Was he a satirist under his Creeping Jesus manner? The notion of Mrs Rundle, a vast bag of flesh now, but still partial to yellow sateen, being *a bit of an interest*, was certainly a difficult thing to picture. 'On Sundays, then, Rundle . . . ?' I prompted, and of course old Rundle had to disappoint me: 'Her last litter was only three pups, but healthy little things, and we sold them all within a week.'

But it was not for chit-chat about pups that Rundle had come to me today.

'Mr Singer, sir, I loathe a gossip above all,' he began earnestly when he had burnt his lip on his tea, trying to put himself at ease by taking a sip. 'I have been hearing gossip now for thirty years, and have never given it any credential.' I nodded understandingly, but did not fill the silence, so that Rundle would finally be unnerved into blurting out whatever little bit of unpleasantness was troubling him. I imagined one of our pretty shop-girls in the family way, perhaps – I quickly did a few sums about the latest girl in Pens, and was reassured by them – or a clerk caught with his hand in the till, something of that order. I made my face bland and expectant while his cheeks sagged in anguished thought, and I could see an edge of shiny inner lip as his mouth struggled to shape itself around the appropriate words.

'I hope you will forgive me, Mr Singer, but your father was as good to me as a brother, and for his sake I am speaking' – *no, you are not, Rundle, you are not speaking, you turnip!* I thought in my own mind, but nodded some more – 'But Mr Singer, please do not take it wrong, if I am doing the wrong thing it is for the best of intentions, I have mentioned it to Mrs Rundle and she was also of the opinion that I should speak.' *Then do it, man, open your silly mouth and be out with it!* I cried in my head, but went on nodding, nodding, only allowing myself to shift in my chair and brush at a bit of fluff on my knee that did not exist, to betray the slightest impatience.

Then for the first time in all those years, Rundle, his big folded face convulsed with uncertainty, surprised me. 'It is about your daughter, Mr Singer,' Rundle said. I could only think that it must be my daughter who was in the family way: in my momentary confusion, a picture sprang to my mind of Lilian lying naked along one of my mahogany counters.

But Rundle was shaping his mouth around more words, trying to pick the right ones. 'I have heard, Mr Singer, on the best of authority, that she – I may be wrong, Mr Singer, but thought I should let you know –' Rundle seemed prepared to let phrases fall out of his mouth endlessly without getting to the point. 'Rundle, out with it!' I cried in what I had intended as a cheerful way, but I heard my voice rasp. 'Just tell me straight out, man, what have you heard?' Before he could tell me, Rundle had to turn away, look out the window, clear his throat, but finally the words were on their way. 'Mr Singer, the word is, that your daughter has been seen intoxicated in Dixon Street with a young man, and also in the Botanical Gardens, lying on the grass with him.' His face was convulsed now, like a twisted shoe, but he was doggedly going on, in an expressionless voice. 'She is selling her textbooks at Fidden's, Mr Singer, and there have been at least four separate occasions, I have it on the best authority.'

I felt my face stiffening, purpling, congesting: I saw Rundle shoot me an apprehensive glance and then stare out the window again. 'I hope I have not done wrong, Mr Singer,' he was bleating, at a vast distance, so that his voice was reedy and insignificant. 'I did not know just what to do for the best.'

I tried, for the sake of the look of things in front of Rundle, to swallow the flame of my rage: I could not have him seeing me pole-axed by betrayal. But what a pain had pierced my heart! I was betrayed. My own daughter had acted as though butter would not melt in her mouth; she had let me waste my time informing her of the facts of the world, and showing a fatherly interest in her studies at the University. And all the time she had been laughing up her sleeve at me. Moreover, it had taken one of my own employees to tell me what half the town probably already knew, that Singer's daughter was a drunken trollop!

I forced my voice to be steady, my face to be mask-like, as I said, 'Thank you, Rundle, you did exactly the right thing. As it happens I have been aware of this for some time, but you did quite right in bringing it to me.'

Rundle was a buffoon, but he was a man with a proper sense of what was fitting, and not a complete fool. He drank off his tea in one searing gulp and got up. 'If there is nothing else, Mr Singer, I have a few invoices to attend to,' he said, and left me alone, closing the door as gently behind him as on a death.

Chapter Twenty-Eight

FOR A START, she was running wild at night. With some solemn tale of her university essays to write and books to read, she went to her room after dinner, but half an hour later, when a father popped his head in to see how his daughter was getting along, and whether she needed a hand with the Wars of the Roses, she was gone. The chair mocked him, innocently empty of the large buttocks it should have been cushioning; the lamp beamed down earnestly on an empty desk, and the window yawned out on the dewy night. When I craned out I could actually see the trail she had left, like a snail, a track of duller slate on the dew-silvered verandah roof.

'I am not a complete fool, Lilian,' I told her next morning, as she fiddled drooping-eyed with her eggs. I was dizzied by my own voice crashing around among the walls. 'I am not entirely obtuse!' But she pouted like any other tease, and would not explain, or apologise, or promise better things for the future. She watched me coldly from her small eyes and said nothing. 'You are toying with me, Lilian,' I exclaimed at

her, 'and I will not have it!' The blank way she stared back
at me did not even do me the honour of being insolent. In
her eyes I was just a little ant dancing up and down, interfering with her breakfast.

◆　◆　◆

Like any cuckolded husband, I burned to know the truth.
A man of coarser feeling might have been able to employ
some sordid fellow in a greasy tweed jacket to follow Lilian
and give me a report, but I was not such a man. A pulse of
excitement began somewhere beneath my waistcoat as I laid
my plans: rage was channelled into cunning.

It was nothing so very strange for us to travel together on
the ferry into the City. 'I seem to be running a little late
today,' I said, making a big show of checking my fob-watch
against the clock on the mantelpiece. Sideways, while winding
the knob, I watched her; as I had suspected would happen,
her face fell somewhat, her eyes went shifty. But the bookbag
was already over her shoulder, her hat was already on her
head. I had timed it well: it was too late for her to avoid me.
'So we will get the ferry together this morning, Lilian,' I said,
and when she did not reply, only fiddled with the buckle of
the bag, I went on, 'That is, if you have no objection,' with
such heavy irony that she was forced to glance at me. Her
eyes skidded across me like a mirror she did not want to look
into, and she muttered ungraciously, 'Of course not, Father,
why on earth should I have any objection.'

It was not really a question, which was as well, because in
my excitement I might have made the mistake of answering

it. 'I know,' I might have crowed. 'You have no secrets from me, my girl, and I know just why you might object: you are going to meet your fancy-boy, that is why!' I smiled in a way that should have warned her, if she had been paying attention, with all my knowledge packed in behind my face, positively buttery with the pleasure of being completely on top of the situation.

The fact had always been the currency of my love for Lilian, and for the sake of allaying any suspicions she might have developed, I wove a web of facts around us so thick that she could not have seen anything behind them. 'Did you know, Lilian,' I asked as the ferry approached, 'did you know that the top speed of one of these ferries is 25 knots? And that in a nor'easter, it is up to half as fast again? And tell me, Lilian, how many tons would you think they displace?' But Lilian was too clever to give me the sport my obtuse son never failed to. 'Oh Father, how should I know?' she cried airily. 'Seventy-four? Six? Four thousand?' and went ahead of me across the gangplank, making it bend like a banana with her weight.

As soon as she sat down she got a book out of her bag and opened it. I had forgotten to bring my newspaper, and regretted it; I would have liked to forestall her by a great rustling and clattering and straightening of pages. As it was, she had the jump on me, and could withdraw from our conversation into her pages, while I did my best to pretend complete absorption in Pinchgut Island going past. *Never mind*, I consoled myself. *She may think she has beaten you now, but she will soon get her come-uppance.*

At the Quay she spoke for the first time. 'Where are you

going now, Father?' she asked, and to the eye that knew, her relief was transparent when I said, 'Oh, along Pitt Street to the office, so I will say goodbye now.'

In her relief, she made a great show of giving me a peck on the cheek. 'Bye bye, Father, see you tonight,' she said, and I was chilled to the bone by her duplicity. She was not kissing me out of any daughterly affection, but as a smokescreen: as clearly as if written upon her face, I could see her thought, 'I will be loving, for I am about to betray him.'

A lifetime of practice at not allowing my feelings to show on my face stood me in good stead now. 'Yes, Lilian, I will see you later on,' I said, and smiled inwardly to think what a short time *later on* I would see her.

I was like a panther in the jungle, here in the streets of my city: I knew every laneway and doorway, and when I wished to, I could be invisible, just one more dark suit and a mouth-slit under a hat. Almost, I would have wished it to be more difficult to lose myself among the serge backs pouring towards Pitt Street. But I did so, and then cut back down through the dog-leg lane that ran behind the tram-sheds. Blood coursed vigorously through my veins, my eyes saw into every corner: I was a healthy animal in hunting mode, padding along between the dustbins. And yes, there she was, a big fat bottom labouring up the hill with the bookbag bouncing against her calves.

It was easy, too easy for excitement, to follow her. I had a newspaper – bought especially for the purpose at the Quay – furled in my hand, ready to whip up in front of my face if necessary; my hat was low on my brow, my face was set in a soapy benign blandness that no eye would glance at twice in a crowd. As we walked up the hill, separate, yet joined by the wire of my watchfulness, I studied the way the shadows fell across the street, and worked out the lanes and doorways I could dart into if she looked back: I considered lines of sight, and invented perfectly good reasons for being here walking up Macquarie Street, rather than in my office ordering seven gross of paper-clips. I relished it all, and suspected I might have a certain aptitude for this spying business.

But I had no need of any of it. My unimaginative daughter simply went on forcing her way up the hill against gravity, brick-like in her solid refusal to speculate on what might be going on behind her.

From one or two little experiences of my own with one or two little friends, I knew of the existence of one or two little hotels in Darlinghurst where guests without luggage were made to feel at home for an hour or two, and I was prepared to see Lilian turn in that direction. But she did not, and I was pleased that I was to be given a run for my money.

Nor did she turn off towards the Gardens, so this was evidently not going to be a day on which she would lie on the grass there, to be observed by sharp-eyed employees of *Singer Enterprises*. My heart fell out of step with itself as I imagined the word getting around the back rooms. *He cannot control her, you know*, they would say. *She laughs in his face.* How dare she, how dare she, my feet beat out on the pavement. How dare you, how dare you, until I had to make myself slow down, for my feet had beaten away so assiduously I had almost run up against my daughter's back.

When Lilian reached the park at the top of the hill, she glanced at her watch and quickened her steps. It was not the Splendide or the Bijou, then, or the Gardens today: it was the geometrical avenues of Hyde Park in which my daughter had her assignation. If there had been any thought in my mind that she was innocent of guile, this clinched it. What might she be doing in the Park, pray, on a Wednesday morning at half-past nine, when a person who had taken a look at her timetable of lectures knew that she should at this moment be sitting with a hundred others in a draughty hall, writing down the salient facts about Peter the Great?

The Park was a challenge to an invisible man, the thoroughfare too wide for clusters of people to form. Even with his hat down to his eyebrows, even with his special hard-to-see buttery blandness in place, a father would be hard to miss. It was now, at this late stage in my life, that I discovered God's purpose in creating fat women. One came along, with a huge silly hat stuck to her head, bearing her enormous bosom in front of her, bound for Mark Foy's, probably, and another silly hat covered with flowers, and I allowed myself to be drawn unobtrusively into her slipstream. Her bulk, and the plumes and foliage of the hat, could have hidden half-a-dozen fathers. When we were as close as I felt I needed to be to Lilian, I lifted the newspaper again, adjusted my hat-brim, and slipped out from her shadow towards a bench from which, peeking around my newspaper, I could watch Lilian sit on the edge of the fountain.

A man invisible is a man with a situation in the palm of his hand: I was grim but buoyant. No man so clever at spying could be made mock of by his daughter for long. Behind my newspaper, behind the smooth-stretched amiable face I had put on, my spirit was fragrant with glee.

From behind my headlines, I watched her with a stranger's eye. Between us was the path, and an expanse of grass, flawlessly green as if rolled out by the yard. Dodging around her, as she sat with her legs sticking out and her bookbag sprawled at her feet, serious folk bustled along with briefcases, handbags and parcels: stolid young men who took their futures seriously, with the sun glinting blankly off their glasses, and parts in their hair as straight as tram-tracks; office-girls neat in navy-and-white, with their sleeve-protectors in their bags, and a cut lunch because they were saving for their glory-box. In all this purposeful bustle, my daughter was conspicuous: she was the fat girl with the stockings wrinkled around her ankles and her hair coming out of its fastenings, squinting into the sun with her skirt trailing in the dust. Above her, various bronze heroes of myth, somewhat larger than life size, clutched lyres and wrestled with bulls. I blushed for my daughter, perching on the rim of the fountain with an arm shading her eyes, in unconscious parody of Apollo far above her, lordly on his column with the water cascading off his private parts.

Now she was shifting her buttocks up off the rim of the fountain, hallooing and waving across the park so pigeons scattered and clerks stared: and there, angling along the path towards her, was that Duncan person from the tennis court, all elbows and ears, in a jacket too short in the arms.

I should not have been surprised, but I was. I had drawn

my own picture of Lilian's seducer, the man who lured her out over rooftops at night, and made her hollow-eyed at breakfast. The man I had drawn for her was possessed of a well-fitting jacket, did not have ears that stuck out, and knew what to do with his elbows. It was even possible that he had a splendid head not unlike my own.

My spirit drooped at seeing that it was not for any proper, red-blooded, manly sort of man that Lilian was betraying me, but for this stalk of a boy, who looked as though he needed a good propping-up with a tomato stake. Now he was bending intimately in towards her ear. His trouser-bottoms flapped and his jacket became twisted as he folded himself down to talk: he was like a praying mantis crouched over her. But she was turning her face submissively up to his, smiling as his mouth opened and closed at her and his hands sketched some kind of suggestion on the air.

◆   ◆   ◆

When they set off towards the tram stop in William Street, I was brazen. A man with metal tips on the soles of his boots hurried along the path beside me, and the self-important sound of his boots on the stone rapped out like a signal across the air: but even then I had no fears. I knew that, even if she were to turn and stare me straight in the face she would not see me, so invisible had I made myself.

It was an easy matter to insinuate myself on the back of the tram. All the long jolting way out to South Head, I watched the backs of their heads and the way their shoulders jostled against each other on every corner, and my steely pleasure grew. From the back they were quite a pair: next to skinny Duncan, Lilian was like an ocean liner, and I felt a throb of the old disgust, seeing the way her vast shoulders squeezed him up against the window. Duncan's head was long, like a bean seed, the back of his neck inflamed and stubbled from a recent encounter with some barber's clippers, and was it my imagination, or did his plate-like ears actually waggle as he talked?

When the conductress came around, Duncan handed her the money for both of them; I saw Lilian turn her head and the side of her face crinkled up in a smile, and I wanted to shout, *For God's sake, girl, it is only a ride on a tram, not the damned Crown Jewels he is buying you!*

By the time the tram neared the end of its journey, I could have told the two in front of me just what they were going to do: could have spelled out every move for them. There was nothing here at South Head – no bohemian coffee-houses, no crowds of lunchtime clerks to scandalise, no pubs that allowed young ladies to drink alongside young men – just a few scattered houses, and a lot of bush. It did not take a genius, only a man who knew the ways of the male and female of the species, to deduce what Lilian and this Duncan person were after. What they were after was bush, secluded bush, the more of it the better, where they would not be interrupted in doing what it was that I was now quite sure they were going to do.

A father might, of course, be called on to provide proof of this thing having taken place, and during the tram ride I enjoyed planning my proof. There was the conductress, I would make sure to engage her in conversation so she would

remember both the fat girl who was with the thin boy, and
also the distinguished man in the grey worsted. Then there
would be significant footprints, perhaps, immortalised in mud
along the way somewhere; and, thinking now further ahead,
to the kind of place a male and female might look for in order
to minimise the discomfort of the thing they were about to
do, there might be a thumbnail of beach somewhere, perhaps
a rock overhang, and under it soft sand which would record
the incriminating groove where two bodies had locked themselves into one another. My scientific turn of mind had even
made me think of plaster casts, and myself with a pointer:
here, ladies and gentlemen, the mark of a head is quite clear,
and if you look closely just here, you will see the shape of
Lilian Singer's bottom, kindly compare it if you please with
the original.

By various rather clever little ruses – a few questions asked
of the conductress, and bending to fasten a bootlace, and above
all trusting to sheer effrontery – I allowed them to get off the
tram ahead of me, and draw ahead, and set off down a track
with a snapped-off sign pointing into the undergrowth.

A hasty man, a thoughtless man, a man who quailed from
finishing an ugly job, would simply stride off after them, and
would be given away by the noise of twigs crushed and leaves
scattered underfoot. I knew better. I was not interested in
rustic strolls, romantic but blameless trysts along sylvan
glades. I was not wasting an entire morning on this, to have
Lilian then go all wide-eyed and pipe at me, *But Father, we
were only admiring the bush flowers, what is wrong with that?* No,
the end of this was going to be unpleasant, but I was not

going to flinch from it. I dallied, and let them draw ahead: I would take my chances on losing them. I would give them time to get to whatever spot they were going to, and commit themselves completely to what it was that they were going to do, because what I wanted was the whole ghastly picture, the entire *flagrante delicto*.

◆   ◆   ◆

Nature was not as friendly to a gentleman wishing to be discreet as were the monuments of man. There was a definite resistance to my progress along the track: my boots slithered on rocks, pebbles rolled beneath them so I had to grab for balance at thick grass that cut the side of my hand; things snagged my trouser-legs, stones rose up before my feet, roots reared to trip me; sticky flies danced in front of my eyes, sat on my lips and explored my nostrils; and in spite of a mass of trees the sun beat down on my back as if through a lens.

The track climbed around among lumpy haunches of stained yellow rock that fell away under your hand if you tried to use it as a support. Then it plunged down into a humid and airless cleft where a creek ran secretively between banks hairy with ferns. I took care not to wet my boots, and yet when I began the climb up the other side, one sock squelched at every step. Now the path skirted around the side of a low cliff above the water, where the waves had eaten away at the land leaving an overhang that one day – in geological terms, any second – would slump into the water below. The path was narrow here, only a boot's width. I could not prevent myself imagining what it would be like to slither off the shoulder of the cliff, and be forced to bleat for help. How Duncan would gape and grin, and how repugnant would be the heat of his hand in mine, hauling me up! I could not afford to slip, and I did not. But I would not have liked anyone to have seen the way I crouched along the path, clinging with both hands to rocks and bits of bush, like a shaky old woman.

Past this difficulty, I paused, for there was a trembling in the air, or in my flesh, that told me I was close. I stopped for a moment to brush down my trousers, pour the water out of my shoe, and try to stop the thudding of my heart.

I heard a cry, but of bird or person, male or female, I could not have said. I peered around me at the vile baffling rubbish of bushes and half-dead bunches of prickles, and out of the corner of my eye saw a flash of white. Irritation dropped away; a metallic calm took hold of me. My moment was upon me I was about to see what so much cleverness with hat-brims and newspapers, so much applied invisibility of featureless bland face, had provided me with: my daughter rutting like a bitch on heat.

Would I see her shake her white dimples at him, would I see the actual flesh exposed to the sun? Would I see him coming towards her bearing his skinny sundial ahead of him, and his thin white nates pumping her full of himself? Would I hear some cry torn from my daughter's throat, the alien voice of a daughter who was a daughter no longer, but a woman, known of man?

But I would wait, I promised myself, wait until the sounds became extreme, wait until the exact animal moment was upon them: yes, then, in the full flight of the uncontrollable urge, when my daughter's eyes were closed, her mouth open, her face turgid, when Duncan was groaning and humping, his eyes rolling, his jaw slack – yes, it was in that moment of the most extreme *flagrant delectation* that I would step in between them and rip them apart like a pair of dogs.

I would not shout, oh no, I myself would not join the beasts: no, I would be the man of perfect control, simply directing my daughter back home, by main force if necessary. Duncan I would deal with through the proper channels. I foresaw with pleasure the meeting with his parents. Shamed and small, they would hunch in their chairs while with my legs apart on the hearthrug, I would let them know that the police and the University authorities would be notified. *I do not see that I have any choice in the matter*, I would say blandly, and enjoyed in my mind how that would sound.

Yes, I would have to be prepared to wait – but how long? I got out my watch and stared at its face. It trembled, and the glass shot a ray of sun painfully into my eyes. I gripped it so hard my knuckles went white around it, for I was a rational man, simply wishing to measure time in a rational way for a rational purpose. I had not planned to become emotional in any way, or to feel the world going grey around my eyes, or to see the watch in my hand trembling as I gripped it: I was a man simply doing what any rational man would be doing under the circumstances.

I stared at the watch, trying to remember how the human species measured the time it might take a male and female to begin the process of coupling. *I will wait exactly five minutes*, I told myself, being systematic about the thing, but I could not seem to remember where the long hand had been when I had first looked, and was it a minute that I had been standing here, or an hour and a minute, or had the watch in fact stopped entirely?

Eventually, I became aware of a line of large white birds perched near me on a branch staring rapaciously, as if I might be a juicy grub; various insects came out from hiding and filled the air with a ragged drone, and above me leaves shivered together secretively. I moved cautiously on; not cautiously enough, however, to prevent all those peering birds bursting up from their branch with a sound like applause that made me cower. When things were quiet again, I tiptoed, as far as a man can tiptoe through tangled grass and crisp tubes of fallen bark, towards the place where I had seen the flashes of garments. As I worked my way down, I came forward in little flurries, so the sound of my crackling and popping and swishing might sound like bursts of wind, or the snap of waves: I positively tangoed down the hill. With infinite caution, I took up position behind a thick-boled tree. My face felt enormous, preparing itself like a plate to receive the sight before me, as I peered around the trunk.

◆   ◆   ◆

The sea, that heaving mother! It was playing cupid for them, or pimp. Lilian and Duncan were sitting below me on a rock shelf, their bare feet dangling in the water, with shoes, socks, stockings, bookbag, sprawled abandoned on the ground behind them. Small waves slapped and pounced at rocks, gulls wheeled and rudely screamed, and the shadow of the trees lay dark on the water. There was a patch of damp sand, garnished with blackened seaweed. There were various rocks among which waves slapped and jerked, and there were three beady-eyed gulls standing on a rock cocking their heads expectantly at the humans, shifting from foot to rubbery foot, ruffling their wings, pecking briefly into their armpits. The sleeve of Duncan's abandoned jacket flapped spasmodically against a bush like a taunt. A gull pecked experimentally at a tube of sock, a butterfly danced around the bookbag and was gone.

I was close enough to see the buttons down the back of my daughter's dress, like her spine made visible, and the tortoise-shell combs slithering out of her hair. I could see her fling out a hand with a gesture I recognised as one of my own, and Duncan in his shirtsleeves tilted back his head and laughed so that I could see his throat convulse. But the mumble of the sea snatched their words away from me. I strained until my ears felt as if out on stalks, but every time a word might have been audible, it was smothered by a wave shattering on a rock, a gull opening its beak with a creaking sound, or the wind whipping the leaves above me into a frenzy. The thing was as if calculated to tease.

Now Lilian was lying back against a boulder with her throat offered up to the lowering sun. Her posture suggested that at any moment she would unbutton her blouse and expose her virginal *titty-bags*, and suck this lad in to fill the void between her thighs. And what sort of travesty of a male was this Duncan? Would not a normal man have taken Lilian up by

now on the invitation she was so obviously offering? A cackling mad laugh from him reached me behind my tree, and I
wondered if he was really all there. Any proper man would
some time ago have progressed from mere talk and convuls-
ing throats to more definite sorts of activities. What more did
the fool need, could he not recognise a come-hither-and-do-
with-me-what-you-will when he saw it? What was he waiting
for, an engraved card?

Thanks to her father's position – her father's pounds in the
bank, to be exact – Lilian could have had her pick of the
boys. She could have chosen some red-blooded young hearty
with a boyhood of team spirit behind him and a sinecure with
Daddy ahead, someone who could listen with the proper show
of respect as a prospective father-in-law set him straight on a
few things. But no, she had chosen this one! Why, she could
have snapped him between her jaws and downed him without
so much as belching.

At the moment it seemed they were doing nothing more
inflammatory than talk. But Lilian was no innocent, and even
Duncan, dim though he was, had to know that this was not
the right way to go about things. They simply talked; but
better than most, I knew where talking could lead. I was
prepared to wait further: unless, it occurred to me now, I had
waited too long back there by the rock, staring at my watch,
and had already missed what I had come for!

I was stuck behind my tree now, committed to outwaiting
and outwitting them, but less and less sure as the time went
by that my moment would ever come. Ants crawled over my

boots, the sun bored into the back of my skull, my eyes began to smart from watching, not wanting to blink in case I missed the thing that I was more and more determined to witness.

◆   ◆   ◆

I was a patient man, but that day would have been too much for any man. As hours wore on, and more and more time was invested in this situation, it became less and less feasible to give up. Even at the risk of throwing good time after bad, I was going to stay here until I was satisfied. I shifted from foot to foot, squatted, finally sat gingerly with my bottom on a tuft of grass. Insects taunted me, lizards crept out of cracks and inspected me unblinkingly, thirst and hunger would have brought a weaker man to his knees: but Albion Gidley Singer with his blood up was a force to be reckoned with.

When they had had enough of talking, they scrambled down and paddled in the shallows, picking things off rocks and showing them to each other, and when they had done that for long enough they came back to their bags and unwrapped sandwiches. When the gulls came they threw them crusts, and when they had done that they sat and talked some more; then Duncan stood up and in a thin reedy voice that cracked and went into squeaks from trying too hard, began to recite something, no doubt the famous poetry of which he was not ashamed.

I could have told him from my own experience that a voice out-of-doors can easily sound insignificant, and become raucous trying to make an impression on such a superfluity of untrammelled air. I could have warned him that there was usually some side-show or other going on, of things tweeting or carolling from trees, or buzzing and shrilling out of the grass: even wind in leaves made a lot of noise when a person had to speak over it. Generally, the human voice was not a match for Nature, and Duncan made a pretty poor fist of his recital. However, Lilian stared up at him, and clapped whenever he stopped, so that he went on far longer than anyone reciting poetry should. I could see his earnest Adam's apple bobbing up and down, but could not hear more than the occasional single word, and gave thanks to the sounds of Nature for this small mercy.

Then Lilian sprang to her feet in a decisive way, crumbs scattering about her, and a fist thumped within my chest. Now! Now! They were going to do it now, at last! Duncan swivelled to watch her, and his hands went to his neck, loosening his tie. I almost shouted at him in my impatience and exasperation: *It is not your neck she is interested in, man, forget about your tie!*

But she only stooped to pick up her bookbag, cheap-looking in the sunlight with its embossed gold initials and fleur-delys, and took out a book. With a grunt I could hear from where I stood, she levered herself up onto a flat slab of rock and took up a pose with the book open in her hand. I recognised the book: it was a volume of the splendid tooled-leather Encyclopedia I myself had given her years ago, the Encyclopedia she had intended to learn by heart, the Encyclopedia that had brought a glow of pride to a father's heart as his daughter had filled the dining-room with her voice, shouting page after page.

'Take a moment to consider the following fact,' she called out, so ringingly that birds fell silent and the bush strained to listen. 'It is a well-established fact that the female of the species is deadlier than the male.' She stopped and lifted a finger admonishingly in the air. 'Consider the following further fact: with admirable economy, the female mantis eats the head of the male while they are copulating.' Duncan let out a sound that was either a laugh, or the sound of a man with an ant in his underpants. There was nothing amusing that I could see, and Lilian pressed on. 'The removal of the head is thought to eliminate inhibitory centres from the male; moreover he provides a useful source of nourishment.' She glanced down at Duncan: he was enraptured, staring up with his mouth ajar, rocking backwards and forwards hugging himself. 'In the next case,' she went on, holding up a second finger, 'let us take the fact of the male tiger slug, whose organ of generation emerges from his ear.' She continued, but I heard no more, in the strangeness of what was happening: before my eyes, my daughter had become someone else altogether.

I knew this person was my daughter, because it was wearing the muslin I had paid for only that week, and those were certainly the two-tone shoes from Fielding's that Norah had thought vulgar, and wanted her to return; and that was the face that I recognised from the years of family life. It was definitely my daughter, but it was not a daughter I had ever known. This face was not the artless enthusiastic face of the child who had watched her father's mouth, admiring the streams of facts it produced. This was not the clever little girl putting her hands together, setting her feet at an angle, and rattling off *The Parts of the Body in Alphabetical Order* for the pleasure of her proud father. This was not the person I had known for so many years around the meal-tables of family life, sitting like a lump of cheese over her food, staring across the damask at her father with unblinking self-possession, as she tried to match him fact for fact!

That Lilian I had known had always been a person who was far too big. She had spent her childhood wearing out chairs, her adolescence being told to suck her stomach in. She had blushed, and tried, and gone red in the face and ashamed, trying to make herself smaller than she was. But now she was like something heroic in bronze, up on her rock. A breeze swept the hair away from her broad forehead and pressed the clothes against her body so that hair and clothes seemed mere accidents, ephemera that had nothing to do with the majestic bulk of her. When she flung out a hand to emphasise something, palm up, elbow down, there was grandeur in it, and her smile said that she knew she was grand.

Her voice swam effortlessly through all this air. This was the voice of someone who was fully in charge of her own being. There was authority in it, but not argument: it was powerful, but not overbearing. It was a voice that did not have to strain or posture: it went on in its own way, but it made you want to listen. A hospitable silence received that voice: birds sat listening on their branches, insects paused in their eating and procreating long enough to hear her out; and Duncan might have come to laugh, but he stayed to listen.

With her voice swelling out through the trees, her majestic

thighs thrusting out against the skirt, her monumental shoulders bearing her up and that enormous depth of bosom swelling with words: at this moment she was not too big. At this moment she was exactly the right size.

By contrast, I was shrunken behind the tree, dwarfed by her as by a force of Nature. The thing was, if she was the right size, then it followed by a matter of simple logic that I was too small. *But it is only Lilian,* I told myself blindly. *Only my daughter Lilian, flesh of my flesh.* What could there be to be afraid of? *She cannot possibly harm you,* I told myself.

I found my own mouth taking on an authoritative sort of shape to utter words. *Silence, Lilian, it is I, your father!* I would call out, and the spell would be broken. She would shrink to her proper size, I would puff up to mine, and we would be again a male and female in proper relation. But somehow I could not make any sound come, and before I could frame the precisely-right words, and gather breath for the task, she had closed the book and was stepping down from the rock.

It was a long way down for a woman of her size, but Duncan was there, holding up his hand, taking her weight as she lowered herself. She did not let go of his hand, even after she had got down, but listened to something Duncan was whispering in her ear that made her smile so her teeth gleamed.

At this distance, and with a young man's arms half around her, my daughter looked every inch a woman. You could see the strong muscles of her back outlined through the stuff of her dress, and one powerful leg, like a small body in itself, was thrust forward to take her weight. Her hem was hanging crooked, and there was a leaf in her hair. Certainly she was enormous, but I looked at her with new eyes, and saw that when out-of-doors, with the soft shadows on her hair, and the blood in her cheeks, Lilian was by no means repugnant.

◆   ◆   ◆

I was coiled, ready, but before I had time to spring out with accusation in my mouth, they had pulled apart, gone to their strewn clothes, and begun to put them on. There was something chillingly matter-of-fact about the way they sat down and methodically went about it. Duncan stuck out his chin and stretched his knobbly neck to tighten his tie; Lilian pushed her hair back into shape, her mouth full of hair-pins: it was like watching an old married couple in a frowsy bedroom.

Rage rose within me in a toxic whiteness. Cheated! I had waited all this time to see them take their clothes off, and here they were putting them back on! I must indeed have waited too long with my watch in my hand, earlier on: even while I had been watching the seconds ticking away they must have been doing it! I had waited all day, and waited in vain: I had missed it, and missed it through my own damned cleverness, when a stupider man would have blundered onwards and caught them bare-bummed!

When they were dressed they looked at each other, and that was worse than anything that had gone before. As Duncan smiled at Lilian, I saw the full radiance of one human sending out a signal to another. His was a soft and lingering look, a look that sealed a promise. There was something obscene in the naked tenderness of his face as it looked at her.

But that flabby look of abject adoration on Duncan's face released in my daughter a person her father had never seen. This new daughter of mine gestured and smiled, tucked her hair behind her ears with an appealing gesture borrowed from some prettier girl, tossed her head so that the hair came loose again and shone in the sunlight. She was flushed and pink, positively winsome as she reached up to brush something off Duncan's shoulder, so that he must have felt her panting breath hot on his cheek. With a pang, watching her, I thought, *When did my daughter last smile at me?*

I watched her with a fullness in my heart I could not name, an ache like hunger or fear: it was some kind of chemical reaction going on within my organism that was new to me, and so painful I thought I might groan aloud.

Lilian picked up her bookbag, Duncan screwed his tie into his neck, and they began to climb, heads bowed, up the hill towards me. I could hear Lilian breathing now, and the bump of her bookbag against her legs, the crackle and clatter as her shoes crushed bark and leaves, the swish of the branches she pushed away in front of her. I was close enough now to hear the hiss of her skirt around her legs; I could almost have reached out a hand and touched her as she passed, stroked her hair, sinuous as it slipped out of its combs and unravelled down her back, and I thought I could even smell the musk of her as she passed.

She was laughing as she went by me, and calling over her shoulder at something Duncan had said. 'Oh no,' she was crying. 'Absolutely not by any manner of means, my dear!' She was as radiant as if there could be no such person in the world as a father.

If I had spoken – *Look over here, Lilian, here I am* – and she had turned, I felt with a chill that she would not have recognised me. Once, in fact, as she glanced back at Duncan, it seemed to me that her eyes met mine, but the awareness of me was pushed away like a bit of flotsam, and her eyes skidded over me. She looked, but she did not see.

Simple invisibility was not what was going on here. Invisibility was only half the picture. I myself had given thought to the matter of being invisible, had applied my not inconsiderable intelligence to the matter, and had succeeded. What was going on here, what was causing the breath to gag in my throat, was something else again. There was my daughter, breathing, laughing, glancing around at Duncan. Her mouth was opening and closing around words, her brain was marshalling thoughts, arranging phrases: and as far as all that vigorous internal activity of hers was concerned, I was simply not a factor. I just did not feature on her map of the world: never had, never would. Watching her, snuffing up the fragrance of her, seeing the corner of her eyes wrinkling as she smiled at Duncan, I saw that she was not Lilian Singer making a monkey of her father. She was not a nice girl with an expensive education, throwing it all away to spite Daddy. She was simply an organism going about its own blind business of seeking out what brought it pleasure.

I was no longer behind the tree; I was now standing boldly right out in the open, staring up the hill at them. If they had cared to turn, if they had so much as glanced my way, they could not have failed to see me. I did not blink, did not move a muscle; my eyes were dry and stiff from watching, my face scraped bare with waiting for her to turn: but she did not turn. I saw my hand make a convulsive gesture like a wave gone wrong. Would they not turn? Would she not see me at all? *Look, Lilian,* I thought, willing the words from my brain into hers. *Turn, Lilian, for God's sake, look, I am here.* But she did not turn.

I watched their backs move steadily away from me up the path and on the breeze I caught gusts of syllables, fragments of laughing, a cry as she flung out an arm with an extravagant gesture. She and Duncan were supremely solid up there, in the sun that made black shadows in their folds: they were etched on the air with needle-sharp clarity. When they moved, or flung out an arm, a weighty black shadow fell away from them, also moving or flinging out an arm.

They became small in the distance, but even small they were still the most convincing elements among all this flimsy vegetation, and their voices cut cleanly through the still air. I, on the other hand, had become transparent, nothing more than a few molecules clinging to the bark of a tree.

◆　　◆　　◆

I watched them until they were out of sight. As they disappeared around the shoulder of the hill, the quality of the air around me underwent a change. All at once I was very completely alone, and alone in a way that was more than simply a man being by himself. It was astonishing just how quickly the bush folded itself around a person. Silence surrounded me like a fluid. The sun went behind a cloud, and there was a sudden chill in the air; the trees loomed over me in an unfriendly way and darkness seeped upwards out of the ground. These spindly ailing bushes, this coarse dead-looking grass, these untidy trees with their random clumps of leaves, swallowed up man and his works the way sand soaks up water: soaked it up and gave nothing back but this watchful silence.

I touched the trunk of one of the trees, just to feel something press against my shell, and it was as cold as a reptile. I was scooped hollow by invisibility and by silence. I was the tiniest, least important bit of rubbish here, just a brittle shell lost among the bush. Everywhere here, nature was getting on with its business: ants hurried around to feed their young, trees strangled each other competing for light, bushes thrust flowers out to tempt bees: everything was blindly going about the endless business of dominion and reproduction. Only I myself was of no account, simply a husk waiting for decay.

Chapter Twenty-Nine

DAWN CAME IN by the front door and fingered my cheek; some bird warbled in a watery way, a kookaburra began to choke, and a day had begun. I awoke from a dream of my daughter in which her lust was made manifest. 'Come to me,' her face, rubbery with dream-lust, mouthed. 'Come to me and make me whole.' From such a dream I awoke choked by my clothes, a twisted body in an armchair like a crumpled doll, stiff in every joint. My boots had an imbecile look sprawled on the carpet and my fingers had congealed in the night.

My daughter had slipped out the previous evening, before I had had a chance to confront her, and I had sat up in an armchair by the front door, for Albion Gidley Singer was not going to be made mock of by his daughter any longer. But she had not returned. I listened now and the house spoke back to me. *She is not here*, it said. *She has not returned.*

I knew then that the dawn was fingering my cheek in a way that meant this day would be like no other, and that those scornful warbling birds knew that something was happening that was new in the world. I stretched and gathered my boots, and tugged at the clothes that had become twisted in the night, roped by dreams, and knew that before darkness fell on the world again, I would have joined myself to my echo and become whole.

Out on the terrace, Norah's wicker chair gaped and the flagstones tried to buckle beneath my feet. My daughter spoke aloud to me here in the shred of pink nightdress-silk, just the shade of flesh, dangling from a splinter in a post of the verandah. *Look*, this flesh-coloured tatter crowed. *Look, Father*. The dawn spoke to me with my daughter's voice. *Yes, Father*, it said. *See what I have left for you to find*, and the pink silk trembled in a breeze from nowhere.

I laughed aloud then, so that birds flew up from the lawn and a cat leapt down from somewhere and ran under a shrub. I laughed to feel the air fill my belly, for my daughter had left me a message, and it was not a message I was going to ignore.

I laughed aloud, and the milkman stared at me from the driveway, standing in a nimbus of steam from his horse's droppings, and I laughed again, and called down to him heartily, 'Fine morning for it,' and the red-faced large-handed man showed me a few teeth and called back in a startled way, 'Too right, sir.'

I stood watching sun swallow the shadows of the grass in the lawn and the dew rising off the flagstones: stood, a father whose hour had come.

◆　　◆　　◆

When John came down, and Alma rang the little brass bell for breakfast, I stood at the head of the table, preparing for a day different from all the others. On the walls, the exotic faces approved. Their eyes all watched me and encouraged. John came in like a sick bird, all sideways and ugly, and gripped his chair until I spoke, so loudly that the exotic faces stared. 'Sit, John,' I said, 'and eat your egg. Your sister will be attended to later.' I had to laugh, thinking of how I would attend to my daughter later, and how somewhere not far away she waited, attentive, for me to attend to her.

'John,' I said, and he spilled the piece of egg that was on its way to his mouth. 'John,' I said when his glasses were turned towards me, listening. 'Lilian cannot be found, John, so you and I will go to the Agricultural Show, as planned, without her.' John was visibly disappointed that I would not abandon the plans I had made for the day. I made him admire the *Largest Egg Ever Laid In Australia*, reproduced in the paper that morning, but it seemed to suggest nothing to him. 'Can you imagine what elastic-sided chook must have given birth to this monstrous egg?' I asked jovially, hoping to create a flicker of interest on my son's face, but his was the blank face I would have had, if I had not learned how to hide behind a frown. 'John,' I said, 'you will be a man one day, does this grotesque egg suggest nothing to you?' but his stare indicated that it meant nothing at all.

For the sake of this feeble son, though, it was necessary to put up a show of looking for Lilian, and although anticipation was beginning to tick along my veins into each fold and pucker of my being, as another kind of plan for the day began to take shape, I acted the part. 'We will look for your sister,' I told John when we had finished our eggs and were standing in the front hall. 'We will give her one last chance.'

I did not join the search myself. That did not seem a necessary part of the ritual, and after all I might have made the mistake of finding her. Close to my shoulder the shred of pink silk hung like a promise. I watched the shadow of my thin son – how insubstantial he was on the grass – wandering crookedly from bush to bush, hesitating, drooping like a weed. His shadow fluttered and faltered, he peered and frowned. The son of a hollow father, he seemed next to nothingness itself.

I waited for John, and would not have him guess at my impatience to be gone. 'Lilian does not have the power to make me change my plans,' I announced to John and to the stairway in general. 'Lilian is not of sufficient importance for that.' John still stared, and in the silence between us, in which I wanted to poke his nose, to see any kind of expression on his face, we heard Cook and Alma downstairs setting out for their day off. 'Hurry up,' Cook called to Alma, and her voice echoed up the stairs to where a father stood with his son.

A band of blood-coloured light lay across the father's boot, from the stained glass beside the front door. Across the chin of the son was a band of leaf-green. Both faces were speckled as if ill from the etched fern pattern in the glass. The father and son stood in this unlikely light, watching each other for a sign, while between them Alma's voice was robust. 'Coming, love, keep your blooming hair on!'

A door slammed down in the scullery and the father made himself move. 'Well, John,' I said, and moved my boot out of the blood-coloured light. 'We are going to enjoy the wonders of Nature today, Lilian or no Lilian.' John blinked and moved so that his whole face was green, then red. 'Yes, Father,' he said, in that way he had, that left me unsatisfied. A robust son with a bit of revolt in him would have made a man of me. 'Yes, Father,' this failed son said, and went upstairs so I was left with nothing, filling some stranger's boots and clothes in coloured light.

We left the house at last, John trailing behind me, my cane decisive on the path. 'Do not look back, John,' I told my son, and pulled at him by his bony elbow. 'Forget about your sister.'

◆　　◆　　◆

At the Show piglets squealed and bulls' balls hung low. There was rank animal carnality everywhere. My hopeless son squinted and blinked and would not look at the dangling bulbs, the hairy pizzles. 'Observe, John,' I told him. 'Observe: it is a visible fact that bulls are the most virile of creatures.' John only blinked and squinted more, and when I jabbed at him, to wake him up, he said, 'What is virile, Father, does it mean hairy?' I would have hit him, but knew nothing more interesting would happen than him sitting on soiled straw, squinting and blinking and rubbing his pathetic bottom. 'Virile, John –' perhaps more forcefully than I intended, so a pair of women looked around and met my eye suggestively – 'virile, John, is what men are. Women are not virile, virility is what we men do to them.' John did not understand, but the ladies behind us did, and one tittered behind a glove. 'Ladies,' I said, and would have gone on: 'Enlighten my son, please, ladies,' I would have said. 'Tell my son about virility,' but they had disappeared behind a cow, and were lost to me with their long lustful eyes.

It was easy to fob John off with a ten-shilling note, brown as dung. 'It is time you had a good time, John,' I told him, but he did nothing but go on blinking at me like a parrot. 'Go and run wild, John,' I told him, and he shuffled his feet in the straw. 'It is time you learned to deal with life, John,' I cried at him. 'Think of Dickens washing those bottles, and Dick Whittington!' My son seemed never to have heard of Dickens or Dick Whittington, but he went on crushing the ten-shilling note in his hand. 'Here,' I said, and gave him another note. 'For God's sake, go away, John.' My son was boring me, and the cows all around us were piddling into the straw.

Chapter *Thirty*

THE HARBOUR sang its sweet song before my feet at the jetty, and a gull bobbed smugly on a swell of green water, watching me with an unblinking beady eye. A smudge on the sky was a fact indicating another fact: that the ferry was on its way. The water appeared to be solid. It sucked in the most leisurely way at the hairy pilings of the jetty, breathing quietly. The gull floated with not a ripple and I was almost sure that I could stride out without so much as wetting my boots, straight across the water to the room where my daughter was waiting for me.

Behind me I heard silk rustling, clinging to some woman's thighs as she moved down to wait for the ferry. I felt her watching my fine manly back: her silk rustled again and I heard her face beating the air behind my head. 'And shall you do it?' she asked in a clear languid voice, and I turned. There was not just one face, but two; two silk dresses, a total of four female thighs, and two mouths turned towards me. Four breasts thrust at me under silk and between those four thighs were two womanly clefts, moist and attentive, waiting. 'Why, Mr Singer,' one of those mouths said, and showed its teeth. Between the teeth the tongue flickered an invitation, lewd, unmistakeable. 'Lovely day, Mr Singer, don't you think?' After the mouth had finished with the words it did not quite close over the teeth and that fleshy tongue, and between those thighs, hot under mauve silk, another mouth was also ajar.

'Good morning, Mr Singer,' the mouth in blue said. 'Oh, that water looks good enough to eat!' This other mouth was not as fleshy as the first but was moister, glistening as it formed the words and winking at me as it opened and closed around sounds. Open, close, open, close.

Our ferry was at the wharf now, and those mouths full of longing had to swallow their lust and trip across a plank and into the ferry. 'Good morning, ladies,' I said, and bowed, and offered my hand to assist them on the plank, and felt the raging fire of their flesh through the gloves of the fingers that grasped my hands. My hand glowed from the scald of their passion, and I watched them walk to the bow, watched four buttocks move up and down against each other under their blue and their mauve. Those buttocks beckoned me to follow, but I smiled, knowing that I would leave the mauve and the blue still panting, longing for male flesh but unfulfilled.

◆   ◆   ◆

Back at the house I did not simply stride in through the front gate. As quiet as the very air, I let myself in by the trades-man's entrance, holding the latch up with my finger so it did not click – I was deft, I could do no wrong! – and slipped quietly in past the dustbins. It was a limpid morning when every atom seemed a fact, when the air was of such a clarity that objects were for once indubitable. My shadow slid ahead of me along the path, up the back steps, and fell upon the door. This is a door, I told myself, and placed my palm flat against it. My shadow lay crisp and authoritative on the wood: today even the shadow of Albion Gidley Singer was a thing of substance.

The air in the house was hushed when I entered, and I slipped from room to room without creating a single ripple. It was a silent house, but it was not an empty house: the silence was full of my daughter. Somewhere, in one of these rooms, she was waiting for me. I had only to go from room to room, systematically, and I would find her.

The air in her bedroom tried to stifle me as I investigated. There was her narrow white bed, that held her large animal body; but it showed nothing. There was no evidence of writhing passion on the virginal white cover, there were no tear-tracks on the pillow. I opened her wardrobe, where filmy frocks hung wistfully, empty, and I thrust my face among them, but there was no one there, no scent, no shiver of self. My daughter's frocks were not what held her: only her skin did that. Her shoes meant more. The leather had been creased and distorted by her feet, and smelled of animal. I put a pair on my hands and walked them across the floor, and for a moment I was my daughter, filling her shoes.

In the drawers of the dresser, smelling of lavender like poor Norah's, lay the things that were secret next to her skin, flesh-coloured snakes of garments with lace and straps that slithered through my hands like living things. Oh, bloomers that held my daughter's secrets! My fingernails caught in these garments and their lavender coolness frightened me.

A curtain tried to take me by surprise, shifting sideways at me in the draught. I jammed the drawer in haste, and caught my wrist in it when it abruptly closed. I saw myself leaving my hands in the drawer, lying cool and wax-like among my daughter's underclothes, lying there like the bags of lavender, my fingers and palms and the hairy backs of my hands forever sliding among the camisoles and bloomers. I thought of how I could go handless to my study and sit thinking blessedly of nothing, of my hands nested and coddled in fine cambric, waiting for my wrists to grow new hands so that I could fill all my daughter's drawers with them, my hands everywhere.

It was a seductive idea, but there was another that beckoned, and I obeyed. I moved through the waiting halls of the house, nothing more substantial than a puff of air floating between the walls, and around each corner I drew closer to the beating heart of my house. There were sounds going on, somewhere: small sounds, but to my knowing ears, large enough.

◆　　◆　　◆

I stood at last outside the door of the bathroom. Within were rustlings and snappings, a slap of fabric on flesh, a sigh of silk slithering over itself, a dry sound of foot-sole on tile. Inclining my head, I found I could see through the gap where the door was not completely closed, and I drew closer. I did not allow a single rustle or heartbeat to give me away; I was nothing but silent cells moving over each other.

I had expected to see Lilian, naturally. But I had not expected three of her, reflected in the three-faced pier-glass, and I had not expected her nude. Her flesh in the mirror was greenish and massive, the light falling on it in soft shadowed ways. Staring-eyed nipples swung around majestically on the points of her bosoms as she moved; the bosoms themselves trembled and shifted, ripples of movement passing across them. They were as soft as water, yet were the most solid and undeniable things I had ever seen. They were like bags of fruit, or skins of water, or sea creatures: faceless, globular, bursting out of their skins, yet each one swung and hung, pointed and lolled, with a weighty will of its own.

Naturally, I had seen bosoms before: the pert titties of Agnes and Una had flirted at me often enough, and Norah's emptied bags had flattened under my grip. But bosoms like this, gigantic, vigorous, bold-eyed, alien! Six of them would be too much for any man.

Then there was the belly, another shock, not like the little belly of Agnes or Una, a neat tame mound under a man's hand. Nor was it that soft belly of Norah's, with the meaty stripes made by her corsets lurid against the white flesh as she lay stretched out on the bed with her face turned away. This belly was a type altogether foreign: much too big for a man's hand to encompass, not flecked and striped, but gigantic, unabashed, sitting up high and round with a smooth glowing complexion like a happy face.

It appalled me to know that all this flesh had always been

underneath her clothes. Norah had poked and prodded, and tried stripes and pintucks, posture exercises and deep-breathing, but under all the expensive fabrics and all the tricks and trompe-l'œil there had always been this flesh: uncompromising, solid, immovable, flesh simply there, flesh that could not be denied, flesh that was not prepared to come to any kind of accommodation with pintucks or dropped waists.

Below was her secret mound, but it was not covered like Norah's with demure little fuzz. Nor was it plucked bald, like the mound of the current Agnes or Una, for the greater enjoyment of her gentlemen friends. This mound was hidden by a great black bush springing out, lush, feral, shocking against her pale skin. Lilian seemed to find it wonderful. She pinched it between her fingers and pulled it out to its uncoiled length, she twisted it around, she fluffed it up, she stroked it down. She played with her own dreadful growth of hair as if it were a pet.

All at once she was gone from the mirror, and I was blinded by the sudden blankness of the glass. I blinked, and she was back, those lolling things on her chest pivoting around on themselves, staring in all directions, and she had my nail scissors in her hand. She bent over double, breasts hanging, belly bulging, and snipped off a pinch of that wiry hair between her thighs. As the scissors closed over the hair she screwed up her face as if she thought it would bleed, but when it was done, she winked at herself in the mirror as if at a lover.

Oh, she loved herself! Her six hands lifted her six great globes of breasts as if weighing them, and she laughed aloud at all the cleavages she could make by pressing them together. She sucked in all her bellies and ran her hands up and down herselves, hands everywhere caressing, congratulating, relishing the way the flesh went in and out. She swept her hair up with her hand, and three heads tilted this way and that, ogling themselves with a leer that showed six sharp eye-teeth. She postured and posed, and blinked her eyelids at herself; she smiled and pouted, frowned and simpered: she tried herself out on herself as if she had never seen herself before.

As perhaps she had not. Lilian's room was the room of a clean-living young girl, who only needed a mirror to tell her whether her hair needed brushing or her face needed washing, and no child of mine was permitted to dally in bathrooms getting up to mischief. I watched my daughter going through this grotesque exercise in self-adoration and realised that this day, with everyone gone from the house, may have been the first time she had ever been alone in the house with a mirror.

As I watched, she lay down and spread her knees apart, opening herself up like a nutcracker, and pressed back the flesh of her thighs with her hands: the girl was actually trying to see in! She could not, of course, no matter how she strained and jerked her hips at the mirror; I could hear her panting from the effort, but a woman's secret place has been designed by Mother Nature to remain unseen by its owner. But Lilian was unstoppable: now she was poking around with her finger, actually probing up inside herself; now she was sniffing at the finger, and now, my God, she was pushing out the tip of her tongue until it came in direct contact with that same finger: she was actually tasting her own slime! It was enough to make anyone sick.

◆　◆　◆

Perhaps my disgust crackled with audible sparks: Lilian froze, and she raised her head so that I could see her face in the mirror, very still, listening. When she rolled over onto her knees and started to get up, clutching at those slippery bosoms, trying vainly to hide their bulk behind her hands, I knew she had seen me.

I opened the door to its full width and came up close to her.

'You are vile and degenerate,' I told her quietly, but she only shook her head and cringed away from me. 'You are disgusting,' I told her, more in sorrow than anger, and joined her in the mirrors. Next to such a crowd of sprawling flesh on display, thighs and titties everywhere you looked, the other person in the mirror with her was large and dark, tightly packaged, bound around with layers of garments that revealed no flicker of flesh.

Lilian met my eyes in the mirror: for a moment all that bulbous flesh dropped away, and it was just Lilian and myself, eye-to-eye in the mirror. If she had spoken to me, or smiled into that private moment, just the two of us, I could have forgiven her everything. But she turned away, and scrabbled on the floor for her clothes, holding them up against her like rags. I laughed aloud, and glimpsed out of the corner of my eye the three laughing mouths of Albion Gidley Singer showing their teeth. 'It will take more than that, my girl, to hide yourself,' I thought, and the men in the mirror stripped the shreds of cloth off all the soft maggot-shapes, and wrestled them to the floor. But as Lilian fell she snatched up Norah's corset from where it lay, and she got it in front of her so that as we all fell together the thing had its whalebone ribs hard against mine. The dark men in the mirror did not seem to feel it, but I did. I ripped it out from between us and threw it across the room: it was a white bird arching through all the mirrors before it fell against the door with a silly twittering of its suspenders.

◆   ◆   ◆

Her flesh under me was not soft, not yielding, not warm and comforting as it had seemed, green in the mirror, giving itself up to her own touch. It was lumpy and resistant, it bucked and arched away under me, it pushed against me with its hands and tried to get away. 'You want it,' I reminded it. 'You have wanted it for years,' but the flesh found its voice now and made a shrill reedy noise, a roaring in my ear like a machine gone wrong. 'No no no!' it said, then louder 'No! No! No!' But I had always known the answer to that one. I felt the muscles of my arms take up the strain as I pinned it down, felt my thighs overwhelm it, and roared my answer so that the voice was drowned: 'Yes! Yes!'

The fight went out of her when I got her arms pinned: her body under mine lay squashy, slack, waiting. Her head was turned away, her hair all over it like a veil: oh, these women and their turnings-away! From having roared and panted in my ear, now there was no evident breathing going on, nothing at all moved, as if all her systems were abdicating in order to allow her to do this. With my palms against her cheeks I swivelled her face to mine and raked the hair off it. There was her face, exposed like a rock in the wind: there were her eyes; but when I forced the head around so that the eyes were looking into mine, all I could see was more of myself, two tiny versions of Albion Gidley Singer looking back at me. Lilian, the daughter I knew, who spoke to me, looked me in the eye, exchanged facts and requests for the salt-shaker, that cranky, obdurate, insolent thorn in my flesh, was withdrawing and leaving only her shell behind, the way a lizard leaves its tail in your hand.

Now that there was nothing more complicated than an empty body in the room with me, I was enabled to motion my inner man to come close. Albion Gidley Singer, pillar of the community, model husband, astute businessman, man with astonishing facts at his fingertips: that person was able to tiptoe away and leave in charge of this situation the nameless secret speck of being who lived within.

Words fell away from me as that nameless secret speck of being expanded to fill the space available to him. He was a being who did not need words, or a past, or a future, or any kind of stories spun around himself about being a model husband or a businessman with facts at his fingertips. The language of this being, no longer a speck, now a colossus straddling this moment of history, was the language of action, and he needed no lessons in the kind of action the situation called for.

Oh, epiphany of flesh! I surrendered myself to myself, and now, as never before, my skin separated me from nothing at all. I and myself were blissfully joined, and for once there was no voice judging, chiding, doubting, fearing: only this warm blank darkness like the inside of a soul, and the sounds of something labouring and panting. I heard a groan forced up from the depths of my self, and felt sweat break out on my skin like tears. I burst with the heat of bliss, and in a blaze of cells like the creation of life from mud, I gave birth to myself.

After I was made whole in my daughter there was silence in heaven. Outside I could hear a bird warbling in an insistent way, over and over tra-la, tra-la. There was a rattle of wind against the window, and a gnashing of the leathery leaves of the eucalypt beyond it. A band of sunlight lay bent across a corner of the wall like a hard problem in geometry, and close to my eye I could see pores, tiny hairs, fine creases on the gleam of skin. The shell of my daughter lay beneath me as empty as a bag. She had collapsed in on herself, proving herself to have been nothing but air in spite of so much bulk.

I levered myself up, and three Albion Gidley Singers stood: the room was full of legs in dark trousers. I looked fearlessly into the mirror, and it was myself looking out from the eyeball-sockets I saw there. It seemed that Albion Gidley Singer and myself had undergone some type of fusion. No longer was it necessary to issue curt commands to the shell I inhabited: the shell and the self were now blessedly one and the same. There was no brittle carapace, vulnerable to the right kind of sharp implement, and no soft jelly within: there was only solid Albion Gidley Singer, Albion Gidley Singer all the way through. 'Albion Gidley Singer,' I told the face in the mirror, whose skin I now inhabited. 'Yes, I am Albion Gidley Singer.'

Chapter *Thirty-One*

NORAH'S TROPICAL cruise left her brown as a savage, and somewhere along the way she had cut off her hair. 'Oh, Albion, it was such a nuisance!' she cried when she saw me looking. 'And everyone agreed how well it suited me,' and she spun around on the ball of her foot like a dancer so that her bangs twirled around her ears. Personally, I found it extremely unfeminine: you could see the shape of her skull now, and her head had a naked look; you noticed her eyes more now, and her mouth. But a gentleman could not be blunt. 'Well, it is your hair, Norah,' I said in my blandest way. 'And if everyone has told you it suits you, then it probably does.' Her hands went up to it then, smoothing it down, and she did not do any more pirouettes. 'Well, Albion, it will grow again, in any case,' she said, and attempted a laugh. 'And it makes a change.'

We lined up to receive poker-worked artefacts from far-flung places, and were presented with large hairy coconuts. Norah handed around tinted postcards of volcanoes, palm

trees, and picturesque natives squinting at the sun, and we all
listened to her tales of waves and waterfalls, fire-walking and
egg-swallowing, with the right expressions of wonderment.
John was particularly interested in the volcanoes. There was
something disturbing in his relish at the idea of the earth
under your feet corking up all that red-hot magma. 'If you
dug down far enough, it would all squirt out!' he exclaimed
with unusual enthusiasm, and when he lapsed into silence it
was easy to imagine him considering spades and promising
spots in the garden.

Lilian was subdued, kept her head down, and did not seem
to appreciate her coconut. She could not even be got to smile
at Norah's stories of the *little scallywag of a monkey* that had
run up her arm and snatched her earring away. No, Lilian
was still determined to go on sulking, as she had been sulking
for several weeks now, and even Norah finally noticed. 'What
is the matter, Lilian?' she asked, 'Is anything wrong, dearest?'
But Lilian just stared at the carpet between her feet and shook
her head mulishly. 'Lilian is going through a little growth
spurt,' I told Norah, 'and I think it has sapped her vitality.
Plenty of eggs will soon put her right.'

We took a turn around the garden, and when Norah noticed
the bars on Lilian's window, I explained. 'It was a terrible
danger,' I told her. 'Why, a man could have shinned up the
verandah-post and got in to her at night!' and Norah had to
nod, 'Yes, Albion, I can see that, now that you point it out.'

But I did not tell Norah about the way Lilian had locked
herself in her room, and bunged up the keyhole with paper,
and refused to come out until finally hunger drove her to join

the family once more. Nor did I bother to tell her about a little runty boy in black – not the Duncan boy – who said he was one of her classmates at University, who had come to the house wanting to know where she was, and rashly offering to marry her. Another admirer! Lilian had certainly been generous with herself.

But even Norah had to notice that Lilian was no longer quite right in the head. 'Albion, there is something wrong with Lilian,' she told me. 'She seems to have some kind of funny idea in her head, but will not tell me what it is.' Of course something was wrong with Lilian: there had always been something wrong with Lilian! But I was bluff and reassuring. 'It is just a funny little phase, Norah,' I told her. 'Perhaps she is having some sort of infatuation with one of the boys in her class, a touch of calf-love. No doubt she will get over it shortly.'

❖ ❖ ❖

But things went from bad to worse. There were silences, there were unexplained disappearances from the house for hours at a time, and there was an increasing slovenliness of personal habits. She spent more and more time in her room with her University books, and although, naturally, we were pleased to see her taking her studies seriously, there was something unhealthy about the way she hunched obsessively over the books, and did not want to come down to dinner.

We took her to O'Hara, but all O'Hara could do was to take her pulse, peer into her ears, and get her to say *Ahhh*. But what was wrong with Lilian was not to be heard in her chest, or seen down her throat. I rather got the impression that in the absence of proper symptoms in a patient, O'Hara had only two remedies: one was *the cruise*, already prescribed in vain for Norah, and the other was *the tonic*. But even a pint of the vile brown stuff made not the slightest difference to Lilian, who became if anything more truculent and withdrawn.

O'Hara then spoke in a vague way of *over-stimulation of the cerebellum*, so we got rid of all her books, and the empty shelves in her room gaped in an ugly way. The desk went, and so did the chair; the telescope, the taipan in its bottle, the globe of the world; all were taken up to the attic. In the end, the room was empty but for the bed, the wardrobe, and the chest of drawers. It was a room lovingly stripped of any incitement to *stimulation of the cerebellum*.

'You must be right, Albion, it is just a little phase,' Norah kept telling me, but to my mind the thing had the look, not so much of a *little phase*, as of deliberate provocation.

In spite of the bars on the windows, and the confiscated shoes, and myself sitting up in an armchair in the hall, she continued to slip out at night. *Nothing!* she shouted when I accused her. *I am doing nothing! Just being!* But I was no fool, and could see the sand on her knees, and the leaves in her hair. What kind of fool did she take me for?

There were visits from men in thick boots, twisting their caps round in their hands and complaining of the noise. 'It is not for myself, Mr Singer,' they would say in the over-loud way of a man put up to something. 'It is my wife, she has a bad back' – or a bad head, or funny turns – 'and the stones on the roof at five in the morning, well, it is a bit much,

Mr Singer.' Then they would remember something else, and know that the wife with the bad back would want to know if everything had been said. 'And the dogs, Mr Singer, it is not right the way she teases them, it is in their nature to bark, of course, but working folk need their sleep.'

There was a visit from a seedy red-faced man who told me he was the proprietor of a cinema in the city, and told me to keep my daughter under my control. 'Next time it will be the police, Mr Singer, I warn you,' he cried, and left before I could quite come up with an answer. Then there was a visit from a smiling smooth man with an armful of expensive shiny books which I recognised. 'I could hardly refuse her, Mr Singer, and gave her a pound each for them, but I thought you might appreciate them back,' and having paid for these unread books once, I was obliged to pay for them again. Once the money was safely in his pocket, he taunted me: 'Your daughter is quite a card, Mr Singer, no doubt about it, she was telling us last time that she is in touch with a higher power, would you believe.' He kept on smiling away insistently, so that I began to think he had some other scheme to make a few quid out of the mad Singer girl. I could imagine him smiling and winking to his wife, 'Fine family, plenty of money, embarrassing sort of thing to get around.' But I would not have any of that, and saw him off the premises very smartly.

I was not provoked by men with caps in their fists, I was not provoked by men with red faces, I was not even provoked by smiling unscrupulous booksellers. But finally, Lilian succeeded, and I was provoked.

When she ran away, and was returned to us with a police-
man on each side of her, and a story of her parading the
streets of Tamworth stark naked, we were forced to intervene.

The best man for this sort of thing was summoned, and
emerged shaking his head. Pink-faced as a baby behind his
muttonchop whiskers, he was bland and uninformative. 'We
may be able to catch it in time,' he said, 'but there must be
absolutely complete rest.' He continued to repeat his formula
as the papers were being signed. 'Rest and routine, Mr Singer,
and Mrs Singer,' he kept saying. 'Rest and routine may work
wonders.'

◆   ◆   ◆

The house was wonderfully peaceful with Lilian gone, and
outside in the garden, the world seemed all sky. Scales fell
from me, so that I felt air against my skin and enjoyed the
caress of my clothes. Sunlight was solid, but so was I: it had
to make way for me as I breasted the air like a ship slicing
through waves. Molecules of air were thrust aside by my chest
and fell into place behind me. As never before I was aware
now of the flights of clouds across vast expanses of blue. I saw
branches thickening with leaves before my very eyes, heard
feathered things shrill and tweet in the dusky depths of trees.

When I thought of Lilian in the place in which she was
undergoing her *rest and routine*, the blood beat exuberantly
through my veins. I strode around the garden, seeing pigeons
scatter in front of my authoritative cane. My boots gleamed
and squeaked as if they enjoyed a life of their own. 'Morning,
Mr Singer,' someone in a cap said, tweaking at it as he came

in the tradesman's entrance, and I nodded, pleased to be recognised by this minion whose life and livelihood were dependent on me.

As I strode, rousing poetry rose into my memory from some pouch filled long ago, and not explored until now. My feet thumped along the path, beating out the lines like a flail. *We sprang to the stirrup, and Jorrock, and he, They galloped, he galloped, we galloped all three*, I said to myself, feeling the powerful muscles in my thighs as I strode faster to keep up with the rhythm. Or was it *I galloped, we galloped, they galloped all three?* I strode around poking at the earth with my cane, a happy man. *All at once I saw, fluttering and dancing in the breeze*, I told myself, seeing some kind of tidy flower jerking at its stem in the breeze, *a something, a something, of golden daffodils!*

Poor old Lilian, I thought when I remembered. She had been made of pretty poor stuff, after all. What she had wanted, she had got, but it had turned out to be all bluster, and now all she could do was sulk and play the fool. She was huge, but she had turned out to be hollow, and it had taken only a single touch to burst her bubble. Personally, I was skeptical of *rest and routine* doing much for her: looking back, I could see that she had always been unstable, and had never fitted in with what was expected. Norah worried, sighing and fidgeting, back on the eternal couch again, and John produced long desperate hoots from his tuba like cries for help, but it seemed to me that the place where Lilian now was, was the best place for her.

She had proved herself to be a viper in my bosom, and had been officially certified to be insane, no longer a member of the human race – but she had left a gap. Life in the Singer household was orderly these days, and no one dreamed of *running wild*: but it was a little dull, and no one took me up on my facts now at the dinner-table, and returned them to me brought to life by disagreement. I decided to visit Lilian, to see if *wonders* had in fact been worked. As I trimmed my nostril-hairs in the mirror before I left the house, I remembered that the colour of her eyes was brown, the curve of her nose mine entirely, the dimple in her left cheek like a third little eye, winking.

◆   ◆   ◆

Into the dim vestibule of the hospital, gleaming with the polish of institutional surfaces, I stepped like a giant among men. There was a mincing nurse bustling and fussing in there, ingratiating himself in a quean's leering way, no doubt lusting after me within his pants. He squeaked suggestively along the linoleum corridor ahead of me in his rubber shoes, his tight white trousers presenting me with two little melons bobbing up and down at every step. 'In here, Mr Singer,' he said, and unlocked a door, and my face began a smile, my lips prepared to form themselves into welcoming words. Even after so long, and after so many vicissitudes, here was my daughter: once a daughter, always a daughter. 'Lilian!' I would cry, and see her look at me in surprise, and in her pleasure at seeing me she would be smiling all over her face and lost for words.

But the person in the room was just an expressionless fat woman in a coarse calico jacket, piled onto a wooden chair, and although her face was turned towards mine as I entered, and her eyes appeared to have me in their sights, she showed no response at seeing me. The nurse was still leering and bustling around, rearranging chairs, opening and closing windows, and heaving at the heap of daughter on the chair, trying to make it more upright: I thought he would bustle around all day, but finally he made to leave the room. He stood in the doorway with one hand round the edge of the door, which I saw had no handle on its inner side, and made large conspiratorial faces at me. 'Mr Singer,' he hissed, as if Lilian would not hear if he hissed, and squeezed up his face in an unpleasantly rubbery sort of way. 'Mr Singer, you must knock when you have finished, just knock and I will unlock you, and if there should be –' he screwed up his face even more so that I wanted to shout at him, his hissing and grimaces were quite spoiling my expansive mood – 'if there should be any kind of problem, Mr Singer, or anythink that worries you, just put your finger on this button –' he showed me, 'and we will be here immediately.'

I thought he had finished, I nodded as he spoke, but in the act of closing the door he opened it again to deliver a large wink at me, as if Lilian behind me could not see it as well, and said, 'Immediately, if not sooner, that is,' and laughed loudly at this display of wit, perhaps louder for the fact that I did not see fit to laugh at all.

Now I was able to give my full attention to Lilian, and I was as banal as a person visiting the insane could possibly be. 'Good morning, Lilian,' I exclaimed in a hearty hospital sort of way. 'And how are we feeling today, my dear?' Lilian stared, but she did not show the slightest flicker of expression, and my bright smile went stale on my face: she was going to be difficult, then!

She was, if possible, even fatter than she had been in her heyday of *running wild*. Her face was puffy and pale, like some bit of offal rolled by the tides, and her eyes were nothing more than wet holes in a bloodless bag of face. I began to be sorry I had come, but could only go forward now, although I could see that if she kept up this thing of not responding, I could be made to look foolish. 'The family is well,' I said, determined to ask no more questions. 'Your mother's researches are going swimmingly.' How normal and admirable it all sounded! No one listening at the window would ever guess at Norah hunched over her stopwatch again, timing the passage of time itself ticking away, and writing her meaningless columns of numbers in the book. 'Yes, she is hard at work.' I was enjoying this! 'And of course John, you remember your brother, he is still as keen as mustard about his music.' How naturally the words rolled out of my mouth! What an utterly convincing sane person I was, concerned with bringing my daughter up-to-date about her brother, when we both knew that he was a blank boy who could hardly ever be extracted from within the coils of a tuba.

Lilian continued to say nothing. Not only did she say nothing, she did not smile, or nod, or shake her head. 'Well, Lilian, you do not have a great deal to say to me,' I said at last, tiring of this game. 'Have you forgotten that I am your father?' Lilian stared and blinked quickly twice, but did nothing else. At least I had made her blink, but I wondered whether it was not I who had done it, but the eyelids themselves, going about their own private business of making sure the eyeballs did not dry out.

I could hear the degenerate's whinnying laugh from outside now, somewhere away beyond the barred window, and moved my chair closer. I brought my face up so close to hers that I could feel the heat coming off her cheeks, and I puffed out a few breaths to see her blink in the breeze of them: she could not fail to notice me now! But not by a single flicker of muscle did she betray that she knew I was there. She could have been quite alone in this gleaming cage of a room, dreaming of times gone by: my head, filling her line of sight, seemed as transparent to her as water, and my voice no more significant to her than the breeze from a moth's wing. I stared at her, checking off the features that had always given me back to myself: the brow, the jaw, that curve of nose and arch of eyebrow. But I could no longer find anything of myself in my daughter's face. I had joined with that person, had become one with her: yet she was a stranger now. No one looking at her at this moment would cry, 'What a chip off the old block!'

I could not have this. I moved around until my lips were close to her ear. 'Come on, Lilian,' I coaxed in my softest way. 'Come on, my dear, give your father a smile.' I was reluctant to touch her flesh, for it had a waxy look and I thought it might be as cold and dry as a snake's skin. But when I put my hands on her face it was not clammy, but warm and firm, muscular under my fingers as I forced her lips up into a winsome smile. 'There, that looks so very much prettier, Lilian,' I said to her kindly. Or was I shouting? Could that be my voice, ringing around the room?

'Lilian,' I cried again, and heard something pleading in my tone. 'Lilian! Buck up, girl, for God's sake,' but Lilian simply sat slouch-shouldered on the chair, staring blankly at my face as if watching the skin grow. I could not bear that inhuman gaze any more, and I pushed back my chair and stood up, so that now her stare was directed at my belt-buckle. 'Come on, Lilian, enough is enough!' I cried, and pushed at her shoulder in a bracing, snap-out-of-it sort of way. But at my touch, Lilian began to crumple, quite slowly, starting with the shoulder I had touched. She folded in on herself and slipped all of a heap onto the lino, like a dead person, and lay there without moving.

I was appalled to hear myself, as if from miles away, utter a strangled sort of exclamation: it appeared that Albion Gidley Singer, that masterpiece of control, was capable of making a quite extraordinary sound, part snort, part squeak. Surely she could not be so lost to me! Surely no one alive – and I could see that she was breathing – could be so dead to the world! Surely in a moment she would get up, dust herself off, and laugh her big throaty laugh. 'Well, Father,' she would exclaim, 'had you fooled, didn't I, and do you know there is a woman here who believes she is made of glass?'

I bent down to look into her face: she was smiling on and on blindly at the linoleum, lying sprawled sideways, one foot tangled with the leg of the chair, the black slipper of the other skewed sideways half-off her foot, both hands palm-down on the floor as if checking its temperature. I stayed bent over until the blood pounded in my temples and my cheeks seemed to hang off my face, but she showed no signs of ever intending to do anything different.

I turned to the door, putting a hand out for the knob. I wanted simply to walk away from this whole situation. But there was no knob there: I stood groping for a way out that did not exist, like an amputee with a phantom limb, trapped in this blank white room containing nothing but two chairs and an empty daughter. For a long airless moment I was given up to fear.

When I got a grip on myself and remembered to knock, the nurse came quickly. He showed some surprise at Lilian having collapsed to the floor, but made no move to pick her up. 'I only just touched her,' I began to explain, but he was not interested. 'Most days she is ever so normal, Mr Singer,' he remarked, and left her there while he took me to the front door. As he unlocked the main door, he winked one last wink, but he had lost interest in me, and the wink was nothing more than habit.

◆　　◆　　◆

It was true that the world was all sky with my daughter gone from it, but a man could have too much sky. Beyond the walls of the hospital, a cold wind had sprung up and I hurried along, clutching my coat together across my chest, looking inward at what I had left behind. A car bore down on me so I had to leap back onto the footpath all of a scramble; then a tram took me by surprise, rounding a corner on top of me, its sudden bell a peal of scorn.

Where to, sir? the tram conductor wanted to know, and for a moment I stared at him, and could not quite think of anywhere I wanted to go.

The thought of the Club did not appeal. Ogilvie was there most days now, his chair drawn up close to Mackenzie's, their corner of the room staked out with their cigar smoke and the way they laughed together and bent over pieces of paper jabbing at numbers with a pencil. Ogilvie would wave to me across the room before bending towards the papers again, but while nothing actually stopped me from drawing up a chair with them, lighting a cigar, and telling them the one about the doctor and the train-driver's wife, somehow I did not wish to do so. Men watched you like hawks at the Club, and I had felt recently that everyone there, including Ogilvie – perhaps especially Ogilvie – was scrutinising me as I ate my steak-and-kidney or read my newspaper. *His daughter is in the madhouse, you know,* I knew they were telling each other behind my back, and I had been finding it a strain to go on making sure that I ate my steak-and-kidney and read my newspaper in a way that was absolutely and perfectly normal.

Nor did I fancy my own home at this moment. Norah would be lying on the chaise-longue, or perhaps even frankly have gone to her bed, where she spent longer and longer these days, in spite of all the specialists with their beautiful embossed prescription-paper. She would give me one of her diffident glances, as if I might bite her if she looked at me too hard, and she would either ask with terrible delicacy, *How did she seem, Albion, and do they think she is improved at all?* or even more delicately ask me nothing at all.

In the end I went to the shop, as usual, but today all its splendours somehow failed to console. I sat at my desk, but was not quite able to come to grips with the papers in front of me. I sat for a long period of time turning a letter this way and that, trying to find the right way up. 'Miss Gidding,' I made to call. 'This letter appears to be in some foreign tongue, Hindustani perhaps, is there someone who can interpret for us?' but stopped myself in time and put the letter away at the bottom of a drawer.

I would have to go back to see Lilian again: I had to know whether she was mad to the point of deafness, or whether she had simply determined to get the better of me. The more I thought it over, becoming calmer as I smoothed the grain on the edge of the desk, the more certain I was. Lilian had not been pretending: surely no one could pretend so well, or for so long. Surely no one would have that kind of will-power. I would visit again, to make quite sure, but I was almost sure now. She was simply beyond the touch of human contact, had slipped away beyond recall. A man was simply wasting his time, if all his daughter could do was fall to the floor in a heap when he visited: I had done my duty by her, and frankly, I washed my hands of her now. I may once have had a daughter, but that thing I had seen with the blank eyes, wasting her smiles on the floor, was not any daughter of mine.

Chapter *Thirty-Two*

SOMETHING HAD happened to facts while I had had my back turned being a *family man*. In the modern world we were in now, it seemed that it was no longer *things* that scientists discovered, but the very absence of *things*: there appeared to be fewer and fewer actual *things* in the world with every discovery that was made. Eminent men, men you could trust, men with degrees from Oxford, were saying that the most solid matter, even a man's boot or a man's 18-carat gold collar stud, was in fact composed of millions of tiny particles of absolutely nothing at all.

Something similar appeared to have happened to the Singer family as the years had gone by since Lilian's removal from it. Where once I had been the core of a solid little family molecule, things seemed now to be breaking down into the constituent parts of their nothingness.

Mother was the first to go, passing away in her sleep in Aunt Daphne's house, after a vigorous day of good works in the form of a cake stall for the Woman's Temperance Union:

one Dundee Seed Cake too many, and she was gone. Daphne sent me a few of her things, and, such is the weakness of the best-regulated man, when I saw Mother's double strand of pearls lying on the worn black velvet, as I had seen them so often lying against her skin, I had to get out my handkerchief and pretend something had gone down the wrong way.

As for Norah, she had tyrannised us for all those many years with her endless *headaches*, her *pains in the joints*, her *weaknesses*, her *fevers*, her *palpitations* and her *rashes*, but I had never thought of her as doing anything as definite as actually dying. With so much practice at it, you would have thought she would have done the thing in style, but all she could do was to shrivel in the bed, go a papery colour, and stare sunken-eyed at the people around her. She did not even manage a proper deathbed speech: she simply withered and shrivelled and stared until the nurse came to me one afternoon with the news that she had *slipped away*.

At the funeral I spoke movingly of my wife's *wit and wisdom*, and even got an affecting huskiness going. I was turning out to be rather good at funerals. Afterwards I stood at the church door with the minister and shook a very large number of hands. Norah seemed to have known more people than I would have imagined, and several of them were able to go one better than me, and produce an actual tear or two. *Oh you will miss her*, they said. *What a gap. What a loss*. I nodded, and looked grave, and pressed the hands between my own, but I grew more and more weary of it. I knew that they were only repeating what they knew were the correct sentiments, but how could they possibly think that her going could leave a gap, when she had performed no actual function in the world? How could they imagine I would miss someone who had never impinged?

Kristabel went too, but not before she had undermined me for one last time. Somehow she had persuaded the doctors that Lilian had had enough *rest and routine*, and that she could now be officially declared sane. Sane! She had never in her life been sane, I could see that now. Certainly it was true that *rest and routine* had been promised to work *wonders*, but *wonders* had not included actually becoming sane!

The last time I saw Kristabel alive was when she came to me with a grim look in her eye and a sheaf of papers she wanted me to sign. 'She will not bother you, Albion, but she must have regular money, I have got it all drawn up here.' There was a look in her eye I did not like, a certain unyielding flat tone in her voice as she reiterated meaningfully that Lilian would not *bother* me, there would be no *interference*, there would be no *unpleasantness of any kind* if I just signed these papers from the bank. I could see she was prepared to stand there frowning in front of my desk all day, and I had several urgent things to get on with, and in any case the money was a trivial sum to a man in my position. In the end I was glad to sign and be rid of them both so cheaply.

Kirstabel's funeral was a pretty small affair, and there was no missing my daughter among the handful of mourners. She had become a gigantic coarse woman with stringy hair and a skirt with a split down the back, no longer young enough to get away with such things: she had gone terribly to seed, and in spite of the regular money she had been getting from me, she looked as though she was sleeping in the park, and probably hearing voices too. To the eye that knew, she was as crazy as she had always been, but she put up a good show. It is a well-known fact that the madder a person is, the better they can pretend to be sane. She had a few words for John, spoke to two old ladies who had been neighbours of Kristabel's, even greeted the Minister, and if you took no notice of the knots in her hair and the mismatched socks visible under the edge of the skirt, she could have appeared almost normal.

I watched her face, watched for her to turn and meet my eyes, and had just the right expression prepared: tolerant, even forgiving, but firm. I was not a man to be taken advantage of in any way, or made to look any kind of fool in public. But in all the time that she talked to John, to the old ladies, and to the Minister, she did not so much as glance over towards me. Not that I wished to speak to her, or have anything to do with her, if the truth were known. Why would I want to approach someone who looked as if she could do with a bath? What would I have to say to someone so obviously a brick short of a full load? Frankly, I was glad she kept her distance, and when I lost sight of her, and realised she must have left, I was not sorry.

When John and I got home from the funeral, he made to go straight up to his room, but I stopped him. He was not much, but he was my only son.

Well, we will have to take care of each other, now, John, I said, in the loud way you had to speak to John to get his attention, and he shot me a stricken look. *Yes, Father*, he said, because he knew better than not to answer when his father spoke, but he was not really paying attention. I had not seen him cry at the funeral: in fact, when I considered it, I had not seen him cry for years. But his eyes seemed shrunken in their sockets and his face was pinched. *Yes, Father*, he said, and blew his nose so loudly the pictures shook on the walls.

When his nose was well and truly blown, I said it again. *Just the two of us*, I told him, *just you and me now*. I made sure we were together a little more, as befitted a widower and his only son. I took him to Dingle for a proper suit, as Father had taken me to Chapman, and lunched him at the Club, and brought him with me more often to the Business. He was at the University now and it was high time he took an interest, but all he could do was sit there like a lump on the chair, and could not even be got to express any enthusiasm for the new-fangled moving stairway. *This will all be yours one day*, I reminded him. *When I am dead and gone, you will be the Mr Singer here*, but I had to laugh at the idea of myself dying, and of John ever being Mr Singer. He shot me a look of surprise, as though the idea of my death had never occurred to him.

◆　◆　◆

Of all the people in the world, John was surely the one least likely to astonish me. And yet it was this gormless son of mine who took the wind right out of my sails. We sat in Norah's dining-room one night, while I explained to John the importance of extravagant public display in business. 'In the business world,' I was saying, 'any reek of thrift is as bad as a rumour of typhus,' and I was pleased with the way I was putting it. I would have liked a better response from John, and said rather sharply, 'Remember that, John, you will be glad of it, when your time comes.' John nodded and said, 'Yes, Father,' in that mechanical unconvinced way he had, but then he suddenly looked up at me and said clearly down the length of the table, 'Well, actually no, Father, I have got a job, you see, and a room in Macleay Street.'

I could not have been more astonished if the mahogany table had opened up the crack between its leaves and nipped me on the nose. But I was not going to give John the satisfaction of seeing me stumped. I did nothing more than nod, and ask him whether he could pass the pepper. It was an insurance company, he told me, as if I had asked, and he was going to *work his way up*, but I did nothing more than nod and chew. 'I will be leaving tomorrow,' he said, although I certainly had not asked.

In order to regain the initiative I went upstairs and came back with my second-best cuff-links, the ones from Father. 'Here you are, John,' I said. 'My father had them from his father, I had them from my father, and now you are having them from your father.' John opened the box and glanced at the cuff-links, but an heirloom was wasted on the boy, and so was an occasion. 'Thank you, Father,' he said with no more feeling than if I had handed him a handkerchief he had dropped. 'I had better go and pack now.'

◆　　◆　　◆

Now that it was just myself to be looked after, I began to think of letting Cook go. Alma could cobble together the simple meals I needed, and do the little cleaning I required, and it seemed an extravagance to employ a cook just for myself. But before I had definitely decided, I was forestalled. Cook and Alma came to me one morning, together, as if giving each other courage, and announced that they were handing in their notice, *What with dear Mrs Singer gone, and now dear little John gone too, Mr Singer sir.* They were puffed up with triumph, both of them, spinning out the business of getting their trunks down to the front door, and doing some definite hovering, saying goodbye several times, and allowing extensive pauses to take place. 'Oh well,' they kept saying, and studied the pattern of the floorboards. It was obvious that they were waiting for me to beg them to stay, and claim I would be *lost without them*, and cry at them about *however would I manage*. I gave them no such satisfaction, and if they were hovering for a *keepsake* or a *little gift* they were not going to get that either: just a week's wages and my best wishes.

Mrs Philpott was found to *do* for me, and she did perfectly well, considering. She was deaf, so chatter was not in her line. I had tried in the beginning. 'It is a well-known fact, Mrs Philpott,' I began, but she had simply left the room and closed the door on my fact. She was surly, which was also fine by me, and made no secret of her feeling that she was doing me a favour coming up the hill twice a day to see to my needs. But she could put a meal on the table in front of me in the cold gleam of the empty dining-room, and kept me in clean shirts. What more could a man need?

It was just what a man needed: it was just what a man wanted: it was an ideal sort of set-up. I did not mind being alone, and I did not miss my family. *All on your own, Mr*

Singer, people sympathised, and tried to get me to break down in front of them. All my life I had felt people watch me tiresomely, their eyes avid on my face, waiting to see me unmanned by emotion. Mother had done it, reading improving stories to me as a boy, of the deaths of angelic children. Norah had done it, bursting into tears over the perfidy of lady-friends or a broken vase, and wanting me to weep too. Even sad old Rundle had watched me as he had spun me hard-luck stories about some drone of an employee, how he had a sick wife and fourteen tubercular children and the bailiffs coming in next week.

Now I brushed away these sympathisers as I had always brushed away false displays of emotion. I was not lonely, I did not miss anyone: a man of inner resources has no need of chatter around him. *Family life* was one of the things expected of a man, and certainly in the abstract it was a fine idea: but in the all-too-concrete flesh of actual *family life*, a man's energies were dissipated. Bills for goods had to be checked against actual objects, and their internal arithmetic checked against the slyness of tradesmen: objects broke, or wore out, with suspect alacrity, and mulish people, mostly women, had to be quizzed about details of cup handles and shoe leather. The children of a *family man* had to be watched closely to ensure they did not slacken in their Irregular Verbs or their Nine-Times Table, and wives had to be kept an eye on in case they *let themselves go*. Finally, the endless minutiae of family life wore a man down.

Now, as the house gradually emptied, I felt as if I could return to my true self as simply Man rather than Family

Man, encumbered on every side. Everything now was just as I had always wanted it. Windows could be open or closed, just as I myself wished: there were no plaintive squeaks from Norah about draughts. *Strengthening liver* and *blood-purifying swedes* could now be entirely removed from my table, and Mrs Philpott could be told to provide tripe once a month, and brains every other week, without Norah murmuring in disgust; if I wished to stay out till all hours, there was no one to whom I needed to explain about *going to see someone on a little business matter*; and after years of distraction and trivia, there was nothing to stop me thinking.

◆　◆　◆

I was free at last, but somehow it seemed that I had almost forgotten how to enjoy my freedom. The tripe was bitter in my mouth, the breezes from every window chilled me to the bone, *seeing someone on a little business matter* seemed somehow more trouble than it was worth, and I could not always settle to a good think. There was something wrong with the air in my study; it was too thick or too thin, so that the print danced before my eyes, the chair wrestled with my spine, the books themselves had to be held open by main force. I would wake up with a brassy taste in my mouth, the shadows falling the wrong way through the window, the book on the floor beside my boots, and I would for a few moments be unable to summon any kind of fact at all. *My name is Albion Gidley Singer*, I would need to remind myself. *And I must have just dropped off for a moment.*

A man's home is his castle, but it seemed that a man's

castle was capable of turning on a man, and making him evaporate. There was silence now from down below where Cook had clashed her saucepans for so many years, silence in the attic where Alma's heavy tread had made the mirrors tremble downstairs, and dust began inexorably to gather. I sat in the dining-room, waiting for Mrs Philpott to bring dinner in, and the sounds as I unfolded my table-napkin, drew in my chair, and swallowed a mouthful of water, were enormous. The room was still *done* as Norah had had it *done* all those years ago: I had never let her *re-do* it again, so it remained a monument to her folly. I had never noticed in the heat of family life what a very chilly room it was. Perhaps there was even a suspicion of damp. I had had the men in, and they had charged me an arm and a leg, but there was still a chill that struck at you as you came in, and a certain stony magnifying silence.

John's leaving had left no trace on the surface of the house. In his room, his tuba tarnished month by month, and the box of cuff-links, forgotten on the windowsill, gathered dust. Some days I found myself going into the room. I would sit on the side of the bed, watching the gleaming bulges of the tuba. Once I even picked it up and got into its coils, but when I tried to produce a sound, I heard only the wind of my own breath whistling emptily through its pipes.

Naturally, I knew I was alone in the house, and simple commonsense told me that if I made no changes to anything, then nothing would change. And yet, as I wandered from room to room, something in me expected evidence of life: somehow I expected the box of cuff-links to have moved from the windowsill, the tuba to be sitting on a different spot on the floor. But even the wrinkle in the bedspread was unchanged: nothing whatsoever had occurred here since I myself had last sat on the bed and got up again, and nothing ever would.

Lilian's was a sad plundered room, with dust thick on the empty bookshelves, and a dead-leaf sort of smell about it. Only around the door was there any mark of a human having inhabited this space. The fingerprints of my daughter's grubby hands could still be seen around the handle, and down near the skirting-board there was a secret known only to myself and perhaps to her: a smear of ink with her thumbprint visible in it. My eye was often drawn back to that fossil evidence that I had once had a daughter. Down on my knees in front of the skirting-board I watched it at close range. The whorls and concentric rings had no end: they drew a man's eye down and down into themselves like an optical illusion. I had read of mystics staring into patterns like this, and going into ecstasies. I was no mystic, but a man of the scientific age, intent on a matter of scientific interest. I knelt before the marks until my knees locked, but no ecstasy occurred.

It was not that I thought much about Lilian these days. If I found myself in that bare pink room more often than one would have expected, it was only that its windows got the best of the sun, and in a house grown dank, it remained warm. Her pink walls were bland, the empty wardrobe gave nothing away, and under the bed was nothing but fluff and a stiff blue sock. Sitting on that bed, feeling it yield under my weight, I could see out across the bay, could hear the kookaburras cackling among the trees, and at the end of the day I could watch the darkness come up from the water.

But nights were no longer safe, for as I sat over the fire downstairs, the dark rooms around me seemed to multiply. Acres of dark doorways yawned into darker rooms, corner after corner of banister curved upwards into dimness, hall-runner after hall-runner vanished into shadows. I hunched closer over the ticking coals of the fire, feeling a draught on my back, stuck there watching the fire die, not able to take the coal-scuttle in hand and venture downstairs to fill it, and not able simply to walk up to bed either. Finally I would creep up as stealthily as if I myself were the intruder, with my back to the wall all the way up the stairs. When I was at last lying under the covers, my heart pounded and sleep would not come.

I would lie in the dark, listening to the humming of the silence, waiting for the clock downstairs to chime out the next quarter-hour, and I would feel myself shrunken away to the size of a pinhead, quite alone in the dark spaces of eternity. I was a small emptiness within a larger one: in my hollow house, I had never been hollower. There were even moments when all the logic against the existence of God was almost insufficient to keep me from calling out to Him like a child for help. That tiny self, my speck of inner man, was now all that kept me company in those terrible hissing nights of long white emptiness.

Even during the day, the silence around me as I considered my facts was like a personality. There was nothing in the house now but the hum of emptiness and the pressure of all those vacant rooms on the skull. I was deafened, browbeaten, goaded by silence: silence was strangling the life out of me: silence had become something toxic. The breath was sucked out of me by a peculiar effect of vacuum in the rooms and the blood turned sluggish in my veins. I felt I needed to sit down, but sitting down did not seem to improve things.

When I stood up too quickly, the blood rushed to my head: everything went grey, and when colour restored itself to the world there was still a sensation of movement in things, as if my eyes had become sensitive to the life of the very atoms on the surface of the world. A wall seethed if I looked at it too hard, the surface visibly teeming; the glass of the window bellied out and back giddily, the boards of the floor undulated beneath my feet.

In such a frame of mind, I was overwhelmed by a sense of something swirling behind the eyes. I left my study and stood at the top of the stairs, aware of the large sounds of my own breathing, hearing other sounds that stopped as soon as I tried to listen to them. Perhaps all those nosey-parkers were right. Perhaps it was true that the house was a little large for a man on his own.

In my dressing-room there was at least myself, large as life in the cheval-glass, with another one behind me in the dressing-table mirror. There was my splendid head, there was my admirable chin; there were the fine shoulders, the good chest, the hands appearing at the ends of the sleeves, the tubes of pants: there I was, and there I was again from behind as well, but it brought me no comfort.

I lifted my hand to smooth my hair over the skull, and the

gesture stuck like a bit of seized machinery. A whistle began in my ear, a small high scream within the skull itself: and now a jerky roaring was starting up in my head, the sound of my frightened blood in tumult within. I stood and watched myself, and could not quite remember how you managed the breathing business. I looked at the waistcoat and the shirt-front moving in and out, and heard a ragged sort of panting, in and out, up and down. *That is all you have to do*, I told myself. *It is really very simple.* One brown shoe advanced towards me in the glass, then the other; the man in the mirror blinked at me rapidly, and the lips twisted under his nose as his mouth formed words I could not hear.

I stood with a bloodless chill around me, as if part of my clothing had fallen away at the back and left me naked to the wind. Here in my own dressing-room, looking at what could only be my own face in the mirror, I was melting away into the void that surrounded me, that hissing whiteness that had always lain at the centre of all things, where there were no voices, no eyes, no reflections: just the void at the heart of self. Loss rose in me like nausea.

Someone else's eyes watched me from the mirror, peering avidly into the transparency that I had become. There he was, Albion Gidley Singer, a man with a splendid head, a man in the finest double-breasted bespoke that money could buy, Albion Gidley Singer, son, brother, father, husband, pillar of the community, leading man of business: there he was, and he had been sucked out of himself like the marrow from a bone. The nothingness within had rushed to join the nothingness without, and the empty husk was collapsing into itself. There it was, Albion Gidley Singer standing hunched under the weight of his own garments, a man in the act of turning into air.